THE ST(

Books by Venezia Miller:

THE FIND SERIES

THE FIND
EVIL BENEATH THE SKIN
RETRIBUTION
THE STORM

COMING SOON:
THE VANISHING

THE STORM

Venezia Miller

THE STORM

Copyright © 2023 by Venezia Miller.

All rights reserved. No part of this book may be used or reproduced in any manner whatsoever without written permission except in the case of brief quotations embodied in critical articles or reviews.

This book is a work of fiction. Names, characters, businesses, organizations, places, events, and incidents either are the product of the author's imagination or are used fictitiously. Any resemblance to actual persons, living or dead, events, or locales is entirely coincidental.

For information contact: Venezia.Miller@gmail.com
ISBN: 9798397184397

Book and Cover design by V. Miller with images taken from www.pixabay.com.

First Edition: June 2023

CHAPTER

1

AS HE GAZED OUTSIDE, a mesmerizing ocean of glittering lights stretched before him. The streets of Gävle were a magnificent spectacle, especially at night in winter. The frosty avenues were bathed in the soft glow of the moon, revealing cars and bustling people braving the bitter cold. The scene was almost otherworldly in its beauty.

Lauri had a profound attachment to Gävle and cherished every aspect of this special place—from its exquisite restaurants and enchanting architecture to its charming alleyways and lively harbor. But what he cherished most were the people—the heart and soul of Gävle. Every time he thought about the fact that he lived two hours away from his childhood home, his heart ached with a mixture of sadness and longing. He couldn't quite remember why they had left this place behind.

He had lived in big cities, both in Sweden and abroad, but he had always dreamt of returning to Gävle. Now, at the age of fifty, memories of his carefree youth came flooding back, overwhelming him with a sense of longing. He closed his eyes, feeling the warmth of the mug in his hand, imagining the joy of going back to his roots.

Everything in his life seemed suffused with a sense of melancholy these days. He yearned for a time when he was free from responsibilities, when his choices had no permanent consequences.

Lauri turned away from the window, placing the mug on the polished wooden desk. When he first started working here, everything had seemed so vital and meaningful. He had felt important. But now, he couldn't shake the feeling that he was missing out on what could have been.

He gazed around the room, taking in the details. The wooden panels, the golden-framed mirrors, the hunting scenes captured in oil paintings, the baroque vase standing tall in front of the magnificent mahogany desk. The desk was a work of art in itself, and behind it, books upon books lined the shelves, covering every imaginable topic.

But all the grandeur felt hollow to him. The same room, not so long ago, was the birthplace of a dangerous scheme, a plan to reshape the world to fit the beliefs of a few, but at the cost of countless lives. Lauri couldn't understand how he could have ever supported such a thing. It took him two decades to see the destruction it would cause. Was it too late to make amends? He couldn't be sure, but one thing was certain: he had to act.

He touched his temple. His headache was mild, but it was starting to become a nuisance, and he was experiencing a sense of discomfort in his stomach that persisted despite his efforts to ignore it.

"... *In an official declaration, Prime Minister Olav Hult confirms that the incident at the Forsmark Nuclear Power Plant two months ago has been classified as an act of terrorism. Investigation of the...*"

He approached the oak cabinet near the wall and silenced the radio.

His gaze then fell upon the painting of a hunting scene, a piece that filled him with distaste. The dark colors and depiction of animal cruelty churned his stomach. On the opposite wall hung a portrait of a gray-haired man adorned in a uniform with golden threading. He was just one of the many forgotten mayors of Gävle, lost to the annals of history.

He let his fingers glide over the ancient wood. A scent of glory from another time filled his nostrils.

Then he returned to the desk, took his briefcase from the floor, and set it beside the glowing lamp. He removed two papers from his briefcase and positioned them on the edge of the desk. Then, with a gaze at his laptop, he hovered his finger above the enter key, ready to make his next move.

He jumped up.

There was a soft noise in the background.

Who was there?

He had lost too much time musing about the past.

"Is anyone there?" he said and waited.

Maybe he should check if anyone was in the hallway. The door hung ajar, and as he pushed it open, the only illumination came from the slivers of light filtering through the windows. The office doors lining the hall were closed, and all he could hear was his own breathing. He paused, straining his ears for any other signs of movement.

It was silent.

He stepped away from the door and returned to the desk. He needed to get a grip. The message on the laptop screen was still pleading for an answer. Continue to print or not? Why was this so hard? It felt like he was betraying the very ideals he had stood for so many years. But he was no longer that man. He grunted and pressed the button, "Print."

The printer in the hall hummed to life, rattling for a moment before spitting out the papers.

When the noise finally stopped, he grabbed the papers from the tray and slid them into his briefcase.

Now, he needed to get out of there.

Leave no trace! They're out to get you.

He jumped up.

There it was again. That sound. That voice.

His eyes scanned the room. His entire body started to ache. He was definitely coming down with the flu. Flashes of warm and cold started to flood his body. He really needed to go home.

Then he froze.

Lauri's heart raced as he took in the strange, warped sight before him. In an instant, the walls of the room seemed to contort and twist, stretching beyond all reason. He rubbed his eyes, wondering if exhaustion was to blame. But as he looked back, the walls remained distorted, pulsing and writhing before his eyes. He felt a wave of dizziness wash over him, and he stumbled back, grasping the edge of his desk for support.

Then the room turned back to normal.

There was no time to waste.

He gripped the handle of his briefcase tightly as he descended the stairs and stepped into the grand hall. The emptiness of the space was unsettling, and he couldn't shake the feeling that something was off. He scanned his surroundings, but the only movement was the flickering of the overhead lights.

His mind raced with uncertainty. Had his senses betrayed him?

He pushed the thoughts aside. The cold air outside helped clear his mind and bring him back to the present. He knew they would soon come after him, and he had to act fast.

He made it to the end of the block and found a surprising amount of life in the small city, even at night. There were already holiday lights up, and the sidewalks were buzzing with people. The next moment he almost fell. He hadn't seen the man who had bumped into him as he passed by.

"Hey!" Lauri shouted.

As he looked up, he saw the man's features morph and twist into a monstrous form. Lauri's heart raced as he stumbled backwards, trying to distance himself from the creature.

This couldn't be.

There was something seriously wrong with him.

He tried to steady himself by closing his eyes, but when he opened them, people were looking at him as if he were crazy.

He pulled up his collar. The snow was coming down heavily now, blanketing the city in a pristine layer of white. Despite the beauty of the scene, Lauri felt overwhelmed and weak. His heart pounded in his chest, and a fierce wave of nausea rose within him. He stumbled forward, struggling to keep his footing on the slippery sidewalk. The blurred vision only added to his sense of disorientation, and he was on the verge of collapsing.

When he finally reached the end of the street, he felt disoriented, as if he was walking in circles. He struggled to recognize his surroundings, his thoughts slow and muddled. With a sigh, he closed his eyes, trying to focus. Suddenly, realization hit him. He knew where he was. He had two options: to turn left towards the train station and go home, or turn right towards the police station. But why did everything seem so distant? He felt sweat trickle down the side of his face. It was hot, and then cold.

He stood there for a minute, stock-still, in doubt. He still couldn't think straight. Everything hurt, his legs felt like jelly, and he collapsed onto the ground. Weird shadows crawled all around him, twisting and stretching in unnatural ways. He tried to shake off the feeling of being watched, but the shadows only grew darker and more menacing. With each passing moment, he felt himself losing touch with reality.

"Are you okay?" someone said.

He looked up and saw a man standing over him, the details of his face obscured by the strange haze that impeded his eyesight.

"Yeah, I'm... fine," Lauri said. "I think I just slipped."

The man gave him one last glance and walked away.

He got up, took the briefcase, and went left.

Home, he wanted to go home.

The strange shadows seemed to dance around him, as if taunting him for his cowardice. He was stuck in a dilemma, torn between doing the right thing and protecting those he loved. The thought of his family being hurt because of his actions was unbearable, yet he couldn't ignore the guilt that bothered him. He knew he had to make a choice, but it seemed like whichever path he took would lead to catastrophe.

* * *

The elastic band came dangerously close to Inspector Isa Lindström's right ear as it skimmed her jaw, making her flinch in response.

"Having fun?" Isa said and frowned as she saw the face of the blond man light up.

Lars grinned and leaned back in his chair, extending the backrest to its limit. She thought the chair would collapse at any moment and he would end up lying on the floor with a severe concussion.

"Between saving Gävle's most precious asset and reprimanding twelve-year olds for shoplifting, I am having the time of my life," Lars said.

"Did they try to put the goat on fire again? Seriously?"

"Yep, luckily some passerby reported it before they could actually do anything. But it will end in flames as usual. It has become a tradition. Gävle's giant Yule goat set on fire!"

"It's arson," she said, "punishable by three months in prison."

"It's just fun," Lars laughed and got up, the chair rolling backward with his movement.

"It's not funny. People might get hurt or even worse... die."

Lars shrugged.

"Anyway, don't stress yourself out," she said with a smile.

"We can't all be such diligent, hardworking employees like that one over there," he said and pointed at the silent figure sitting at the desk in the corner.

She turned her head and threw a quick glance at the dark-haired man who was probably listening to everything they said. But Inspector Timo Paikkala chose to ignore them and kept his blue eyes focused on the computer screen.

She let out a sigh. "Mmm, I know."

Then she draped her jacket over the backrest and sat down. "How long has Timo been sitting there?"

Lars moved closer, lowering his voice. "I don't know, and I don't want to ask. He's not exactly Mr. Sunshine these days."

"I know," she said, taking the laptop out of her bag. "It's not easy having to accept someone else as boss."

She settled into the chair across from him at the desk in the sparsely populated police station. The three of them were the only occupants in the otherwise deserted space. The only sounds that filled the air were the occasional hum of a passing car and the gentle clicking of computer keys coming from the nearby corner.

Lars frowned. "You're going to sit here? Your desk is over there."

She smiled and said, "You have a problem with that? I'd rather not interfere with Mr. Sunshine's activities."

Timo's eyes flicked up to meet hers before he hastily turned his gaze back to the computer screen.

"Timo was a good boss," Lars said. "I don't understand why they chose Finn Heimersson over him. And why would Finn take this job when he could have a better one in Uppsala? It makes no sense!"

"Politics," Isa shrugged and turned to her laptop.

"Yeah, politics... the best way to lose good people."

They worked in silence for a while, until her phone beeped.

After two months of radio silence, Nick had finally replied to Isa's messages. In his first message to her, he revealed that he had checked himself into a psychiatric hospital. Isa had sent him at least ten messages in the past two days, but she still felt a sense of disbelief as she read his reply.

"Dear Isa," the message began, "I know you're worried about me, but I can't talk right now. It's best for me. Please don't worry. I'll be fine."

Isa stared at her phone, struggling to understand the words on the screen. The formality of the message was striking. The use of 'Dear' was so distant, as if they were strangers, rather than two people who had once shared their deepest emotions and lived together. The message felt like a slap in the face, and she couldn't shake the feeling that something was amiss.

She missed him more than she had expected. The man she had picked up in a nightclub, whom she had solely wanted to use for sex. The man who, just like her, had been only interested in one-night stands and uncommitted relationships. That same man had been confronted with his own mortality when he had seen his colleagues die in a violent shooting at the law firm where he had been working. She had given him the space and the time to reflect. They had kept in contact, but this message confused her.

She was curious to know why he had taken such a drastic step. "Don't worry," he had written. But she couldn't help worrying.

Nick may no longer have romantic feelings for her, but she couldn't shake him from her mind. Especially now that her infatuation with Timo Paikkala had faded or, at least, subsided. She wouldn't even classify it as a crush anymore. It was just a heightened interest that went beyond the bounds of professional friendship.

She cast a quick glance at Timo, her former boss, who looked as handsome as ever, even in his casual attire of faded jeans and a black T-shirt with short sleeves. He seemed to wear the same outfit year-round, whether it was summer or winter. She had a soft spot for good-looking men, but with Timo, it was different. He possessed an enigmatic charm that effortlessly put others at ease, while his directness and perceptiveness allowed him to see through people. Despite any initial reservations, both men and women found themselves willingly sharing their deepest secrets with him.

But Lars was right: Timo seemed more reserved and burdened these days. She wondered why he had decided to stay on as chief inspector and work for the new Superintendent Finn Heimersson.

She put the phone on the desk and turned to her laptop.

"Did you hear about Berger?" Lars said.

"What about him?"

"He's getting married."

"What? Our Berger is getting married?"

"Yes, and they have already set a date," Lars said.

"When?"

"In a month from now."

"Jesus, they seem to be moving fast," Isa said.

Lars leaned back. "Yeah, they have known each other less than six months."

"Well, sometimes you know."

"Or sometimes you make the biggest mistake of your life."

"You still don't like her," Isa said and smiled.

"I don't know... it's probably me. Ingrid likes her, and you too. It's just... maybe I just miss my friend."

In the many years she had known Lars, he had always kept their interactions professional and distant. He was laser-focused on his work and rarely shared personal details. Although he and Berger were close friends, there was always a competitive edge to their relationship. The jealousy he was now displaying towards Berger's girlfriend was a familiar scenario, reminding her of how love interests can put a strain on even the closest of friendships.

Berger's fiancé, Mila, was a forensic assistant for Dr. Ingrid Olsson and had met Inspector Berger Karlsson while working on a case. It was love at first sight. Within weeks of meeting, they had moved in together and were now in the midst of planning their wedding. Although the pace of their relationship might have seemed fast, Isa knew all too well about moving quickly in relationships—or, as she preferred to think of them, flings.

"Why don't you just be there for him? I know he would like his friend to be happy for him."

"I am," Lars sighed, "in a way... it's just... never mind."

She shook her head. Why was he so obsessed with Mila? He couldn't even voice the reason he was so suspicious about her.

But maybe he saw what none of them could see?

* * *

Where was he? This wasn't the way to the train station. He was lost. How could this be? It was a road he took almost every day. Lauri had never been to this part of town before, and it was all unfamiliar. As he stumbled around in pain, he occasionally threw up, but he kept going. The pain was so bad he could hardly breathe, let alone think straight. People walking past offered to help him, but he ignored them. Their faces looked strange, as if they were from another world, and their words sounded distant and garbled. Lauri's vision started to blur, and he was about to pass out. He leaned against a nearby wall, trying to catch his breath and regain his bearings.

He just needed to get home and then everything would be okay.

His wife. She wasn't going to be happy if he came home late. She was never happy these days and he couldn't blame her, leaving her alone with two young kids, a demanding mother-in-law, and an entire household that she had to manage on her own. He had let her down by leaving her alone for so long, but he didn't have time to make amends now—he needed to keep himself and his family alive.

He was close. He could hear trains in the distance, but he still couldn't make out where he was. And all this time, he had a feeling that someone was watching him, following him.

Lauri, Lauri!

Voices assaulted him from every direction as the shadows crept closer.

He stumbled down the alley. Its walls were covered with graffiti and the air was thick with smells of urine and vomit. His head was swimming with hallucinations. He knew the movement in the shadows wasn't real, but his heart was still racing with the thought that something ominous lurked in the dark.

He leaned against the wall, trying to catch his breath.

He couldn't go on for much longer.

"Hey, mister... are you okay?"

He jumped up, and the briefcase fell, with all its content spreading on the snowy ground.

He looked down. A cardboard box lay near his feet.

In an instant, the box burst open, and what emerged was like something out of a nightmare. A monstrous hand, covered in slick, oily skin and writhing with veins and sinews, reached out towards him, its fingers stretched wide as if to grab hold of him.

He tried to run, but his legs wouldn't move. The hand was too close, too terrifying, and he was frozen in place, helpless to defend himself.

"What the hell is this?" He took two steps back, then stumbled and fell against the wall.

Only then he noticed the girl—a teenager, with messy black hair and bright blue eyes. She was wearing black boots with an old pink dress that was torn at the bottom and had stains all over it. Only the bodywarmer looked new and clean.

"Are you alright?" she asked, helping him up with a tender smile, but he gave her a denigrating look, pushed her hand away and growled: "Don't touch me! Go away!"

Then he knelt and started, almost like a madman, collecting the papers.

He had to get out of there.

Lauri, Lauri. You can't escape. He's coming for you.

"I didn't mean to...," she said, her eyes big and concerned.

"Stay away from me!" he snapped, his breath coming out in short desperate puffs. "I mean it!"

She backed away, but said, "You're not well."

"You've been following me." He let his hand run over his face, sweat beading on his forehead.

"I haven't...," the girl stammered. She knelt next to him and handed him the papers she had quickly picked up from the floor, almost in a desperate attempt to placate him.

"Give it to me!" he screamed as he yanked the papers from her hands. "The only thing you're after is my money," he repeated as he patted the pockets of his coat. The wallet and phone were still there.

"I just wanted to help," the young woman said and brushed the dirt and snow off her dress.

He quickly crammed the papers into the briefcase and skid off without giving her another look, deeper into the dark alley.

"Well, thank you very much," the girl said, her tone dripping with sarcasm, as she prepared to continue on her way. But something caught her eye. Two papers were lying on the ground between the dumpsters, and she felt a strange urge to investigate.

"Hey, mister," she called out, but he didn't hear her.

As she crouched between the metal containers searching for more papers, she didn't see the dark figure passing by.

Quiet, like a ghost.

Nothing made sense. Lauri tried to regain his balance. The sounds he was hearing, the blurred images he saw.

Frightening shadows, moving closer and closer.

He couldn't trust his senses. Was the girl even real? Was it just a figment of his imagination? He turned around, stumbled, and fell over an empty bottle. It rolled away into the dark. The next moment he was lying in the snow.

He couldn't move. He couldn't feel his arms and legs anymore. His body ached horribly, and he gasped for air. He stared at the yellow light of the lamppost. If he didn't get up, he would freeze to death.

His wife. His daughters. He couldn't do that to them.

Everything will be okay.

But he couldn't move.

A dark figure suddenly blocked his sight.

"Help... me," he said.

The figure didn't move or speak, just stared at him with empty eyes. Was this another hallucination?

"Help me," he pleaded.

"Now, now, Lauri, you know what's going to happen. It's best you accept it."

He recognized the voice.

"It's all right, Lauri. I won't let you suffer. I promise. It'll be over soon."

The man in black began to fade into the darkness of his own mind, and Lauri felt tears streaming down his face as reality seeped in.

"My girls...," Lauri let out.

He couldn't even feel the pain anymore. His eyes were failing him.

"It's like falling asleep," the man said.

"But why... I... don't... understand..."

The man smiled.

Then the darkness was complete.

His heart stopped and a puff of air escaped his mouth.

* * *

The man sighed, then looked down at the body and pulled the briefcase from Lauri's hand. Next, he took his wallet and phone. But when he turned around, he found himself face to face with the young woman who had collided with Lauri moments before and was now standing there frozen with fear. For a moment, neither of them knew what to do.

She couldn't see his face. The hat and scarf were pulled tightly over his head and mouth.

A faceless killer.

She curled her fingers around the papers in her right hand and said, "What did you do to him?"

But the question needed no answer. She knew, and she also knew she didn't have much time. Time to get out of there and save her life.

Then the man sprang forward, but the soles of his polished shoes slipped over the frozen puddles, and he fell with a thud to the ground.

She turned and sprinted through the alley until she reached the main street. It was so quiet. This part of town was deserted. There were no signs of life anywhere. The only sound came from the wind howling through the trees and whistling between the buildings. The moonlight glinted off the snow-covered street, giving it an almost surreal view, with the shadows of trees stretching across the road almost like arms reaching out for help.

She heard the man closing in on her and panic flared inside her chest.

In the distance men were shouting.

There was a tunnel on her right. She ran toward it and ducked inside, then turned and looked back at the street. She couldn't see him, but it was only a matter of time before he caught up.

The tunnel was dark and damp. There was a smell of decay that made her stomach turn. She could hear rats scurrying about in the distance.

This wouldn't work. She couldn't keep running.

But where could she go?

The tracks. He wouldn't follow her down there. She had been to the tracks enough times to know where she could go. No one would find her there.

The police? They wouldn't believe her. She was just a homeless kid who had to steal, deal drugs, and sell her body to survive.

Minutes later she reached the tracks.

Her body ached. With every step it became more difficult to move forward. She heard the snow crunch beneath her boots, but not a single other sound pierced the silence around her. Her boots slid off the metal tracks with a clang, and she turned around. She was now hundreds of meters away from where she had seen the man. In the dark, all she could see were trees stretching high into the sky on one side, and an old service building and the overhead lines of the train track on the other side.

Her breath ghosted in front of her face. He couldn't have just disappeared. She knew he was out there somewhere, watching her—no doubt waiting for the perfect moment to strike.

It was too quiet.

Suddenly, a dark figure materialized out of the shadows, launching himself at her with a savage ferocity that took her by surprise. She screamed and kicked, trying desperately to hold on to the papers, but the attacker was too strong, and she soon found herself tumbling to the ground.

The briefcase, which he had been clutching tightly, landed with a sickening thump against the side of her head, causing her vision to blur and her head to swim. Dazed and disoriented, she struggled to regain her footing, but before she could even stand up, the attacker was upon her.

With a guttural growl, he clamped his hands around her throat, cutting off her air supply. She choked and gasped for breath. She fought back with all the strength she could muster, but he was too powerful, and she soon found herself slipping into darkness.

"Hey, what's going on there?" a voice yelled.

A sudden beam of light pierced the darkness, illuminating their struggle in a harsh, unforgiving glare. The dark man, momentarily blinded by the sudden brightness, froze in his tracks, giving her a momentary advantage.

With a sudden burst of adrenaline-fueled strength, she lashed out at her attacker, striking him hard across the face with a savage blow that sent him reeling backwards. He stumbled and fell, his eyes wide with surprise and pain.

As she caught her breath and struggled to regain her composure, she noticed that in the struggle, she had pulled down the scarf covering the man's face. Squinting in the harsh light, she could hardly believe what she was seeing.

"You?" she gasped in disbelief, her mind racing with a jumble of conflicting thoughts and emotions.

The man, his eyes darting back and forth in panic, looked towards the source of the light. He could hear voices in the distance, getting closer by the moment. With a sudden burst of energy, he leapt to his feet, snatched up the briefcase, and bolted into the darkness.

By the time the men arrived at the scene of the fight, there was no sign of the attacker or the woman, only a series of footprints leading into the snowy night.

CHAPTER

2

"WHAT'S HEIMERSSON DOING HERE?"

Isa rubbed her hands together, trying to warm them in the freezing morning air. As she checked her watch and saw it was already 7 a.m., she couldn't help but shiver. She looked at her partner Timo who had asked the question. She was always surprised by how tall he was— it seemed like all police officers had to be over 190 centimeters these days, but Timo still didn't quite measure up to Finn Heimersson, who towered over everyone at a massive two meters.

Timo's face was scrunched up in a scowl, and Isa could tell that he wasn't too thrilled about being called out on a snowy winter morning. She sighed, wishing she had gotten more sleep the night before, and braced herself for the long day ahead.

"He's the boss," she said, "and if I remember correctly, you also used to show up everywhere, unannounced, when you were superintendent."

Timo let out a growl. "Not for a drunk who obviously froze to death because he passed out."

"I'm not sure he's a drunk," Dr. Ingrid Olsson said as she saw Timo approaching the demarcated zone, her face registering a look of horror. "And I would appreciate it if you would not disturb the crime scene."

Timo looked down at his feet and saw the yellow evidence marker, dangerously close to the nose of his black boots. He turned to her and said, "Uh... sorry... doctor."

Ingrid gave him a quick look of irritation.

"What do you have?" Isa moved closer.

A chill ran down Isa's spine as she approached the body. The man lay sprawled on the ground, eyes tightly shut in a frozen grimace of terror. Despite the frost that coated his features, she could tell he was middle-aged, maybe in his late forties or early fifties. His attire suggested he was an upper-class man, dressed in a dark blue coat, black pants, and boots, but something was off. A strange substance leaked from the corner of his mouth, which puzzled her. She took a closer look, trying to identify the mysterious substance.

"Expensive shoes, leather gloves, fashionable coat," Isa said, "this doesn't look like your typical drunk."

Ingrid, in a white coverall, wearing latex gloves and overshoes, stood up examining the dead man's body. She paused to glance at the frozen corpse before walking to where Isa and Timo were standing.

"I'm not convinced this was an accident," Ingrid said, her brow furrowed.

"What's troubling you?" Isa asked.

"He has lesions in his face. The skin seems swollen, but hard to tell because of the cold, and he was vomiting blood before he collapsed."

"Oh, that's what's in the corner of his mouth," Isa said and pointed at the man.

"We found more vomit in the alley," Ingrid said. "Not sure if it is his."

With a steady gaze, Isa turned to her. "So, he was ill. Then he collapsed over here and died of the cold. An unfortunate accident?"

"His wallet and phone are gone," Ingrid said quickly.

"Someone could have stolen them after he collapsed," Isa said. "It's not exactly the safest neighborhood in Gävle."

Ingrid nodded. "But the result is that we don't know who this man is."

"I know him," Timo said suddenly.

The two women looked at him in surprise. He ignored them, moved closer and kept staring at the lifeless body.

"This is Lauri Valkama. I met him a month ago to talk about Karst Engersson."

"The Global Law shooting?" Isa asked.

The mass shooting at one of Sweden's most prestigious law firms still lingered in people's minds. The tragedy had claimed the lives of ten people, including the founder and CEO Karst Engersson, and even after two months, the investigation was yet to reveal the true culprit or the motive behind the attack. There were still many unanswered questions.

"When I spoke to him, he was working at the City Hall in Gävle," Timo said. "He used to be Engersson's accountant, but he wasn't very forthcoming with information that could help with the case. I got the sense that he was hiding something."

"You think this is more than just an accident?"

He shrugged. "It could be that he was sick, but it could also be that he was poisoned."

Ingrid frowned. "Oh, is that so? Maybe you should do my job then?"

"Just saying," he replied and then without giving the two women another glance walked away.

Isa shook her head, let out a deep sigh to get her growing irritation with her partner under control and then turned to Ingrid. "And what do you think?"

"I hate to say it, but he could be right. This doesn't feel like an accident. There are distinctive footprints of at least three different people. It's hard to say if they were made at the same time but it could show that someone was here and witnessed what happened to him."

"It looks like the alley doesn't get much foot traffic. It's not a popular neighborhood and there are only dumpsters here. Maybe some of the residents from the nearby apartment blocks come through here," Isa said.

Ingrid scanned the surroundings. "Well, I wouldn't want to be here… at least not at night."

"Temperatures were still above zero during the day," Isa said. "It started freezing around 4 p.m. and a few hours later it was snowing. To make prints that deep, it must have been snowing heavily."

"I'd say he died between 7 and 10 p.m. But I can give you a more accurate estimate after I examined the body."

"When can you do the autopsy?"

"Likely still today."

"Let me know what you find." Isa gave her a friendly nod before turning to Timo, who was still strolling around like a kid in a bad mood.

She then walked over to the young police officer standing near the wall full of graffiti. He looked unsure of himself and kept throwing glances at the body. He appeared to be a newbie, looking barely eighteen, with freckles on his face and red hair messily tucked under his police cap. He stood still, as if guarding the dead man with his life.

She tried to suppress a grin. Those newbies always looked so terrified and ill at ease. But then again, she remembered her first day, and not much had changed. At least this one hadn't thrown up… yet.

"Sergeant?"

He jumped up, straightened his back, and looked at her with wide eyes. "Yes, ma'am."

His voice was a little hoarse and deeper than expected, but it was still young and surprisingly full of energy. He looked scared, like a little boy thrown into something that was beyond him, but the way he had addressed her said something different. A certain ambitious ruthlessness shone through, and she found herself intrigued.

"Who found him?" she said.

"One of the neighbors. Inspector Karlsson is talking to him."

"Any CCTV?"

The young man gave her an incredulous look. "Here? No, I don't think so. People don't really..."

"Many of them want to protect their property in a neighborhood like this... like the shop owner over there." She pointed to the building on the main street, across the entrance to the alley, barely visible between the dumpsters. The windows were covered with metal roller shutters, and one might have thought it was abandoned, but Isa had seen in the light of the lamppost someone close the curtain on the upper floor when she had arrived. "Likely our victim came in from the main street, so I need to know if there are any cameras on that side that could have picked up our victim."

"Why? Isn't this just an accident?"

Isa frowned. "I expect a report on my desk tomorrow morning."

"Yes, ma'am." The young man turned and walked, as a good little soldier, in the direction of the main street.

"The CCTV will be useless," Timo said.

She crossed her arms. Her limbs felt cold and stiff from the cold.

"I doubt there is a camera, and even if there is one, I doubt the owner would admit it. There is too much stuff going on here that they don't want police to see."

"We can only try," Isa said.

"Well, I think this is more interesting." He gestured for her to come closer.

He didn't look up when she joined him, keeping his gaze fixed on the dark object on the floor between two dumpsters. "What does this seem to you?"

"Uh... it's a bag," she said, a bit surprised. "It's just some trash."

"No." He took out the latex gloves from his pocket and knelt.

As Isa observed her partner, she felt a twinge of sadness. Despite his occasional bizarre thoughts and exhausting conversations, he was usually right on the money. But now, as he quietly absorbed the scene before him, she sensed they were losing him. His loneliness and surliness were symptoms of a deeper issue. He was discontented with not being promoted to superintendent, and his heart was shattered after finding his girlfriend's killers eight years after her death. But there was more to his troubles than just those things, and she couldn't quite pinpoint what it was. After visiting the psychiatric hospital and speaking with the murderer who they believed avenged his girlfriend Caijsa, he had become even more withdrawn and silent.

She turned to him. "Why is this significant?"

"The temperature is below freezing and it's snowing," he said, gesturing at the swirling flakes. "For a wanderer, a bag with food, clothes, and an extra blanket are precious possessions. So why would he leave them behind?"

"You think there's a witness?"

"Maybe. The owner of this stuff left it here and hasn't come back to pick it up. We need to find him or her."

"Let's not jump to conclusions just yet. It doesn't mean this was left here when Valkama died."

She quickly put on a pair of latex gloves and knelt beside the bag. It was a common bag for hikers. Everything was frozen stiff from the cold and moisture.

"Let's see," Timo said.

"So, Paikkala, what do we have?" a deep voice thundered through the air.

It was Finn, their new boss, and Timo's pained expression revealed how much he despised facing him.

"Likely just an accident," Timo said, trying to sound casual.

Isa's eyes widened and opened her mouth to intervene, but Timo's frown signaled her to keep quiet.

Finn's expression was unreadable. "Okay but keep me up to date."

And then he walked away.

Timo let out a deep sigh. "Why was he even here?"

Isa shrugged. "And why didn't you tell him about the bag?"

Timo's voice dripped with sarcasm as he replied, "Because I don't want him to meddle. This is our case."

Isa gave him a puzzled look. "But whether you like it or not, he's still the boss. He'll find out anyway."

* * *

Timo looked at Dr. Olsson's cluttered desk and felt a sense of claustrophobia settle in. Despite Ingrid's impressive ability to balance a full-time job and motherhood, her workspace was a study in controlled chaos. In contrast, Isa preferred a pristine workspace, especially when working on a big case.

Isa often told him it made her think better. Although he had to say that his partner, with her perpetual procrastination, tended to pass the pile of files, screaming for her attention, almost unnoticed to her neighbor's desk, which was his. He had recently moved from an individual office—now that he was no longer the superintendent—to the open space and was now very aware of Isa Lindström's annoying little habits.

"So, you're in charge of the investigation," Ingrid said.

"Yep, together with Isa. Why do you ask?"

"Well, there are rumors."

"What rumors?" he said in a stern voice.

"That you're leaving."

He gazed at her for a moment and then lowered himself into the swivel chair at her desk. "Do you want me to leave?"

He was aware he had placed the emphasis a little too much on 'you'.

She stood there for a few moments, silent and showing a glance of awkwardness. Her eyes were cast down, focused on the latex gloves in her hands. She began to fidget with them nervously, before finally throwing them into the bin and walking over to the desk where he was sitting. She opened the file lying in the middle of the table.

"Okay. Lauri Valkama died of a heart attack, but I cannot rule out poisoning. There was damage to his heart, but for the rest he was in perfect shape. No blockages in the arteries or signs of inflammation. His medical history didn't reveal any underlying conditions that could have led to the heart attack. I sent samples of blood, urine, hair, and tissue to the lab for further analysis."

In his mind, he was still trying to process the silence, her not answering the question he wanted answered. He had to put his frustration aside and move on. "So, we cannot rule out an accident, neither foul play."

"I can't say for sure until we get the toxicology report," she replied, handing him the file. "But I'd say the damage to his heart was that unusual that you can almost assume it is something else than natural causes."

He opened the file and quickly scanned through it. Although, he had to admit, he didn't really understand what he was reading.

"Analysis of the hair could tell us when the exposure started."

"You think he was being poisoned over a longer period of time?"

"Could be, although there wasn't substantial damage to the other organs."

He continued to go through the file. "This must have something to do with Karst Engersson. It can't be a coincidence."

"Do you think Valkama was involved in the shooting?"

"I don't know," he said, shaking his head. "But when I talked to him, I had the feeling he wasn't completely honest with me. We were never able to identify who ordered the attack, but I think Valkama knew something."

"And now someone decided to kill him," Ingrid said as she walked up to where he was sitting and leaned over to look at the file in his hands. He smelled her soft, sweet scent and realized that this was new. She had changed her perfume. Then he remembered the passionate kiss on the doorstep of his lake house weeks ago. And then a farewell kiss days later in his office when he still had been superintendent.

He gave her the file and got up. He couldn't stand being so close to her. Everything about her bothered him. The seemingly emotionless expression on her face, the conversation that didn't allude to the sexual tension still present between them—or maybe that was all in his head—and the unilateral decision she had taken to end things before they had even started.

"When you have the full report, let me know," he said.

As he reached for the door handle, she blurted out, "No, I don't want you to go." His annoyance grew as he turned to face her.

"Are you serious?" he snapped.

She looked away. "I just... I don't want you to leave."

He could feel his anger boiling inside him as he asked, "And why is that?"

After a moment of hesitation, she replied, "I don't know... I just don't want you to leave."

He sighed and shook his head. "Nothing has changed, right?"

She hesitated before answering, "Nothing has changed."

"Okay then," he said, reaching for the door again.

But before he could open it, she spoke up. "I miss you. I miss talking to you."

He was taken aback, but then disappointed as she clarified, "I miss my friend."

He looked down, feeling a mix of frustration and sadness. "We haven't talked in weeks. I tried to reach out to you, but you were always busy. It seemed like you were avoiding me."

He took a deep breath before continuing, "You made a decision. We're colleagues, not friends. Nothing has changed on my end either."

You broke my heart.

As he looked at her, he struggled to find the words. She was so beautiful, with a unique charm that defied conventional standards of attractiveness. He felt foolish and naïve for ever believing she would leave her husband for him.

"I'm sorry," she whispered.

In that moment, he finally understood the depth of her pain. He had been so wrapped up in his own desires that he never stopped to consider the emotional turmoil she must have endured when deciding whether or not to leave her family and marriage. It was a decision that could not have been easy, and he felt ashamed for never acknowledging that.

As his fingers relaxed their grip on the doorknob, he looked at her with newfound empathy. He knew that he couldn't undo the hurt he had caused, but he could start by showing her that he understood. "I'm sorry. How have you been?"

A faint smile crossed her lips as she replied, "Kjell, my youngest, is doing much better now. The nightmares are gone. Benno, on the other hand, is acting like a typical teenager—frustrated and annoying most of the time. Anton, as always, is busy with work and struggling with everything that's happened at Global Law."

She let out a heavy sigh.

"I heard Global Law is going through some tough times," he said.

Her expression grew solemn as she confirmed his suspicions. "Yes, it's been a difficult time for everyone. The other partners have taken over, and they're considering downsizing the company and changing its name. As for Anton, he can't seem to decide whether he wants to stay or leave. He's been spending most of his time commuting to the Uppsala office, sometimes staying there overnight. So, I'm mostly alone."

As she spoke, his mind replayed the hurtful words someone had said to him just months earlier.

"... I guess she must be frustrated with Anton's exploits. I understand her. If I had a husband who slept around like he does, I'd do the same..."

He knew Lyn Hjort, his deceased girlfriend's half-sister, was trying to manipulate him, but her words still stung. Despite his reservations, he couldn't shake the feeling that Anton had a hidden side, and he needed to protect Ingrid.

He had tried to share his concerns with Isa, but her unwavering loyalty to the couple left her blind to the truth. Anton and Ingrid were the picture of a successful marriage in Isa's eyes, and she had even scolded him for suggesting otherwise.

He didn't want to come across as bitter or vengeful, but he couldn't shake his unease about the situation.

"But I want to talk about you," he said. "How are you feeling?"

"I'm..." She stared with furrowed brows at the screen of the computer. "I know you're angry and you talk about not being friends, but I need my friend right now," Ingrid whispered and then looked at him, eyes watery with tears.

"What's wrong?"

"I'm scared," she admitted, bowing her head. "I try to tell myself it's all in my head, but I can still feel her breath on my face... the gun... I thought I was going to die."

The abduction.

"Why didn't you tell me?" He felt guilty for not realizing something was wrong.

"I'm sorry... it's not your problem," she whispered, wiping away her tears.

He was astonished at what Ingrid had kept to herself. How could he have been so careless? He was a police officer; he knew how to handle life-death situations, but Ingrid had never dealt with a real threat to her life.

"Of course it's my problem," he said firmly.

He hesitated, his mind a jumbled mess of conflicting emotions, but then walked up to her. She let out all the feelings she had bottled up for weeks—the anger, the fear, the terror. Her body was shaking as he took her in his arms.

"It is my problem." He felt responsible for the abduction. He had failed to protect her. Because of him, she had gone through agonizing hours of not knowing if she would survive. She had talked about her son's nightmares starting after her abduction, but how could he have been so blind to her fears?

She looked up at him, and he felt a familiar pull towards her. He knew it was wrong, but he couldn't help it. Her lips were so close, and he wanted to kiss her so badly. But he couldn't. He had to remind himself of the reality of the situation.

He gently pushed her away. "We can't do this. You need to talk to Anton."

Her face fell, and he could see the disappointment in her eyes. "Timo, I...," she started to say, but he cut her off.

"I can't be the one to comfort you. Not like this. You need to talk to your husband." Then he turned and walked away, feeling a sense of emptiness inside him.

***

"Where is Heimersson?" Lars said.

"In Stockholm," Timo answered.

"I don't understand. He's the new superintendent, but we've hardly seen him."

Timo shrugged, uninterested in Lars' displeasure, and turned his attention to the whiteboard where Isa had posted the victim's picture. She had scheduled the first briefing for the new case, but Lars had been trying to intervene since he stepped into the room. Alongside Lars, Berger and Timo, the IT expert Sivert and two rookie police officers were present. Isa recognized the red-haired officer from the crime scene and gave him a faint smile, but he met her gaze with a look of terror.

The room was a testament to modernity and functionality. An oval-shaped table with a light oak laminate top and black sled-frame chairs dominated the center of the space. On one wall, a large whiteboard stood, and on the ceiling hung a beamer, ready to project any images or presentations required for the briefing. The building's renovation had taken months, but the result was impressive. Gone were the days of peeling paint and rickety doors that barely opened or closed.

Timo occupied the head of the table, and none had dared to assume his spot. Although Finn Heimersson held the title of superintendent, it was clear that Timo was still perceived as the leader in his absence. He was the one they relied on to spearhead the investigation, but Isa believed she wasn't doing too bad herself.

She focused her attention on the victim's photograph. The man in the picture had a narrow face with small eyes that appeared sad and distant. He was middle-aged and quite unremarkable looking.

"Lauri Valkama, fifty years old, married, two young daughters," she said. "He was born in Sweden—he's actually a local—but his parents are Finnish. It might be a good idea for you to talk to them, Timo, since you're a native speaker."

Timo raised an eyebrow. "Why? I assume the police already told them about their son's death."

"Yes, but it seems he called his parents just before leaving the office. At least that's what they told us, and his phone records confirm this. I'm not sure if it's the accent, old age, or something else, but I think they're hiding something. What they did mention was that he sounded different... panicky, stressed."

Timo nodded. "Okay, I'll talk to them."

Isa walked over to the whiteboard and tapped it with her marker. "Lauri Valkama. A man who has managed to stay under the radar most of his life. No criminal record, not even a parking ticket. The toxicology report is still pending, but we're treating this as a suspicious death for now. He used to work at the Finnish embassy in Stockholm but left the job after meeting his wife. This was about ten years ago. He's been with the mayor's team at the Gävle Town Hall for a year, but before that, he worked at Global Law."

"That's quite a change in career," Lars said.

"No one knows for sure what he did in Stockholm. They're not making it easy for us to find out."

Timo said, "Diplomats don't like to share information and they don't think they need to work with the police. But I can help... I have my network."

Isa's frown deepened as she spoke, her eyes flicking over to each member of the team. "Valkama's name was linked to the Global Law shooting. We have to investigate whether his death is related to that incident."

Sivert chimed in, "He handled the company's finances, and there were some shady dealings involving complicated business arrangements."

Then Sivert turned his attention to his laptop, his fingers tapping quickly on the keys. The room fell silent, and it was only then that Isa noticed the cluttered table, strewn with papers, files, and empty coffee cups.

"And I talked to Kristoffer Solberg," Isa said.

"Your SÄPO buddy?" Berger let out.

Isa threw him an angry look, and then said, "He's not my buddy. One partner is more than enough."

Isa tried to nail Timo with an I-had-enough-of-your-whining look, a silent but meaningful glare that hinted at her frustration with his behavior these days. He had pushed her to the point where she found it increasingly difficult to put in the energy needed to keep their professional relationship going, after another incident that morning where he had started complaining about her messy paperwork.

He kept looking at the file in front of him, seemingly ignoring her little expression of annoyance.

"Why is national intelligence involved anyway?" Berger said.

Timo looked up. "They were zooming in on Valkama after the Global Law shooting. He might be the one who paid Nils Vollan to orchestrate the attack, which resulted in the death of Karst Engersson and several others."

"I don't get it," Isa said. "Valkama was close to Engersson."

Timo explained, "According to Lyn Hjort, Engersson wasn't the primary target, but Leif Berg, the Minister of Justice, was."

"But then Lyn took matters in her own hands and killed Engersson," Berger said.

"So, Valkama might not have realized that he was enabling the murder of his friend and past employer." Timo leaned back in his chair, allowing his eyes to rest upon the white ceiling for a moment.

Lars crossed his arms and leaned against the wall. "Who are we looking for? Someone who wants to avenge Engersson's death?"

Timo straightened up. "Lyn Hjort killed Engersson. There is no doubt about it. But we're looking for the person who set the whole thing up. The one who wanted to kill Leif Berg."

Isa's expression turned serious. "Let's not make any assumptions here. Timo, you'll talk to the parents. Lars and I will speak with his wife. She may have more information for us. And what's the status on the CCTV footage?" She turned her gaze to the young police officer who had been quietly taking notes in the back of the room.

The officer looked up, his face flushed with embarrassment from being caught off guard. "Uh... what, ma'am?" he replied nervously, trying to collect himself.

"What's your name?" Isa asked.

"Uh... Varg Mårtensson," he replied after a moment of hesitation.

Isa's frustration was apparent as she addressed sergeant Mårtensson again. "The CCTV footage from the night of the murder. Have we received it yet?"

Mårtensson appeared confused and embarrassed, causing everyone in the room to stare at him. "I gave it to Dr. Sivert," he said, pointing to the man with glasses and greasy hair who always sat a bit too close to Isa.

Isa frowned. "Doctor? Since when are you a doctor?"

Rumors had it that Sivert had finally found a girlfriend, but Isa wasn't sure she believed them. She gave him an inquiring look, taking in his greasy man bun and his Star Wars T-shirt. If he took better care of his appearance, had a better sense of style, and didn't exhibit behavior that was dangerously close to crossing boundaries, she might even go as far as to say that he was an interesting man.

"I have a Ph.D. in information technology," Sivert stated.

"I didn't know that."

"I'm not surprised," Sivert snorted. "Anyway, I still need to go through all the material."

Isa turned to Timo, a hint of satisfaction in her voice. "So, there was CCTV after all?" She relished the opportunity to prove him wrong for once. But Timo ignored her, engrossed in his own thoughts.

"What about the bag?" Berger asked.

Isa stepped up to the whiteboard and pinned a photo of a black bag to the board. "Okay, let's review what we know so far. DNA samples were taken from the bag, and we should have the results in a few days. We also have reports from neighbors who say they've seen a young girl, around eighteen or twenty years old, hanging around the area where the body was found. She's been spotted carrying a similar black bag, but nobody knows her name."

"It could be her," Berger said.

"But they haven't seen her since the night Valkama died," Isa added.

"We need to find her," Timo said.

"Wait a minute!" Lars shuffled through the papers in front of him before settling into his seat next to Berger. Isa braced herself for a long-winded report.

"Three railway workers reported an incident the same evening Valkama died," Lars began. "They were working on a broken rail about a kilometer away from the station. They finished early and were packing up when they heard a commotion on the tracks."

Isa leaned forward. "What kind of commotion?"

Lars hesitated for a moment before continuing. "They saw a man assaulting a woman. He had his hands around her neck. When the workers tried to intervene, both the man and woman disappeared."

"Could they identify them?" Timo asked.

"They couldn't," Lars said. "They were too far away, but the woman could be our witness. We could have the station staff work with our sketch artist to get a first drawing."

Timo stood up and leaned against the wall. "If she's a witness, we need to find her."

Isa sighed. "A witness to what? Poisoning is a great way to kill someone from a distance. It's doubtful the killer was even there. Maybe she stole his wallet and phone and fled the scene, leaving the bag behind."

"Maybe," Timo said. "But we can't rule anything out. We need to analyze that CCTV footage as soon as possible."

Sivert spoke up. "I'll get started right away."

Timo looked at the picture on the board and then turned to the others. "We need to assume Valkama was going to the train station to go home like he did every day. Did he make a stop somewhere? Did he talk to anyone? Was there something unusual? If the lab results confirm he died of acute poisoning, he must have been exposed to the toxin about one or two hours before dying. Where did that happen? At work or somewhere else?"

He took a deep breath and continued. "Sivert, check his phone records and financials. Lars, talk to the railway workers again. I'll talk to the parents, and Isa can talk to his wife and colleagues. Someone wanted Valkama dead. We need to find out who it was."

* * *

"They still see you as the boss," Isa said when she and Timo were alone. She dropped in the chair next to him.

"But I'm not and they need to realize that. Heimersson and I are different; he likes his soldiers to be in line."

"I've noticed. I didn't like him when he tried to steal the Sandviken case from me back when he was in Uppsala, and I don't like him now. But I'll do what he expects me to do."

Timo raised an eyebrow. "That doesn't sound like you."

"I've been suspended too many times. Besides, I thought you'd be more supportive of your friend."

He sat up and collected the papers scattered across the table. Suddenly, Isa sprang to her feet as if a forgotten thought had struck her. "Wait, I need to give you something!" With that, she hurriedly exited the room.

Timo stared out the window at the falling snow and sighed. Christmas was just a few weeks away, and he dreaded being alone. Had he made the right decision to stay? Wasn't he better off in Stockholm? At least he had friends there, and if he were lucky, he could visit his family now and then. Not that he yearned to see his overly dramatic mother and villainous brother, but he needed to talk to someone, really talk.

He scrunched the papers in frustration before tossing them back on the table. He still had to write a report on a violent burglary, and he was feeling overwhelmed. Procrastination had taken over his life the past weeks, and now he was feeling the consequences. He had been staring too many times at Caijsa's file. Now, he felt numb, and nothing could hold his interest. It was so unlike him—he used to be so passionate and energetic.

Where had all of that gone?

"Happy birthday!" he heard someone say, and the next moment a tartlet with a single burning candle was placed under his nose.

He looked up and saw a smiling Isa. "Uh... thank you," he said, staring at the flame. "Besides the fact that this is a fire hazard... how do you know?"

"Fire hazard? As always, optimism is one of your best qualities," Isa said with a smile. "I know because I've seen your file, Timotheus Yefgeni Nikolai Aukusti Gunnvaldur Paikkala."

He laughed. "Oh, wow. You've been studying."

"Timotheus, seriously, five names?"

"My mother got a little carried away, but I hope you'll be able to forget this. Otherwise, I'll have to call you Isabel, and I don't think you like that name any more than I like Timotheus."

She smiled. "Fair enough. Forgotten already."

"But it's much appreciated." He looked at the candle and tried to force a smile on his face. "Thirty-six."

At thirty-six, he felt like he hadn't reached any significant milestones in his life. His father, on the other hand, had already accomplished so much by that age—he was married with children and had traveled the world. His father was a prominent figure with big aspirations and a successful reputation, while he felt like he had nothing to show for himself. His mother may not have expressed it explicitly, but he could sense her disappointment in his lack of achievement.

"Make a wish," Isa said.

"Lindström, seriously?"

"It's your birthday, so you're allowed to make a wish." She moved the candle closer to him. "You never know, wishes can come true, but maybe not always in the way you had hoped."

He shrugged and blew out the candle.

"Any plans?"

"Not really," he said. "But if you want, I can offer you a great curry."

She made a strange face. "With all due respect, I'm still reeling from your last attempt."

A warm smile graced his face. Over the past weeks, Timo had found himself growing closer to Isa. Perhaps it was the shared sense of loneliness that had brought them together. They had gone climbing on weekends, and he had even invited her to his house to taste his latest culinary experiments. Timo had a passion for experimenting with various flavors and cuisines, although at times he tended to go overboard with it.

"Why don't you invite your mom?" she asked.

"My mother always forgets my birthday—not that I mind. She usually calls the next day to make up for it. My brother knows not to call."

"Speaking of your brother... I have a meeting with a certain Fredrik Paikkala tomorrow. Do you know him by any chance?"

He looked at her surprised. "Yeah, that's my dear brother, but why?"

"This morning, Heimersson called me into his office and gave me a new assignment. I'll still be working on the Valkama case, but I also need to keep an eye on Leif Berg."

He frowned "What does that have to do with my brother?"

"Didn't you know? He's Berg's chief of staff."

Timo's head shook in disbelief. "What? Leif Berg is a centrist. My brother is as right-wing as anyone can be. This has to be a mistake."

"I'm meeting Fredrik tomorrow to discuss the New Year's convention of the Social Democrats in January. We have been asked to set up security for Minister Berg. It's a quite intense program, with a bunch of meetings and TV interviews."

Timo sighed. "What is it with this guy? He's in the news all the time. And wasn't there a convention last September?"

"I know," Isa said and leaned backward. "But it seems there is a real threat that someone is trying to kill him. Lyn Hjort wasn't lying."

"Leif Berg is in trouble. He has problems within his own party. He had a few run-ins with Prime Minister Olav Hult."

"And there is the Eirik Lunde scandal."

"Who is that?" Timo asked.

"His campaign manager. Two women have accused him of inappropriate behavior."

"Oh, okay," Timo stammered.

"You're not interested in politics? Strange for the son of a former diplomat."

"I am interested in politics, not gossip," he said with a straight face.

"Anyway, I see you're not a fan of Leif Berg."

"I'm not and neither should you. He's abusing his power to get the Sandviken case reopened and he's going to succeed."

"He does remind me of you," Isa said and stood up.

"Why?"

"He has these strange blue eyes."

"Everyone has blue eyes here," Timo said, his voice stern.

"Not everyone, and not everyone has these peculiar—how shall I put it—icy blue eyes that can pierce right through your soul."

A look of annoyance crossed his face. "Icy? Soul?"

"Never mind." She quickly glanced at her watch. "I need to go."

"A date?"

"Not really. I want to talk to Nick's parents since he doesn't want to talk to me."

"Nick Petrini? How is he? Where has he been?"

"Everywhere and nowhere, trying to find his inner voice, and now he's back. He checked into a psychiatric hospital and... obviously he's ignoring me."

"Lindström, the guy checked into a psychiatric hospital! This means he's not okay. This means he needs professional help. It's not about you."

"I just want to know how he is," she whispered. "I'm worried."

"I know you are," Timo said, putting his hand on her shoulder. "But maybe you should give him the time and the space to heal. He's been through a lot—seeing his colleagues die in that senseless shooting and being taken at gunpoint. He doesn't know how to deal with something like that. Give him time!"

"You're right," she said and smiled. "You're always right."

"Not always, but most of the time."

"Yeah, yeah." She got up and walked to the door. "Anyway, enjoy the evening and what's left of your birthday."

"Thank you for the cake," he said, but she had already left.

He stared at it before discarding the remaining bits into the bin. He felt even more alone than before. Life just moved on and his was at a standstill again.

* * *

It was pitch-black outside. The kind of darkness that descended on the Nordic countries in the middle of the afternoon. A reminder of the brutal power of nature that could bring the world to a halt. Timo always had mixed feelings about winter. He hated the short days and the perpetual darkness that hung over the Scandinavian lands. Snow and ice were no longer things he enjoyed since his father had died in a horrific car accident caused by black ice just a few days after Timo's birthday.

He could try to distract himself by returning to Caijsa's file, but it wouldn't help him escape the thoughts of her death, her betrayal, and the falsehood of the life he had thought they shared. It was eating away at him, consuming him, dragging him into a black hole of depression and despair, day by day.

If only he could confide in someone.

The thought of Ingrid immediately came to mind, but he had pushed her away with his foolish pride and resentment after she had dumped him. He knew he should get over it, but the realization that he was only human and could be brutally egocentric and vindictive disappointed him.

He gathered the papers, switched off the light, and made his way to his desk, resigned to another night of pondering about Caijsa's death and his purpose in life.

CHAPTER

3

FREDRIK PAIKKALA WAS the polar opposite of his younger brother, Timo. Average height, blond hair, and brown-green eyes. He exuded a polished and charming demeanor that showed off his privileged upbringing. As she sat across from him in one of the most expensive restaurants in Gävle, she couldn't help but observe the constant and annoyingly charming smile that never seemed to leave Fredrik's face.

It was clear why he and Timo didn't get along.

She gazed at the oversized cappuccino placed in front of her, then shifted her attention to Frederik, who was finishing his breakfast. Leif Berg's chief of staff was a man who believed in starting the day with an elaborate meal. Politely declining his offer to treat her to breakfast, she had almost expected him to deliver a Timo-like sermon on the importance of a healthy breakfast, but he hadn't. The coffee was lackluster, and she knew it wouldn't do much to alleviate her exhaustion. Last night was a long one. Ignoring Timo's advice, she had contacted Nick's parents at 10 p.m. They had been gracious and understanding when they explained why Nick had made the difficult decision to seek professional help. After their separation, Nick had been doing well, or so everyone thought. Pro bono work had given him a sense of purpose in life, but he had hidden his night terrors and insecurities from them, and it had gradually eroded his confidence. His mother had been horrified when she found him lying in his own vomit on the floor of his apartment. It had become apparent that Nick had been concealing his addiction to alcohol, and he was now in a very dark place where they couldn't help him.

Timo was right. She was again so caught up in her own life.

"So, you work with Timotheus," Fredrik interrupted her musing, as he signaled the waiter to clear the table and bring him another coffee.

"Yes, I work with Timo."

"Timo? His name is Timotheus. He hates it, but that's why I keep calling him that way."

She took a sip of her coffee. "Yeah, you guys seem like a really great and loving family."

"Like any other family I guess."

"Any other privileged family," she corrected.

"You think we are a privileged family?"

"When I first met Timo, it seemed as though he had an entire fleet of cars. He was staying in hotels, trying to find a house. He was like a poor little rich guy, always talking about fighting against the upper-class mentality of his family, but he couldn't really detach himself from his family's money and status."

"That's my brother. Saint Timotheus is always the one to point out our flaws and how much he hates our lifestyle, but he's not perfect. He's not an angel, and he has secrets too."

"Secrets?"

He gave her a teasingly mysterious smile.

"Oh, come on! You can't say A without B."

He looked at the cup of coffee in front of him. "I was going to call him when I heard about Caijsa, but I didn't. I feel bad about it. The reopening of the case must have been tough. How did he take it?"

"Bad. Of course, he tried not to show it, but it hit him hard and even now I think he can't get it out of his head. I guess you knew Caijsa."

"Oh yeah, I knew her," he said, a bit too expressly.

"Interesting. You didn't like her?"

"Well, mom didn't like her, but there was a good reason for it."

"And that is?"

"Caijsa was my girlfriend."

"What?" She almost dropped the cup of coffee.

"Before she was Timo's girlfriend, she was mine."

"What happened?"

He shrugged and continued, "I don't know. My parents hired her to tutor us when we moved back to Sweden, and we fell in love. But then, out of the blue, she suddenly broke it off. Six months later, Timo and Caijsa were a couple. He had always been jealous of our relationship."

Isa frowned. "You think he took her from you, on purpose?"

That didn't seem like the Timo she knew.

He waited for a moment and then said, "She was the most beautiful woman I had ever seen. She was my first girlfriend. It was hard to get over her."

The rivalry between the brothers was definitely Cain and Abel-esque. Fredrik might have been the easy bad guy—pretentious, rude, arrogant—but maybe she shouldn't underestimate Timo.

But she also knew Fredrik had designed this whole scene to make her feel sorry for him. After all, Fredrik and Timo were the sons of Valesca

Ignatova, the infamous Russian movie star. Born actors.

"I'm married now. I have a beautiful wife, Pamela, and three incredible children. But the humiliation is still there, after all these years and after everything that's happened. Maybe I will never forgive my brother."

"So, Leif Berg," she interrupted his lamentation.

He sighed. "Yes. Let's talk business. As you know, SÄPO considers the Global Law drama as an attempt to kill Leif Berg."

"That's not entirely accurate," Isa said, leaning back in her chair. "It was an attempt to kill Karst Engersson. But besides one rather untrustworthy testimony, there is no actual evidence they wanted to kill Leif Berg. And there is a link with the sabotage at Forsmark, the nuclear plant."

"That is still under investigation, but it might be totally unrelated."

"The plans were found on the laptop of one of the attackers. So, there is a link, and the motive might have been something else than Leif Berg."

"Not my concern. My priority is keeping Leif Berg alive."

"Isn't there a conflict of interest?"

"What do you mean?" Fredrik said, surprised.

"SÄPO falls under the authority of the Ministry of Justice, led by your employer. Looks to me these concerns about his safety are a bit excessive and he's using—or rather abusing—his power to get SÄPO involved."

"So what? He's the Minister of Justice. His safety should be guaranteed regardless. This is not just a faint hunch. He has gotten several emails and letters."

"What did they say?"

"The emails were sent in a span of several weeks, full of details about the organization of the convention. Things only insiders know, and... they knew about the accident."

"Which accident?"

"Berg was driving in Stockholm about a month ago when he lost control of his car, and it ran off the road near Uppsala. Luckily, he wasn't injured. Later we discovered someone had messed with the brakes."

"Does he usually go off alone?"

"Rarely, especially this last year when he became Minister."

"So, this was well planned," Isa said.

Fredrik nodded. "There were two other incidents. Two weeks after the car accident, someone broke into the headquarters."

"Anything stolen?"

"No, but they seemed to be searching for something. In fact, the first incident occurred a week before the car accident. Berg was visiting the City Hall here in Gävle when he suddenly complained of a sharp headache and earache. We discovered he had been grazed by a bullet on the side of his head. The wound was only superficial. No one saw or heard anything, and the attacker disappeared. We found the bullet casing, but no other clues."

"So, it looks like someone is really targeting Berg."

"Berg isn't a saint. Everyone knows that. He loves money, fast cars, and women. And you can argue about it, but he horribly abused his daughter Anna's disappearance and murder to get the favor of the public. Yet, who will go that far to kill him?"

"Send me the emails and give me the details about the incidents. I'd like to dig a little deeper myself. If these incidents are connected, the perpetrator has left traces."

"I'll ask my assistant to send you the input you need," he said.

Isa shifted her gaze to the window. A man outside the restaurant was pressing his face against the glass, almost as if he were searching for someone inside. As soon as he noticed Isa looking back at him, he quickly took a step back and disappeared into the crowd.

Strange. She didn't know what to think of it but quickly pushed the incident out of her mind.

"So why Gävle?" Isa asked.

"It was Leif's idea. Nobody else wanted it here, but he insisted."

"Do you know why?"

Fredrik shrugged. "No. Maybe he thought it would be safer than Stockholm."

"That seems unlikely. There must be some other reason."

"It's not my job to know. Our job is to make sure he stays safe."

"When does the convention start?" Isa asked, flipping through her notebook.

"Mid-January. It's a week-long event with a lot of high-profile guests from Sweden and other countries."

Isa leaned in closer. "If you want us to do our job, you need to tell me everything you know."

"I've told you everything. You can trust me."

"With all due respect, I'm not sure I can. Your brother was surprised to hear that you were working for Berg."

"I'm sure he was. But he doesn't know me as well as he thinks he does."

Isa let out a sigh. "Send me any information you have, and I'll get back to you by the end of the week with our plan for the convention."

"Will do. And in case you're interested in anything other than work... maybe we could have dinner?"

Isa raised a brow. "Just so you know, your brother and I are only colleagues and friends. Nothing more. And if you're thinking about getting revenge on him for Caijsa, I suggest you think twice. Besides, aren't you a happily married man?"

He gave her a half-hearted smile and took a card from his pocket, sliding it across the table to her. "Too bad... but if you change your mind," he said. "Anyway, it was nice meeting you."

Fredrik got up.

She looked at the card. This was her old life. She could take it and acknowledge that her good intentions were just a scam, something that lived in her head, but she could never live up to.

Yes? No?

She got up and started to walk to the exit, the card still lying on the table. But she couldn't just leave it and went back to take it. Temptation was stronger than herself. She told herself that this didn't mean she'd go back to the one-nightstands and meaningless relationships where it was all about sex. This didn't mean anything. She didn't even find him attractive.

But meeting Fredrik Paikkala left an impression. She only didn't know if it was a good or a bad one.

***

"Most of the people at the homeless shelters only know her by her first name, Tuva. Nobody seems to know her last name."

Lars stood next to Timo's desk, waiting patiently. Timo closed his laptop and looked up at the young man. "Okay, let's wait for the DNA results to come back. Maybe we will find a name. But the more I think about it, the more I'm convinced we need to find her... fast."

"I've been told she has a close friend. A girl she spends most of her time with. A Greta... something. She might know where Tuva is."

"I'm not sure if this is the best way to go about finding Tuva, but it's worth a shot," Timo said. "So, yeah, see if you can find this Greta."

"The guy from the shelter said she's been hanging around the docks a lot. He said he'd contact us when she shows up. By the way, Dr. Olsson called me. The toxicology report is in. I'm going to the lab now."

"Ingrid called you?"

"Is there a problem?" Lars asked.

"No, no... it's fine."

Five minutes later, Timo and Lars found themselves walking down the hallway in silence.

"Did she say anything about the results?" Timo grumbled.

"No, nothing." Lars opened the door to the forensics lab.

Timo felt himself tense with every step, dreading the prospect of seeing Ingrid. There was a time when the thought of seeing her filled him with anticipation, but now it was painful and awkward.

As they entered the forensics lab, Mila, Dr. Olsson's assistant and Berger's fiancé, greeted them with a radiant smile. But Lars' face became noticeably grim at the sight of her.

"Good afternoon, Inspector Paikkala," Mila said.

Her smile disappeared, and she said with a deep voice, "Lars."

Timo had never noticed before but these two were not friends.

"You have something for us," Timo said.

Ingrid, who Timo had not noticed in the back of the room, interrupted, "The toxicology report."

Timo's anxiety rose.

Ingrid signaled for the two men to come closer as she walked to the desk, straightening her back. Mila joined her at the other side of the table, her expression turning gloomy and distant as she looked at the men.

Ingrid said, "Mila, is there something wrong?"

Mila stammered, "Nothing. But do you want me to stay? I have a lot of work to do."

Ingrid said in a stern voice, "It would be nice if you could stay... since you work here."

Timo frowned. Ingrid was being irritable and cold, and he didn't like it.

Mila nodded. "Of course, Dr. Olsson."

"So?" Timo said.

And he too did not escape Ingrid's wrath when she glared at him. "The lab results confirm he had large amounts of scopolamine in his system."

"Scopolamine?" Lars said.

"It's a drug, also known as 'Devil's Breath'," Ingrid said, her tone sharp. "It's derived from a plant found in South America and is known for its ability to cause amnesia, hallucinations, and suggestibility. It's often used in robberies, kidnappings, and sexual assaults. Just like atropine it is a tropane alkaloid, but it is much more potent and longer lasting, and it has more prominent effects on the central nervous system."

Lars' face grew serious as he directed his gaze towards Ingrid.

She continued, "The amount of scopolamine was quite high, so it's likely he was given a significant dose of it. The scopolamine triggered the heart attack and caused his death."

Timo rubbed his temples, feeling a headache coming on. "Why would anyone use scopolamine?"

Ingrid rolled her eyes. "Like I already said, this drug renders its victims susceptible. Likely his killer wanted to control him in some way, perhaps to get information or force him to do something."

"How did the drug get into his system?" Timo asked.

Ingrid said. "Mila?"

"Uh... I, uh...," Mila stammered. "What?"

The young woman looked at Ingrid with big eyes.

Ingrid took a deep breath before speaking, obviously annoyed with her assistant. "It can be ingested but scopolamine can be administered just by a small number of particles blown in someone's face, making it a highly effective and dangerous tool in the wrong hands. It's a very tricky drug to dose, though. Even a slightly higher amount can have severe consequences, such as causing a heart attack. It's a delicate balance between controlling someone and killing them. It's not something you want to mess around with."

"Dr. Olsson, you mentioned the poisoning could have started a while ago," Lars said.

Ingrid turned to the frail, slender woman standing next to her.

"Mila?"

"Uh...," Mila started and looked confused.

"The hair analysis?" Ingrid said with a straight face.

"I... haven't read the report yet," Mila had to admit.

Ingrid gave her another irritated look. "We can determine when the poison was administered by looking at the hair. But you have to keep in mind that hair analysis is not as reliable for detecting exposure to the drug, as it takes time for the drug to be incorporated into the hair fibers. Blood and urine are better indicators for detecting acute exposure to scopolamine. On top of that, scopolamine is rapidly metabolized and excreted from the body. So, it depends on the dose and individual factors like the victim's metabolism. Anyway, we did find traces of scopolamine at the root of the hair, but not at the tip."

"So, the poisoning started recently," Timo said.

"Well done," Ingrid said with a faint smile, but he could sense the sarcasm behind her words. "I'd say a few weeks ago to a month, but it could be longer. The fact that we find so many traces in the hair samples suggest that it was not a one-time event, and that Valkama was exposed to high doses of the drug."

"But he died of acute scopolamine poisoning," Lars said.

Ingrid nodded. "Yes. The last one was fatal."

Timo furrowed his brow. "Our killer was pressured into taking swift action. How long does it take to work?"

"It depends on how the scopolamine was administered. If given intravenously, it can take effect within minutes. If taken orally, it may take up to an hour to take effect," Dr. Olsson explained.

Timo turned to Lars. There was a sense of urgency in his voice. "I know you're focused on finding Tuva, but we need to talk to Lauri's colleagues and his wife. We can't rule anyone out, especially those closest to him."

Lars nodded in agreement.

Ingrid's face still showed her annoyance, and Timo felt the tension in the air.

After a moment of silence, Timo looked at Ingrid and Mila. "Thank you for the report. We have work to do. But Dr. Olsson, can I talk to you for a moment?"

"I'm busy," Ingrid said and looked at the paperwork on the desk.

"Uh, I'll just go back to the office," Lars said.

Timo saw Lars and Mila disappear. "Can we please talk?"

She looked up and sighed. "Okay then. So, talk!"

"You are too hard on her. She was clearly overwhelmed."

"Mila? I'm sorry, but Mila is my assistant, and she needs to learn. This was unprofessional of her. She wasn't prepared. And I would appreciate it if you stayed out of this."

"Okay, okay." He didn't want to have a fight.

"Anything else?"

"And I think... I need to apologize. I didn't want to be so blunt the other day. And..."

"And?"

"I need your help," he said quickly.

She frowned. "About what?"

"Can you check Caijsa's autopsy report?"

She stared at him for a moment, dumbfounded. "Why?"

"I... I need to know if she killed my child," he blurted. "If it was my child at all."

"I don't understand."

For weeks, a voice had been steadily growing louder in his head, taunting him with the idea that the love of his life had betrayed him, that she had wanted to leave him before her death. He tried to ignore it, to push it aside and focus on the good memories, but it was too persistent, too convincing. As time went on, it felt like everything he had built up over the years was crumbling around him, leaving him with nothing but the unbearable weight of his suspicions and grief.

"I want to know if she had an abortion."

"Timo, where is this coming from?"

He took a deep breath. "I think she had an affair."

She walked up to him and took his hand. "This is Lyn, right? Why do you let her get to you? She's a manipulator. Why do you believe her? Caijsa loved you. Why do you doubt that?"

He fixed her with a stare and then shook his head. "I did some digging, and the conferences and workshops Caijsa supposedly attended the year before her death don't even exist. Where was she? Everything Lyn has told me seems to be true."

And that also meant that what Lyn had said about Anton, Ingrid's husband, was true. Anton was an adulterous man.

"I'm begging you." He held her hands tightly as if he never wanted to let her go. "Please. I'm going crazy."

"Timo... I...," she started and then looked at the floor. "I don't know what to say. Even if I looked at her file, I don't think I can give you the answer. It's difficult to say if someone had a miscarriage or an abortion."

"Then how?"

"Her medical records. If she had an abortion, she must have had the procedure in a hospital. Do you have them?"

Timo shook his head.

"Her parents?"

"I can ask Marcel, her dad. But it's been so long. There was nothing mentioned in her case file. Maybe I can get a warrant to get access to her records. Maybe..."

"Stop this! Don't let this get to you! Time to move on, don't you think?"

He muttered in defeat. "I can't. I'm stuck. I'm completely stuck, and I don't know how to change it."

She let go of his hands. "I wish I could help you, but..."

"It's fine."

"No, it's not fine. You're not fine."

"Thanks," he said and then turned. With determined pace, he walked out of the room.

"Timo," he heard her say, but he couldn't turn back.

He didn't only feel stuck, he felt useless, inadequate. Why was he bothering her with his insecurities and doubts?

She had enough problems of her own.

CHAPTER

4

OUTSIDE, THE WIND WHIPPED fiercely and drove swirls and shards of snow through the air. Rolf—the man Tuva was looking for—jumped up and down to stay warm, but the thin pants and shirt he'd stolen from various dumpsters offered little protection from the cold.

The building was a squat, rusted-orange shell, a hulk of metal and concrete, just big enough to house a few people. The lone lightbulb that dangled precariously from the ceiling was broken, casting the room in darkness. She couldn't even remember what the building had been used for before it became a homeless shelter. There was a man balled up on the icy floor, his cap pulled over his head so deep that no one would even recognize him.

Rolf stepped outside when he saw her, and she followed. He leaned against the concrete wall, next to the entrance, and put a cigarette in his mouth. Smoke came out in small clouds, dissipating into the cold air.

Tuva gazed down at her hands; they were throbbing, and she could barely move her fingers. She lost one glove during the fight, and the other was now torn and barely hanging on. She shoved her hands into her pockets, where she could feel the paper. It was all that was left after the fight. She had stared at it a dozen times over the past days, but it never made any sense. The words were random and unconnected, with no context.

The bruises around her neck ached. After three nights freezing inside one of the abandoned train wagons, she'd finally worked up the courage to leave. She had been wandering around town for a while, not knowing what to do. Danger could be lurking around every corner. The man was still looking for her. She could feel it.

Greta would know what to do, but she hadn't seen her friend for days.

Rolf would surely know where she was. Rolf knew everything.

"Hey, you look like you need to let loose, and I know just the party where you can have a good time," he called out to a passerby who gave him a dirty look.

Rolf bared his teeth. They were yellow and black. He probably hadn't brushed them in over a decade.

"Look who the dog dragged in," he said.

"Cat."

He frowned. "What?"

"It doesn't matter. Rolf, I need your help."

He grinned. "My help? You never needed my help before. You know it comes at a price."

"I have no money," she snapped.

"Something else then?" He looked at her from top to toe.

"I have nothing. No hash, no meth, nothing."

He was propped up against the wall, looking like he hadn't eaten in days. His next fix was always more important than food.

She moved closer. "But I see you don't need me to provide your next shot. You're high."

He cast his eyes down and took another drag of his cigarette. "None of your business. What do you want anyway?"

"Greta. Where is she?"

"Haven't seen her for days."

"Come on, Rolf, she usually hangs around Boulognerskogen park or the docks. She wasn't there. What's going on?"

He gave her a sarcastic grin. "I saw her a few days ago, talking with two men. Didn't hear what they were talking about."

"Two men? Clients?"

He shook his head.

"Who then?" She shoved him against the wall. She was done with him constantly avoiding her questions.

"Oh, oh, harassment... of the worst kind," he said indignantly and then let out one of the scariest laughs she had heard in a long while.

"Don't be a baby! So, Greta and the men?"

"She sold you out," he said. "She's always been a ruthless bitch."

"I thought you didn't hear what they said?"

She stepped back and had another glance at him. "No, it's you. You sold me out! What did they promise you?"

He was so zoned out that it took him a minute to realize what she had said. With a blank stare, he looked ahead of him.

Tuva grabbed him by the arms and shook him. "Tell me!"

"They were looking for you."

"Who are they? Why were they looking for me?"

"I don't know. One had a beard and mustache. The other one was fat and tall."

"And did you tell them?"

He freed himself from her grasp. "No... how could I? I didn't even know where you were." He let his bony fingers run along her face and then continued, "Such a pretty girl... if only you had money... I could show you a good time."

Tuva pushed his hands away. "But they'll be back, and you'll give them all the information they want. Jeez, Rolf! For what?"

He grinned. "What did you do? They really... really want to find you."

She stepped back, fear washing over her. They were out to get her. And as she ran away from him, with the cold seeping through every fiber of her clothes and body, she realized she would never be safe. Rolf, Greta. She couldn't trust anyone. For the first time in a long while, she thought about her mother. The warmth of the fireplace, the warmth of her arms, her perfume. Her soft voice, the way her mother sang to her when she was scared, her encouragements. She desperately needed her. She missed her so much.

Who were these men? Were they allies of the man who had tried to kill her? Or maybe not? She stopped and stared at the snow on the ground. A bearded man. A tall, fat man. She had seen them before.

She couldn't trust Rolf. But Greta?

She needed to disappear for a while, and with Greta's connections, she could ensure that no one would be able to track her down.

* * *

Hannele Valkama almost tore the fabric of her seat as Isa and Lars told her the details of her husband's last moments. While Mrs. Valkama wallowed in drama, Isa tried to figure out if her grief was genuine.

Mrs. Valkama was the type of woman who loved status and money. She had a law degree but never worked a day in her life. She was beautiful, with long blonde hair styled in the latest fashion. She put it behind her ear to show off her diamond earrings. Her red nails were flawless, and she wore a white designer jumpsuit like she was about to attend a cocktail party. She had demanded a certain level of admiration from her husband. And Isa could see that Lauri Valkama, who had not been blessed with high cheekbones and a perfect nose, would have done anything for his wife to keep her happy.

"Mrs. Valkama, we think your husband's death was murder," Isa said.

"Murder?"

Mrs. Valkama gazed at the light-gray wall in her living room and then turned her attention to the floor-to-ceiling windows that looked out onto the garden. A beautiful white snow-covered garden, where the children had made their first attempt to build a snowman.

"It looks like your husband was poisoned," Lars said. "Scopolamine."

She kept her eyes on the garden. "I don't understand. Why?"

"That's what we're trying to find out," Isa said. "We're trying to figure out if it happened here, at work, or somewhere else."

"Here?" Mrs. Valkama said. "Is that why you want to turn my house inside out? Am I a suspect? How long does this poison last anyway?"

"We can't rule out anything. Poison is usually a woman's weapon."

Mrs. Valkama shouted, "That's bullshit! Prove it! And by the way, scopolamine can be found in prescription medication to treat motion sickness and nausea."

Isa raised her eyebrows. "You seem to know a lot about scopolamine."

"My grandfather was a pharmacist. I learned a few things from him."

"Interesting," Isa said.

"That doesn't mean I killed him," Hannele Valkama stammered.

"And did your husband take scopolamine as prescribed medication?" Isa asked.

"No... not that I know of."

"We ruled out an accident. That leaves murder."

"Was there anything out of the ordinary the day Lauri died?" Lars asked.

Mrs. Valkama narrowed her eyes before answering Lars' question. "No, but he wasn't feeling well. He hadn't been himself for weeks. I had been urging him to go see a doctor, but he refused. He was also quite nervous that day. When I asked him about it, he just said he had an important meeting and that he would be home late."

Isa leaned forward. "What was he feeling specifically? Can you tell me more?"

"He was always tired and drowsy, and he had a persistent cough. He was also losing weight. I was really worried about him, but he didn't listen to me. He was always busy with work and didn't take good care of himself."

Then Mrs. Valkama's eyes widened with fear as she spoke. "The blackouts. Oh my God, could it have been scopolamine?"

"Blackouts?" Isa asked, intrigued.

Mrs. Valkama's voice trembled as she spoke. "He mentioned to me that he often had blackouts and memory loss. He couldn't remember how he got places or what he had done. I didn't think much of it at the time. I just assumed he was overworked, but maybe I should have paid more attention."

"Can you think of any reason why he might have been nervous about the meeting?"

Mrs. Valkama thought for a moment and said with a quavering voice, her emotions barely under control. "He was always quite private about his work, so I don't know the specifics." Tears began to stream down her face. "Why would anyone want to kill Lauri? He was just a simple accountant."

Isa leaned back on the sofa, a designer piece that had caught her attention as soon as she had entered the room. She liked the style and simplicity, but she couldn't agree with Mrs. Valkama's statement that a simple accountant could have built a house like this.

"A simple accountant who can afford a house of ten million kronor," Isa said. "Lauri must have been doing something exceptional to have that much money."

Mrs. Valkama wiped the tears from her face. The mascara had smudged, leaving dark streaks down her cheeks. She took a deep breath, trying to compose herself. "My family is well off, and Lauri's grandmother left him a lot of money when she died, and we were lucky with our investments."

"We've looked into your finances, and we know that he has been doing quite well since he started working at Global Law. The money was pouring in."

"Okay, okay," she sighed and bowed her head. "He was Karst Engersson's special accountant."

"Special accountant? What does that mean?"

Mrs. Valkama shifted in her seat before continuing. "I met my husband while he was working at the Finnish embassy in Stockholm. My father was on the Finnish ambassador's staff, and we were often invited to the events they held. I met Lauri there. We got married two years later. These were good times."

Isa said with a straight face, "So why did your husband left his well-paid job and went to work for Global Law?"

"He wanted to move closer to his parents. I just found out I was pregnant..." She sighed before going on. "We wanted kids, but things didn't go so smoothly. You can tell we're not the youngest parents. I had my first kid when I was forty and my second one three years later. The money was just better."

She looked at the pictures of her husband and their daughters on the white cupboard.

"How he loved his girls," she let out and then wiped a tear away.

"Global Law, Mrs. Valkama?" Isa said.

The woman was getting on her nerves. Maybe she was a bit too touchy. After the phone call from her ex-husband Viktor that morning, Isa felt bad, but she didn't know why. She didn't have a good feeling about Viktor's request to meet. He was in Gävle, and he wanted to see her. She hadn't talked to him since he had sent her a letter announcing his marriage and asking his new wife to adopt their two kids, Olivia and Felix. Isa had left them when her ex-husband had moved to the UK five years ago and she hadn't seen them since.

She wanted to reach out to her children, but there was always an excuse not to. She wasn't a good mother. She was not good enough for them. They didn't even remember her. All of these were good reasons to take her parental rights away.

The court order had come with a date, in a month from now. She had put the paper in the cupboard. Before leaving, Nick had found her a lawyer, but ultimately, she still didn't know what she wanted. She still hoped to build a relationship with her children.

"Global Law, right," Mrs. Valkama said. "Karst approached him about ten years ago. He needed an accountant to arrange Global Law's finances, and he offered him a ton of money."

"To arrange the illegal accounts in the Bahamas. Does the name Nils Vollan or Sven Toksund sound familiar?"

"Sven Toksund. Yes. One of my husband's colleagues. He called a few times, and he came here once. I remember him. He was very rude."

Isa took a picture of Nils Vollan from the file in her hands and showed it to Mrs. Valkama.

"Is this the man?"

Mrs. Valkama nodded.

"Nils Vollan goes by the name Sven Toksund. We believe your husband was tasked with creating accounts that were used to finance illegal activities."

"What? No. This was Karst Engersson, Sweden's most renowned

lawyer!"

Isa's attention oscillated between the unfolding conversation and the wintry scene outside the large floor-to-ceiling windows. As if in response to the escalating tension, it started to snow again. The snowflakes were swirling in a mesmerizing flurry, painting a picturesque tableau beyond the glass. Then she turned her attention back to the woman sitting on the other side. "Does the name Rune Breiner ring a bell?"

"The dirty cop Engersson defended and who got murdered? Yes, from the news, but that's all."

"Your husband never talked about him?" Isa asked.

"No. That happened... about a year ago or so. By then, Lauri was already working at the City Hall in Gävle."

"Strange career move," Lars said. "Why?"

"He wanted to spend more time with the kids, and we had decided to move and build this house. But then he got this opportunity."

"It takes two hours to commute from Ljusdal to Gävle. That doesn't sound like he would get to spend much time with his family. Mrs. Valkama, why did he take the job?"

Mrs. Valkama stared at them for a moment and then said, "Karst forced him into it. Engersson fired him and then, on the same day, he was offered the job in Gävle. Little did we know Engersson was behind it."

"But why? What did he do there that was so important?"

"He was staff member and personal assistant to the mayor."

"So, he had access to confidential documents?"

"I'm not sure what you're trying to say, but it sounds like you think my husband is a criminal. Let me be clear: if that's what you think, then you can talk to my lawyer from now on. But if I were you, I'd start looking for my husband's murderer. Or..."

"Is that a threat?" Lars said.

She fell back in her seat and put her hands over her face. "This is a nightmare!"

65

"Mrs. Valkama, if you want to clear your husband's name, you need to help us. The warrant to search your home is..."

"Just do it," she yelled, before turning away from them and staring out the window. "His study is upstairs."

Her eyes glistened with tears as she turned her attention to the window.

Isa placed the official document on the glass table. Half an hour later, the forensics team arrived to begin their search.

* * *

Lars put up his collar and followed Isa to the car. "It's a bit strange. Karst Engersson hiring Nils Vollan. He practically paid for his own murder."

"But likely Engersson didn't know Vollan had other plans. Valkama's role is not clear to me. Maybe he was playing a double game. He worked for Engersson, but at the same time hired Vollan to plan an attack on Global Law and kill Engersson."

"But who killed Valkama?" Lars said as he got in the car.

Isa stared at the key in the ignition. "His client? Maybe Valkama had become a liability."

"There was nothing in that house. It was clean as a whistle. Nothing on the laptop except for a few files, no papers of any importance. Either she hid it, or he knew what was coming."

"Maybe there was nothing to hide," Isa said.

"Let's see what the forensics report shows. I'm curious to know if they'd found traces of scopolamine in that house."

"I doubt it."

"Great car by the way. Quite an upgrade."

"I guess," Isa said, and drove off to the south, direction Gävle.

She despised the car. It wasn't her grandmother's beloved Volkswagen anymore. The car had been destroyed beyond repair after

Lyn Hjort had rammed into it. It was as if she had to let go of her grandmother too. Timo had advised her that she didn't require a car to hold onto her grandmother's memory, but she was the kind of person who needed physical things to remember. The car and the house reminded her of her grandmother, the sweater reminded her of Alex, her dead love.

That's why she had burned everything associated with her former partner, who was currently confined to a psychiatric hospital for killing his romantic rival. As if she could erase him from her life that easily. It was foolish to believe it would work. Sometimes reality struck her hard, and it felt like it would knock her down.

As she drove along the coast to Gävle, her grandmother's memories faded. She'd matured since Nick had put a stop to their relationship. She had not engaged in any flings, one-night stands, or meaningless sex. She was proud of herself for maintaining her standards. The only thing she hadn't been able to cope with were her children. The thought of meeting Viktor heightened her anxiety.

She glanced over at Lars, who sat with his head against the window, unusually silent. The situation with Mila and Berger had disturbed him more than she had thought.

For a moment, she considered starting a discussion on the subject but decided against it. She wanted to keep her peace of mind.

The snow-covered scenery flashed by, and she felt a sense of warmth and anticipation. She adored everything about Christmas and New Year. Spending time with her friends, and even her parents. She needed that moment, far away from all the drama that had engulfed her life in the past year.

She grinned and grasped the steering wheel tightly.

Maybe Lars was right. The car wasn't as terrible as she had initially thought.

* * *

"What have we found out?" Finn's voice thundered across the room, jerking everyone to attention.

"His wife is hiding something," Lars said and put down the pen he'd been playing with. Berger was sitting on his left. Sivert, sitting across from him on the other side, was distracted and kept looking at his laptop.

"I agree; I don't think she's being completely honest with us." Isa was standing in the back of the room, leaning against the wall. "She knows the real reasons for his frequent career changes, but she chooses to ignore them. She's fond of luxury and status. If she has that, no matter where the money comes from, she doesn't care."

Finn dropped his two-meter tall and more than hundred kilo energy-draining body in one of the chairs. "So, our theory is that Valkama was paid to arrange illegal activities, and they killed him to make sure he kept quiet about it."

Isa nodded in agreement. "That might explain why scopolamine or burundanga was used to kill him. It's a drug used by criminal organizations to incapacitate their victims and make them more susceptible to suggestion."

"Money always leaves traces," Timo said and joined Isa in the back of the room.

Leaning back in his seat Finn chimed in, "I see your point. But at this stage, we shouldn't limit ourselves to just one theory. There could be multiple potential leads we haven't explored yet. For example, what if Valkama had an affair and the wife found out? We need to keep an open mind and consider all possibilities. What about the forensics report of the Valkama house?"

Lars said, "No traces of scopolamine were found. If someone was poisoning him, it must have been done somewhere else."

"Actually... Finn is not bad," Isa whispered and looked at Timo.

"I guess," Timo said. "When he decides to show up..."

She gave her partner another look. "Man, you look bad. What happened?"

Timo shrugged. "Not enough sleep."

"Do you have anything to add, Inspector Paikkala?" the deep voice said. "You two seem to be having a cozy chat over there. I'd like everyone's attention here. We're not a kindergarten."

"Yes... sir," Timo stammered.

Isa was taken aback by Timo's uncharacteristic behavior. He seemed lost, unsure, and lacking his usual confidence. She knew him as a natural-born leader who would take charge, inspire, and motivate his team to achieve results. But now that he was no longer in charge, it seemed like he had lost a part of himself.

She knew he was trying his best. It must have been difficult for him to watch someone else take over his role and oversee the team he used to lead. She wished she could find the right words to comfort him.

Finn continued, "Valkama called his parents just before his death. Do we know why?"

"It was a tense meeting," Timo said. "I was able to talk to them, but I could tell the father didn't appreciate my visit. The old man became a little cranky and would have kicked me out of the house if the mother hadn't stopped him."

"Your Finnish charm didn't work then," Isa grinned.

Finn gave her an angry look.

Then Timo said in his most serious voice, "Obviously not. What I wanted to say was, Valkama called his parents just before he went to the train station. He told them that Hannele and the kids would stay with them for a while."

"His wife didn't mention that," Isa remarked.

Timo said, "I assume Valkama knew that if he stayed, not only his life, but his family's lives would be in danger, so he told his parents he was going to disappear for a while."

"Did he say why?" Finn asked.

"No, but I probed a bit more and that's when Mr. Valkama got really nervous. The father used to have a transport company. Many years ago, before his retirement, he was accused of fraud, and guess who helped him with his judicial problems?"

"Engersson?"

"Exactly, and miraculously the case got suspended."

"You think Engersson used Valkama's father as leverage?"

"This happened right before Lauri moved to Global Law. I bet Engersson had him in his pocket."

"Valkama's father must have been in serious trouble," Lars said.

"I tried to find out," Timo said, "but the old man ended up throwing me out of his house. I won't say it, but the Finnish language can have some spicy words to express... well, let's say one's displeasure."

"Do you know that Finns swear more than Swedish people?" Berger said and gave him a smile.

"Then I guess I've got some learning to do. Though, I'm only half Finnish."

"The same level of profanity as Scots and Russians," Berger continued.

"Then I definitely have some catching up to do," Timo replied.

When Finn slammed his fist on the table, Isa could sense the tension in the air. She watched as his face turned red with anger and his eyes blazed with intensity. "We need to stay focused here, people. We don't have time to waste on pointless conversations. We have a murderer to catch, and every moment we spend dawdling is a moment that he gets further away from us."

Timo let out a sigh. "I think Engersson was blackmailing Valkama into working for him. Valkama seems to be some sort of whiz when it comes to financial accounting."

"And Engersson wanted the whiz," Isa said.

"What did we find out about Engersson's finances?" Finn turned to Sivert, who was clearly not listening. He jumped up and started nervously shuffling in his chair.

"Uh... there was the link with Brissitone, the subsidiary of Global Law, but there are many entities Engersson set up to transfer money and support certain activities."

"Illegal?"

"Apart from the link to Nils Vollan, no. Everything seems to be done nicely by the book. But I'm not there yet. This is a huge tangle of ghost companies, all linking to others. I need time."

"And all set up by Valkama?" Finn said.

Sivert met Finn's gaze, nodded, and then turned his face to the whiteboard. Lauri Valkama's picture loomed large in the center, a stark reminder of the man they were seeking justice for.

Timo said, "All to hide something bigger. We need to find out what it is. What is at the core of this?"

The next moment Timo was the subject of Finn's harsh gaze. "... sir." That one word was dripping with sarcasm.

"Rune Breiner," Isa said. "This might be about him."

"Breiner is dead, his file is classified," Finn said.

"But..."

"We need to focus on finding Valkama's killer. Sivert, keep tracking the money and let me know if you find anything. Inspectors Karlsson and Nyquist, look into Valkama's family and see what Engersson had on them. Isa, I need you to focus on Leif Berg from now on."

"But...," Isa started. Timo gave her a kick and a frown to keep quiet.

"What about the girl... sir?" Timo said.

Finn frowned. "What girl?"

"The witness. Has she been identified?"

Finn looked at the papers on the table and then quickly skipped through them.

"Dr. Olsson sent the DNA analysis report yesterday," Berger said. "She has been identified as Tuva Norling, nineteen years old. It's a sad story. She ended up in foster care at the age of twelve when her mother died. She has a history of running away from home and has been living on the street most of the time since she was sixteen."

"Criminal record?"

Berger said, "Shoplifting mostly. She was once accused of attacking a woman—that's why her DNA was in the system—but she was acquitted. We don't know the details. Strangely, that part of her file is sealed. She shows up now and then. People tolerate her. She's usually polite and nice. In summer, she can be found by the docks, with her friend Greta. In the winter, she usually hangs around the train station."

"I think it's a dead end," Finn blurted. "Unreliable witness."

"Why?" Timo said.

"Because I say so. Now, let's get back to work. I want a report from each of you on my desk by tomorrow morning. You can go."

Isa gave Timo a quick look and then headed for the door.

"Not you, Inspector Paikkala," Finn said. "My office. Now."

* * *

Finn Heimersson's office was a museum of his long and illustrious career in law enforcement. His impressive medals and decorations were displayed prominently in the cupboard behind his desk, reminding visitors of his many achievements. Along the walls hung framed photos of Finn posing with celebrities and high-ranking officials he had met throughout his career. Amidst these displays of accomplishment, there was only one picture of Finn's family, his wife and their three children.

Timo felt intimidated. As a former superintendent himself, Timo knew how hard it was to climb the ranks, and he compared his own stalled career to Finn's success. And yet, as he looked around Finn's office, he felt a sense of sadness. For all of Finn's accomplishments, he was alone in this impressive space, surrounded by mementos of his achievements but lacking the warmth of companionship.

"Why do you want to talk to me... sir?" Timo said.

"Spill it! Say what you need to say."

"I'm not sure..."

Finn gave him an annoyed look and leaned back in his chair. Timo had always liked that swivel chair; every time he gave it a spin, all his problems disappeared for a few seconds. He doubted it would survive another week.

"You and Lindström were having a nice conversation in the back. I'd like to hear it... off the record. Between friends."

At one point in time, Timo would have taken his friend's word for it. But now, after everything that had happened, he didn't know who this man was anymore. His long-time friend had changed and there was no going back to the way things used to be.

"Okay then," Timo started, "I don't think this is the way to gain their trust. The small jokes and friendly teasing just show how close we are as a team. I know we need to be professional, but the job is hard enough."

"Look, you and Anders Larsen failed because you showed them too much favor. I don't need to gain their trust. They just have to do their jobs. This is not a democracy. I am the boss. They must listen... and you too for that matter. And that's why you'll help me."

"Oh, really? I just wonder... forcing me to call you sir as you so clearly spelled out the last time we had a conversation, is that a way to humiliate me?"

"What? No. I want you to set the example. They'll follow you; they listen to you."

"So, you're using me to make sure they nicely walk in line?"

As he questioned Finn's intentions, a surge of defiance coursed through Timo's veins. He refused to be a mere pawn in Finn's game of power and manipulation. The thought of being reduced to a tool for enforcing conformity ignited a flicker of rebellion in him.

"It's no secret they hate me. I need an ally."

"They don't hate you. Just give them some credit."

"That I can't do. Not after last year. And I hold you responsible if they screw up. Is that understood?"

Timo was speechless. Maybe he hadn't been strict enough when he had been the boss, but was this how you treated people?

Or maybe Finn wanted to save them, just as he had once thought he would.

But why the hostility?

"Yes... sir."

"And you know who—besides yourself—is going to go down first," Finn said with a smile on his face.

"Is that why she needs to babysit Leif Berg?"

"Perhaps not," Finn replied. "It's nothing you need to concern yourself with. You have more important matters to attend to."

"What things?"

Finn gave him another sarcastic grin and turned to his computer. "Close the door when you leave."

CHAPTER

5

HE LOOKED OLDER THAN ISA HAD IMAGINED. In her head, they were still twenty and sharing a small one-bedroom apartment in the center of Gävle. She noticed the wrinkles around his eyes. His hair was almost completely gray. She had always found his black hair one of his more appealing traits, but now it was almost gone. The hairline was pulled back a little further, but his cheekbones and eyes still made an impression on her. She would be lying if she said there weren't any feelings. There were plenty. She just couldn't let them take over.

He had changed. It was nothing tangible, but she could see it, in his manners, even without talking to him. He seemed more reserved.

Viktor stood up when he saw her coming. The day before they had agreed to meet in the small café close to the police station.

Her thoughts had immediately trailed off to her partner. Timo loved that place. As a coffee lover or rather addict, he always took a moment to breathe in the scent of fresh beans before he dropped in the chair at the table closest to the bar where he could see the barista work. The waitress made sure the table was reserved especially for him. She suspected the woman had a crush on her partner.

"Isa," he said.

"Viktor, it's good to see you." She removed her jacket and put it over the back of the chair before taking a seat.

"You look good," he said, while fidgeting with the coffee cup. "You want something to drink?"

"Just some water." Isa signaled the waitress to take her order. "You look so... mature," she continued and gave him a smile.

"Well, we all have to grow up eventually."

"One a little faster than the other."

"You said it." He looked at his hands again.

There was an awkward silence after the waitress left them alone with their drinks.

"I wanted to call but...," Isa started. "I know the hearing is in a month and..."

"That's not what I wanted to talk about."

A look of confusion crossed Isa's face.

"Look, the kids and I will be in Gävle until the end of January... at least. We'll spend Christmas and New Year with my mother."

"I thought you were getting married."

"The marriage is off... for good."

He looked at his hands and took a deep breath.

"What happened?"

"I wasn't the man of her dreams." He couldn't hide the sarcastic undertone.

She took his hand and for a moment they just sat there in silence.

"We might move back to Sweden. It all depends on whether I can find a job here. I've got a few interviews lined up."

She didn't know what to think. Was this good or bad? The hearing and the adoption were off the table, but there was something else going on. She could feel it.

"So, is this what you wanted to talk to me about?" she said.

"No. I want to talk about Felix."

"Felix? Why? What's wrong with him?"

"He's been asking about you... a lot. He wants to meet you."

Witnessing the unmistakable signs of relief and fear on his face, her gaze shifted to the glass of water, as if silently demanding a pause to make sense of her jumbled emotions. "He was three. He doesn't know me, and I don't know him."

"He's been watching the tapes, the videos from when he and Olivia were little. He's been asking about you. It's been really hard."

"And Olivia?"

He shook his head. "Just him. So, I'm wondering if you'll meet him."

She took a deep breath. "I don't know, Viktor. I need to think about this. It's hard for me."

"It's hard for you?" he said in a stern voice.

"Uh, I didn't mean..."

"It's hard for you. Really? What about me? Us? You left us. You decided to leave your family. I've been raising the children on my own and it's hard on you?"

She sighed, took the glass of water, and emptied it in one go. "This was a mistake."

"Just leave like you always do!" he said, grabbing her arm as she tried to stand up. "Do you ever think of us?"

The anger left her when she looked in his eyes and saw the deep sadness, but she couldn't say the words.

77

"How can I tell Felix that the mother he idealizes has left him, his sister, and his father so mercilessly? So, yes, figure out what you want to do, but don't think I'll be as patient as before. You need to choose if you want to be in his life or not. You need to choose quickly."

"You know why I had to go," she said softly.

She pulled away, grabbed her jacket, and ran out of the café.

Outside, she welcomed the cold, but it wasn't enough to calm the anxiety. He was right. It was time to choose. But if she let them into her life, she'd have to admit to herself and her kids how selfish she'd been.

And was she ready to do that?

* * *

That night, as Timo walked to his car, he noticed the snowflakes dancing in the light of the lampposts. He could hear the snow crunching with each step. A fresh layer of snow had covered the street and sidewalk, and only his footprints marred the perfect scene. As he walked to his car, he thought back to when he was younger, and his brother and friends would target him in snowball fights. His mother had been surprised at the bruises on his body, but he had kept quiet about the continuous harassment. There had been good times, moments when they had been real siblings, and he cherished them even more than the disturbing memories, but until this day the mode of interacting with his brother was based on rivalry and jealousy.

He got to his car and noticed how old and battered it looked in comparison to the cars he used to have. He was disappointed to realize that even though he said he could do without comfort and flashy things, he felt uneasy sitting in a car that didn't make him feel like he had a certain status. The gears didn't work properly, his head almost touched the ceiling, and the fabric on the seats was torn in some places. He felt embarrassed driving through the streets of Gävle in this old, beaten-up car. His family friend and mentor, George, had laughed at him and said it wouldn't last more than six months. Maybe George was right. He always had good intentions, but he could never escape his family's wealth. Maybe it was time to embrace those things and stop trying to be someone he wasn't.

But as he pulled out of the car park, his heart and mood were rejoicing with anticipation. He knew exactly where he wanted to be. In the distance, between the trees and the heavy snowfall, which was clouding most of his vision, he saw the lights of the house. And as he approached the end goal of his nightly drive, he felt the butterflies, the surge of longing rushing through his body. He would see her soon.

He parked the car by the house, away from sight, and turned off the engine. He had sat there so many times before, watching Ingrid through the windows of the big house. He loved how her hair bounced over her shoulders as she moved from the living room to the kitchen. He rarely got to see that at work. She usually wore her hair in a bun.

Suddenly he remembered how beautiful she had looked with her hair down, in that green jumpsuit, on the steps of the opera house. His heart raced, yearning for the moments when he was blissfully unaware of how to navigate these emerging feelings.

Now he was a stalker.

He smiled to himself, seeing her walk around and looking so happy. The youngest son was telling a story, looking very agitated, and she laughed while she rubbed his hair.

A wave of sadness suddenly hit him. A tear slowly made its way down his cheek, which he quickly brushed away.

He couldn't understand how she could be so happy. If only she knew.

Anton, the adulterer.

He shook his head, not knowing what to believe anymore. He refused to follow the path of jealousy. But when he saw her like that, doubt began to creep into his mind. Maybe he should tell her. She deserved to know.

His phone beeped with a new message. It was Isa. She needed to talk to him about Leif Berg. She was home, and he could still meet with her if he wanted. He put the phone away and looked up, about to put the key in the ignition when he saw Anton standing in front of the window looking almost directly at him. It was almost as if Anton knew he was out there, staring at his wife and imagining the most inappropriate things.

He froze.

His mind went blank, and everything seemed to pause when he saw those eyes staring at him. Anton knew. He knew Timo was out there. Still, he did nothing. This was a threat if anything else.

Anton suddenly turned around and walked back to join his wife in the living room. He kissed her. But there was this moment. Just before Anton put his lips on hers, he stared outside again, saying she was his and only his.

For a few seconds, Timo couldn't even hear his own breath. It was as if the world around him had shown him glimpses of the darkest and most terrifying secrets. The masks fell off for a moment. Decent Anton was a calculated and not to be underestimated man. A dangerous man. He felt it, he knew it. But Anton had done nothing but stare into the darkness. A darkness colored by the white of the snow. A whiteness that intensified as Timo drove home.

Isa had to wait.

He needed time to think.

* * *

Lars sat on the couch in the small apartment, wondering if this would be one of the last boy's nights out before Berger got married. They had ordered pizza and planned to stay in for the night, but Lars felt a little sad at the thought of his friend getting married and leaving him behind. A great thriller was on TV, and they had plenty of beer, but it wasn't enough to take Lars' mind off his friend's impending marriage.

"You look happy," Lars remarked.

Berger was surprised. Their conversations usually didn't go beyond jokes and arguments about movies, sports, and work. Nothing like this, about happiness and feelings.

Berger smiled. "I'm happy. In a few weeks, I am marrying the most beautiful woman in the world."

Lars looked down at the slice of pizza in his hand. "Look, Berger, I know I haven't always been so supportive of your relationship with Mila, but I just want to tell you that I wish you both all the best."

"Thanks. I really appreciate it. I know. Mila told me."

Lars frowned and straightened his back. "What do you mean?"

"You and Mila," Berger said and opened another can of beer. The pizza was already cold, but he took the last piece.

Lars had been suspicious of Mila for a while, but he thought he had come to terms with her marrying his friend. Now, all his doubts came flooding back.

"There is nothing between Mila and me," Lars said calmly.

"She said that you don't like her because you are... in love with her."

This was preposterous! How could she claim that? He found her attractive and smart, but after those few dates, it was like all the alarm bells had gone off. He didn't trust her then and he still didn't trust her now.

"I can assure you that I don't have any romantic feelings for her. You shouldn't worry about me getting in the way of your relationship."

Berger should worry about her. A lot. But he couldn't go through that discussion again. His friend was love-struck, blinded by happiness.

Then Lars said, "Are you sure?"

"About what? Mila?"

"No, about getting married. It's all happening so quickly."

"You know we're not that young anymore."

"Jesus, Berger, come on. It's not like you're an old man. You've still got plenty of time to find the right person and settle down. You're a great guy, and Mila is lucky to have you. You deserve it. Sorry for being so annoying about it, but after everything that's happened lately, it's hard not to be cautious."

"Thanks, man," Berger said and gave him an approving nod.

"So, are you guys going to live here?"

"For the time being, but when the kids come, we'll probably have to look for a house."

"Kids? Is she...? Are you...?"

Berger smiled. "No, no, but we don't want to wait too long."

Berger's life had become so real. With marriage and children, Lars sometimes found himself jealous of those who were in a steady relationship. People who weren't alone like himself.

Then Lars said, "How are your parents doing? Is your mother able to come? With her surgery and all."

"Yeah, she's a lot better now. She's driving my dad crazy. I think they'll be able to come. I think she would regret it if she would miss it."

"That's great. I assume Mila's parents will be there as well?"

"No," Berger said, eyes cast down, "they are dead, and she is an only child."

"Dead? But I thought..."

Why did he think her parents were still alive? He couldn't remember. She must have told him. Or was it a mere assumption from his side?

"That's hard," Lars said. "What happened?"

"They died in a car accident when she was eleven."

There was a moment of silence before Berger got up and went to the kitchen. A few minutes later, he came back with a bottle of champagne in his hands.

"For all these years of friendship and healthy competition," he said, "I'd be honored if you would share a few glasses of champagne with me."

"Berger, my God, you can really make a man cry," Lars said, got up and threw his arms around his friend.

His best friend.

And they shared the champagne while recalling good memories and swore they would never forget them, whatever happened.

***

"Mayor Ek cannot be with you today. He has an urgent meeting."

The woman who had let Isa and Lars in Valkama's office was a secretary who was not used to talking to police officers. The moment she had seen the police badges she became flustered, and her voice started trembling.

"He really wanted to talk to you, but this couldn't wait," she said.

Isa observed the woman with a sharp gaze, noting the piercing glint in her ashen-grey eyes. Her attire was unremarkable, neither trendy nor outdated, but her demeanor exuded a sense of understated dignity. Despite her unassuming appearance, Isa sensed an air of wisdom and experience about her, as if she held a trove of secrets close to her chest. It was clear that this woman was not one to gossip or betray confidences lightly.

"And you are?" Isa asked.

"Olga Morosov."

When she merely got a stern look from Isa, she continued by saying, "We were all so shocked."

"This was Mr. Valkama's office?"

Olga nodded.

"Not bad," Lars said and walked to the window.

"All the offices are about the same," she said.

"And you were Mr. Valkama's secretary?" Isa continued.

"Only the last months before he... died. Mrs. Petersson, his regular secretary, had an accident and is recovering at home. I took over temporarily. I am actually the mayor's management assistant."

Isa looked at her with sympathy. "How was Mr. Valkama as a boss?"

"He was okay. Nothing special. I didn't really have time to get to know him."

"Any particular habits?" Lars said with his back towards her, while he scanned the bookcase.

"No, he was quiet. He never said much, but he was polite and considerate."

"The day he died, was there anything out of the ordinary?"

She shook her head. "Nothing special. He was just as usual."

"He didn't go out or...?" Isa said, with her eyes fixed on the woman.

There was hesitation. Doubt.

"It was around noon. He wanted to be left alone. No phone calls, no visitors. I thought he would just stay in. I went for lunch, and when I came back, Mayor Ek called. He urgently wanted to talk to Mr. Valkama. I went into his office, but he wasn't there."

"He had gone out? Do you have any idea where?"

The woman shook her head again, the strands of hair coming loose from the knot. "But last month he started to eat outside, sometimes twice or three times a week. That was unusual."

"Where did he go?"

"No idea, but it mustn't have been far. He has no car, and he was usually back within the hour."

"A mistress?" Lars said with a grin on his face.

The secretary frowned. "He wouldn't do anything like that. He adored his wife."

Isa exchanged a glance of annoyance with Lars and then turned to the woman again. "What did Ek want to talk to him about?"

"The same issue he's trying to deal with today. The planned construction of an apartment block at the harbor. The construction company didn't get a license and there was a meeting that day where Mr. Valkama was supposed to be present, but he didn't show up. I saw him later that day. He didn't say where he had been, but he didn't look well. Pale and tired, and... worried. I made him a tea before I went home."

"And that's the last time you saw him?"

She nodded.

"His wife told us he had blackouts. Did you notice any signs of memory loss or confusion during your interactions with him?"

Olga shook her head. "Blackouts? No, I never noticed anything like that."

Isa stared at the mahogany desk. The forensics team had already dusted it for fingerprints but found nothing suspicious. The desk was wiped clean every morning, and the same had happened that day when his body was found.

Lars' brow furrowed in concern. "Do you have his work computer? We've only found his personal one so far."

With a face full of confusion, the woman said, "Uh... I know. The laptop should have been in the drawer. He never took it home."

"Well, it isn't. Who has access to his office?"

"Everyone working here. You need a badge to enter the building, but once you are in, you can basically go into every room."

"There wasn't a single document on his desk or in any of the drawers. It was as if Valkama had never worked here." Then Isa turned to the woman in front of her, "Who removed them?"

"I don't know... I swear," Olga replied in a low voice.

"Could it have been Ek?" Isa asked.

"No, of course not. He was just as surprised as I was. He launched an investigation, questioned the guards, and reviewed the footage, but..."

"Footage?" Lars interjected.

Olga nodded, "There are cameras at the entrance and in the hallways."

Isa thanked Olga and turned to Lars. "We need to find out who removed Valkama's work belongings and why. And we need to review that CCTV footage and conduct background checks on everyone who works here."

CHAPTER

6

ISA FOUND THE YOUNG MAN cleaning Minister Berg's car in the garage of his Stockholm mansion. She had shown him her badge and he had seemed lost for words. He looked to be just below twenty, and he was not unattractive. He was either a second or third generation immigrant and his Rinkeby-Swedish dialect gave away where he was from. He tried to mask it with a stilted, formal Swedish that ended up making him look both clumsy and endearing. She had to fight the urge to smile.

"So, you work for Minister Berg?"

He nodded.

"How long have you been working for him? You seem quite young to me."

"Six months, his previous driver retired," he stammered.

Isa wrote a few words in the notebook she had taken from her pocket. "More than a month ago, there was an incident. A car accident."

After glancing over the shiny black metal, the man rubbed off a small stain with his glove and slammed the door shut. Isa thought of Timo and his love for fast cars. She wondered how he was coping with driving around in a scraped Volvo. Timo had once confided that his passion for cars started at an early age when his father would take him on car rides, racing through towns and the countryside just to feel the power of the vehicle. And there was his fascination with Miami Vice, which made him think every cop had a Ferrari in the garage. As much as he tried to deny it, Timo could be superficial and status-sensitive at times.

After the mention of the car accident, she gave the young man an inquisitive look.

"I've heard of it," he said. "I had nothing to do with it."

She frowned and gave him a stern look. "No one says you did."

She turned away and quickly scanned the room. It was unusually tidy for a garage. The gray-tiled floor was cleaner than her living room, and the white walls were lined with mounted storage bins. The space was huge—larger than one would need to host the three cars that were parked inside. When she walked around, the echo of her footsteps bounced off the walls.

"Which one was it?"

He pointed to a dark-blue Mercedes standing in the far-right corner. "It took a while to fix it."

"So, this is his own car?"

"All of them are, except the gray BMW. That's his wife's car, but she hardly ever uses it."

"Why is that?" Isa stopped in front of the Mercedes.

He walked up to her. "Mrs. Berg ain't doin' too good. Since her daughter went missin' and was found dead, she's been shuttin' herself inside. She hardly ever comes out, let alone drives somewhere."

He stared at the floor, almost embarrassed he had let his dialect slip through.

"Do you chauffeur the Minister around to his appointments?"

"Pretty much everywhere he goes, except for some fancy events when he likes driving himself. But usually, it's just for work meetings and political stuff."

"So, he doesn't get behind the wheel that often?"

The driver nodded.

"Then why did he take the car out in November and drive up to Uppsala? What was so important?"

"You would have to ask him, ma'am. But that afternoon they got into a fight."

"Who?"

"Minister Berg and his right hand."

"Fredrik Paikkala?"

"No, the one before. The one he was sleeping with."

Isa smiled. "I see. What's her name?"

"Sandra... something. I think it's Arvidsson."

"And she was Berg's mistress?"

"Yeah, Minister Berg is a bit of a ladies' man. I can't blame him. He isn't getting any from the missus."

"What were they fighting about?"

He shrugged. "Dunno."

She crossed her arms and faced him. "Come on. Don't tell me you know they were fighting and not know why?"

"He fired her," he said reluctantly.

"Mmm, interesting. Why?"

"Dunno, but she was yelling that he couldn't do that, and she would expose him. After that, she ran out of the house. He went upstairs and, about an hour later, he drove off."

"Would Ms. Arvidsson have access to the garage and the car?"

"Yeah, I suppose so. She was here all the time. There was even a time when the house was used as a campaign center. At least, that's what I heard."

"But why the Mercedes? The likelihood that he would use that car was low. Why not his ministerial car if they really wanted him dead?"

The young man stared at her, saying nothing.

She needed to talk to the man himself, but before entering the house she turned and asked, "Are there any cameras?"

"Yes, outside at the gate, the front door and the garage."

"I assume the images were checked?"

"Yeah, nothing special. No intruder. But like I said everyone in the house had access to the cars."

"Including yourself," she remarked.

"Why... why would I?"

Isa gave him a sarcastic smile and then opened the door to the hallway.

* * *

"So, you're the police officer who is supposed to keep me alive?" Leif asked.

As he picked up the cup of steaming coffee from the table, he crossed his legs and fixed his pale blue eyes on her. Isa was struck by his undeniable sex appeal, even though he could have been her father. The way he looked at her sent a shiver down her spine. Though she had seen him on talk shows and in the news before, it wasn't until this moment, sitting face to face with him, she realized just how attractive he was.

She took a moment to survey the room. It was spacious and inviting, and, unlike her usual disinterest in classic interior designs, this room spoke to her. The elegant furnishings blended harmoniously, and a magnificent chandelier gracefully hung from the ceiling, casting a soft and inviting glow. The walls were adorned with tasteful artwork, each piece carefully chosen to enhance the room's ambiance.

In one corner, a grand piano commanded attention, exuding an air of artistic sophistication. Across from it, a large sofa and two cozy armchairs faced a crackling fireplace, casting flickering shadows on the walls. It was in this atmosphere that Isa felt a deep sense of comfort and serenity. A coffee table proudly displayed a beautiful bouquet of fresh flowers, adding a vibrant touch to the overall aesthetics.

Despite its grandeur, the room emitted a warm and welcoming atmosphere that resonated with Isa. It wasn't just a showcase; it felt like a space meant to be lived in. The personal touches, such as cherished family photos and mementos, scattered throughout the room further reinforced this feeling. It was clear that this room reflected the esteemed public figure Leif Berg, but it also served as a sanctuary—a place where he could find solace and peace.

He continued, "I heard about you. You found the so-called killer of my daughter."

"So-called? He is the killer."

"You work with Fredrik's brother. He told me all about it."

"Yes, but I'm not here to discuss the Paikkala family."

"Of course. How can I help you?"

"The attacks on your life," she said and put the notebook on her lap.

He placed the cup down and met her gaze. She felt a confusing mix of emotions, fascination but also a hint of fear. He looked harmless and even charming, but she knew better than to underestimate him.

"I have enemies. Many enemies. That's the price I must pay for the job I do. But let's not get overly dramatic here. I know my team means well but I don't need a babysitter, and I don't need you."

"I'm not pretending to be your babysitter, but you're right you don't need me. Why exactly do you need the Gävle police to help you?"

"They thought it was a good idea to have someone local to coordinate and help with the conference in Gävle."

"That's always a smart thing to do. And with they... you mean?"

"My team... Fredrik."

"It was Fredrik's idea?"

He nodded. "But not to investigate these stupid incidents."

Isa leaned forward, her expression grave. "The attacks you're facing are no longer just idle threats," she said, her voice low and serious. "It seems that some of your enemies have taken things to a new level. We need to discuss this."

"Okay, if you think it will help, but this has already been investigated by SÄPO and they found nothing."

"The car accident. Why did you take the Mercedes that afternoon and drive to Uppsala?"

"I got a call," he said, then stopped and looked down at the floor in front of him.

"About?"

"It's a family matter," he said.

"Mr. Secretary, I need to know. Witnesses told me you had a fight with Ms. Arvidsson just before the incident."

"She has nothing to do with it," he said quickly. "There's no way she could have tampered with the brakes. It's not that straightforward."

"How would you know?"

"I used to work in a garage when I was a law student many... many years ago."

"It's possible that the car was tampered with well before the incident, even weeks in advance," Isa suggested. "The question is, who has access to the garage?"

"Everyone in the house. My wife, my son, the housekeeper, my campaign team, my cabinet members."

"Why were you in Uppsala?"

He fell silent, his gaze dropping to his hands. After a few moments, he spoke softly. "It was my mother," he said. "She's ninety years old and currently living in a nursing home in Uppsala. Her health has been deteriorating rapidly, and I received an urgent message that she had been admitted to the hospital. I immediately got into my car, but as you know, I never made it."

"Your mother was admitted to the hospital?"

"No, it was a trick. The person who called wanted me to drive off the road," Leif said.

"Was it a man or a woman?"

"Woman."

"We can try to trace back the call and..."

"Forget it. It's pointless. SÄPO already tried and failed. You're just going to end up wasting your time. All these incidents were investigated. The car, the shooting, the threatening emails, the burglary. They all turned up nothing."

"Does the name Lauri Valkama mean anything to you?"

He frowned. "The name sounds familiar."

"He worked at the City Hall in Gävle. He's dead."

"I remember now. He was working for the mayor. What happened?"

"He was murdered."

"Was he the guy found in an alley? It was all over the news."

Isa nodded.

"He was there... when the shooting incident happened."

"Really? Where exactly was he?"

"Uh... what do you mean?"

"Next to you?"

"Yes, I think so."

He turned his head and looked at the pictures on the cupboard, then closed his eyes as if to recall the scene. "We stepped outside. We were about to go down the stairs, when..."

He suddenly opened his eyes. "He pushed me."

"Valkama?"

"I thought he wanted to protect me, but maybe..."

He swallowed a few times before continuing. It sounded like he was trying to decide about something, but she wasn't sure what. "Maybe he wanted to put me in the line of fire."

"Any reason why he would do that?"

"People don't always like what I stand for. The far-right groups have been attacking my ideas for years."

"Who else was there?"

"Mayor Pehr Ek, Sandra Arvidsson and Fredrik Paikkala."

"Fredrik Paikkala? He was already working for you?"

He smiled and gave her a sarcastic grin. "I hired him about three months ago."

"I still don't understand. People tell me his political ambitions are diametrically opposed to what your party stands for. Left versus right."

"There is no left or right. There never is. And if I can convince someone like Fredrik Paikkala, I can convince everyone."

"I don't see what's in it for both of you."

He smiled, closing his eyes before saying, "Of course you're right. I've been losing the support of the center-right constituency. They don't particularly like my proposal on migration and asylum. I knew Fredrik's father Yrjo. He wasn't much of a politician, but he was a good diplomat, and he was respected by many, left and right. He was extremely good at building a network. Maybe because many saw him truly as... neutral ground. He couldn't do much, but he was able to build a good relationship between Finland and Sweden."

"But that was Yrjo, not Fredrik."

"The Paikkala name still carries a lot of weight in Sweden, even if Fredrik might not be as palatable to the center as his father was. I would say he's more in line with the far-right Sweden Democrats. But having him on my team gives me a much better chance of convincing people."

"And what's in it for him?"

"To work with me. He doesn't seem ethically bound to a certain Party."

"Going back to the conference. Why Gävle? Why on earth do you want to have your party convention there?"

"It's personal and it's political. You don't need to know why."

He fixed his gaze on her once again, his eyes gleaming with an intensity that caused her skin to crawl. It was as though he were a predator, poised to strike his prey. The sudden shift in his demeanor shocked and surprised her, leaving her momentarily speechless.

She rose to her feet, eager to bring the meeting to a close. "Thank you for your time," she said quickly. "If you think of anything else, feel free to give me a call."

As she turned to leave, he stood up, revealing his imposing height. He took her hand and met her gaze with an intense stare. "Perhaps we could discuss this further over dinner?"

She stammered nervously, feeling uneasy about his sudden shift in tone. "I don't think that would be appropriate."

Before he could respond, the door to the sitting room burst open, and a confused elderly woman stumbled into the room. She had wrapped a blanket around her nightgown and long gray hair hung in strands around her face. The bloodshot eyes and thick walls under her eyelids showed she hadn't slept in days. She pointed a finger at Isa and then started screaming. "Whore! You won't get away with this!"

And then she turned to Leif. "Another one? Really? You just can't keep your hands to yourself. The previous one is only gone for a few weeks and the next one is already in your bed!"

Leif's gaze changed, but it was a more comforting, soft expression that appeared on his face. Quite different from how he had looked at Isa at the end of their conversation.

"Masja, you're not feeling well. I'll bring you to your room. Then you can go back and rest."

He grabbed her arm, but she wrapped them around him. "I'm not sick. I know very well what's going on."

"Sorry, my wife is going through a tough time." He embraced his wife and looked her in the eye. "Everything will be alright."

Suddenly Masja wrenched herself free from his grasp and darted towards Isa, her eyes locking onto hers. "Don't trust him!" she blurted out. "He's insane."

"Masja," Leif said. "Stop it. Let's go upstairs, so you can rest."

He glanced over at Isa, who was in complete shock, unable to say anything. He took Masja by the hand and led her to the door while calling out, "Tanja!"

Through the half open door, Isa saw how a woman quickly came down the stairs. Leif spoke to her firmly, and then Tanja, whom Isa gathered was some sort of nurse, disappeared with Masja upstairs.

"I apologize for my wife's outburst," he said, his voice heavy with sadness. "Ever since our daughter disappeared and passed away, she has been struggling with confusion and guilt. She blames herself for leaving Anna alone that day, and after all these years, it still weighs heavily on her mind. She has good days and bad days, but lately, the bad seem to outnumber the good. It's difficult for her to distinguish reality from delusion, and for that, I am truly sorry."

"And does she know her husband is trying to get her daughter's murderer go free?" Isa said in a harsh voice.

He sighed, straightened his back, and spoke to her calmly. "The Sandviken killer isn't Anna's murderer. Her real killer has been in prison for more than twenty years."

"You put an innocent man in jail."

"I didn't do anything. Justice did."

"Really? There was almost no evidence and still... he ended up in prison."

As she walked to the door, he opened it for her and added, "I agree the jury should get all the facts. The unbiased, untampered evidence. But I can't say the Sandviken investigation isn't without its flaws either. Can you?"

She looked at him, dumbfounded, as he said, "Goodbye, inspector."

She stepped out of the house with an uncomfortable feeling. There was something more behind this seemingly boring task to keep the Secretary safe. Leif Berg was an intriguing yet scary man. He had left her with more questions than answers.

* * *

"Why exactly did I have to come along?"

Timo grumbled to himself as he tried to brush the snow off his pants, casting a frustrated glance at the car that Isa had parked in an inconvenient spot. The worry of potential difficulties in getting the car out later gnawed at him, exacerbating his annoyance over even the smallest of inconveniences that seemed to irk him these days.

As he looked out at the surrounding area, Timo admired the picturesque scene before him. The white apartment buildings, with their neat balconies overlooking the water, were now covered in a blanket of snow. The neatly kept parks in front of the buildings were filled with rows of parked cars, adding a sense of orderliness to the otherwise wintry landscape.

Hägernäs Strand, the suburb where they were located, was a modern and affluent area situated in the inner archipelago of Stockholm. He knew that Sandra Arvidsson, the woman they were here to meet, had moved here two years ago.

He took a deep breath, filling his lungs with the crisp, fresh air, and felt a sense of calm wash over him.

"Well, aren't you a little ray of sunshine!" Isa said while she slammed the door of the car shut.

And in seconds his peace of mind was gone. "I don't see why you and I for that matter should waste time on this. It's not your job to investigate these incidents. You just make sure the guy stays in one piece. There are other things to do."

"You should really do something about that terrible mood of yours," she leaned against her car while pulling up the collar of her jacket.

He shrugged but said nothing.

"Just don't take it out on us... on me."

He frowned. "I'm not."

She sighed and then walked steadily past him to the entrance hall of the apartment building where Ms. Arvidsson lived.

When Sandra Arvidsson opened the door, she looked at the two inspectors in astonishment. "Yes?"

Sandra Arvidsson was a tall, slender woman with bright blue eyes and long, light-brown hair that almost reached her hips. She was wearing a gray cashmere sweater and black pants.

"Ms. Arvidsson, I am Inspector Isa Lindström." Isa showed her badge. "This is my colleague Inspector Timo Paikkala. We would like to talk to you about Leif Berg."

"Paikkala? Are you family of Fredrik Paikkala?"

"My brother," Timo said.

Sandra's frown deepened as she appeared lost in thought for a moment. "I'm sorry, what was it you wanted to talk to me about?"

"Leif Berg," Isa said firmly.

"I can't say anything about him, I'm sorry."

"We're investigating the attacks on his life and the threats that have been made."

"You should be talking to him about it," she said as she tried to close the door, but Isa quickly interjected, "He fired you. Why?"

Sandra's eyebrows shot up and her eyes widened in surprise. "He didn't fire me. I quit."

Isa said calmly, "Can we just come in to talk to you? It won't take long. I promise."

Sandra dropped her shoulders, opened the door wider and signaled them to come in. She led them through the hallway to the spacious kitchen.

Isa's attention was immediately drawn to the kitchen island, which was covered with medication blister packs. "You're ill?"

"No," Sandra said and quickly grabbed the medication and put it back in the box. "I'm pregnant, and it's not going well."

"Is it Berg's?" Isa said.

Sandra's eyes widened and her features momentarily were frozen in surprise. But she swiftly straightened her posture and managed to regain control of her facial expressions. "You wanted to talk about Leif Berg. So, what you want to ask?"

"Why did he fire you?"

"As I already told you, he didn't fire me. I left. It was better that way."

"Because of the baby?"

Sandra sighed. "Berg has nothing to do with my pregnancy. I left because it was better for me and the baby."

"Still, I wonder... isn't that the real reason he let you go?" Isa tried.

"I can't talk about Berg," she said suddenly with a serious expression on her face.

"Why?"

"He'll come after me," Sandra said.

"Did he pay you to keep quiet?" Timo asked.

Sandra's face broke into a smile, and she locked eyes with Timo. "Leif doesn't pay anyone. You should count yourself lucky he's not destroying you. He has that power. I'm not the only one. There are dozens of us. This has been going on for years, decades even, and since his daughter's death it's been even worse. He's charming and convincing at first, but women are disposable to him. He takes what he wants and when he doesn't need us anymore, he gets rid of us. But I guess you already know that."

"What do you mean?" There was a subtle flicker in Timo's eyes and a barely perceptible shift in his stance that betrayed his true reaction.

She shrugged and turned to Isa who had been watching the entire scene with increasing interest.

"In a #metoo era, where these things are so easily brought in the open, where a public figure like Berg needs to be extra careful... it's hard to believe," Isa said. "He's been very direct and clear about the Eirik Lunde case. He openly condemned his misconduct."

Sandra shook her head and turned to Timo. "It's cute how naïve she is!"

Then Sandra continued, "And before Lunde there was Martinsson and Holm, and... Berg has a whole list of guinea pigs lined up. They don't know it, but he makes sure they take the fall before he does."

Isa's eyes widened in surprise. A look of disbelief crossed her face as she spoke with a slight frown. "Are you suggesting that Lunde is innocent?"

"No, I'm not saying that. I don't know the full story, but I'm saying Berg knows very well how to pick his confidants. That interesting blend of sexual predators and political geniuses."

"But that surely does him more harm than good," Isa said.

Sandra gave her an ironic grin. "And do you see him getting bad reviews? He's even gone up in the polls. People loved the way he handled Lunde. Decisive, with tact and consideration for the victims. Only... one of the victims wasn't a victim. She told me it was consensual, and the only thing Lunde is guilty of is his own stupidity. She's married and they got caught. You don't need much these days to damage someone's reputation. There is still an investigation going on, but the damage is already done. And the other woman... I wouldn't be surprised if Berg himself had something to do with this. By the way, it was Prime Minister Hult who hired Lunde, not Berg. Hult is going to take the hit."

"Why do you let Berg get away with this?" Isa asked.

Sandra took a sip of the cup in front of her. "Because... Ask me a question I can answer. Otherwise leave!"

Timo quickly said, "The incident at the City Hall."

"That was weeks ago."

"Why were you at the meeting?" Isa asked.

"Pehr Ek is a Social-Democrat. He and Berg have been allies and friends since the beginning. Berg wants to give Ek a prominent role in his campaign for the next elections."

"But why was Valkama there?" Timo asked.

"Lauri Valkama? He wasn't there for Berg. He had a meeting with Fredrik."

A faint twitch at the corner of Timo's mouth betrayed a hint of astonishment.

"Why did he want to talk to Fredrik Paikkala?" Isa asked quickly.

"I don't know but they knew each other. They talked for about an hour. I stayed with Berg and Pehr Ek. Why is that important?"

"When you went outside, someone took a shot at Berg. Where were Valkama and Paikkala?"

Sandra looked at the floor for a moment and then shook her head. "They were next to Berg. Fredrik was on his left and Valkama was on his right-hand side."

"Did you see any of them push Berg or do anything strange?" Isa said.

"Isa?" Timo interrupted. "Why..."

She signaled him to keep quiet.

Sandra gave him a sarcastic grin. "Relax, your brother didn't do anything wrong. I saw nothing. Only when Berg grabbed his ear, I saw he was bleeding."

Sandra frowned. "No, wait! That's not right. We came down the stairs. I was talking to Pehr, but Valkama missed a step and lost balance. He grabbed Leif's sleeve and pulled him down. That's when the shot happened."

"You think it was on purpose?" Isa inquired.

"I didn't think so at the time. It all happened so fast."

"And you didn't hear the shot?" Timo pressed.

"Afterwards, SÄPO found the bullet and conducted a thorough sweep of the buildings surrounding the City Hall, but they didn't find anything."

"What about the car accident in Uppsala? Is that related?"

"That couldn't have been an attack," Sandra said quickly.

"Why do you say that?" Isa asked.

"He may claim that it was an accident, but Berg likes to race and he's not exactly the most careful driver. Plus, he hardly ever uses that car anymore. I don't see why anyone would tamper with it."

"That's not what Leif said."

"I've already said more than I should have. And by the way, I'll deny everything if you try to implicate me in this investigation." Sandra flopped down on the kitchen chair and pointed to the front door. "You know where the exit is."

"One more thing," Isa said. "Karst Engersson."

Sandra looked up surprised. "What about him?"

"What was his connection to Leif Berg?"

"There was no connection. As far as I could see Engersson was Hult's puppet."

"Are you sure? The day of the Global Law shooting, Berg was supposed to meet Engersson. And they had many telephone calls before."

Sandra gave them a faint smile. "I set up the meeting. Engersson was desperately trying to get into Berg's good graces. Engersson wanted a career in politics. God knows why. He was a creep and a bloodsucker."

"But Berg never showed up," Timo said.

"An hour before the meeting, Berg calls me and says the meeting is off." She bowed her head. "It was just luck. If Berg hadn't called off the meeting, we would all be dead."

"Did Berg give a reason?" Isa asked.

"Not really and to be honest, after the shooting I was so shocked I let it go. The only thing Berg mentioned is that Fredrik didn't think it was appropriate for us to engage with Engersson due to his association with Anna Wallman."

Isa looked up from her notebook. "The far-right anti-abortion activist who's always making headlines with her demonstrations?"

"Yep." Sandra turned her attention from Isa to Timo.

Timo's face was flushed with a mixture of embarrassment and shock. The constant mention of his brother was seemingly making him uncomfortable.

"Don't look so shocked," Sandra said. "Your brother did nothing wrong besides being a total asshole... but I guess you already knew that."

Then she got up and faced him. "I'd be more concerned about you and your mom."

"Why?" he stammered.

"Ask her," Sandra said.

"I don't like these cryptic messages. Say what you want to say."

She gave him another mocking smile. "I need to rest. Please leave!"

He straightened his back and then looked at Isa, who started to walk toward the front door, but then turned back and said, "Ms. Arvidsson, are you going to be all right?"

Sandra's expression changed from surprise to a smile. "I knew my career was over when he hired Fredrik, but I'll be okay. I've dealt with worse before."

As Isa left the building, she wasn't sure whether she should feel anger or sympathy towards Sandra Arvidsson.

The snow was coming down hard, making it difficult to walk through the thick layer that now covered the street and sidewalk.

They stepped into the car. She let her hands rest on the steering wheel for a moment and then said without looking at Timo, "You were awfully quiet."

"I don't trust that woman."

She turned her head to face him. "Why?"

"She forgot to tell us she got a nice position in the board of directors of the Riksbank. Guess who got her there?"

"Berg?"

He nodded.

"How do you know?"

He smiled. "What are brothers for?"

"Do you trust Fredrik?"

"Fredrik hates her. That's obvious. But I tend to believe him when he says she's as manipulative as Berg. She doesn't want to talk about Berg, still in subtle ways, she reveals he's a sexual predator and master manipulator. I wonder what Berg would think of her little confessions?"

She stared before tackling the subject that was floating between them. It was daunting, she knew, but she had to ask. She had to find out what was going on. "Does your mother know Leif Berg?"

He looked at the gloves on his lap and then said, "Why do you ask?"

"Look, Timo, there is no denying it. You look like him. Sandra saw it too. I know you were very close with your dad but..."

"You're right. My mom had an affair."

She turned her head and studied his face. There was pain and humiliation.

"How long have you known?"

"Since I was a teenager. My dad knew too. She refuses to tell me who my real father is. Berg comes awfully close, but then again, I've been looking and comparing men in my mother's entourage who somewhat resembled me my whole adult life, thinking they might be my real father."

"Why don't you ask her?"

"Every time I try, it ends with a huge fight. I don't have the energy anymore. What I do know is that I don't like Fredrik working for Leif Berg. I don't trust Berg."

"That bothers me as well," Isa said.

"Valkama's murder and these strange incidents must be connected. I just don't see how, and I wonder who the target in the City Hall incident was. Valkama or Berg?"

"Or Valkama knew about the attack on Berg as he was in on it."

CHAPTER

7

THE IMAGE ON THE SCREEN FLICKERED to life, displaying a grainy black-and-white view of the main street where Lauri Valkama's lifeless body had been discovered in a nearby alleyway. The footage was marred by pixelation, which Sivert had dismissively referred to as 'stone age' technology multiple times during their meeting. Despite this, Sivert had used his extensive expertise in digital enhancement to sharpen the image, and now Isa and Lars could finally make sense of the scene before them.

The man in the image strolled down the sidewalk with his back facing the camera. Due to the poor lighting, his features were shrouded in mystery. Isa propped herself against the wall behind Sivert and Lars, who were intently watching the footage.

"This was when?" she asked, as Lars sat to Sivert's left, looking visibly agitated by his neighbor's bragging.

"This was 9 p.m.," Sivert said, pressing the key to stop the image.

"That sounds about right," Isa said. "Ingrid put the time of death between 7 and 10 p.m."

Lars pointed at the screen. "He's in pain."

The man on the screen was hunched over, his body wracked with the unmistakable signs of impending nausea. Sivert's fingers danced across the keyboard, and the group watched as the man crumpled to the ground, dropping to his knees. He remained there for a few tense seconds, before slowly pushing himself back to his feet, using the wall for support.

Isa moved closer and stared at the screen, narrowing her eyes. "And he looks confused. He's looking around continuously and... who is he talking to?"

"Scopolamine causes hallucinations," Lars said.

As the man walked out of frame, the camera captured an eerie stillness of the empty white sidewalk. The occasional flickering and jumping of the bad quality footage interrupted the image now and then.

Lars broke the silence. "That's when he stumbled into the alley."

Isa's excitement was palpable as she watched the scene from the moment the camera first captured the man. "Can you go back? What does he have in his hands?"

A spark of enthusiasm flickered in Lars' voice as he shouted, "It's a briefcase... but we didn't find it."

Isa closed her eyes for a second, throwing her head back. "Someone took it."

Sivert chimed in, "This is only the boring part. Watch a bit longer, and you'll see this."

A few minutes later, a dark figure appeared on the screen, pausing for a moment before crossing the street and disappearing.

"Who is that?" Lars asked, leaning in for a closer look.

Sivert shrugged.

"Looks like he was following Valkama," Lars said.

Isa let out a sigh. "So, there was someone else, but we were wrong about the girl, Tuva."

"No, we weren't," Sivert interjected, drawing their attention back to the screen. Moments passed without any significant action, until a young girl suddenly appeared.

"She looks frightened," Lars observed, leaning forward with his elbow resting on the desk, much to Sivert's annoyance who was now pushed against the wall.

"And there is the other guy. He's chasing her, and he seems to have the briefcase." Isa was now leaning over the back of Sivert's chair, watching the footage with bated breath.

"We didn't see her before," Lars said in a hushed tone, looking up at Isa. Her eyes were fixed on the screen that now showed only the street.

Sivert said, "We see her on camera about fifteen minutes before Valkama walks into the alley. When we look at the footage again, it becomes clear that she was already there. But there is something else."

"Show me," Isa said.

The screen displayed a section of the main street where a dark SUV pulled up and stopped. A young girl stepped out, holding a large backpack, and walked across the street, disappearing into the darkness.

Isa furrowed her brow. "It looks like it's her, and the bag we found is hers. But whose car is this? We can only see a partial license plate. Can you zoom in on it?"

"I can give it one more shot," Sivert said, "but I'm afraid that's as good as it's going to get."

"It could be a client," Lars said.

"Maybe... but she's not a prostitute."

Lars shook his head. "No, but she's homeless and maybe desperate.

She might do anything to survive."

"Mm, maybe." Isa leaned against the wall.

Sivert turned his head from one to the other and asked: "Do you still want to see the footage of the City Hall?"

Isa's eyes brightened. "Yeah, what did you find?"

Sivert closed the window, opened a new file, and began typing. "So, three weeks before his death, Valkama started to go out during lunchtime. Two times a week, sometimes three times. There was no particular pattern to his behavior."

The high-angle image showed Valkama standing on the stairs outside the City Hall. He put up the collar of his coat and then walked away.

"And he never used to do that before?" Isa asked.

"That's correct."

With a puzzled expression, Lars locked eyes with him. "Then where did he go?"

"Hard to say. You can see him going toward the bridge, but that's about it."

"Do we have CCTV anywhere else in town?"

"Yeah, at the Castle and the Yule Goat, maybe a few restaurants and shops, but it's possible he didn't go to any of those areas. And this might be totally unrelated to his death."

Isa shook her head. "It was a change in habit. People don't change their habits that often. There was a reason. We need to find out. I'll have our guys check the area for CCTV."

"And did you notice anything unusual on the day after Valkama's murder that could explain why his computer and files were missing?" Isa asked.

"I didn't see anything that stands out," Sivert replied. "I haven't been able to identify everyone yet, but it doesn't look like there were any intruders or unexpected guests that showed up that day."

"Thank you, Sivert," Lars said, placing a reassuring hand on the young man's shoulder.

"Wait," Isa said suddenly. "Can you show the footage of three weeks ago? I believe it was the Monday, around 2 or 3 p.m."

"Why?" Sivert said, confused.

"Just do it."

Sivert sighed and pushed the buttons on the computer, and the screen filled with footage from the surveillance camera outside the City Hall. "What am I looking for?"

Isa leaned over and for a second time Sivert started to shuffle in his chair. His face turned red, and he moved closer to Lars.

"There it is," Isa yelled.

Fredrik Paikkala, Leif Berg, and Lauri Valkama appeared on screen, followed by mayor Ek and Sandra Arvidsson. They were now standing at the top of the stairs and seemed to be engaged in a friendly conversation. Then they started shaking hands as if to say goodbye.

But Isa kept her focus on Valkama who stood next to Berg. Valkama turned to Berg, looking surprised. The next moment she saw how he lost his balance and grabbed Leif's arm to prevent himself from falling. Then Leif put his hands over his face, and everyone gathered around him. While the Minister of Justice was in obvious pain, Valkama moved away from the crowd, his stare fixed on something on the other side, something they couldn't see.

"Do you have sound?"

Sivert shook his head.

"What did we just witness?" Lars asked and looked at Isa.

"An assassination attempt on Leif Berg's life," Isa whispered. "Or at least that's what they want us to believe."

"Who are they?" Lars asked.

She didn't answer and kept staring at the screen. There was something off about the images.

***

Timo stood awkwardly in the barren waiting room, surrounded by empty cubicles and uninspiring beige walls. The stern receptionist, reminiscent of a character straight out of a 1960s film, peered over her glasses at him. Her gray hair was pulled back, and her white blouse covered as much skin as possible, adding to the room's dull monotony and Timo's growing sense of unease. "Does Mr. Paikkala expect you?" she asked.

"No, I'm his brother."

The receptionist gave him a scrutinizing look. "Mr. Paikkala is very busy, family or not. I'll check with him, but please take a seat over there."

She gestured towards the black leather sofa, and Timo begrudgingly walked over, sinking into it as he leaned back. A glass door to his left offered a view of the empty desks on the other side of the room.

The Social Democratic Party's office was located on Sveavägen, a busy street in Stockholm. Despite the unremarkable exterior of the six-story building sandwiched between apartment buildings, the interior was a different story. The entrance hall boasted sleek, modern design with marble floors and clean lines, in stark contrast to the dated pale exterior walls that seemed to date back to the 1960s.

He closed his eyes for a moment, trying to calm down the whirlwind of stress raging through his body. Then he glanced over at the woman at the desk, but she was now absorbed in the papers in front of her. He was about to ask if she had contacted his brother when he saw Anton, Ingrid's husband, on the other side of the glass door.

Anton was dressed in a polished suit and tie, looking every bit like a successful lawyer. His cold and distant expression was a stark contrast to the warm and welcoming demeanor he had shown when they first met at his house.

Feeling scrutinized, Timo didn't quite know how to behave. "Inspector, what brings you here?" Anton said, while he quickly straightened his tie, although it was already perfectly in place.

"My brother."

"Oh, yes. Fredrik Paikkala." A twisted smile spread across his face as he kept his eyes fixed on Timo. "It's interesting how two brothers can be so different."

Timo's blood heated up. "What are you doing here?" He stood up, his voice louder and more forceful than he had intended, despite his efforts to remain composed.

"Minister Berg requested to see me."

"Ah, yes, I heard you are thinking about leaving your job at Global Law."

Anton's eyes narrowed. "Where did you hear that? Who told you?"

Timo swallowed, not sure what to say. He had heard it from Ingrid, but if there was someone he didn't want to bring up, it was her.

"Uh... I think Isa told me," Timo said.

"Isa? Right."

Anton seemed to ease up as he nodded. Despite not being as tall as Timo, who at a height of 190 centimeters often towered over others, Anton's toned and fit physique gave him a commanding presence. He unbuttoned his jacket, giving him a more relaxed appearance and supporting Timo's belief that he had not fully transitioned from being a lawyer to a politician yet.

"I want to thank you again," Anton said suddenly.

"For what?"

"For taking such good care of my wife."

It was like a bolt of lightning hit him. Timo's face fell. Anton knew, just like he knew Timo had been outside his home, watching his wife. Every word in that sentence felt like a threat.

Then Anton turned his back to Timo and gave the secretary, who quickly looked up, a wave, before stepping into the hall without looking back.

"Timotheus."

Timo, still reeling from Anton's words, glanced toward the elevator. The doors parted and Timo watched Anton enter, somehow looking pleased with himself.

Then Timo turned to his brother and said, "Fred."

"What brings you here?"

"Official police business."

It had been some time since he had spoken Finnish, so it felt strange to hear himself using what he still considered his first language. Nowadays, he even did his thinking in Swedish. Just like in the conversation with Valkama's parents, he found himself looking for the right words.

"By the way... I have visitors, but I'll think you want to meet them," Fredrik said and signaled him to follow him.

As he pushed through the glass doors, Timo's eyes were drawn to the blue carpet. It didn't match the rest of the interior. The bright, sterile lights overhead cast an unforgiving white glow over the neat rows of empty desks. The room was quiet, save for the soft hum of the fluorescent lights and the rhythmic tapping of a lone figure hunched over a keyboard in the corner.

"Not much activity," Timo said.

"It's a slow day."

Fredrik led Timo to a corner office, where two people were engaged in an intimate conversation. The couple looked startled when the two brothers entered, and Timo immediately recognized one of them.

"Mom?" Timo said.

The woman, slender and middle-aged, gaped at him before recovering her composure. She was dressed in red. He was always amazed at how youthful she appeared, despite being in her early sixties. She had a sharp mind and quick wit, never holding back her thoughts and opinions, sometimes to the dismay of her sons.

She took his head in her hands and placed a kiss on his forehead. "Timofey, what brings you here?" she asked in Russian.

He had never been fluent in Russian, but Timo responded in his mother's native language. "I could ask the same of you. I am here on police business. What brings you here?"

She spun around and introduced him to the older man standing near the window. "This is my youngest son, Timotheus."

He recognized Leif Berg.

The man looked directly at him with piercing blue eyes, and for a moment, it felt as though the man could see right through him. Timo wasn't sure, but he thought he detected a hint of annoyance and anger in the man's expression before he regained his composure and smiled. He extended his hand.

"Well, nice to meet you. Leif Berg."

Timo took the man's hand, feeling a sudden jolt of surprise. The man had walked with the energy of a thirty-year-old, but the deep lines on his face showed he was much older. The same age as his mother.

"You have handsome boys, Valesca," Leif said.

"You know each other?" Timo stammered.

"We met before, a few times, but I, of course, know your mother best as the famous actress she was."

"Really?" Timo turned to his mother. He felt the tension, the lies that were buried behind the polite words. Was Berg the one?

"You are here on police business?" Leif asked.

"Yes."

"I've heard all about the plans for the convention. I like it."

"We'll do everything we can to keep you and your entourage safe," Timo said. "But that's not why I'm here. I need to talk to Fredrik."

Leif said goodbye and headed for the door.

But before leaving, he turned to Valesca. "If you are still in Stockholm, I'd like to have dinner this evening."

There was shock on her face. "Uh... yes, of course. It's my pleasure."

"Excellent. My assistant will give you the time and address. See you this evening."

With poise, the man exited the room, leaving the mother and her sons behind in the impeccably designed office. Timo surveyed the space, recognizing his mother's handiwork. Despite her efforts, she had been unable to fully instill in her sons her appreciation for art, fashion, and style to the degree she had hoped.

"Here we are," Fredrik said.

"You knew he was working for Berg?" Timo turned to his mother.

"Yes," she said, sitting down on the white leather two-seater next to the desk.

"What else should I know?" Timo didn't realize how wronged he sounded until he heard his own voice. It reminded him of a whiny, little child.

"I knew you would react this way. But Timofey, how have you been? You look tired and skinny. Have you been eating well?"

"How have I been?" he repeated and threw his hands in the air, "Jesus, mom, I don't know. Splendid, just splendid. Couldn't be better! Oh, no, wait... there are a few things like Caijsa's murder case being reopened, being treated as a suspect and..."

He stopped to catch his breath before continuing. "Just terrific!"

"I heard about that," she said calmly.

"You heard about that!" His voice was rising. "And I guess you were too busy to pick up the phone or visit?"

After a moment of silence, she finally spoke up. "The last time we talked, you made it very clear that you didn't want my help."

Rising to her feet, she addressed Fredrik, who had remained silent throughout the exchange. "I need to go, but I'll call you tonight."

She walked past Timo, hesitated for a moment, then said, "It was good to see you. Take care of yourself."

A wave of regret washed over Timo as his mother made a sudden exit, leaving him feeling both surprised and remorseful for his harsh words. He looked towards Fredrik, who was sitting behind the desk, a smirk on his face. Timo fought the urge to lash out, knowing that his brother always found a way to mock him at the most inappropriate moments.

"I hadn't expected you to come," Fredrik said. "First a phone call, now a visit. It seems like we're making up for lost time. I've had more interaction with you in the past days than I have in years."

Timo managed a weak grin in response. "Well, I was in the neighborhood. So, I thought I would drop by and say hello."

"I doubt that."

"Leif Berg."

"What about him?"

"Since when are you working for him?"

"Since this year," Frederik said, glancing over the papers on his desk.

Timo leaned over, hands on the table. "I don't get it. Leif is a socialist. When did you switch sides?"

Fredrik looked up with a smile. "You're always so naïve! I go where the opportunities bring me."

"What about what you believe in? Does that get abandoned so easily?"

"Look, I don't agree with everything Berg does and says. He contacted me a year ago and we made a deal. He figured that if he could convince someone like me to join him, he would be able to convince anyone."

"And what's in it for you?"

"Money, glory."

"Leif has a hidden agenda. I don't trust him."

"We all have our agendas. I don't trust him either, but we have an understanding. I lead him to victory in the next elections, and he'll open doors for me."

"Victory? He's in office. What more does he want?"

"Being Prime Minister."

"Meanwhile, we have to babysit him. We have other things to do. Since there have been attempts on his life, why don't you postpone the convention?"

"He doesn't want to." Fredrik got up and paced across the room. "We've been careful the last weeks. He hasn't been in the spotlight often, but he can't stay hidden forever."

"Who could be so determined to kill him? I mean... the man has some rather radical ideas. Why don't just wait until he commits political suicide?"

Fredrik gave him a faint grin, "It's my job to prevent his political suicide. Leif has a lot of enemies. He's not exactly the most diplomatic guy. We often have to bend over backwards to soften his words or put them into context. At the same time, that makes him a popular guy. He says what he thinks, and he says it in simple words, so most people understand. He was doing okay until the Sandviken saga started."

"Yeah, the serial killer. Leif is going through a lot of trouble to get that case reopened. Why? The man killed Berg's daughter."

"Allegedly. Remember: innocent until proven guilty. Besides, he had nothing to do with reopening the case. Separation of powers. Remember."

"Sure. And I have to believe that?"

Fredrik shrugged. "Believe whatever you must."

"So, most of his enemies are political?"

"Not just political... police officials, judges, companies, the gun lobby... you name it, but constituents love him."

"Does the name Lauri Valkama ring any bell?"

"Lauri Valkama," Fredrik repeated. "The name sounds somewhat familiar. Why?"

"He was murdered a week ago in Gävle. Used to work for the Finnish embassy when dad was still alive. I can't remember him. Do you?"

Fredrik stared at the wall for a moment and then shook his head. "No, but then again, we didn't know everyone who worked there."

"And now you're lying to me. I know you met with him." The frustration was evident in his voice.

Fredrik's brow furrowed in confusion. "Met with who?"

"Don't play dumb with me, Fredrik. I'm talking about Valkama. Sandra Arvidsson told me you had a separate meeting with him at the City Hall in Gävle."

Fredrik let out a dismissive snort. "Sandra? If I were you, I wouldn't believe a word that comes out of that woman's mouth."

"So, you deny talking to him?"

"I didn't say that. I talked to him briefly about the construction project," Fredrik admitted.

"Why?"

"It's a community project. I was just curious about the details and the financial impact."

"Really? Again... why?"

"Mayor Ek didn't particularly handle the situation well. Berg was furious."

"Berg shouldn't meddle in local politics."

"There are so many things we shouldn't do, but we just do anyway."

Timo shook his head in exasperation. "What is it with you people? You talk in riddles and mysterious sentences. Can't you just say it clearly? Anyway, I think Valkama's death has something to do with Engersson."

"Like in the late Karst Engersson? The idiot that fell off his throne?"

"Don't be such a schmuck about it. Your boss was willing to welcome Engersson with open arms. And the way I see it, you weren't the only one Berg was trying to convince. What did Berg want with two right-wingers?"

"Engersson was not right-wing," Fredrik snapped.

"I'm not too sure about that. His link with Anna Wallman? You knew all too well he was right-wing. What do you know of the link between Engersson and Berg?"

"Nothing. Berg was wooing Engersson to step into the party. As far as I know he needed Engersson's network and money."

Timo frowned. "Berg was wooing Engersson? I rather had the impression it was the opposite. And they had a fall-out before Engersson's death. And you... you again decided to call off the meeting with Engersson the day that Global Law was attacked. That's quite a coincidence."

"Where did you get all of this? Lies, nothing but lies."

"Fred, this is serious! If you knew about the attack..."

"I didn't cancel the meeting, someone else did. I know Sandra is trying to undermine my reputation, but I don't care. My only concern is Leif Berg's safety. I hope that sexy colleague of yours is doing everything she can to guarantee his safety?"

"The name is Inspector Lindström, and she's my partner," Timo said in a stern voice.

"I hope she is as smart as she is beautiful... my dear Timotheus."

"Stop doing that!" His brother's subtle insults and references to how much he disapproved of Timo made him so angry he could barely breathe. "You never think about me as your equal."

"Because you are not," Fredrik said, "you're my little brother."

Timo frowned. "What are you saying?"

"And... I... never mind," Fredrik dropped in the seat. "I've spent enough time on you today. Just go and leave me alone!"

"Fine, I need to be somewhere else anyway," Timo said and looked at his phone. But the message he had been waiting for wasn't there.

"Where?"

"The cemetery."

Fredrik gave him a cold look that made him almost gasp for air. "Caijsa?"

"Yes, Caijsa. Send Pamela and the kids my regards."

"Sure, as if she's going to believe that."

* * *

The snow crunched underfoot as Timo walked away from the building, his mind occupied with recent events. It had been a mistake to come here, to try and find closure. Everything was still so raw, so filled with insecurity and doubt. It had been hard enough when he was living in Stockholm, and when he could visit Caijsa's final resting place whenever his heart desired. Nothing had mattered more to him than being with her, pouring out his thoughts, even though he held no belief in an afterlife. He told her the things he would never tell anyone else—the silly things, the crazy things, and the most terrible things. In her company, he felt like he could simply be himself without judgement. Even if she wasn't there anymore.

Now he stared at the marble plate with her name on it, and the vase with the withered rose. This time, he felt anger instead of sadness. He was confused. He felt betrayed. He had adored her for many years, and now he doubted her. A doubt that had been planted there by a manipulator, a murderer. He knew that, but still…

He had started to doubt if any of it had been real—the love, the whispers, the touches, the kisses. He wanted to ask her if it had meant something, but he couldn't get the words out. With a heavy heart, he left the cemetery, carrying an indescribable mix of longing, emptiness, and unresolved emotions.

With Ingrid's words about Caijsa's medical records echoing in his mind, he set off towards Caijsa's father's house. Marcel had been living with his late ex-wife's husband, Nelvin, and things seemed eerily perfect. The kind of calm that usually preceded a police call about a fight that's gotten out of hand.

"Timo, my dear boy, what are you doing here?" Marcel had said when he found him on the doorstep.

"I'm sorry for disturbing you," Timo said, "but I called you a few times and you didn't answer, so I thought I'd come over in person."

"I'm not very good with cell phones," Marcel explained. "And neither is Nelvin," he added, gesturing to the other man who was sitting on the couch and had been following the conversation in silence.

Nelvin looked tired and distracted. His daughter Lyn was on trial for murder, but Marcel had told Timo that the ordeal had brought the two men closer together. Nelvin's daughter avenging the death of her half-sister forged a bond, but not with Timo. Nelvin hadn't looked at him since he had set foot in their home. Tension was high, and Marcel was trying to bury it with everyday conversation.

"I'm looking for Caijsa's medical files," Timo said.

"Why do you need her medical records?"

"I just need to check something."

"Is it about Lyn's case?" Marcel glanced at Nelvin.

"Yes."

"I don't think I have her medical files. It's been more than eight years. Maybe Paulina had them. Do you remember, Nelvin?"

The old man shrugged and said nothing.

"Can you have a look? Please."

Marcel took Timo's hand and smiled. "I can't promise you anything."

Timo stayed for a little while, and they talked about the things going on in their lives. Marcel loved having Timo over, but the conversation had left him feeling uneasy.

When Marcel closed the door after Timo left, Nelvin walked up to him and said, "You're going to have to tell him at some point."

Marcel looked down at his hands, which were still gripping the doorknob. "No, it'll destroy him."

"He deserves to know."

Marcel turned to look at him before speaking. "I know you're still upset about what happened with Lyn and that's why you don't like him, but it wasn't his fault. You can't blame him for her choices. I need to protect him."

"That's not what this is about, and you know it," Nelvin said, his voice low and angry. "You're just doing this because you feel guilty. You need to tell him the truth."

And with that, Nelvin turned and walked back into the living room, leaving Marcel alone with his thoughts.

Marcel sighed. No, this was a burden he would have to carry alone, one he would take to his grave if needed.

* * *

Isa's gaze lifted, drawn to the towering building that stood above the surrounding structures. It had seen better days. Its brick facade was chipped and worn, and the large windows on the upper levels were streaked with grime. The entrance, once grand and imposing, was now marred by peeling paint and a rusted doorknob. Above the doorway, a faded sign read 'Maplewood Apartments'.

The courtyard, visible through a dingy window, was overgrown with weeds and littered with broken bottles. The fence surrounding it was made of two rough planks of wood, barely held together by rusty nails.

Inside, the air was thick with the scent of dust and musty old carpet. An old wooden staircase curved upwards; its banister worn smooth by generations of tenants.

Despite the disrepair, there was a strange beauty to the building. Its faded grandeur hinted at a bygone era when it was a bustling hub of activity. But now, it was a forgotten relic, slowly succumbing to the ravages of time.

"Anna Wallman?"

The woman, in her forties, looked up from the papers on her desk. Isa and Lars had come to visit her at the campaign bureau.

"Yes?" she said.

Isa couldn't take her eyes off the perfectly symmetrical face. Black medium-length straight hair, red lips, and dark eyes staring at her from beneath long lashes. A beautiful woman. Only she could not relate to the ideas that the woman loudly proclaimed on every news channel and radio station. She was a fervent anti-abortion supporter.

"We're with the police, ma'am," Isa said and showed her badge.

"Police? Everything I do is legal. So, I don't see how…"

"We'd like to talk to you about Karst Engersson?" Isa said.

A grin appeared on Anna's face before she got up and signaled them to follow her. "Let's talk a bit more privately."

They made their way down a long hallway, their footsteps echoing against the scuffed hardwood floors. The wallpaper was peeling in places, revealing the bare plaster beneath. A few scattered light fixtures flickered overhead, casting strange shadows on the walls.

They finally entered a small room that smelled of coffee and food. The table was covered with wrappers, plastic plates, and cutlery.

"Sorry for the mess, we don't have much space. We only rent this floor."

"Why did you move here… to Gävle?"

"Our offices in Stockholm and Malmö were vandalized. They broke in and threatened our employees. We'll try again here. Let's see how long it lasts."

Anna let out a deep sigh and then looked at the inspectors again.

"Your organization is facing several charges of harassment and intimidation," Isa said.

"They're pending. I'm confident they'll be dropped. They were all unfounded. So, what do you want to know about Engersson?"

"What was your relationship with him?"

Anna's lips curled into a sarcastic smile, and for a moment, it seemed like she was on the verge of bursting out laughing. "Karst and I go way back," she said, her tone dripping with irony. "It was a... how shall I put it, love-hate thing."

"You were his mistress."

"One of many. He was a powerful man and always got what he wanted. I was still a young girl when he first fucked me... in his home office, with his wife sitting in the next room. You never said no to him."

"But the relationship was an on-off thing," Isa said.

Anna removed a strand of hair from her face. "When he didn't need you anymore, you got dumped."

"But he always came back to you."

"Well, I used him the same way he used me."

"What did you use him for?" Lars asked.

"Money, power, influence."

Lars said Engersson was not known for his far-right ideas and was instead considered a center figure.

Anna countered him. "But that's only because he wanted to pursue a career in politics and couldn't be associated with more extreme right-wing beliefs."

Isa nodded thoughtfully. "He was hiding his true views?"

"Exactly. In reality, Engersson was an ultra-conservative. He believed in traditional gender roles, where women were expected to be submissive and stay at home. And while he agreed with the ideas of our group, he took it one step further."

A chill ran down Isa's spine as she imagined what 'one step further' meant in this context. People like Engersson were dangerous precisely because they blended in with society, hiding their true beliefs behind a veneer of respectability.

"What do you mean?" Isa asked.

"I think he was involved in more... illegal activities. There have been rumors about a group that preaches complete dominance of the white race... Swedish race. They don't shy away from violence, and some say they have been behind several big incidents. We don't want to have anything to do with them."

"What incidents?"

"I don't know," Anna said. "But take Forsmark. The sabotage of the nuclear plant. That sounds like something they would plan."

"But why?" Lars asked.

"Anarchy, chaos, to put the blame on the foreigners, and then a coup d'état to put it all right."

"And what about Berg?"

"They need someone to victimize. Berg is in a good spot. He's got power and influence, but he has also been a little too trusting of outsiders and criminals. Engersson needed to make Berg think they're friends, get him to lower his guard and then boom, take everything away from him."

"Could they go this far as to murder Berg?"

"They are capable of everything," Anna said. "And you need to realize that just by telling you this, I've put our lives in danger."

"Why do you tell us?"

"This group is dangerous and needs to be stopped. I am willing to fight for my ideas, but with words and debate, not violence."

"Why didn't you go to the police?"

"Police? You don't get it... they are everywhere. Police, politicians, judges, CEOs. Everywhere. They are capable to have everything and everyone disappear, including myself."

"Do you know who they are?"

Anna shook her head and spun toward the sounds of footsteps in the hallway. She leaned over and whispered, "It would be unwise to trust anyone, detectives. Be careful."

CHAPTER

8

TWO MEN WALKED THROUGH the white double doors and into the sitting area. They were familiar with the small castle outside of Stockholm, having met there many times before. The older of the two men was clearly nearing seventy, as evidenced by his thinning gray hair, which was spread sparsely over his balding head, and the deep wrinkles etched into his tanned skin. Despite his short and slightly overweight build, he had sharp dark eyes and a face that hinted at a past as a ladies' man. The other man, who was younger, tall, and athletic, had piercing blue eyes and blond hair that was beginning to turn gray at the temples. The wrinkles on his face were the result of years spent squinting in the sun.

After pouring himself a glass of scotch, the younger man took a seat on the sofa near the fireplace, across from the older man.

"It's a mess," the older man said. He took a sip of his drink, with an arrogance that seemed to come with position and power.

"Olav, I...," the young man said, and then stopped. His conversation partner gave him a frowned look.

"Prime Minister," he corrected, "we are doing the best we can, but the Forsmark sabotage is a complicated..."

"Excuses, nothing but excuses I hear these days," Olav Hult said. "If the far-right groups are involved I need to know. Fast. This could be damaging now we're trying to get the Sweden Democrats' support for the new legislation on health care."

"Why do you need their support?" the other man said. "Does Berg know you're talking to the far-right?"

Olav gave him another deadly look and then said, "Let me do the politics, Eriksson. You are the police commissioner. You take care of police business!"

"And Valkama...," his companion said hesitantly.

"Another disaster." Olav leaned forward. He almost looked like a predator, out to attack his prey. "Is it true about Engersson?"

"Yeah."

"I trusted that man. Berg is going to use this."

"But he was the one who approached Engersson and wanted to give him a prominent role in the party."

"But I suggested it to him. Damn it!" Olav took a sip of his whiskey and then said, "Who killed Valkama?"

Eriksson bowed his head. "We don't know. Heimersson is busy with it."

The man's voice was so loud it filled the room. After all these years, Olav still wondered how this man could be so irritating that it would make all the hairs on the back of his neck stand up.

"Then Heimersson needs to step it up and find whoever did this... fast," Olav said, his voice showing the frustration that had been building up. He almost dropped his glass of whiskey. "And I'm not sure Heimersson's the right person. It was a mistake to put him in Gävle. Your mistake."

"You wanted someone in Gävle that supported our cause," Eriksson said without blinking an eye. "By the way, SÄPO reopened the Breiner case."

"Solberg?"

Eriksson nodded.

"Why?"

"It seems they have new evidence and... an informant who has come forward."

"Interesting," Olav said. "Who is the informant?"

"We don't know. Internal affairs and SÄPO are keeping this confidential. Basically, the police are under investigation."

"Remind Solberg where his priorities lie and find out what new information they have."

Eriksson's eyes widened in astonishment; his gaze fixed on him. "You are venturing into dangerous territory. If word gets out that you've been manipulating an internal investigation..."

"I'm not manipulating an investigation. I just want to know what they know."

"Why? Is there something I should know? Are you involved?"

Olav rose from his seat and made his way to the fireplace, where the flames were dancing and flickering against the wood. He retrieved a cigarette from the pocket of his jacket and lit it. As he took a drag, he said, "I think this one could backfire."

"Olav, what's going on?"

The older man spoke in a calm tone, "I'm not paying you to ask questions. Do what I ask you to do!" He took another drag of his cigarette, his cold and piercing eyes locked onto the other man.

Olav walked back to the sofa, the cancer stick precariously dangling from his mouth, smoke trailing from his nostrils. He should have stopped ages ago, but at sixty-six there was no incentive anymore. The damage was already done. "Now let's get back to business. We need to find out who's responsible for Forsmark. Who did this? Engersson and Valkama are dead. See what our guys in Stockholm and Gävle can find out. We need to contain this. I need to know if the far-right is involved. And what about Lunde?"

"The investigation is still going on."

"And? Is Berg involved?"

"Don't underestimate Berg," Eriksson said. "He covered his tracks well. He has been successful in dodging that bullet before. And he will this time. Besides, one of the women has changed her story and claims it was consensual. And…"

Eriksson took a sip of his whiskey, his expression turning grim. "… Lunde was your man, and now Berg is exploiting that. He's invited his own supporters to the convention in January, and if you're not careful, he'll use them to overpower you. Why did you need a convention anyway… so soon after the elections?"

Olav kept quiet, leaned back, and closed his eyes, while his mouth folded in a sarcastic smile.

* * *

Tuva stood in a desolate section of the harbor, surrounded by low houses. In the distance, the blaring sirens of fire trucks could be heard, while an orange glow illuminated the horizon, casting an eerie light on the surroundings. It was a familiar sight, one that she had seen before. Once again, the Yule Goat in Castle Square, a cherished holiday tradition, had fallen victim to vandals and been set ablaze, ensuring that it would not make it to Christmas for yet another year. The smaller goat, its sibling, had already met the same fate a week earlier.

At first, the glow brought a sense of warmth and comfort, but soon Tuva was consumed by panic. She turned around to face a pristine, white carpet of snow before her.

But it wasn't perfect.

She saw the trail of red spots in the snow, which grew larger as she walked on. Her body trembled, and her breath came out in white puffs as she approached the gleaming blade on the ground. The redness contrasted sharply with the whiteness of the snow, and she felt the chill of the snowflakes on her face as she looked at the peaceful water on the other side. In the distance, she saw a docked ship. Everything was so quiet and dark.

For hours, she had wandered along the docks searching for Greta. She had seen the fully loaded ships and the men who had looked at her either with horror or with a look that betrayed they wanted to do something more with her than chat. With every step she took, the image of the man, his hands, his smell, and the anger in his eyes flashed by.

She gazed at the knife on the ground, saw the blood and then the stains on her dress. She remembered the day Greta had given her the dress as a birthday gift.

Greta. She approached the figure lying meters away from her. As she followed the trail of blood, the drops had turned into smears, and the snow was trampled where the body had fallen and dragged itself through the ice and mud.

Eyes open, skin as pale as the snow. But the expression was what frightened her most. A face contorted in a grotesque manner, as if someone had forcibly removed the skin and clumsily attempted to reattach it, only for it to appear mismatched and ill-fitting.

"Greta," she whispered.

She removed her glove and leaned over to touch Greta's face. It was so cold. There was no doubt about it, Greta was dead.

She got up and started to run.

She needed to get out of there... fast.

But each step she took was fraught with difficulty, as the soles of her boots fought for traction on the slippery surface. The wet snow offered no support, causing her feet to slide and sink with each stride. She struggled to maintain balance, her legs threatening to give way beneath her with every gust of wind.

The cold air filled her lungs, each breath a sharp reminder of the chilling reality she was fleeing from. She could hear her own labored breaths, intermingled with the crunching sound of her boots struggling against the snow.

Someone called out behind her, but she ignored them and kept running.

Run! Run as fast as you can!

* * *

The snowflakes drifted down like feathers from a pillow fight that slowly found their way to the ground. Isa had been staring at it for more than five minutes. The whiteness and the silence that came with the snowfall were mesmerizing. Cleansing almost.

"Knoch snowflake," she whispered.

It had been almost a year since that evening in the pub when Alexander Nordin had told her about one of the first fractal curves. She remembered it all so well. And now, here she was, standing in silence, watching the snowflakes fall to the ground. That evening, she had fallen in love with him, the man who had died at the hands of her partner. And she had been the reason. She felt a deep melancholic sadness that she couldn't shake.

"What did you say?"

In the background, she heard the sizzling of butter. She turned around and saw Timo bent over the pan where he tossed chopped onions. His black T-shirt and blue jeans always looked good on him. She respected him as a colleague and friend, but there were feelings. Her little crush was back. But even though they shared common interests, she knew that his heart belonged to another woman. He always looked lonely and sad, just like she felt herself. She didn't know for sure, but it probably had something to do with Ingrid. Only, she didn't dare to ask him about it. If she did, it would make it too clear that his mind and heart weren't really with her. She longed for someone—someone who could give her the warmth, thrill, and excitement of love. She longed for Alex. But he wasn't there anymore; he was only a ghost of the past. Someone she desperately wanted to forget and replace.

"What did you say?" he repeated.

"Nothing, never mind." Isa walked to the open kitchen. She took the glass of red wine, he had offered her when she had arrived, from the living room table.

"It smells nice." She took a seat at the counter in front of the cooking hob where he was busy stirring the vegetables.

"Now that you're here," he said, placing a cutting board in front of her with tomatoes. "I assume you know how it works."

She wasn't the best cook but cutting tomatoes couldn't be that hard. "I went through Valkama's file again."

He looked at her with his sharp blue eyes and then said calmly, "And?"

"Nothing new. But I was thinking. Anna Wallman gave us an address where the so-called secret meetings of this far-right group take place. We should take a look."

"That's for SÄPO."

"Come on, Timo. You're curious like I am. You want to know."

"Finn made it clear. Let SÄPO investigate it."

She frowned and looked at him. "You and Finn. I thought you were friends, but you're afraid of him. Why? So what if he threatens to fire me? It's not like it hasn't been done before."

He put the wooden spoon down. "I'm not afraid of him but of what he represents."

"What are you saying?"

"I haven't told you everything. He warned me. There are people out there who are playing dirty games, and we seem to be in the middle of it."

"Timo, you can't ignore this."

"I need to protect the team, everyone. You."

He peered down at the vegetable mixture and closed his eyes, letting the scent of the herbs take him away. She smiled. Three hours ago, he had talked her into trying his healthy vegetable curry. After his last cooking fiasco, when she had spent half the night hugging the toilet, she had been hesitant to accept. But with all the emotions and memories of Alex flooding her days, she had said yes.

"I can perfectly protect myself," Isa said.

"I'm sure you can. Still..."

She took another sip of the wine and then looked at him closely. "So, you and Ingrid."

He sighed but didn't look up. "As you so blatantly pointed out to me, there is no Ingrid and I... so let's leave it at that."

"He's been asking about you."

"Who?" Timo said, his face pale. He knew very well who she was talking about.

"Anton. About the two of you."

"And what did you say?" Timo stammered.

She took another sip of the wine. "Nothing, but he knows or at least suspects something."

"Shit. I don't want Ingrid to get into trouble."

"Then stop running after her like a lovesick puppy."

"I'm not!"

She gave him a mocking smile. "Sure."

He narrowed his eyes. "That reminds me: how did your talk with Viktor go? Last time you successfully moved the conversation away from that topic."

"For good reason. I don't want to talk about it. Not yet."

He put the steamy pot on the table, and she joined him in the living room. She liked the living area. It was pleasant and stylish at the same time. It was warm and inviting, even though it had an open feel. There was a small table in the corner for drinks and food, where he had put the plates and pot, and it had a spectacular view of the lake. The kitchen was a level below the living area, which was a fun little detail in the design.

It had two big gray sofas in the center facing away from each other and a coffee table in front of the sofas. There was a wall mounted flat screen, and a bookshelf with old DVDs and CDs stacked on top of it. The only thing that irritated her was the picture of the beach with the palm tree. It looked like he had bought the frame and never had removed the picture that had come with it.

But she missed something. Caijsa's pictures were gone. They had been there the last time.

Puzzled, she found herself sinking onto a nearby chair. When the food was presented to her, she took a bite and remarked, "This is really good."

But despite the pleasant taste, the nagging questions continued to tug at her mind. Timo's recent behavior had been puzzling and left her with many unanswered questions. The deep love he once shared with Caijsa now felt distant. There was an unexplained change in his demeanor. Was he truly moving on? Or was there an underlying current of anger and frustration that had led him to bury all memories of her?

He smiled. "I told you. This is great food. But... since you're going to keep changing the subject, I just want to say that I'm here for you if you need to talk."

She had to let it go, at least for the moment, and instead embraced the comfort and support he was offering. "I thought we were just people who are getting less and less annoyed with each other?"

"I think we can safely say that we're partners and friends at this point."

She smiled. "Yeah, I know. And thank you for the offer."

As she poured herself another glass of wine, her gaze shifted to the almost empty bottle, while his glass remained mostly untouched. A realization washed over her—a growing awareness of her recent habit of consuming more wine, particularly on weekends and after challenging days.

As the familiar taste graced her lips once again, she recognized the need for change. She needed to cut down on her drinking.

* * *

After dinner, she settled on the couch. It was dark outside, and through the window, she saw the lights of the houses on the shore of the lake.

"Lindström, you had too much to drink," he said with a stern voice as he put the two cups of coffee on the small table.

"I'm okay."

"Either I drive you home or you stay here."

He wasn't joking. Letting her loose on the road was asking for trouble. He couldn't take that responsibility.

"I have a room available. It's not the Ritz, but if you don't mind the boxes, there's a perfectly decent bed where you can sleep."

"Thank you, that sounds great."

"How's Nick?" Timo asked.

"I talked to him a few days ago. He's okay. Well, maybe that's stretching it. He's getting therapy. The road to recovery will be long."

"PTSD is a serious thing, and it doesn't blow over that easily. I remember he was in a very bad shape when he left."

After giving it some thought, she realized Nick had just picked up exactly where he had left off after his two-month sabbatical. And that turned out to be a mistake. Too fast, too early.

"In any case, I'm glad you didn't miss out on this delicious curry," Timo said with a grin.

She smiled in response. "It was very good. Thank you."

She sat in silence, her gaze fixed on the steaming cup of coffee in front of her.

"Anton," he suddenly said.

"What about him?"

"Is he good to her?"

"Ingrid?"

He took a sip of coffee. "Do they have a good marriage?"

"I think they're great together."

She took his hand, and he looked up in surprise. "Ingrid is not the right woman. I think you're looking for a new Caijsa."

He shook his head. "Ingrid is not Caijsa. Everything about Caijsa is so... never mind."

* * *

Isa awoke to the sound of heavy breathing coming from the adjacent room and was instantly reminded of her partner's snoring. It wasn't that bad, but it wasn't exactly music to her ears. At least there was something comforting in the fact that the guy wasn't perfect. As Isa lay there, she felt disoriented by a headache that kept intensifying. Struggling to recall how she ended up in this situation, memories of dinner and wine slowly returned. Relieved that she hadn't woken up next to Timo, Isa remembered him helping her up the stairs and into bed before the rest of the night became a blur.

Then a wave of panic washed over her as she remembered kissing him and how he had taken her head in his hands. For a moment, he had hesitated before telling her she should lie down and rest. Or maybe it was all in her head? Maybe she had wanted it to be something else than it actually was.

Thirsty, Isa reached for her phone on the nightstand and saw it was 2 a.m. She got up, using her phone's light function to guide her way. As she walked out of the room, she saw her partner sleeping soundly through the open door on her right.

She stood there for a moment. In the moonlight, she saw his face, eyes closed, unaware she was staring at him. Her eyes then descended, tracing the contours of his naked torso that peeked out from beneath the blanket. Every part of his exposed skin exuded a certain allure—a sculpted physique that hinted at strength and vitality. The play of moonlight on his smooth skin highlighted his natural curves and defined muscles. It was as if he was meticulously crafted by an artist's hand. From the gentle slope of his shoulders to the chiseled lines of his chest.

The surge of lust she was feeling at that moment clashed with her attempts to resist and she took a deep breath. Then she walked down the stairs and made her way to the kitchen, but the open study door caught her attention. The full moon's light shone through the curtains, casting an eerie glow on the strange drawings and papers pinned to the whiteboard at the other end of the room. She couldn't shake the feeling that she was still in a dream as she approached the wall, using her phone as a makeshift flashlight. As she neared, she recognized the central image on the board.

"Caijsa," she whispered.

Next to a picture of Caijsa, she saw scribblings. Although some of the writing was illegible, the words she could make out sent a shiver down her spine. They read: 'Abortion' and 'Unfaithful'.

Suddenly she heard the bed creak upstairs. A brief silence followed and then the resumption of snoring. With a heavy heart, she backed away from the board and exited the study, silently closing the door behind her.

Timo was an odd man. He had come in as an outsider, asked by Stockholm to clean up the mess after the serial killer debacle. But he hadn't done what his superiors had expected of him: Fire her and the rest of the team. He tried to protect them, he believed in them, and he had paid for it with his job. Why would he stay? If it hadn't been for Ingrid, he would have gone back to Stockholm.

But the clippings on the whiteboard made her uneasy, and she couldn't shake the feeling that Timo was keeping secrets from her. As she filled a glass with water from the kitchen sink, she made up her mind to uncover the truth before things got out of hand. Timo's obsession with Caijsa's case was far from healthy.

CHAPTER

9

"**WE'RE HERE,**" Timo said as he stopped the car under the bridge. He looked over at Isa next to him and said, "You can open your eyes now."

She moaned and then looked at him.

"Are you sure you want to be here?" he asked. "I can drive you home. No need for both of us to be here."

Isa rubbed her face. "It's my own stupid mistake. I'll be fine."

"Are you sure?"

"Yeah, yeah," she said, but sounded irritated.

"Isa, I know you're going through a rough time, but alcohol is not the answer."

"Do you really think this is the time for a lecture?" she asked, narrowing her eyes.

Ignoring her comment, he said, "And kissing me isn't the answer either."

She was suddenly fully awake and gaped at him.

"Oh... you remember," she said.

"You were drunk. Not me."

"I'm sorry," she said, stumbling over her words. "This was not the intention. I don't know what came over me."

"It's time to grow up don't you think," he said, opening the door and stepping out.

And there he was, good old Timo, with his raised finger and pedantic remarks. Maybe she deserved the lecture, but she remembered the moment when she kissed him, and he hesitated. That told her something.

She got out of the car and followed him to where most of the police officers were gathered.

Despite the appearance of a bright and sunny day, the biting wind was unforgivingly cold, causing her fingers to numb and tingle even with thick gloves on.

"Berger, what have we got here?" Timo asked.

When the bearded man turned, they saw the dead body lying on the ground, and Dr. Olsson, dressed in a protective suit, sitting next to it.

"Woman, early twenties, stabbed multiple times," Ingrid said quickly before Berger could open his mouth. She continued to examine the body without giving Isa nor Timo a look.

"Who is she?" Timo asked.

"The body was discovered by two dockworkers who were loading a ship. They recognized her as Greta Almstedt," Berger said.

"Tuva Norling's friend?"

"Yes, they knew her," Berger said. "She worked as a prostitute."

Timo knelt next to Ingrid and stared at the body. "There's a look of surprise on her face."

"More like... a look of pain," Ingrid said. "The first wounds were superficial, in her arms, hands and shoulder. She tried to defend herself and tried to flee, but her attacker caught up with her. That was when he stabbed her one final time. That stab was fatal as it likely severed the hepatic artery. The victim bled out in minutes."

Timo looked at the blood-soaked snow, and a sudden pang of horror gripped him.

She continued, "Then the attacker removed the knife."

"Was the murder weapon found?" he asked, his voice hoarse.

"It was lying a few meters away from her. Over there. There were footprints as well. Several of them, but I can't use them. The snow covered most of them. Some are old, others probably from the time of the murder."

"Fingerprints?"

"Yes, on the knife, and if we're lucky they're in the database."

"If we're lucky... yes." Timo stood up, then stared at the warehouse and the water. The bright reflection of the sun blinded him, so he closed his eyes.

Lars spoke up, "The dockers saw someone flee. From the description, it could be Tuva."

"Tuva?" Isa's eyes widened. "Why was she here? Maybe the people who attacked Greta were after her. Maybe she was the real target."

"We're not entirely sure of Tuva's role in this," Berger interrupted. "Is she a witness or a suspect?"

Timo scowled. "But Greta was the victim, not Tuva."

"Greta and Tuva look very much alike," Berger pointed out.

Turning to Lars, Timo asked, "What did your source reveal?"

Lars rubbed his chin. "Not much. Tuva's often seen with Greta. There's a guy named Rolf, don't know his last name, who's been seen with them. He's a drug addict."

"Where is Rolf now?"

Lars shrugged. "I don't know. He hasn't been seen for days."

"And Tuva?"

"Neither of them."

"We need to consider the possibility that she might be dead if she witnessed Greta's murder," Isa said.

"Or that she might have killed both Greta and Rolf," Berger added.

"You don't like Tuva," Isa said as she looked at him.

Berger maintained his composure and replied casually, "I'm just following the evidence. She was there when Valkama died, and she was there when Greta died."

Timo sighed. "But someone was chasing her. If she didn't do it, she could be in danger. Valkama's murderer might be after her. We need to find her as soon as possible. Lars, I want everyone out looking for her."

"Heimersson won't be happy about that," Isa remarked.

"Let me take care of our superintendent," Timo said and then turned to Ingrid who had quietly followed the conversation. "Dr. Olsson, this case is a priority. A young woman is in danger. If you find anything, please let me know."

"Very well," Ingrid said with a straight face.

He gazed at the body. "I just hope we're not too late."

* * *

Two days after the discovery of Greta's body, Timo decided it was time to visit the Lager family. According to Tuva's file they had been the foster family where she stayed before she decided life on the street was better than having a house and family.

Isa had to admit it intrigued her, because on paper the Lagers were a caring family who had hosted troubled kids for more than fifteen years.

As they arrived at the Lager's residence, Isa felt a sense of unease. Tuva's file hinted at a troubled past, and she knew that getting information from the Lagers might not be easy.

A somber and slightly annoyed looking Mr. Lager answered the door. He invited them inside and offered the perfunctory drink which they politely declined.

The living room was cozy, with a couch placed by the window, where Mrs. Lager sat, her hands folded in her lap. There was a strange tension in the air. Though the Lagers were cordial in their greetings, and their home was warm and inviting, there was an undercurrent of unease that Isa couldn't quite place.

Next to Mrs. Lager, their only child Petra was sitting.

Petra Lager was a young woman in her mid-twenties, with long, dark hair that cascaded down her shoulders in loose waves. She had a sharp, angular jawline and high cheekbones, giving her a striking, elegant appearance. When she introduced herself, she spoke in a measured tone, and she seemed to choose her words carefully. She looked at her father, who was standing in the doorway between the living room and kitchen, as if she had to get his approval.

"So, Tuva stayed with you for two years," Isa started.

"Sad story. Mother died of cancer when she was twelve. She had been with several foster families when she came to us," Mrs. Lager said.

"And her father?'

Mrs. Lager shook her head. "Tuva never talked about him. I don't think she knew her father. At least he wasn't in the picture."

"After two years, she ran away," Isa said.

"We thought she was happy, but then one day she didn't come home from school. She was seventeen... no, I'm mistaken, she was sixteen. We've been worried sick ever since."

"Did you try to find her?"

Mrs. Lager sighed. "I can't tell you how many times we've scanned the streets to look for her. We filed a missing person's report, but they didn't do anything. Uh... no offense."

"None taken," Timo said. "But do you know why she suddenly ran off like that?"

"It wasn't the first time," Petra intervened.

"Oh, when did that happen?" Isa asked.

"Six months after she came to stay with us."

"But she came back."

"We found her near the docks... with that friend of hers... I think she was... Greta."

"Greta Almstedt?"

Petra shrugged. "Could be."

"I knew from the start that girl was no good," Mr. Lager suddenly said. "She was poisoning Tuva's mind with nonsense. That's why she filed that complaint and later withdrew it."

Isa gave Timo a quick look. There was nothing mentioned about a complaint in Tuva's file.

"Yes, let's talk about the complaint for a moment," Timo said with a straight face.

Petra looked up at her father, eyes wide with horror.

"There is nothing to tell. All lies. Accusing me of racism and bullying! Good God! Luckily, the police dismissed it as the fantasies of a troubled kid."

"It was a period Tuva didn't feel good about herself," Mrs. Lager intervened. "She was sad and... lonely. Almost nostalgic. And we had many fights... mostly about small things."

"A stupid, annoying, ungrateful teenager," Mr. Lager let out.

"No bullying... right," Timo said. "And I assume you forced her to withdraw the complaint?"

Isa felt the tension rising.

"I didn't do anything," the man yelled. He walked over to where Timo was sitting and stood in front of him, with his arms crossed. "What was your name again? Paikkala? Finnish?"

"Yes, I am," Timo said calmly.

"Of course, a bloody foreigner!" Mr. Lager spat out.

"Timo...," Isa tried to prevent her partner from trailing off in a dangerous discussion that could escalate, but it was too late.

"I guess you don't like foreigners that much, Mr. Lager?" Timo asked, his tone now more assertive.

"They take our jobs, our women, our money. I don't trust them. Finns, Russians, Muslims... you're all the same. Parasites, living off the wealth we, real Swedes, have established over decades with decent, hard work."

The shocked expressions on his wife's and daughter's faces showed they wanted him to stop talking.

"I'm sure my father didn't have anything or anyone specific in mind," Petra spoke up.

"I see," Timo replied.

"What do you mean by that?" the old man asked.

"Nothing in particular," Isa said quickly, trying to keep the peace. "We just want to find Tuva. We don't care about these allegations. Can you think of a place where she would go or hide?"

She quickly glanced at Timo who was struggling to control his anger and frustration. Thankfully, he kept quiet.

"No, I'm sorry," Petra said.

"Was there anyone she was close to when she was here? Besides Greta?"

Mrs. Lager closed her eyes briefly as if to recall fragments of her memory. "We had one more foster child when she was here. An older girl, but they weren't close. I can't remember her name. She left a few months after Tuva arrived. And for the rest, Tuva was a bit of a loner. I think you, Petra, were probably closest to her."

"I wouldn't say I was her friend. We talked now and then, but she never really talked much about herself."

"Okay," Isa said. "If something comes to mind, let us know."

And she gave her card to Petra.

Petra's voice quivered with worry, "What will happen now?"

"We'll keep on looking for her," Isa said.

"Is she in any danger?"

"Maybe." Isa looked the young woman in the eye. A look of confusion had settled on Petra's face.

Mrs. Lager stood up. "I hope you find her."

"I'll see you out," Petra said, got up and walked to the living room door, followed by the inspectors.

As she stepped into the hallway and closed the door to the living room, Petra suddenly turned around and said: "You should talk to Mahmoud Najm."

She quickly let her eyes glance over the door that was still shut, afraid her parents could come into the hallway at any time.

Isa signaled that it was best to walk to the front door and then asked her: "Who is that?"

"He works at the youth center," Petra said in a soft voice. "He was close to Tuva. She started to go there after she came to live with us. She liked it there."

"But?" Timo asked.

"My dad found out. He thought Mahmoud was her boyfriend and... well, you've heard him."

"Yep, I did," Timo let out. "He doesn't like Mahmouds."

"I don't want to make excuses for my dad, but he had a tough childhood. I understand why he is the way he is. Anyway, he forbade Tuva to go to the youth center."

"And that's when she filed the complaint," Timo remarked.

"Yes... just talk to him. He might know where Tuva is."

The father walked in and looked surprised. "Are you still here?"

"Call me if you think of anything else," Isa said, ignoring the man's frowns.

* * *

Isa put her collar up, looked at the house again, and then walked to the car with Timo next to her. There was an unusual silence, like they both needed time to let everything sink in. She looked up. The lampposts started to cast shadows over the streets that had suddenly turned silent. An eerie silence before the storm. She just didn't know what storm.

"The man is a racist," Timo said.

"I'm sorry."

"What are you sorry for?" he said in his no-nonsense Timo-like way.

"I can see why you felt addressed. I didn't even know people had something against Finns."

"Oh, you'd be surprised. I can imagine he wants to go back to the time Sweden ruled Finland. But it's not just about Finns in particular. Anyone who doesn't fit their worldview is considered a threat. Probably he's angry with you too, being a woman in what once was considered a man's job."

"The problem is these people raise the next generation of racists, and the cycle continues."

Timo stopped and looked at the house again. "There's a whole lot of anger and fear in that house. Did you notice how scared the daughter was?"

"The father rules his family like a dictator. His view is the only one that counts. Tuva escaped, but these people have been foster parents for years. I wonder how many children they've poisoned with these ideas.

How did social services not catch this?"

"They stopped fostering children two years ago. We need to check with social services for the reason."

"Why didn't they look into this when Tuva filed the complaint?"

"She was a troubled kid with zero credibility. And she was forced to withdraw the complaint. But she was a brave kid."

"I wouldn't be surprised the father is member of a far-right group."

"Let's find this Mahmoud Najm," Timo said, "and see what he has to tell us."

* * *

Mahmoud Najm was sitting in his office at the youth center, trying to focus on the paperwork in front of him. Just as he was about to take a break, he saw two unfamiliar faces entering the building. Isa and Timo introduced themselves as police officers trying to find a homeless teenager named Tuva Norling.

"Tuva? Yeah, I know her... knew her. I haven't seen her for a while."

"Do you know where she could have gone? To hide?" Isa asked.

Mahmoud thought about it for a few moments and then shook his head. "No. Like I said I haven't seen her for a while. Maybe you can check with her friend Greta."

Timo hesitated for a moment before finally speaking, "Tuva. Did you know her well? What was she like?"

"She was okay. There was a time when she would come to the center almost every day. She was a good kid. Always willing to help others, and she had a strong sense of community. She just had a tough life. She was struggling with not having a family anymore and not belonging anywhere. She was always a bit reserved and sometimes... how shall I put it... obsessive."

"Obsessive," Timo said. "About what?"

"Her father. She was trying to find her father."

"She knew who he was?"

"I think she met him once or twice. She was always using the computer here. The Lagers didn't allow her to have a computer or phone. She was trying to get information about him."

"And did she find him?" Isa asked.

"No, she didn't, and that upset her."

Mahmoud leaned back in his chair, a feeling of unease creeping over him. He knew the dangers of being a homeless teenager on the streets and the thought of Tuva being out there alone worried him.

"There was an incident," Isa said.

Mahmoud looked at his hands and then said, "Her foster father thought Tuva and I were in a relationship."

"And were you?" Timo asked.

Mahmoud jumped up. "No, of course not. I was twenty-five and she was not even sixteen."

Mahmoud could feel the anger rising in his chest. "He's a racist. One afternoon he suddenly showed up here, calling me names, threatening to report me to the police. They had to escort him out of the building. Two days after that, someone threw a brick through the window of my parents' house. It almost hit my mother. I knew it was him. And then... I was here alone one night, when two men came in and beat me up. They didn't take anything, they just wanted to hurt me."

"Did you report it to the police?"

He shook his head. "No, but Tuva filed a complaint against her foster father accusing him of racism."

"And she retracted her testimony later," Timo said.

"I asked her. I knew it would only make things worse. She didn't want to at first, but I begged her."

"And what happened then?"

"She started coming less and less. And then... not anymore. I felt sorry for her. The Lagers... it didn't click. You could feel it. Those people scared her. She didn't feel safe."

"Did you never consider filing a complaint with child welfare?"

"I... no. Maybe I should have, but to be honest, there was no evidence of abuse, psychological or physical."

Timo flipped through his notebook. "There was another incident. Tuva was arrested for attacking a woman."

Mahmoud sighed. "Yes, I remember. This happened when she was already homeless. It was a difficult time for her. She was going through a lot, and I think she just snapped. But she never spoke about it to me, but I know she broke into a house. The woman who was home at that time caught her and claimed Tuva attacked her, but I'm not sure what exactly happened or what led to it. All I know is that it was a confusing time for her, and she needed help. Unfortunately, the system failed her. I failed her."

"Mr. Najm, if you know anything, if you know where we could find her, you need to tell us. We believe she is in danger."

Mahmoud's expression hardened. "I wish I knew where she was. I would tell you."

He paused for a moment, his eyes misting with emotion. "But I will do everything in my power to help you find her. If there's anything else I can do, just let me know."

* * *

The 'Mille Birre' pub was in the heart of the city, nestled among a bustling strip of shops on the main street. As Christmas was fast approaching, it was a highly sought-after destination on this December evening. Even at 6 p.m., the street was still teeming with people, cars, and holiday shoppers.

The pub itself was an impressive, square-shaped, older building, its facade painted in a deep red color with contrasting black accents. Inside, the atmosphere was lively and boisterous, with the sounds of chatter and laughter filling the room. Everyone seemed to be in high spirits and enjoying themselves.

Isa had braced herself for a room full of menacing and disreputable individuals, but as she walked in, she was surprised to find that the men and women at the meeting appeared to be perfectly ordinary. She struggled to reconcile the idea that these seemingly normal people harbored conservative and far-right beliefs.

Isa and Timo blended in seamlessly, and nobody had taken notice of them or questioned their presence. As Timo and she took a seat, Isa couldn't help but glance at her partner who had remained silent during their walk to the pub.

"Timo, we didn't have the time to talk after Greta's body was found, but I'm truly sorry."

"About what?"

"The drinking and... the kiss."

No, that wasn't true. She didn't regret the kiss. She just wished it hadn't been marred by pointless, juvenile drama.

"When did it start?" he asked.

"What?"

"The drinking."

"I don't... after Alex died."

"You need to do something about it."

"I did... I tried but I just can't forget. It's almost a year."

She looked at her hands.

Timo stared at her, and the expression on his face softened, "I forgot. I'm sorry. The first anniversary is tough. Aren't the sessions with Dr. Wikholm helping?"

She quickly cast her eyes. Time to confess. "About that..."

Lines of concern appeared on his forehead. "You're not going anymore?"

She let down her shoulders. "It's hard."

"Yeah, it's hard. Jeezes, Lindström, are you..."

She felt the anger boiling. "Look, he wanted to talk about things I didn't want to talk about."

"That's the idea of therapy. To talk about things, you're afraid to talk about. Wikholm is there to help you think about things you've avoided, like the loss of Alex or... why you go so easily from one man to another, like we... men are disposable."

This was a conversation they hadn't had before. At least, not so openly.

She looked up at him, her eyes flashing with anger. "That's not fair and... none of your business."

"It is my business because I... care about you and I want to help you."

She didn't know what to say. He avoided looking at her. The silence between them grew heavy, filled with unspoken thoughts and emotions.

Isa finally broke the silence by saying, "I... guess I want the ultimate dream, the ultimate love. And I'm afraid there's always going to be someone better, a true soulmate. Alex came close, but he died."

"I wonder if you'd think the same thing if Alex were still alive."

She stared at the stains on the table. "Maybe not. But you're doing the same thing, although in a different way. Waiting for the next Caijsa to come along. Timo, this isn't healthy either. There is nothing stopping you from moving on. Her real killers have been found and..."

"Maybe," he said, his gaze shifting to the crowd of people entering the pub. "But let me tell you something, something I haven't shared with anyone yet. I've started seeing my therapist again. I'm willing to admit that I need help. I'm not happy and I want to be. I want to build a life that I can be proud of, but I don't know how to get there. I don't know how to fix it, but I'm willing to accept that I'm broken. And maybe you should consider doing the same."

The weight of the world settled on her shoulders. "I'm not broken," Isa said and shook her head. Then she looked at him, the tears brimming in her eyes. She was fighting hard to keep them back. But she was losing the battle.

"You can be cruel sometimes," she sneered.

"And what if I am," he answered. "I'm just trying to make you see that you're living in a fantasy world. You're living a fantasy with a man who doesn't exist, probably never even existed. And I get it... it's so much more comforting to believe that than to live in the real world, but it will consume you. I've been there."

"I think you're still there. You're moody and angry. And it's not just Ingrid you're angry about. You're hiding something."

The picture on the wall in his study came to mind.

He hesitated for a moment before saying, "I'm going to tell you something that I only told one other person, and I'd appreciate it if you keep it to yourself."

"Okay," she said.

He told her about his conversation with Lyn Hjort, Caijsa's half-sister, and the insinuations of betrayal. And as he talked, she couldn't stop thinking about the telephone records of Rune Breiner that Kristoffer Solberg had given her, and the names that had popped up: Nelvin and Paulina Hjort.

Should she tell him? Should she tell him that his parents-in-law had hired Breiner to kill the presumed murderer of their daughter?

"You can't believe a word she says. She wants you to come back to her. This will bind you to her. She knows that. A manipulator never stops manipulating others."

He put both hands on the table. "But I think she's right."

"Why?"

"That last year, our relationship was so... toxic. Caijsa traveled more than usual. Conferences, workshops. She had a new supervisor, an opportunity to make a career. He took her to those events, but half of them didn't exist. It could be him."

Isa took a deep breath. "Are you sure?"

"Why else would she lie about it? But the worst thing is... the baby."

"Sometimes our mind tricks us into believing things that aren't real. Right now, it's filling in the blanks and supporting your theory about an affair. You need to think about this with a clear mind. Would Caijsa really have an abortion?"

"Maybe..."

She wasn't sure if this was the right moment to ask, but she went ahead anyway. "Paulina, Nelvin, Marcel. Can you trust them?"

"Of course."

Then the expression on his face froze. His mouth fell open and he quickly got up to peer past the crowd of people that were coming in.

"What's wrong?" Isa asked.

"I... just thought that I saw someone I know," he said and turned around a couple of times, but he couldn't see the person anymore who he was looking for.

He sat down again, but he seemed nervous.

"Who was it?"

But before Timo could respond, the lights dimmed, casting a hushed atmosphere over the room. As anticipation filled the air, a middle-aged man stepped onto the stage, immediately capturing the attention of the audience. The room erupted in thunderous applause. It was an intriguing sight, as the small, frail-looking figure appeared more like a wise professor than a conventional celebrity. As the applause echoed throughout the venue, Timo observed the peculiar scene unfolding before him.

"Who is that man?" Isa whispered.

"I really don't know," Timo said, scanning the room.

People were already giving them weird looks. He leaned over and whispered into her ear, "I think we need to participate."

The sensation of his warm breath on her skin sent shivers down her spine, leaving her in a daze. It was a small gesture, but its impact was undeniable. She rose to her feet and began clapping.

"We could take a picture and use facial recognition to identify him," Timo suggested.

"Well, you can try," Isa said softly without looking at him.

The standing ovation continued.

"Dear friends," the old man started, "dear, dear friends, it's good to see so many of you here at the final meeting before the end of the year."

Another round of cheering and clapping.

"But my dear friends, it's time for action! And I need your help…"

The rest of the man's words were lost on Timo as he noticed a handful of men moving to the back of the room and disappearing through a small door in the corner.

"Isa," he whispered, "five o'clock."

She was just in time to see the last man disappear through the door.

"We need to get in there. The action is going on there, not here. This guy is full of bullshit."

And off she went.

"What the…" He tried to chase after her as she deftly navigated through the throngs of people. Suddenly, he caught a glimpse of a familiar figure disappearing through the same door. Could it be him? It couldn't be. This was the second time that he thought he saw Ingrid's husband.

Isa tried to make her way towards the door, but her progress was hindered by a towering man who blocked her path. He was significantly wider and taller than her, making it difficult for her to move past him.

"No entrance," the man said and crossed his arms.

"Uh, I am just looking for the restroom," Isa explained.

"That's not here."

His eyes were locked onto the slender woman, so focused that he didn't even notice Timo slip past him and enter the next room.

Timo pushed through the door, descending a dimly lit set of stairs to a hallway. He passed beneath a stone archway and found himself in what appeared to be an old wine cellar. The air was thick with the musty scent of aging bottles, and he could hear muffled voices coming from the back. He inched his way between the racks, careful not to brush the dust-covered bottles. Some of them carried price tags that exceeded his monthly earnings.

He could make out nothing except a confused murmur of indistinguishable words. The only light in the room was dim and red, coming from small lamps scattered over the ceiling. His gun pressed against his side, and an uneasiness washed over him. He had no one to guard his back.

"We should postpone," a voice said.

"There is no reason to panic," said another voice.

"This is a setback, nothing more," a third man answered.

"Forsmark was a disaster and it's not the first time this has happened."

"Relax. We have a plan."

"Yeah, yeah, another fucking plan that's going to fail. I'm out."

Timo didn't recognize any of the voices. It wasn't Anton after all. How his mind was playing tricks on him.

The next moment there was a noise as if someone was thrown against a wall. And then there was silence.

"Nobody... nobody leaves. Do you hear me?"

"Yeah... okay," one of the men stammered.

Timo scanned the room but still couldn't see the men. It was almost like the voices came from everywhere.

He crept forward and arrived at an open door. It was a storage room, full of crates of wine and boxes of assorted bottles. He stepped inside.

But where were the men?

"What the hell is he doing here?" a deep voice sounded. There was a noise coming from the back and the next moment everything turned black.

* * *

As Timo opened his eyes, Isa was kneeling beside him.

"It doesn't look too bad," she said, meanwhile assessing his injuries.

"What happened?" he mumbled, struggling to sit up. His head was spinning, and his legs felt like rubber.

"Take it easy," Isa said, steadying him with her arm. "You need to rest."

"I need to sit down," he groaned, his hand clutching his throbbing head.

"We need to get you to a doctor."

"I don't remember much," he said, trying to piece together the events leading to his blackout.

"I was getting worried when a group of men came out and disappeared into the crowd. I found you here, unconscious."

He looked at his badge on the floor and breathed a sigh of relief. His gun was still in its holster. Isa handed him his badge and showed him the cell phone pictures.

"I'll run these through facial recognition," she said.

"It's so quiet. Where is everyone?"

"The meeting is over. There are only a few people left in the bar."

"I doubt they'll come back here," he said, slowly getting to his feet. "But you're right, I need to see a doctor."

CHAPTER

10

CHRISTMAS CAME SOONER than anyone thought it would, but no one felt like celebrating.

Timo had really wanted to turn down George's offer to spend Christmas evening together, but as always, his friend had been very convincing. Even after Timo had warned George that he wouldn't be great company, the older man had been insistent on having him over to his new place in Stockholm. Timo couldn't keep track of the many houses George had bought and sold over the years, but from the way his friend talked on the phone, Timo had expected a small house five kilometers north of Stockholm. Instead, he found himself driving his Volvo through an iron gate to a mansion.

This wasn't the small house he had in mind.

As Timo drove through the gates, he couldn't believe what he was seeing. The driveway meandered through the gardens, which had been expertly cared for but were now blanketed in snow, and past a fountain that sparkled with colored lights. In front of him, the house loomed large, its brick facade illuminated by soft, warm light.

The mansion was a stunning sight. It was three stories tall, with an impressive entrance featuring two large, wooden doors that looked like they belonged in a castle. The windows were tall and narrow, with white frames that contrasted beautifully against the red brick. The roof was tiled with dark slate, and a tall chimney towered above the highest point of the house.

As he parked the car, Timo felt a little intimidated by the grandeur of the place. He had known George for years, but he had never imagined that his friend could afford such a luxurious home. He took a deep breath and got out of the car.

"Welcome, welcome!" George appeared from somewhere within the house, a wide smile on his face. "Come in, come in!"

"Small house?" Timo said when he entered.

"Timo, Jesus. You look pale! Are you ill or something?"

"Just recovering from a mild concussion," Timo laughed and offered him the bottle of wine. He had spent a full afternoon picking out the right bottle, but it probably wasn't good enough for a Burgundian like George, who had spent his lifetime finding the best restaurants and getting the advice of world-renowned sommeliers.

"Concussion? Again? Don't tell your mom."

"Mom?"

Timo's mother appeared, visibly loaded with diamonds, and dressed in a long red cocktail dress. Her make-up was immaculate as always.

"Timofey, my boy," she yelled and put out her hands.

The next moment Timo found himself in her tight embrace, being kissed wildly on the cheeks. He gave George an angry look as his mother kept kissing and hugging him.

"You don't look good," she said in what was a mixture between Swedish, Finnish, and Russian, as she pulled his sleeve to get him into the living room. "I told you before... you've lost weight."

"Mom, wait... let me take off my jacket."

"The same old outfit as usual," she said disparagingly.

"I'm sorry, I didn't know she was going to come," George whispered as he helped him and took the jacket to hang on the coat rack in the hall.

"Well, you invited her," Timo said calmly.

"Not really. Your aunt Lilia did."

"Aunt Lilia? Why?"

George sighed. "Well, she and..."

"It's so good to see you, Timo," Lilia smiled as she walked up to him. She was his mother's youngest sister. They were complete opposites in every way. His mother was an overacting drama queen while his aunt was level-headed and thought through everything carefully.

"Auntie Lilia, you look fantastic," Timo said.

"All because of my new man." She looked at George and gave him a quick kiss.

This wasn't what he had expected. Lilia and George.

"My new girlfriend." George's eyes twinkled.

This was good. Timo had been afraid for a moment that George had succumbed to his mother's charms, but this was marvelous news. Mom and George would never have been a match, although in the past he had had his suspicions about their relationship.

"I'm really happy for you," Timo said.

Dinner went well, amicably. They wanted to have a nice evening, and the grievances and frustrations, especially the ones that played between mother and son, had moved to the background.

"I'm sorry to hear about Caijsa," Lilia said when dessert came.

Timo could tell she had been hemming and hawing for a while if she would touch on the subject or not. He couldn't blame her. There was a time when he hadn't been able to get through a conversation about his dead fiancé without running off. And it had usually been his mom who had found some joy in revisiting the painful memories for her son.

But even though he tried to hide it, the shocked look on his face was obvious and he saw that Lilia wondered if she had made the wrong choice.

"George told me what happened. I know it must have been hard for you."

"Yes, it was," Timo said calmly.

"Surely, you must be glad now the real killers are found. You can finally move on," his mom said.

Of course, his mother needed attention. She couldn't give him five minutes to talk about one of the most difficult times in his life. Those were five minutes taken away from her.

She looked at him and then continued, "Timsy, I wanted to call you, but I wasn't sure if you wanted to talk to me."

"You could have called or visited me regardless." Timo looked down at his hands.

"But, darling, I was in Russia. I can't just drop everything and come running every time you need me."

"Is that so? That's not what I heard."

And he calmly turned his head to give her a sharp, accusing gaze.

"What?"

"Marcel, Caijsa's dad, told me he saw you in Stockholm a few months ago. And you certainly knew where to find Fredrik."

"I was only briefly in Sweden. I didn't have time."

"But you had time to spend with Fredrik?"

"I...," she stammered.

Fredrik had always been her favorite. He, on the other hand, was just an annoyance. A mistake. Maybe he reminded her too much of his real father.

"But it's fine," he said with a painful smile, "you never liked Caijsa anyway."

George and Lilia remained transfixed in silence as the conversation between mother and son escalated into a profound and unyielding intensity.

"I did," Valesca said, "but she was sometimes so... much Caijsa."

"So much Caijsa? What do you mean by that?"

"So soft, so unambitious. I think you were... are better off with a woman who is strong and decisive, who can support you and guide you in the right direction."

"Do I seem off-track to you? I guess you want me to be more like Fredrik."

"Timofey, I don't want you to be like him," she leaned over to take his head in her hands. "I love you both so much. I just want you to be happy."

It had been a long time since his mother had spoken to him with such kindness. Their relationship had been so strained in recent years that he started to doubt her love for him. The last months had been incredibly difficult, and he needed his mother. He needed her to tell him that everything would be okay. But nothing was okay right now. He was so disappointed in Caijsa. She had kept secrets from him. Maybe they were nothing, but the doubt had grown in his mind and put him at an all-time low. He looked at George and Lilia. At least, George was happy.

* * *

Isa brushed the snow off the granite and looked around. It was peaceful here. She understood why no one would want to spend Christmas Eve at the cemetery, but it was better than spending the evening with her parents and having to answer all their questions about Viktor and the kids, her work, her non-existent love life, about everything she didn't want to talk about. Or spending the evening alone, with bottles of wine on the table next to the couch, watching movies she didn't like anyway.

She liked Christmas but this year she wanted to be alone.

She looked at the grave. Alexander Nordin, the man she couldn't get over, the man she had to forget. She removed the glove and let her fingers rub the granite. The cold stone cut into her flesh, but she didn't feel the pain.

Isa lowered her gaze, unsure why she was even there. Timo had told her that visiting the grave of a loved one could have a cleansing effect. But as Isa looked upon the stone, surrounded by snow and frozen earth, she felt skeptical. It all seemed so distant, so disconnected from her own grief.

"Everyone tells me I need to move on," she whispered. "But you know..."

She gasped. She could tell herself it was the cold, but the emotions were getting the upper hand, and tears were forming in her eyes.

"Jeezes, what is it about you that I can't? We didn't even know each other if I must be honest. I don't want to cry; I don't want to feel this miserable... all the time!"

Isa wiped her eyes and tried to compose herself.

"Paikkala is right. I don't have this under control anymore. I sometimes imagine how our life together could have been, and it's too fucking perfect. I would have left you. I would have been unfaithful to you because that's who I am."

She longed for his warmth, his voice, his smell, and most of all his lips. She missed the closeness and intimacy. She missed making love. But with Alex, she knew there was always a dark side, a tragedy she had been good at pushing to the background. A darkness she rarely allowed to surface.

"Your mother keeps calling me. For a woman who had a tough time loving her own son, she seems very determined to make your killer pay. She's been collecting signatures to revoke his sentence. Being locked up in a psychiatric unit isn't a proper punishment, in her opinion, and I must agree with her. Still, I don't want to help her. She scares me. I know she has a hidden agenda. I just don't know what it is... yet. I just don't think she's doing it for the right reasons."

A strange feeling crept up on her. It was as if someone was watching her. With a sudden twist, she became aware of the encroaching darkness. She looked around, but nothing stirred in the cemetery. A shiver ran down her spine. It felt like someone was close.

Imagination or was it real? She took a few deep breaths to calm herself down, and she felt a little foolish for getting scared. It was, after all, a cemetery. It was the same feeling she used to get when she was a little girl and her parents used to take her to see the graves of dead relatives. People she didn't even know.

She threw a last glance at the tombstone and decided to leave. As she walked away, she couldn't shake the feeling someone was still watching her.

She quickened her pace.

* * *

"What do you think about the political storm hitting this country?"

The journalist on TV looked like a movie star in a tailored suit and matching tie. His serious expression seemed carefully guarded, but when he smiled, his ivory-white teeth had an almost unnatural glow.

His conversation partner, however, was another story. The political science professor wore a wrinkled shirt, as if he had just rolled out of bed. His tie was crooked, his hair unkempt, almost as if he had rushed over without bothering to comb it or even run the fingers through his thinning strands. The contrast couldn't have been greater.

"I wouldn't call it a storm... a hurricane maybe," the professor grinned.

"You mean the Eirik Lunde case?" the reporter said without showing a hint of emotion.

"One should not underestimate the damage Lunde has done to the Social Democrats. The party is already divided with Prime Minister Hult on one hand trying to keep his more right-wing constituents happy and Leif Berg on the other side, with a more moderate, centrum-oriented program. They seem to clash all the time."

The reporter raised a brow. "But with Berg's right hand Eirik Lunde under suspicion of having inappropriate relationships with women during the time he was campaign manager, Hult seems to have the winning hand."

"At least that's what our Prime Minister thinks. In recent months he has been making overtures to the Sweden Democrats..."

"What are you watching?" Ingrid said and threw herself on the couch next to her father.

He smiled and switched off the TV. "Ah, just some political stuff."

She tilted her head and then said without taking her eyes off him, "You look puzzled."

"You know, I don't understand this country anymore. It all used to be so simple. Left or right. Now, everything is so convoluted, and you can't trust any of them."

"Yeah, I know, but it must be difficult though, leading a country, making decisions, making compromises. That's why I would never consider going into politics. Anton on the other hand..."

Her father turned his head to see if his son-in-law was there but couldn't find him. "Is he really considering going into politics?"

"Maybe. Anyway, it's Christmas Eve. We haven't been able to talk much, but how have you been?"

He smiled. "Your mom and I are fine. Getting old but we're fine."

Christmas Eve had traditionally been a time when her family would get together at her parents' house, but her parents were getting up there in age and were not as spry as they used to be. This year, Anton and Ingrid had offered to host it at their place. This meant that three extra kids—her brother's kids— would be running around, in addition to her own two boys, but she didn't mind.

The children were unpacking the presents. The eight-year-old and the young teenager, almost twelve. They suddenly seemed so grown up. Even the young ones. Life was fragile, more than Ingrid had realized. After coming close to dying, the way she approached things these days had changed. She made sure she never left the house without having discussed things through and without leaving things unresolved.

"But are you okay?" her father said suddenly.

"Yes, I am," she smiled as she saw her husband come in with another bottle of wine. Her mother, an avid wine lover, was the first to hold up her glass to get a refill. She was so un-Finnish. Sometimes Ingrid thought that she was a passionate Italian in a typical northern body.

"Thank you, my dear son-in-law," her mother said in fluent Swedish.

Her mother had come to Sweden when she was only twenty, following the man she had fallen in love with head-over-heels. Finnish was spoken at home, Swedish everywhere else. Her mother didn't like Finland though. She found it much duller than her life in Gävle, although Ingrid didn't see much difference. Timo should talk to her mom. He could spin the most intriguing stories about Finland, a country he could hardly call his own. It was his dad's country. He often had to remind himself of that. He, on the other hand, belonged nowhere.

She wasn't sure why he kept popping into her head. Thoughts of him had interrupted her focus so many times during dinner that it was probably the reason why her father kept giving her concerned looks. He finally got up and came to sit closer to her.

167

"Something's wrong," he whispered, watching the children sit around the Christmas tree, comparing presents.

"There's been a lot going on," she said quietly. "It's a lot to take in."

He took her hand. "I just want to make sure you're okay. Your mom and I are worried."

But her dad didn't know the whole story. The terror, the pain, the thought of dying. She hadn't even told Anton how horrifying it had been. The shooting at Global Law had been dramatic and her husband had lost many friends and colleagues, but he hadn't experienced death first-hand.

She had, and not once had he asked her about it. Timo had, even after she had so cruelly turned him down. And she had used her son's nightmares as an excuse. But the reality was she was scared. Scared that her life would be put upside down by giving into her feelings for this gorgeous man who wasn't her husband.

But she had hurt Timo more than she had imagined, and she couldn't stand that either. What did she want? That they would be friends? That they would go back to how it had been before, flirting with each other, longing to be with each other but not daring to make the first move, constantly looking for each other's company.

"If you need to talk, I'm here for you," her dad said, giving her a kiss on the cheek.

She appreciated the offer, but she wasn't in the mood to discuss it. Not now. Not on Christmas Eve.

He got up and walked to the tree where the children were still enjoying themselves. Grandpa was especially popular with the youngest. They loved his stupid jokes, his loud laughter, and just the fact that he made time for them.

Ingrid stared at her phone, opened WhatsApp, and scrolled to find Timo Paikkala. For a moment, Ingrid doubted whether she should send the message. But she finally made up her mind and decided to go ahead with it.

"Merry Christmas," she wrote and sent it.

The least she could do was send him a kind message. For a moment, she thought about asking him how he was doing but decided against it. It would have been too cruel, after kissing him and then telling him it was a mistake.

* * *

All attention shifted back to Valesca. Timo was okay with that; at least he had gotten five minutes of her time and energy. That was more than he could have hoped for. The two women laughed and chatted away in Russian, while George sat nearby, bored out of his mind because he couldn't understand a word. Timo joined him at the dinner table and said, "Thank you for inviting me. Dinner was great."

George smiled in response, "I thought you could use some company on Christmas Eve. And I'm sorry. I really didn't know Lilia would bring her. I guess she was tricked into it."

Timo shook his head and gave him a smile. "It's okay. At least we got to talk."

"That wasn't talking."

"That's as far as she can go."

"But what's going on? You look so... down. Is it Caijsa?"

"George, I really don't want to talk about it."

"Fair enough, but I'm here if you want to."

"I appreciate that." Timo gave him another smile.

Valesca dropped herself on the chair next to her son. "So, Timofey, it's not so bad that I'm here, is it?"

She took his hand and for a moment held it.

"How do you know Leif Berg?" Timo said and looked her in the eye.

Her fingers tightened around his hand.

"Why do you ask?"

"I had the impression you knew him when I saw you in Fredrik's office."

"Fredrik?" George said.

Timo turned to George and saw the same expression of astonishment on his face.

George continued, "Does Fredrik work for Berg? Why? I don't understand."

"I don't understand it either," Timo said and then looked at his mother again.

"I think it's a great opportunity for him. Berg will advance his career."

"You didn't answer my question," Timo said in a stern voice.

"What question?"

"Do you know Berg?"

"No... I mean yes. Your father knew him."

There were so many things going through his head. George, Yrjo, Leif Berg. Which one?

"Yeah, we all know him," George said quickly.

She let go of her son's hand, pressed her lips together and then got up.

"Timo," George exclaimed, his voice tinged with annoyance.

Timo shrugged in response. "I didn't say or do anything."

"You didn't have to say anything. She knows what you're thinking."

"And you know something."

George shook his head. "You need to put this stuff aside and move on. Otherwise, you risk losing your mom."

Timo ran his hands through his hair. In just a single minute, his emotions plummeted from the buoyant state he had been in after dinner to the all-time low he now found himself in. George was right, but it was just beyond himself.

His phone beeped with a WhatsApp alert. It was Ingrid.

Timo felt a pang in his chest as he stared at the message. It was nothing special, just a general greeting she probably sent to a lot of people. But it meant so much to him because it meant she hadn't forgotten him. They hadn't talked in a while, and she had been avoiding him.

"Merry Christmas to you too," he wrote and sent it.

He hesitated for a moment and then continued, "And to your family."

He put the phone back into the pocket of his jeans and joined the rest of the company.

"And to my family," Ingrid whispered. Her family. Her beautiful, safe family. Her sons, whom she loved more than anything in the world. And her overly excited, sometimes hyper husband who would do anything for her. She smiled. She had made the right decision.

This was where she wanted to be.

* * *

Tuva looked at the candle whose flame danced back and forth with the draft that blew through the carriage. It gave a comfy and Christmas-like atmosphere. But the memories of Christmases past brought a wave of sadness and longing. Last year, she and Greta shared a piece of cake, laughing and enjoying each other's company.

But now, Greta was gone. Her death had left her feeling alone and adrift. The memory of Greta's twisted face, drenched in blood, haunted her every waking moment. She couldn't shake the image from her mind, and the thought of it made her gag.

Christmas had once been a time of joy and celebration with her family, but now it was a lonely and painful reminder of all she had lost. Her mother's death had left her without a family, bounced from one foster home to the next. The simple act of putting up a Christmas tree now felt bittersweet, and the holiday feast her mother used to lovingly prepare was a distant memory. Tuva felt the weight of her loss and the loneliness that went with it.

She held her hand over the flame.

Blood. Stains on the side of her glove. Greta's blood.

There was a noise. Soft, but it was there. Quickly she blew out the candle and pressed her body against the metal wall of the wagon, just in time to hide herself when she saw, through the rusted half-open doors, the dark figure pass by. The train looked ancient. She couldn't even guess when it had last been used, and it looked more like a freight train than anything else. The track had not been used for years and everything she touched was covered with a thick layer of rust.

Could it be him? She couldn't tell. How did he find her?

The man stopped and stared at the broken window for a while. His face was hidden under the hood, and in the faint light of the lamppost, she saw something glistening. A knife.

Rolf. The snitch. He must have told them. She knew he couldn't keep quiet. This was it. The killer found her.

But then the figure moved on. She stayed hiding in the shadow for a moment. She was never going to be safe. Never. And she had to think carefully about what to do next. Going to the police wasn't such a bad thing, but could she trust them now that she knew who was behind it?

* * *

The police officer at the counter was chatting with a female colleague, both of whom were volunteers or rather victims forced to spend Christmas Eve at the station.

Lars sat down in a chair, finding the silence oddly comforting. Hours ago, he had visited his father, who was living in a nursing home. He had set up a small Christmas tree in the room, but his father remained unresponsive as usual, lost in his own thoughts and memories. Seeing his once proud and intelligent father reduced to this state broke Lars' heart every time. His father was the only remaining member of his family, as his mother had left them when Lars was a baby. Though his father had never admitted it, Lars knew that he had spent years searching for her. His mother had been a drug addict and had gone through rehab out of love for his father, but the responsibility of motherhood had led her back to her old habits. Lars blamed himself for her leaving.

He switched on the computer and saw the blue envelope on the desk. Berger and Mila's wedding invitation. He felt the shiny smooth paper, and then turned to the screen. He opened the internal search engine and typed 'Mila Hillborg'. Seconds later the page filled the screen. Mila Hillborg, twenty-five, master's degree in forensic science, started about six months ago at the National Forensic Centre.

He scrolled down the file. It revealed nothing new about her. Copies of her degrees and qualifications were attached. And Berger was right. Her parents were dead. They had died in a car accident when she was eleven years old. After that, she spent most of her teenage years in foster homes. But when she turned eighteen, she went out on her own and basically worked herself through university, which was admirable.

He closed the file and leaned backward. Why couldn't he let it go? There was nothing wrong with Mila. Her file was clean. Maybe too clean. Was his intuition letting him down?

He'd agreed to be Berger's best man.

He couldn't let his friend down.

CHAPTER

11

As they combed through the seemingly endless lines of code, the IT team felt like they were making no progress at all. Despite their best efforts, they had only managed to decipher two files from Lauri Valkama's laptop. These files had remained encrypted until now.

But the investigation into the death of Lauri Valkama was about to get a whole lot more complicated. With new evidence pointing to connections between Valkama's death, the Global Law shooting, and potential threats against Minister of Justice Leif Berg, the stakes were higher than ever.

"What the hell is this?" Isa asked, her voice filled with frustration as she sat behind the computer screen with Timo and Lars. The police station was eerily quiet, with only the sound of the howling wind outside breaking the silence. The severe weather conditions were causing concern as people braced themselves for a harsh winter.

Isa and her colleagues poured over the encrypted files, trying to make sense of the list of names they had found. But as they studied the hundreds of names, including politicians, lawyers, judges, actors, and doctors, they were coming up empty.

"Do these people belong to the organization plotting these attacks?" Timo asked.

Before anyone could answer, Isa let out a scream, "Shit!" Her finger pointed at the screen, her name now staring back at her. She couldn't believe her eyes. Was she being framed? Why?

Her mind was reeling with questions and possibilities as she tried to understand how her name had ended up on this list.

"Isabel Lindström, that's you," Lars quickly pointed out.

"But why is my name there? I have nothing to do with this," she asked, struggling to make sense of it all.

"Unless you're secretly plotting more attacks, this isn't a list of members of that so-called secret group," Timo said.

"What is it then?" she asked with a hint of desperation in her voice.

"Maybe it's a target list?" Timo suggested.

"A hitlist? There must be hundreds of names," Isa whispered.

Timo took a deep breath and straightened his posture. "Check on Paikkala."

Before anyone could say anything, Isa quickly typed Timo's name into the search bar and found a match. "Timotheus Paikkala. Looks like you're on the list too."

"Guess I'm a dangerous man," Timo said with a sarcastic smirk. "Check Finn Heimersson."

Isa gave him a confused look, but quickly complied and searched for the name. To her surprise, there was no mention of Finn Heimersson in either of the files.

"Why are there two files?" she asked.

Timo shrugged. "The good guys and the bad guys."

"I doubt that," Isa said with a shake of her head.

"Mila Hillborg," Lars read out loud, a look of concern on his face.

Isa glanced at him, realizing that perhaps Mila wasn't as innocent as she seemed. But they were all on this list, except for Lars and Ingrid.

"And... Fredrik Paikkala," Isa said, looking at Timo.

Timo closed his eyes and ran his hands through his hair.

"Are you okay?" Isa asked softly, getting up from her seat.

"Yes, but I'm not sure what it means. I do have the feeling my brother is involved in something fishy."

"Do you really think that?"

"I know he was lying to me the last time we spoke. He knows more than he's letting on. He says it's to protect me, but I've seen this before, when we were kids."

"But you're not kids anymore. This is no longer a game."

"I don't think he's capable of planning something like this, but I believe he's gotten himself into something he can't control, and he doesn't fully understand the consequences," Timo explained.

With a deep sigh, Isa turned to the computer screen. "We need to go through each name on this list. This is going to take forever."

"That's why we have our sergeants."

A smile spread across Isa's face as she thought of the red-haired Varg Mårtensson.

Lars stepped up to the screen, scrolling through the list once more. "I still don't understand why Lauri Valkama would keep these lists," he said.

"To protect himself. This was his insurance policy," Timo said.

"Well, it didn't work out too well for him," Isa noted.

"Or maybe he intended to use them for blackmail."

"That's more likely."

"Wait, go back!" Timo suddenly said.

Isa stared at the name on the screen. "Nicolas Petrini. Why is Nick on the list?"

"And Karst Engersson and... Anton," Timo added.

"They're all from Global Law. They're all on the same list," Isa said, her voice rising with alarm.

"High-profile lawyers and politicians," Timo added.

"And simple police officers," Lars said.

"We need to get them protection." Isa sounded out of breath.

"Lindström, if we do that, we'll have to protect everyone on these lists, including ourselves. There's no sign that any of these people are actually in danger. We don't know what these lists mean."

"But Timo, we have to at least tell Finn," Isa argued.

"Finn won't do anything," Timo said, getting to his feet. "We need Solberg's help... again."

* * *

"I don't understand. Why is Nick's name on that list?" Isa paced back and forth as Timo watched her. She had sent Lars away and wanted to talk to Timo in private.

"We were all on that list. It doesn't mean anything. He's a good lawyer. Maybe they consider him as someone to watch or...?"

"Lyn Hjort told you she wanted to use him in her plans. Is that why he's on that list?"

She dropped back in the chair and spun it around a few times, finally facing Timo.

"Shouldn't you be more worried about why you're on that list?"

"I can handle it, but not Nick. I need to warn him."

"Just leave him in peace. He's in the hospital."

"No, he's not," Isa said.

"What do you mean he's not?" Timo sat up in his chair.

Isa had a look in her eye that said she knew something Timo didn't. She finally told him that Nick had been released from the hospital days ago, but he had refused to tell anyone where he was staying. Isa had found him in a cottage outside of Gävle, owned by his parents. They talked for hours about his feelings, his alcohol addiction, and the PTSD that still haunted him—dead bodies, dead colleagues, the damaged body of his management assistant Kim against the wall, an image he just couldn't leave behind.

Nick had told her he was done with the law, that he couldn't go back and face all those people, the survivors, like nothing had happened.

"He's fine. You'll see. He'll be at the wedding," she said with a forced smile.

But Timo was having none of it. "You asked him to be at Berger's wedding?" he said, his tone rising in disbelief.

"He just knew about it, and I can't remember any more if I asked him or not."

"As always, you only think about yourself. Do you think he wants to be around people who remind him of one of the most traumatic moments in his life? And you're going to put him in a situation where alcohol will flow freely."

"So, you're speaking on behalf of him now? Nick is a grown man. He can make his own decisions," she replied, crossing her arms. "I understand it's difficult for Nick, but if he needs my help, I'll be there. And I didn't force him to come. He actually said he's looking forward to talking to you."

"I'm not going."

"But why?"

"I don't feel like it," he said, looking down at his hands on the white table. "And I don't have anyone to go with, so..."

"Neither does Lars. Does it matter? It's just us. Ingrid and Anton will be there. It's about having fun and... dancing."

And that was the problem. Ingrid and Anton.

"I'll think about it," he grumbled.

"Just saying, everyone will be there. We'll miss you if you don't show up," Isa said with a smile.

"If the wedding even goes through. The weather isn't great."

"They'll manage."

Turning their attention back to work, Timo asked, "What are we going to do with these lists? And we need to investigate this far-right group. But apart from the pictures you took, we have nothing."

Timo glanced out the window, witnessing the snow-laden trees, gracefully bending under the weight of the relentless storm. With the snowstorm intensifying, he knew his drive home would be challenging. Yesterday, he had toiled for hours clearing a path for his car and shoveling snow from his patio. The storm was expected to last for days, causing widespread disruption to the community.

He turned to Isa and spoke, "Karst Engersson died in a mass shooting a year after his client Rune Breiner was killed."

Isa nodded. "Yeah, what about him?"

"Engersson unknowingly paid for his own murder. Rune Breiner was about to blow the whistle on a network of dirty cops. Nils Vollan, one of the attackers, was paid with Global Law money through an account set up by Lauri Valkama."

"So, Valkama had an accomplice or a client. Someone who turned on him and killed him."

After a moment of contemplation, Timo replied, "We need to find Tuva Norling, but it's like she doesn't want to be found. And now with the weather..."

"She's learned to survive on the streets and knows how to stay under the radar. I've learned that if people don't want to be found, they won't be found."

"But she's in a vulnerable position, and... she could be dead already."

"Let's hope not," Isa said. "We need to find her before it's too late."

* * *

Finn Heimersson sat across from Timo, his silence deafening. Timo felt the weight of disappointment and shame bearing down on him as he realized that he hadn't been allowed to become superintendent, but that the man chosen for the position had proved to be a disappointment, disappearing for weeks on end, and lacking any real impact when he finally reappeared.

"Your focus should be on the Valkama case," Finn said firmly. "Have you found this Tuva yet?"

"No." Frustration crept into Timo's voice. "We've put out an APB, but so far, nothing."

Why was Finn suddenly so interested in Tuva? Weeks ago, he had told them she was a dead end. But he couldn't ignore the fact that Tuva was seen on the CCTV moments before Valkama had died. Together with the mysterious man.

"A young woman doesn't just disappear like that," Finn said, leaning forward in his chair.

Timo nodded. "I know, but we have to face the reality that she might already be dead."

"What about the crime scene where Greta was found? Did forensics find anything?"

"Besides Tuva's fingerprints... nothing. I think we need to take a step back and reconsider our approach. I want to take another look at Engersson and Leif Berg."

Finn's eyes narrowed, and he rose from his chair. "Hands off Berg and Engersson. They have nothing to do with this."

"How do you know?"

"I just do," Finn said, his voice steady but firm. "The only reason you're interested in Berg is because of Fredrik," Finn added, cutting off Timo's protest.

"Fredrik is the last person on my mind."

"Find the girl, and you'll find the murderer," Finn said, pointing to the door. "I have other business to attend to."

Timo left the room, his mind racing with questions. As he walked to his office, he heard hasty footsteps echoing through the hallway. He turned to see Kristina Rapp rushing into Finn's office, her eyes meeting his briefly before she disappeared.

Kristina Rapp, forensic profiler, old colleague, friend, and Timo's biggest fan. She'd always had a soft spot for him, but he tried to keep his distance after she confessed her love. He would never be able to reciprocate those feelings. She was a good friend and nothing more. Their conversations often ended in some dramatic climax, where he felt guilty, and she left looking even more depressed. But he'd love to see her again and reminisce about the time in Stockholm when he was a beginner and Caijsa was still around.

Half an hour later she was standing at his desk.

"Kristina, what are you doing here?" he said surprised.

"Looking for you," she said with a big smile on her face.

There was something different about her, and it wasn't just the haircut—her brown hair was neatly modeled in a fashionable bob—but she looked even more sad and lonely than usual.

"I'm honored. But you didn't drive two hundred kilometers in a snowstorm to see me. What's up?"

"Oh, a case. I just needed some information, and Finn was happy to help me out."

Seeing how loaded she was with a black bag hanging over her shoulder and a pile of papers and a coat in her arms, he offered her a chair. "Sounds mysterious."

She signaled to him it was fine and put the bag on the floor. "It's not, but I can't say much about it."

"So, you arrived this morning?"

"No, actually... I came last Sunday."

He frowned and then asked why she hadn't told him.

"It was a last-minute decision, and I didn't want to bother you."

Although Timo wanted to offer her a place to stay, he knew it would be complicated. "Where are you staying?"

"At the Regency Hotel," Kristina replied, finally taking a seat in the chair Timo had offered her.

"The Regency. Nice!"

"It's a bit outdated, but it'll do."

"When do you plan on leaving? How about we grab dinner tonight?"

"Normally I'd be leaving tomorrow, but with the weather, who knows," Kristina said, gazing out the window. "Dinner sounds good though."

"Great, I'll pick you up at the Regency at eight."

With a nod, Kristina grabbed her bag and made her way to the exit, leaving Timo with a million questions running through his mind. Why was she so secretive about her visit? And why did she come during a snowstorm, predicted a week ago? He couldn't shake the feeling that her poor planning was intentional.

CHAPTER

12

AS THE BLIZZARD RAGED ON OUTSIDE, the Grand Hotel in Gävle was alive with excitement. Mila and Berger were finally tying the knot, in an intimate ceremony surrounded by close family and friends. Although Berger was initially hesitant due to the harsh weather conditions, Mila's unwavering determination to become Mrs. Karlsson that very day left him with no choice.

Mila appeared absolutely breathtaking in her exquisite gown and delicate veil. Crafted from pure silk adorned with intricate lace accents, the dress accentuated her beauty flawlessly. And as the bride walked down the aisle full of people, Isa looked at the groom, dressed in black tails. Isa had never witnessed him exude such radiant joy before. Overwhelmed by the moment, tears gently streamed down her cheeks.

She thought about her own wedding.

Isa's wedding had been an intimate affair, attended only by her now ex-husband Viktor, and their parents. They had met during their secondary school years and decided to get married shortly after Viktor's graduation from university. While Viktor had landed a job as an engineer in a British company, Isa was pursuing her passion for linguistics, which she later gave up joining the police force. Some might view her career transition as a sign of indecision, but Isa knew exactly what she wanted. While her parents initially disapproved of her career choice, Viktor had always supported her decision.

Despite Viktor's Catholic upbringing Isa had convinced him to hold the ceremony under the trees near their apartment, where they could watch the sunset together. She now shook her head, regretting her youthful naivety.

As the ceremony began, she noticed Lars standing nearby, appearing troubled and struggling to maintain a smile. When he took his seat next to a mysterious dark-skinned woman, a sense of unease washed over her. A strange, uncomfortable feeling of imminent danger. A deep panic that something was going to happen—that all this happiness would be taken away from them.

She shook it off, but it only lasted for a few seconds before returning. She tried to focus on what was going on in the room around her—the music playing, the soft hum of people whispering—but it was no use; her mind kept drifting back to that sensation of doom.

The seat next to her was empty. Somehow, she had imagined Timo would show up.

She had taken his advice to heart and told Nick that it was better for him to stay home and concentrate on getting well.

Ingrid and Anton hadn't shown up either. Securing a babysitter for their eight-year-old and eleven-year-old had proven to be a daunting task, and Ingrid had told her they would only be able to join the evening party.

The rest of the ceremony she observed with a mix of emotions.

* * *

That evening the Grand Hotel was bustling with activity as more guests arrived for the evening celebrations. Many of them were planning to stay the night, eager to be a part of the joyous occasion. But the ominous feeling in Isa's heart refused to fade.

She stood in the entrance hall, scanning the surroundings. She spotted the reception desk positioned on the left. A grand staircase, draped in luxurious red carpet, ascended to the upper level where elevators awaited to transport guests to their rooms. As she pivoted to locate the ballroom, she was taken aback by the multitude of guests dressed in elegant evening wear, seemingly unaffected by the raging snowstorm outside.

Isa caught a glimpse of a familiar face in the crowd, and she felt a jolt of recognition. The blonde woman was dressed in a sleek, black gown and her expression was neutral, almost guarded. Isa couldn't recall where she had seen her before, but she felt sure she should know her. She scoured her memory, trying to recall if they had met at a previous event or if she was a colleague from her time at the police academy. The woman walked up the stairs to the upper floor and disappeared.

Isa shook her head. Maybe she was mistaken.

She walked on.

As she approached the right-hand side of the venue, Isa was greeted by grand doors adorned with golden ornaments and gleaming gold handles. Behind them, a ballroom awaited, filled with tables that could comfortably seat ten guests each. In the center of the room, a space had been cleared for dancing, where a DJ bounced energetically, one side of his headphones pressed firmly to his ear. An upbeat tune echoed throughout the room, filling the air with a sense of excitement and energy as Isa stepped inside, alone. Though she couldn't quite place the song, it felt familiar to her all the same.

Berger had meticulously arranged for everyone to be seated together at the same table, but one key member was missing. Finn Heimersson had unexpectedly cancelled due to an urgent last-minute engagement. He had voiced his displeasure to Isa about how most of his senior inspectors were attending the wedding despite a nationwide alarm being instated because of the snowstorm.

As Isa approached the round table, she saw that Lars was already seated, accompanied by the mysterious woman she had spotted at the ceremony. The woman looked older than Lars, with short, dark hair and glasses adorning her face. She was dressed in a simple yet elegant black dress. As Lars introduced her as one of his childhood friends, she exuded a welcoming and amiable demeanor that immediately seemed to put everyone at ease. She was a schoolteacher-turned-editor, working at a prominent publishing company.

Ingrid and Anton joined them a few minutes later.

"The weather's terrible," Anton said as he stamped the snow from his shiny black shoes and sat down.

"Mila really looks magnificent," Ingrid said and looked at the young woman in her princess-like bridal gown with embroidered silk.

Isa nodded in agreement, then struck up a conversation with Lars' friend while Lars and Anton fell into a discussion about police work. Despite his sudden change in attitude, Lars appeared grumpy once again, much like his mood swings in recent days. It was as if his emotions were a tumultuous sea, constantly surging and receding.

Ingrid noticed the two empty seats at the table. "Where's Timo?"

Lars shrugged. "No idea."

But before Ingrid could press further, a voice rang out, "Sorry we're late."

As she turned, she saw Timo and a mysterious woman making their way toward the table.

"Finding a parking spot in this weather was a bit of a challenge," Timo explained as he pulled out a chair for the woman, offering her a warm smile.

She grinned back, taking in her new surroundings. "Nice to finally meet you all. I'm Kristina Rapp."

When she caught sight of Ingrid, Kristina's eyes widened with a mixture of shock and awe. She quickly regained her composure and put on a charming smile, as Timo, discreetly and efficiently, poured water into the glasses at the table.

Clad in a shimmering green-satin dress that accentuated her curves, Kristina was a vision of beauty. Her delicate features were enhanced by subtle yet striking makeup, making her high cheekbones glimmer and her eyes sparkle. The famous Kristina Rapp was a sight to behold.

And Timo had made an effort that evening. He looked dapper in his simple black shirt and trousers. His dark hair and fair skin complemented each other, creating a refined look that perfectly suited him.

"It's great to finally meet the renowned Dr. Rapp," Anton grinned, but his words set off alarm bells for Ingrid, causing her to feel wary and on edge.

Kristina's brow furrowed as she turned to Timo. "Famous? What did you tell them?"

"Uh... I didn't say anything," Timo said confused and gave Anton an inquiring glance.

"You've written a book about killer profiling," Anton continued and took a sip of his wine. "Fascinating stuff! I hope to talk to you about it some time."

Kristina's lips curled into a pleased smile. "It seems I've found the one person who took the time to actually read it."

For a moment, Ingrid detected a hint of disdain on Timo's face. She felt increasingly uneasy as she listened to her husband's remarks, which seemed insincere and overbearing, like someone trying to assert dominance.

She didn't like Kristina Rapp.

"You must have made an impression on good old Anton over here," Lars said. "By the way, be careful, he's a lawyer."

Kristina's sly grin spread across her face. "Well, well, well," she said, tracing a finger along the rim of her glass with a hint of mischief in her eyes. "Looks like things just got interesting."

Anton gave her a quick smile and then stood up. He raised his glass and toasted the newlyweds. "To Mila and Berger!"

The rest of the table followed suit.

"Don't drink too much," Ingrid whispered.

Anton looked puzzled. "Why? We have a room here."

"Just... don't get drunk," she said firmly. "You'll embarrass yourself."

"Alright, alright," Anton held up his hands in defeat as he turned to Ingrid. But before she could scold him another time, he spun back around to Kristina, a glimmer of excitement in his eyes. "So, tell me, how did you get landed with Paikkala over here?" he asked, gesturing towards Timo.

"Anton," Ingrid said and frowned.

But Anton ignored her and launched into a riveting discussion about serial killers, fully engrossed in his conversation with Kristina.

As the night went on, Anton shined as the life of the party, regaling everyone with his witty anecdotes and charm. Despite Ingrid's efforts to draw Lars into the conversation, he remained quiet and reserved, offering only curt responses. Timo, sandwiched between Kristina and Isa, seemed almost invisible, barely speaking throughout dinner. But Ingrid noticed his eyes occasionally wander over to her.

Once the first dance was over, Anton, already feeling the effects of too much wine, pulled Ingrid onto the dance floor, leading a throng of guests to follow their example. Kristina made several attempts to convince Timo to join in, but he steadfastly refused, insisting that she enjoy herself without him. And Lars retreated to the bar, turning down the invitation to join the dancing crowd.

Left alone at the table with Isa, Timo turned to her and offered a warm, reassuring smile.

"No Nick?" he asked with a hint of casual curiosity.

She nodded. "You were right. It was too early."

Timo took a sip of his drink, then looked up at Isa. "You look beautiful."

She smiled at his words, even though they seemed strange coming from him. But the sincerity in his voice made his words seem honest and genuine, taking her aback.

"You're looking sharp tonight as well," she complimented him with a hint of playful teasing. "It seems like you've finally discovered the wonders of a clothing store."

He couldn't hold his laughter and nodded. "Funny!"

Isa's gaze shifted between the dancers, taking in the wild arm swings of Anton and the rigid stance of Ingrid who gazed at the floor.

Isa turned to her partner and pointed at the dancers, "So, you don't dance?"

He curtly replied, "Yep."

"Can't or won't?" she asked, intrigued by his aversion to the dance floor.

"Seriously, Lindström, do I look like someone who'd hang around the dancefloor?"

She ignored his comment and continued, "You can't, or you won't?"

He gave her a faint smile. "I can."

"But you won't?"

"I don't just dance with anybody. That is something... special."

She turned her gaze towards the lively dancers on the floor, taking in the scene. Anton, drunken and carefree, embraced Ingrid while laughing, a side of him she rarely saw. His flirtatious advances toward Kristina were plain to see. On the other side of the room, Lars was seated at the bar, nursing his beer and sulking.

Isa raised an eyebrow as she observed the scene, then with a hint of sarcasm, she pointed to Kristina, "I guess she's not special enough to warrant a dance with you."

He was lost in his thoughts, fixated on the woman at the edge of the dancefloor. Ingrid appeared out of place amidst the joyful revelers, her discomfort unmistakable. Their eyes briefly met before she turned away, focusing on the throngs of people gyrating to the beat of the music.

Then Isa spoke up. "I'm going to say it again. Don't waste your time on her. It's clear she's not the one for you."

She leaned in, placing her hand over his. It was a gentle, comforting gesture, a sign of friendship and support. Months ago, he would have recoiled from such intimacy.

"Come," she said and signaled him to get up. "Show me your moves, mister 'I can, but I won't'."

He smiled, rising to his feet, and trailed behind her as Chris De Burgh's 'Lady in Red' filled the air. She took his hand, leading him confidently to the heart of the dance floor. But as he placed his hand on her waist, she suddenly jolted back, a hint of fear in her eyes. The confusion was evident on his face as well, mirroring her emotions. Maybe they both realized it at the same moment: dancing was intimate, and the rush of being close to each other, the bliss of moving in perfect harmony, was a feeling she had only experienced once before—when she had kissed him.

He was a skilled dancer, poised and graceful. Yet, he held her too closely for her comfort. As she attempted to decipher her feelings, he suddenly pivoted towards the commotion behind them.

Anton, with Kristina in his embrace, whispered something in her ear that elicited an unnatural outburst of laughter. Timo's expression darkened.

"So, Kristina Rapp," Isa began, her gaze fixed on the couple who had caught Timo's attention.

"What about her?" he replied, his tone distant.

"Are you friends?" she asked, intrigued by his sudden shift in demeanor.

Timo sighed heavily; his eyes cast down as they continued to twirl around the dance floor.

"What's wrong?" Isa asked, surprised by his reaction.

"It's amusing how everyone starts that conversation the same way," he said.

She inhaled sharply as he tightened his grip, then said in a voice that was meant to sound innocent: "What exactly do you mean by that?"

Ingrid was by herself, holding a glass, observing the crowd. Anton and Kristina continued to cackle and jest with each other, oblivious to the boundaries they were crossing. Isa noticed her friend's simmering anger as she shifted her gaze from Timo to Anton and Kristina.

Timo faced Isa and said, "Why beat around the bush? Do you want to know if there's something between Kristina and me?"

"I didn't want to imply that."

The sound of Chris De Burgh's 'Lady in Red' faded as Ed Sheeran's 'Perfect' took over and Timo effortlessly adjusted his steps to the new beat.

"Well, I'll put your mind at ease," he said, twirling her in a graceful spin. "Kristina and I are just friends. Nothing more, nothing less."

As they danced, Timo's foot missed a step and he almost stepped on her toes. He apologized and added, "Why can't men and women just be friends? It seems like society has this notion that there's always something more."

"I know," she said, a hint of regret in her voice, but then added, "But in my experience, it always seems to lead to something more, and that never ends well."

"But you and I are friends," he said and looked her straight in the eye.

She couldn't shake the emotions he stirred within her, but she understood he was genuinely convinced that their relationship was limited to friendship and professionalism. She forced a smile and nodded, but the sound of another outburst of laughter nearby only intensified Timo's frustration.

He released her, spun on his heel, and strode towards Anton with determination, barely avoiding other dancers in his path.

"Hey, Paikkala," Anton slurred, placing a hand on Timo's shoulder. Timo pushed Anton's hand away and stepped forward, glaring at him.

"What the hell are you doing?" Timo demanded.

Isa noticed the steam practically rising from Timo's head.

"Uh... just having a good time," Anton said, glancing at Kristina who no longer appeared as relaxed as before.

Anton chuckled, "You're jealous." He attempted to drape an arm over Kristina's shoulder, but she stepped back and fixed her gaze on the floor.

"Timo...," Isa tried to intervene, but he ignored her.

"Get a hold of yourself, man. Show some respect. Your wife is right over there!"

Anton scowled as he leaned in, invading Timo's personal space. "It's just for fun. Ingrid knows that."

Timo's eyebrows rose in disbelief. "Really? Does she?"

"Of course, she does," Anton said, his tone growing defensive. "And you should watch your own behavior before trying to play the hero. Keep your hands off my wife."

Timo stepped back, his expression blank. He glanced around the room before focusing back on Anton.

"It seems like the big talker is at a loss for words," Anton said.

Without another word, Timo turned and made his way through the crowd that had gathered. He approached Ingrid and asked, "How could you let him treat you this way?"

Ingrid frowned. "What are you talking about?"

"He humiliates you and takes you for granted. How can you stand for that? I would never do that to you. Never."

Ingrid tried to speak, but Timo cut her off. "Don't tell me it doesn't hurt. I can see it in your eyes." He took a deep breath and then continued, "I need to get out of here. I just…"

She took his arm, but he pushed her away.

He needed a breath of fresh air. The kind that came with an ice-cold breeze and a resetting of one's state of mind.

He headed for the exit but was met with a throng of people blocking his way.

He managed to get out. The wind was picking up, bringing with it a barrage of snow. He wished he had worn his boots instead of the shiny black shoes he had found tucked away in one of the cabinets.

The cold air did little to clear his mind.

"Timo," a voice called out, and he turned to see Isa making her way down the snow-covered sidewalk towards him, buttoning up her coat and gingerly trying to maintain her balance on her stilettos.

"Are you crazy… going outside in this weather?" she exclaimed. "Come back inside so we can talk about it."

He wiped the snowflakes from his face and shot her an irritated look. "I didn't ask you to follow me. Just go back inside."

"No, not until you come with me," she persisted, still making her way towards him.

"What are you going to do? Chase me in those heels? You're going to break your neck," he warned.

Despite her struggles, she continued toward him, and when she nearly stumbled, he quickly reached out to steady her.

"What's going on?" she gasped. "Why were you so angry with Anton?"

He fixed her with a scathing glare. "Is it normal for a husband to publicly humiliate his wife like that?"

"It was just for fun. Ingrid knows that."

"You're really quick to forgive Anton."

"And you're acting like a jealous idiot," she retorted.

"Jealous idiot? That man is sleeping around," Timo raised his voice.

"Anton? I've never seen a man more devoted to his wife."

"Really? That's not what Lyn..." Timo trailed off, averting his gaze.

"Lyn Hjort. The woman who's infatuated with you and would do anything to manipulate you. Haven't you learned your lesson? She spread the same lies about Caijsa."

Timo remained silent, looking down at the ground as the wind picked up, whipping snowflakes around them.

"Timo, try to keep things in perspective. Your negative attitude isn't helping anyone," she urged.

"Let's see... I'm no longer a superintendent, the woman I loved betrayed me, and the woman I want doesn't want me. Why should I be happy?"

Before she could respond, he spun on his heel and strode away, determined to put distance between them.

"Timo, let's talk...," she called after him, but he didn't slow down.

The next moment, he was thrown forward and landed on the ground with a thud. A deafening explosion followed, and a sharp pain ripped through his jaw. He instinctively tried to protect his face with his arms.

Car alarms blared.

People screamed.

Glass shattered all around him.

As Timo stumbled to his feet, his surroundings came into focus.

The street was in chaos, with debris scattered everywhere.

He frantically searched for Isa. He spotted her lying nearby, clutching her arm to her chest, and grimacing in pain.

He rushed over to her and knelt beside her. "Lindström, are you okay?"

She winced and whispered, "My arm."

Broken pieces of stone were scattered around her. The debris must have hit her.

Timo helped her up, but as he stood, he saw the massive hole in the wall of the hotel. Glass and debris filled the street and small fires burned all around. He couldn't believe the devastation that had occurred in such a short amount of time. But as he surveyed the damage, a sudden fear gripped him—people he cared for were in that building.

Timo felt a strong urge to rush into the building to check on them, but his legs felt unsteady, and he couldn't leave Isa like that.

He turned to her and looked at her arm, "How bad is it?"

"Don't worry about me, help the others."

When she saw him waver, she said, "Go."

CHAPTER

13

AS TIMO STOOD THERE, FROZEN IN SHOCK, his mind raced with conflicting thoughts and emotions. He had never witnessed such destruction and chaos before, and he was overwhelmed by the enormity of the situation. He had to do something, but he didn't know where to start. His training and experience had prepared him for many scenarios, but nothing could have prepared him for this.

His attention was drawn to a group struggling to escape through the entrance hall. He could hear their cries for help. Behind him, he heard the ambulances and police cars arriving. Impressive how fast they had been there. The police station was nearby. Amidst the chaos, he spotted Berger's mother, dressed in a stunning crimson outfit that shone like a beacon in the light reflected off the snow. Just as she was about to be hit by a falling stone, a stranger leapt into action, pulling her to safety.

"Mrs. Karlsson!" Timo shouted, his voice ringing out in the chaos.

The sound of ambulance and police car doors slamming echoed through the air, and as Timo began to make his way up the stairs, a police officer stopped him.

"Sir, you can't go in," the officer warned, but then he was surprised when he realized who was trying to enter the dangerous scene. "Inspector Paikkala? What are you doing here?"

But Timo wasn't about to let bureaucracy get in his way. Recognizing the young officer, he asked, "Varg, right?"

The officer nodded, and Timo pointed to the woman standing under a tree. "Lindström is over there. Get her into an ambulance!"

The young officer hesitated, but Timo's urgency was impossible to ignore. "You can't go in there, it's too unstable," Varg said. "The gas explosion..."

"Gas explosion?" Timo cut him off, his eyes narrowing. "This is no gas explosion."

The young officer's eyes widened in terror. "Then what is it? A bomb?"

"Get a specialized bomb squad over here," Timo commanded. "There may be more. And get these people out of here." He gestured towards the men and women who were gathered at the entrance.

"What are you going to do?"

"I'm trying to find my team," Timo replied, before charging up the stairs. He pushed his way through the stream of people escaping the building, his mind focused solely on finding his missing team. Debris rained down from above, but he pressed on. Time was running out, and he couldn't let his team down.

"Uh... inspector," he heard a shaky voice behind him. He turned around and saw a woman, the companion of Lars. He couldn't recall her name. Fear and confusion were written all over her face.

"Are you okay?" Timo asked.

She nodded but couldn't speak.

"Where are the others?"

The woman just stared ahead, tears streaming down her face.

"What happened?" Timo pressed.

"I don't know," she replied, her voice trembling. "We were dancing and then there was a loud noise and... chaos. I lost Lars. I don't know where he is."

Timo took her by the hand and guided her down the steps, her shoes slipping on the ice-covered ground. He took her to one of the ambulances.

Meanwhile, he spotted Ingrid and their eyes met. Like many others, she looked confused.

Anton, still struggling to remain composed despite being drunk, tried to console a frantic woman who was searching for her missing husband and son. She was sobbing and pleading for help.

It was Mrs. Karlsson. Timo had overlooked her presence until now. The chaos and destruction made it hard for him to focus. He walked up to them. Mrs. Karlsson was shaking, and only now he saw that she was missing her shoes and that her clothing was torn exposing a portion of her bra. She had a deep gash across her forehead.

"Mrs. Karlsson," Timo said softly, as the woman quieted down and focused her attention on him.

"You... know me?"

"Yes, I'm a colleague of your son, Timo Paikkala," he replied.

"Oh, yes... Timo Paikkala..." She appeared disoriented, her gaze flickering across Timo's face, seemingly attempting to recognize him.

"This is what we're going to do: I'll take you to the paramedics. That cut on your forehead needs attention, and I'll look for your husband and son," he said firmly, shaking his head as Mrs. Karlsson tried to object.

With a determined step, Timo led Mrs. Karlsson to the waiting ambulance.

He only vaguely remembered her husband, a man who was nearly cartoonish in appearance, with glasses and a mustache. The man didn't seem to match the woman in front of him, who was crying and pouring out her fears. Her voice was soft and gentle, unlike Berger's.

Turning to Anton, Timo spoke firmly, "You're drunk and not helping anyone by hanging around. It's best you get out of the way."

He gave the insulted-looking man one final glance and walked back to survey the area. Ingrid was walking towards him, supporting an older man.

Timo might have told Berger's mother that everything would be okay, but he was no longer so confident. He realized he had taken on more than he could handle.

"Timo!" someone yelled, and he turned to see Kristina. "You were gone," Kristina said.

"I'm sorry... I... didn't feel well."

Kristina frowned. "I was so worried. I didn't know where you were... you idiot!"

Timo wanted to say something but changed his mind. "Are you hurt?"

Kristina shook her head.

Another gust of wind and snow made him gasp for air. "Stay here. I need to find Berger and Lars."

Ingrid was looking at him and Kristina's expression became serious.

He looked at the building. The firefighters were trying to extinguish the fire that continued to rage on the second floor.

"Where are Berger and Mila?" Timo asked.

"I don't know," Kristina stammered.

He rubbed the snowflakes from his face and shouted at Ingrid, "Have you seen Berger and Mila?"

She came closer.

"No," Ingrid said.

"Did you see them before the explosion?"

"I can't remember."

Meanwhile Kristina had wandered off to the ambulances.

"But... I'm so happy you're okay," Ingrid whispered and reached out to take his hand but then changed her mind.

"Me too," he said.

Then a man shouted, "Be careful! The structure is going to collapse!"

The firefighters suddenly retreated.

The front of the hotel came down.

Timo took Ingrid's hand. "We need to get out of here!" he shouted.

Timo's heart pounded with adrenaline as he witnessed the hotel crumbling before his eyes. The deafening noise and the sheer force of the falling debris engulfed the scene. In that moment, an overwhelming determination surged within him—a fierce resolve to shield her from harm, whatever the cost.

* * *

Anton's relentless pacing echoed down the hospital corridor, eyes heavy with exhaustion and fear. Ingrid watched him closely, noting the dark circles around his eyes. But neither of them, nor the rest of the group, would leave until every member was accounted for. Ingrid didn't know what time it was, but it looked like hours had passed since they arrived at the hospital. Mila, Berger, and Lars were still missing.

Despite Timo's persistent pleas for Isa to go home, she refused to leave until her colleagues were found. Though her own injuries, evidenced by the brace on her left arm, had been treated and deemed minor, she refused to let it stand in the way of finding those who were still missing.

"Sit down," Ingrid said to Anton.

"There should be something we can do!" Anton shouted.

"The best thing you can do is go home," Timo said calmly.

Anton ignored Timo's words and approached Ingrid. "We should be out there, helping those in need."

Ingrid snapped, "And what good will you do in your current state? The best thing you can do right now is sit down and stop pacing. You're making me nervous."

The waiting room was overflowing with patients, some seated in chairs, others on the floor. Some cradled their heads in their hands, while others paced or walked aimlessly.

A man near the entrance, his head and arm bandaged, and his shirt stained with blood, sat in a trance-like state with a blank expression. At the other end of the room, another man appeared to have been crying, while a woman with scratches on her face sat against a wall, softly whimpering as she gazed at the floor. Her husband stood close, offering comfort and support as he held her hand tightly.

The paramedics brought in more wounded people on stretchers.

"So many people," Ingrid whispered.

Timo looked at her and nodded. "I know."

Then, he let his hands slide up to cover his face as he rubbed his tired eyes. He was overwhelmed by fatigue, so much so that if he were to close his eyes, he feared he would collapse and fall asleep where he stood. His body was weighed down by exhaustion, every muscle yearning for rest. The stress of the past weeks had taken a toll on him and now, he struggled to keep his eyes open and his mind alert. Just the thought of sleep made him want to lean against a wall and drift off into a deep slumber.

"Maybe you should go home too," Ingrid suggested, her voice soft and compassionate.

"Not until I know what's happening."

"Kristoffer Solberg is here," Isa interjected.

"I know," Timo acknowledged. "I saw him when we were evacuated."

"SÄPO is fast," Isa said. "I just hope they'll include us in the investigation."

"This one isn't for us. I think it's a bomb. That's SÄPO's area of expertise."

Isa let out a sigh. "I just don't understand why anyone would want to target the Grand Hotel."

Timo shrugged, equally puzzled.

The next moment, Finn entered the waiting room, and Timo felt a pang of irritation as he saw his boss, impeccably dressed as usual. Why wasn't Finn there earlier? The thought that Finn may have been conveniently absent during the chaos only added to Timo's anger.

"They've found Berger," Finn announced calmly.

His words were met with silence.

"He's alive, but critically injured. He's been in the hospital for a few hours."

"Thank God," Ingrid breathed a sigh of relief.

"And Lars? And Mila?" Timo asked.

Finn looked down before continuing, "Mila didn't make it. She was killed in the explosion."

"But how...," Isa stammered. "The dance hall was intact. The explosion happened on the second floor. Everyone was able to evacuate. Did Mila get trapped under the rubble?"

"I don't know," Finn admitted. "We need to inform her next of kin. Is her family okay?"

"She was an orphan, a foster child," Isa replied.

Finn turned to Timo, "Can I speak with you for a moment?"

Timo followed him into the hallway.

Finn rubbed his face and took a moment before saying, "They found them on the second floor."

"Berger and Mila?" Timo asked.

"Yes."

"What were they doing there?"

"I don't know, but Solberg wants to talk to us."

"And we're sure this is a bomb?"

"Yes. The bomb went off in one of the rooms on the second floor."

"Whose room?"

"We're still trying to figure out which room, but the National Counter-terrorism Center has already issued a high-level warning for potential terrorist attacks. Security has been heightened at all key sites across the country."

"But are we sure this was a terrorist attack? We've been wrong before, like with the shooting at Global Law," Timo pointed out.

"We don't know yet, but SÄPO has requested our assistance in the investigation."

"Well, it seems Solberg learned his lesson."

Finn's face turned serious, "I'm not sure how we can help them."

Just then, a nurse approached them. "Are you colleagues of Mr. Karlsson?"

"Yes, we are," Timo answered.

"He's conscious and asking to speak with someone," she informed them.

"I'll go," Finn offered.

"Are you Timo?" the nurse asked.

"No, that's him," Finn said and pointed to Timo.

"He specifically asked to speak with you," the nurse added with a gentle smile. "You can come with me, Mr. Timo."

Surprised, Timo followed the nurse down a long and chaotic hallway filled with people sitting in chairs and mobile beds, and even on the floor. As they made their way to Berger's room, Timo felt a sense of unease at what the man wanted to tell him.

"Now, just to warn you: Mr. Karlsson is in really bad shape," the nurse said as they walked through the double doors to the intensive care unit.

"How bad is it?"

The nurse stopped. "Third and second-degree burns cover over half of his body. His Total Body Surface Area, TBSA, is at 54%."

Timo furrowed his brows in confusion. "TBSA?"

"It refers to the total percentage of a person's body that has been affected by burns," the nurse explained. "The doctors want to put him in an induced coma, but Mr. Karlsson insisted on speaking to you before that. Unfortunately, there's a possibility that they may need to amputate his right arm."

Timo's heart sank at the news. "I saw his mother earlier. Has she been informed?"

"Yes. She has seen him briefly, but now she is attending to her husband, who is also receiving treatment here at the hospital."

"Her husband is injured too?"

"Yes," the nurse answered. "But I don't have any information on his condition."

They finally arrived at a large double door, behind which Timo could see patients lying in beds, hooked up to machines and tubes.

"The doctor will be with you in a few minutes. Please wait here," the nurse said before leaving and closing the door behind her.

Timo sat down and stared at the floor, feeling overwhelmed. Just yesterday, Berger was joyfully dancing with his bride, and now he was lying in a room of pain and suffering.

"Mr. Timo Paikkala?" a voice called out, breaking Timo's thoughts.

"Yes," Timo responded, as the door opened to reveal a doctor, a young woman with dark hair and blue eyes.

He felt a chill run down his spine as the doctor approached him. She was dressed in protective gear and handed him a similar outfit. In a quiet, even tone, she informed Timo that he would only have ten minutes with Berger and that he needed to wear protective clothing as the patient was highly vulnerable. The doctor also explained that Berger had been given morphine for the pain and might appear unresponsive and incoherent.

The doctor then revealed that Mr. Karlsson had been asking about his wife, but they had told him that she was injured. They wanted to keep it that way for now. Timo nodded, struggling to process the information.

He put on the protective suit and mouth mask. The stiff, bulky material was uncomfortable. The mask felt tight around his face, but he knew it was necessary.

When Timo finally entered the room, he was struck by the sound of the breathing machines and heart monitors, which beeped and hummed in a steady rhythm. The ten hospital beds were all occupied, and a sense of danger and death permeated the air.

The doctor led him to one of the beds in the corner, where he was confronted with the extent of Berger's injuries. The blistered skin on Berger's face was a painful sight to behold, and Timo could only imagine the excruciating pain Berger was going through.

"Timo," Berger whispered, his hand reaching out. Timo tried to move closer but was stopped by the doctor, who signaled for him to keep his distance.

"I'm here, Berger," Timo replied, trying to hide the sadness in his voice.

"It was a bomb," Berger wheezed.

"Why were you there?"

"I don't know... I can't recall. I think I went for a walk. Everything is a bit of a blur, but I remember the explosion. And Lars... is he okay?"

"What's with Lars?"

"I think he was there." The nasal cannula was seemingly annoying him, restricting his movement as Berger tried to pull it away from his face. The doctor intervened and repositioned it.

Berger closed his eyes, taking deep breaths before continuing. "I followed Mila... It's all so blurred. I can't think straight. You can ask her."

Timo's heart sank.

"Then the explosion... the walls collapsing, the fire, the smoke," Berger continued, his breathing becoming more labored.

"Where exactly were you? Were Mila and Lars there too?"

"In the hallway... on the second floor," Berger replied, his eyes searching Timo's face. "Lars was there... I think."

Berger started coughing and gasping for air. The doctor quickly attended to him, and Timo stepped back, feeling helpless. He found it hard to breathe through the protective suit and mouth mask, the tightness making him feel suffocated.

"Maybe I should go," Timo said softly. "Give you some rest."

"No," Berger replied, his dark eyes locking onto Timo's. "I don't think I'll make it. But you can ask Mila what happened. I can't remember. Is she okay? They said she was injured."

Timo struggled with the weight of the responsibility placed upon him.

"Timo?" Berger asked, his voice weak and raspy.

The doctor shot Timo a worried look, a silent reminder of the agreement they had made before entering the unit. Timo's conscience tugged at him, torn between his duty to follow instructions and his loyalty to Berger. He knew he owed his friend the truth, no matter the cost.

"She is... okay," Timo finally whispered.

As tears streamed down Berger's face, Timo felt his own eyes well up. He couldn't bear to see the pain and longing in Berger's expression.

"Can I see her?" Berger whispered and turned to the doctor.

"Not now," the doctor said. "You need your rest. Maybe later."

"I don't think I'll make it," Berger said, choking on his words.

"I see what I can do," the doctor finally said.

Then Berger turned to Timo. "Tell her... I love her... so very much...

I just wished we had more time... our time together was so... wonderful, the best of my life. Tell her... I understand. It'll be okay."

Timo frowned. "Berger?"

"Please take care of her... for me," Berger continued.

Timo nodded, unable to speak.

"It's time for Mr. Paikkala to go," the doctor intervened gently. "You need to rest."

"Tell her I love her," Berger said, his voice growing weaker.

"I will... I promise," Timo said, forcing himself to leave the room.

* * *

Ingrid walked down the hospital hallway and saw Timo leaning against the wall, looking defeated. His eyes were bloodshot and heavy with exhaustion, and his breathing was labored. He looked like he was on the brink of a breakdown, as if the weight of the world was pressing down on him. His clothes were rumpled, and his hair was disheveled. Ingrid could see the pain imprinted on his face and she felt a deep sadness for him. She wasn't sure how to approach him. Should she ask him about Berger or give him a moment to compose himself?

"Timo?" she said softly.

He jolted at the sound of her voice, and she could see tears in his eyes.

"Berger?" she asked.

Timo nodded silently and she stepped closer to him, pulling him into a comforting embrace. He broke down in sobs, his body shaking with emotion.

"It's okay," she whispered.

"No, it's not," he said between sobs. "I just had to tell a dying man his wife was okay. But she's not. She's dead."

"You did what you had to do. There's no right way to handle this kind of situation."

"It's unforgivable," he said, wiping his eyes. "I'm so sorry. This is embarrassing."

"It's okay," Ingrid said, placing a hand on his cheek. "I'm just glad you're okay. I was so worried about you."

Then Isa's voice broke through their conversation, drawing their attention. "I'm sorry to interrupt," she said, stepping closer to them.

"Yes?" Ingrid said and moved away from Timo.

"They found Lars," Isa said.

"How is he? Where is he? In the hospital?" Timo asked.

But when Isa lowered her head and took a deep breath, the answer was clear. "He's dead. They couldn't save him."

At that moment, Ingrid looked out of the window, and stared at the orange and pink hues that slowly filled the sky. The storm had finally passed, leaving a peaceful silence in its wake. But the world seemed to have lost its color and vibrancy. She closed her eyes, trying to steady her breathing. She took a deep breath and opened her eyes again, but the sunrise didn't bring the peace it usually did. This morning was different, this sunrise was a painful reminder of what had been lost.

CHAPTER

14

"**INSPECTOR SOLBERG.**" Finn walked over to shake his hand.

Timo sat in stony silence as Finn spoke with Kristoffer about the explosion. His mind was a tempest of emotions—anger towards Finn, who appeared unaffected by the loss of one of their own, sadness for the loss of Lars, and frustration at the seeming lack of urgency in finding those responsible.

"Nasty business," Kristoffer said. "It was indeed a bomb explosion."

"But why?" Timo asked.

Kristoffer took a seat next to Timo. "This stays between these four walls."

Timo and Finn nodded in agreement.

"The explosion took place just outside Leif Berg's room," Kristoffer revealed with a serious expression.

"Berg was there?" Timo asked.

"He was supposed to be there, but changed his mind and went back to Stockholm at the last minute."

"How come we didn't know?"

"It was supposed to be a secret meeting between Leif Berg and a member of a criminal organization which I cannot reveal. The man in question is seeking immunity from prosecution in exchange for information on Rune Breiner and his network of dirty cops. It was the first breakthrough we had in years, but there were demands. He only wanted to talk to Berg. We have been planning this for months. We had taken all precautions, but... it was obviously a disaster."

"Who knew about it?"

"SÄPO and a few confidants in Berg's entourage."

"And my brother Fredrik?"

"He knew. He went with Berg back to Stockholm."

As relief washed over him, knowing his brother was safe, his thoughts quickly shifted to Berg's sudden and hurried departure from Gävle. Timo, with a thoughtful expression etched on his face, pondered aloud, "Was Berg the intended target or the informant? And what compelled him to return to Stockholm?"

A sense of skepticism clouded his mind as he continued, "It all appears oddly convenient. This is at least the fourth occasion where he narrowly escaped an attempt on his life. Could it be possible that he has access to inside information?"

"Never mind that," Finn interjected. "The important thing is that he wasn't harmed."

"But many people were," Kristoffer added. "Four of them are in critical condition, and two lost their lives: Inspector Lars Nyquist and Mila Hillborg. We're fortunate the casualty count wasn't higher."

"It's a sad case," Finn said as he took a seat behind his desk. "Dr. Olsson is doing Lars' autopsy as we speak."

"Is that a good idea? She was a colleague," Timo said.

"She's professional enough," Finn replied in a firm tone. "Back to the investigation. Any leads?"

"We do think they were after Berg," Kristoffer said. "The convention is in a few weeks, they're likely to try again."

"Who are they?" Timo asked.

"We now know the right-wing group Aktivisterna is behind the Forsmark sabotage. Three people have meanwhile been arrested, including someone from the plant. Berg's name is on a hitlist and popping up everywhere. We can safely say they also planned this attack. We were just... too late."

Timo shook his head. "What do they gain from killing Leif Berg? If he dies, ten more Social Democrats will take his place."

Kristoffer looked at the wall of photographs on the cabinet. "Berg has connections and power, if he dies, the party won't recover so easily."

Timo's hand instinctively rubbed his chin as he mused, "So someone from Aktivisterna planted the bomb?"

Kristoffer nodded. "At least someone who had knowledge of Berg's presence at the hotel. I think we have a mole. Few people knew about the meeting."

Timo added. "Who tipped off Berg?"

Finn began to answer, but Kristoffer interjected, "Not us. We were aware of plans to target Berg, but all our intel pointed towards the convention. We must begin investigating our own ranks to find the mole."

"Maybe the meeting was a setup," Timo said. "How far can you trust your informant?"

"You can never really trust a man like that, but we were confident he really wanted to come clean. This has been the culmination of years of undercover work. Now it's all destroyed. The man is scared and doesn't want to talk anymore. He disappeared and we've been unable to contact him."

"Let's say Aktivisterna is responsible, I still don't see how Berg knew."

"It's just a coincidence," Finn said.

"We need to question Berg's entourage," Kristoffer said. "They were the only ones who knew he was staying at the Grand Hotel."

"And SÄPO," Timo remarked.

Weariness tinged Kristoffer's words as he lamented, "Yep, I know. That's the scary part. I can't trust anyone anymore."

Timo kept quiet, but he wasn't too sure about the other man in the room either. Could he trust Finn?

Kristoffer got up, exchanged a few last words with Finn, and then walked out the room.

Timo was deep in thought when Finn spoke. "Olsson is doing the autopsies on Lars and Mila. Maybe you're right. Maybe she is too close to this case."

"Why are you defending Berg?"

Finn looked at him, surprised.

"I don't have to answer to you, a simple inspector," Finn said, his voice low and almost threatening. "Mind your own business and that business is Lauri Valkama. I don't see many results coming from you. And you know where the door is if you want to leave."

Timo anxiously awaited a response from Finn, but the room fell into a disconcerting silence as Finn remained fixated on his computer screen. It wasn't just Finn's questionable professional decisions that troubled Timo; it was also the hateful undertone directed at him. Timo could sense the overwhelming presence of animosity and envy permeating Finn's words.

Overwhelmed with a mix of frustration and simmering anger, Timo abruptly stormed out of Finn's office, his emotions churning in him.

* * *

Timo found himself standing in the parking lot of the police station, his mind tangled in a web of thoughts. If he had been one to indulge in smoking, this would have been the precise instant to retrieve a cigarette and let the wisps of smoke carry his worries away.

Suddenly, a car pulled into the lot, and as the door opened, a wave of surprise washed over Timo. It was the last person he expected to see.

"What are you doing here?" he asked, his voice still tight with emotion.

"My dad brought me," Isa said and looked at her left arm. She had removed the brace and was now holding it up with her right hand.

"Aren't you supposed to stay at home?" He sounded angry and frustrated, and barely looked at her.

"Why are you out here in the cold?"

"I need to think."

There was a moment of silence.

"I called the hospital," she said softly, as if she was trying to get his attention.

"And?"

"Berger is still in a coma. They brought him to Uppsala, and they managed to save his arm. But the next days will be critical."

For some reason, his mind wandered off to the conversation with Berger in the hospital. It had been lingering in the back of his mind, but there was something about Berger's words that had struck him as peculiar.

"Well, at least there's some good news," he remarked, his voice carrying a touch of relief. After a brief pause, he continued, "They're currently conducting Mila's autopsy."

She stepped inside and he followed her.

"What's wrong?" she asked.

Timo led her into one of the meeting rooms, closing the door behind him. "Everything is wrong. Finn is hiding something. I think Berg put him here to gather information. And Finn conveniently wasn't at the wedding. I don't know what to think of it."

Isa's eyes widened in surprise, her voice tinged with astonishment as she struggled with her injured arm while removing her coat. "Wow, where is this coming from? How would Finn know about the explosion?"

"I don't know... yet," Timo said with a shrug. "But I have to do something before this gets out of hand. Finn warned Berg about the explosion but allowed innocent people to be harmed. Two of our own."

"Timo, don't let your anger and disappointment in Finn cloud your judgement. Accusing your boss without solid evidence is a dangerous path to follow."

"That's why I couldn't be the superintendent. Berg needed a puppet," Timo said, his eyes hardening with determination. "But I'll have to play it through Solberg."

Isa's voice carried a mix of concern and skepticism as she countered, "What if Solberg is in on it too?"

"I don't think so. But you know him better than I do."

"I'm not so sure I know him that well. Nevertheless, I believe he is a decent man. But since when are you so quick to bend the rules? It's so unlike you. Must be my bad influence."

He gave her a wry smile.

Suddenly his cell phone rang, breaking the moment of levity.

"Paikkala," he answered.

After a short conversation, he hung up. "Tuva Norling was seen at the train station about an hour ago. With luck, we'll find her and get some answers."

She grabbed her coat and strode towards the door. "I'm coming with you."

***

The young woman next to Ingrid shook her head and, with tears in her eyes, whispered, "She was so young. My age."

Mila's broken body lay on the cold, metal table. It was the most devastating destruction of a human being Ingrid had ever seen. She struggled to make sense of what she saw before her.

The same impersonal words as always, the same procedures, echoed through the room, "The victim has been identified as Mila Hillborg, 25 years old..."

Mila's charred wedding dress caught Ingrid's eye. Sparkling fibers glimmered in the light like silver wires. Ingrid remembered the beautiful white princess gown Mila had worn, now reduced to scraps.

The wire she was looking at was thick, insulated by a white rubber-like polymer that exposed the core only here and there.

As she looked at it, she couldn't tell whether the shards of metal had become lodged in the dress due to the sheer force of the explosion. But upon closer inspection, she came to the realization the wires had been intricately woven into the very fabric of the dress—not just a few, but a lot of them.

She placed the wire and piece of fabric in a plastic evidence bag. "We need to get this analyzed,"

Her colleague, Dr. Einarsson, looked at her. "What does this mean?"

Ingrid took a deep breath, trying to stay calm. "Let's not jump to conclusions, and let the police investigate this."

But in her mind, Mila Hillborg had just gone from victim to suspect.

***

Timo took another sip of his coffee, frustration evident on his face. Despite their best efforts, Tuva Norling had escaped once again. Timo and Isa had spent most of the morning searching for her, but to no avail. The mood was bleak, and Timo's emotions were all over the place.

He opened the file before him, his eyes scanning the pages. "Mila's body was heavily damaged. She must have been close to the explosion."

Seated across from him, Ingrid gracefully crossed her legs, her face etched with a visibly concerned expression. As Timo absorbed the information contained within the file, she patiently waited, her gaze gently drifting towards the plain white walls of the meeting room.

"The fibers in Mila's dress are electrical wires?" he asked.

"Yes, and residues of the explosives were found on her body and clothes."

He put the file down and stood, leaving the room without saying another word. Ingrid waited patiently for him to return. When he came back, he was carrying a stack of handwritten papers. He quickly went through them, his eyes fixed on the pages.

"What are you looking for?" Ingrid asked.

Timo didn't answer, his mind preoccupied with the notes.

"What's this?" she tried again.

"Notes," he finally answered, as he found the page he was searching for. "We need to have Ragnvald Strand—the Chief Technology Officer of Tech4You—look at these wires. Maybe he can tell us if they are used in their technology. Remember the Global Law shooting?"

Ingrid nodded. "How can I forget?"

"We always suspected someone from Tech4You was involved. The attackers escaped through the doors connecting the two buildings."

"But what is the connection with Mila?"

Mila, the young, cheerful woman was now a suspect in a murder case. Was it even possible?

"Maybe someone wants us to think that Mila is involved. Her background was clean, but Lars accessed her file just before the New Year. Why did he do that? Maybe he discovered something about Mila."

Ingrid sighed. "Lars didn't like her. It's not a secret he didn't trust her."

"Perhaps he had valid reasons," Timo mused.

Ingrid shook her head, a look of disbelief crossing her face. "There's something wrong. I find it hard to believe that Mila would be the mastermind behind all of this."

"We have to be prepared that SÄPO will consider Berger a suspect," Timo warned her.

"Solberg already asked about Mila."

Timo's icy blue eyes fixed on her. "How does he know?"

"He requested regular updates."

"So, Solberg thinks the same thing. I need to talk to Berger before rumors start to spread and his reputation is damaged beyond repair."

"He's still in a coma. What did he say when you talked to him in the hospital? Does he remember anything?"

Timo shook his head. "Nothing... just that Lars was there."

Ingrid clasped her hands together tightly, her knuckles turning white, as she leaned closer to Timo, her gaze unwavering and resolute. "We need to help him. I don't believe he had anything to do with this."

Timo's breath escaped in a weighted exhale, carrying the gravity of the circumstances. He couldn't bring himself to fully suspect Berger, but the seed of doubt lingered in the back of his mind.

Was it possible that the man he had worked with, the man he respected and trusted, could be involved in such a heinous crime?

He shook his head, trying to clear the thoughts. He needed to focus and find concrete evidence to prove Berger's innocence.

He couldn't give up on him just yet.

CHAPTER

15

FINN SHOUTED, "What part of 'Leave it up to SÄPO' didn't you understand?"

Timo sat calmly across the table; his hands tightly clasped together. He was determined to get to the bottom of this mystery, even if it meant going against his former friend and boss, Finn.

"Is that what you want to talk to me about... sir?" Timo asked, a hint of defiance in his voice.

He was no stranger to dealing with bosses who didn't appreciate his stubbornness. He had once been superintendent himself. And for the first time, he had been faced with the delicate balance of compromise and authenticity he held dear to his heart. From the genuine shock and words of gratitude when he had told the team he would no longer be the superintendent, he knew he hadn't done a bad job. Of course, he had been disappointed, and perhaps he could have achieved more, but he believed, more than ever, that sticking to one's moral standards was ultimately the best thing to do. But he wasn't naïve either. In a position as superintendent, there were politics to navigate around, which he had failed to do.

"Spill it! Say what you need to say and then get on with what I ask you to do," Finn demanded, his voice raised in anger.

Timo could sense that Finn was scared. He frowned, studying his friend's face. "Why did you keep me?"

"What do you mean?"

"Did they ask you to keep an eye on me? Is that what this is?"

"You were perfect to replace Magnus Wieland, Isa's old partner," Finn replied.

"I was, wasn't I? Did Berg order you to keep me close?"

"What are you accusing me of exactly?"

"The explosion, Lauri Valkama, Karst Engersson, Rune Breiner. They are all connected. I can feel it," Timo said, his eyes locked on Finn's.

"Think what you want. You do what I say. And if I find you're meddling with the SÄPO case, don't think I'll hesitate to suspend you."

But Timo refused to be intimidated. He got up from his chair and leaned over the table. "Finn, don't do this! Whatever it is, it can't be that bad."

Finn's lips curled into a sarcastic smile. "You seem to confuse plain professionalism with preposterous notions of a conspiracy. I'm simply following orders, not hiding anything. This is the way it should be. As the boss, I expect you to comply. Now, kindly leave my office."

"Oh, really?" Timo said. "You might want to show up now and then."

"One more word, Paikkala, and I'll put you on the bench.

Understood?"

"Loud and clear," Timo replied, pushing his chair aside and walking out the door.

He was more determined than ever to uncover the truth.

He knew he was right.

* * *

Sivert Zavadsky had a tense relationship with Timo Paikkala, the chief inspector who had repeatedly scolded him for his behavior towards women. When Timo stormed into his office, Sivert was confused.

"I need you to tell me you found something more on that laptop or else I..." Timo trailed off, but he stopped short of kicking a chair when he saw Sivert's bewildered expression.

"I didn't find anything new in the files," Sivert said.

"Fuck!"

Sivert had never seen him so upset. But before he could ask what was going on, Timo composed himself and sat down.

Sivert had no idea what was going on, but he decided to try and help. "But I did find something in Valkama's private mailbox."

Timo leaned forward. "Why didn't I hear about this before?"

"I just found it. I wanted to tell you and Inspector Lindström..."

"Okay, okay, what is it?"

"Valkama deleted these emails, but I was able to recover them. They're from a year ago."

"And?" Timo prompted.

"Take a look for yourself," Sivert said, pulling up the email browser. "Engersson sent Valkama emails asking to deposit large sums of money into Breiner's account, our dirty cop. This was months before Breiner was killed."

"That confirms my suspicions. Breiner was working for Engersson."

"And Engersson kept him out of the hands of the authorities until he could no longer protect him. Valkama was the middleman," Sivert added.

"That's a good assumption, but we need more than this."

Sivert's brows furrowed. "Then we need to do a more thorough background check on Engersson, but we won't get approval for it."

"Let me worry about that. What else do you have?"

"Some of the threatening emails to Leif Berg were sent from an account that Valkama created a year ago and that was closed the day after Valkama's death, but I managed to retrieve it," Sivert said.

"Show me."

Sivert pulled up another file. "Most emails were sent in October and November, months after Engersson's death."

"Berg told me that SÄPO wasn't able to figure out who sent them."

Sivert could hardly contain the sarcasm in his voice. "I told you before, they are amateurs."

Timo frowned. "I'm not sure... anyway, are we now saying Valkama is behind the attacks on Berg?"

Sivert opened another file on his computer. "No, not really. Valkama received instructions from a certain Ty2779."

Timo paused for a moment to read the emails on the screen. "This is more than threatening emails. It's about Forsmark, the convention... other targets. Everything. You have no idea who sent this?"

"I have the IP address," Sivert replied. "Most of the emails were sent from a computer inside the Party building of the Social Democrats in Stockholm."

Timo sat up with a start. "Someone in Berg's inner circle? Do you know who it is?"

"We need a court order to find out the identity of the user."

"And that won't happen," Timo sighed. "But Solberg can help us."

"Can you really trust SÄPO?"

"I have no other choice."

"Valkama downloaded and printed these emails an hour before his death," Sivert said.

"Looks like Valkama wanted to come clean."

"Or he wanted to blackmail his client."

* * *

"Hey, do you know when Inspector Heimersson will be back?" Timo asked the young woman at the reception of the police station.

She looked up from her computer, a smile appearing on her face as she saw him. Timo had noticed this before, every time he spoke to her, she would give him a confused look and then a twinkle of infatuation would appear in her eyes. Isa, in her characteristic indiscretion, had once told him that there wasn't a woman in the police station who hadn't had wild sexy dreams about him.

He wondered if Isa was one of them. There had been a drunken kiss and subtle hints that she was interested in him romantically. It didn't surprise Timo much, as Isa was an attractive woman, and he had to admit there was a spark of interest. But he knew that getting involved with Isa Lindström would only lead to heartache.

"Uh, I... uh..." she stammered, caught off guard by Timo's attention.

"Sylvia, right?"

She nodded and took a deep breath. "Yes... I'm Sylvia Ahlgren. The superintendent is out for the rest of the day. Do you need him? Can I call him for you, sir?"

Timo looked at the floor for a moment and then shook his head. "No, I'll call him myself, thanks."

He thought about the argument he had with Finn in his office and felt ashamed for losing his temper. He wanted to make things right with him, but Finn was stubborn and biased, traits that Timo had never noticed before. He wasn't sure if he could still call Finn a friend. Their friendship was just a facade, something his mother had warned him about. It saddened him that it took twenty years to see Finn for who he really was and now he questioned his own ability to judge character.

He had uttered words to his boss that were unjust and laden with bitterness, aware that they stemmed from a place deeper than the mere frustration of witnessing a crucial case slipping away.

Sylvia pointed to a boy sitting on a bench in the entrance hall, "Inspector Paikkala, before you go, maybe you can help this young man."

The young boy, seemingly around the age of seven, was attired in a blue parka, black jeans, boots, and a knitted cap. His slightly overgrown brown hair curled up at the nape of his neck. He stared at the door, waiting expectantly for someone to enter at any moment.

"Why is he here?"

Sylvia shrugged. "He's waiting for someone, but he wouldn't say who. Maybe you can talk to him. Otherwise, I'll have to call child services."

"Why me?"

"You're good at that." Sylvia quickly added, "Sorry, I mean…"

"It's fine." Timo walked up to the child.

The boy suddenly turned his head and looked straight at Timo. For a moment, Timo was taken by surprise and didn't know what to say. There was something familiar about him.

"I hear you're waiting for someone," Timo said and put himself next to the boy.

The child nodded.

"Okay, maybe I can help you. My name is Timo Paikkala."

The boy said nothing and continued to stare at the door.

"Maybe you can tell me your name and who you are looking for."

"My name is Felix Clausen and I'm waiting for my mom."

Felix Clausen. Why did the name sound familiar?

"And your mom is where?"

"She works here. Inspector Isabel Lindström."

Now Timo remembered. Viktor Clausen. Isa's ex-husband.

"Isa Lindström?"

Felix turned his head, "Do you know her?"

"I'm her partner. But she's not here. She's in Stockholm."

"I'll wait," Felix said with a determined expression on his face.

"Okay, you can't wait here. It's too cold. Come with me!"

Timo got up and when Felix didn't move, he motioned the boy to follow him.

Five minutes later, Felix was at the table in the coffee corner, watching Timo get a cup of hot chocolate from the vending machine.

"It's not too bad," Timo said as he put the plastic cup in front of Felix. "Better than the coffee."

"When will she be back?" Felix asked as he took a sip of the hot chocolate. He scrunched and blew on it to cool it down.

"I don't know. It might be late."

"So, you work with my mom. You catch the bad guys?"

Timo smiled, "At least we try." He watched as the boy sat across from him, trying to understand what might have brought him here.

He resembled his mother. Sharp, green eyes with a mischievous twinkle, light-brown hair, soft, almost angelic features. A classic beauty. A boy who'd in his later years break many hearts.

"Shouldn't you be in school?" Timo asked.

"No, we just moved to Sweden, and we haven't found a new school yet. We're staying with grandma, and dad's looking for a job," Felix replied, his soft English accent noticeable.

"Does your grandma know you're gone?"

"No... I don't think she'll like it."

"Is that why you came here alone?"

"She doesn't get along with my mom."

"How did you get here?"

"By bus. I have some money." Felix showed him the banknotes.

"Why not call your mom instead?"

"It's too difficult for dad, I just want to tell her we're back, and she can visit us. She doesn't know it yet," Felix said.

Timo knew that Felix's hope was like a fly on the wall, doomed to be crushed by the truth. Crushed by Isa's truth.

"Your grandma and dad must be worried," Timo said.

"They'll understand. And I think dad needs some cheering up. He'll be happy when he sees mom. He and Ellen are not getting married. I think it's because of me."

"Why do you think that?"

"I talked about my mom a lot to Ellen and then she got really upset. They had a big fight and Ellen said that my dad still loves my mom more than her, and she doesn't want to be in second place."

Timo didn't know what to say.

"I just want to talk to my mom," Felix said.

"Moms... it's complicated."

"Did yours leave too?"

"No, but my mom can be... complicated," Timo said with a faint smile. "She means well, but sometimes it has the opposite effect."

"Like my mom. She thinks she helps by being gone, but she's not. I miss her."

"Give her time," Timo said. "Sometimes moms don't know what to do and we need to help them."

Felix smiled.

"Do you have a cell phone?" Timo asked.

"Yes, in my pocket," Felix answered, pulling it out and putting it on the table.

"Call your dad," Timo said with a straight face.

* * *

"Thank you for taking care of him," Viktor said as he shook Timo's hand. "It won't happen again."

"He's a great kid," Timo said.

Felix stood a few meters away from them, watching the snow fall through the window.

Viktor's face flushed as he looked down at the ground. He wasn't what Timo had imagined Isa's ex-husband to be. The man in front of him, smaller by a good ten centimeters, was handsome with soft features and a kind but sad expression on his face. Timo had expected someone more like Nick or Magnus: passionate, confident, maybe even arrogant. But Viktor was none of those things. Instead, he reminded Timo of the stories he'd heard about Alex: intelligent, timid, and serious.

"He thinks it's his fault the wedding was cancelled," Timo said.

"What?" Viktor quickly turned to his son. "Why would he think that? Ellen and I decided to break it off. It had nothing to do with him."

Viktor's growing discomfort showed as he averted his gaze from Felix to the floor.

"He wants to see Isa," Timo added.

Then Viktor looked at Timo with sadness in his eyes. "She doesn't want to see him."

"Did you ask her?"

"Yes. Coming back to Sweden may not have been the best idea. Being in the UK, I could always use distance as an excuse. But now it's going to be painful. I don't know how to tell him."

Felix was laughing and chatting with Sylvia, who seemed genuinely interested in his stories about chess.

"Give her time," Timo suggested.

"Time... that's what she always asks for. No, I won't give her time. She's had enough."

Felix's sudden outburst of laughter echoed through the room, drawing the attention of those around him.

"I understand she's scared, but after so many years...," Viktor said.

"Scared of what?"

Viktor looked at Timo with furrowed brows, then shook his head. "She probably didn't tell you. PPD."

"PPD?"

"Postpartum depression. Isa suffered from it after Felix was born. I blame myself. I pressured her into having children too soon. I knew she wasn't ready, maybe never would be. It was severe, so severe that we had to put distance between her and the kids for fear she might harm herself or them. She stayed with her parents before ultimately ending our marriage. I thought that with time and space, everything would go back to normal, but it never did. And now, I've run out of patience and energy."

As Viktor spoke, Timo realized he didn't really know Isa. Despite Viktor claiming he no longer wanted to reconnect with her, his eyes betrayed his love for his former wife.

"You left five years ago," Timo pointed out. "Felix was what... three?"

"Yes, and Olivia four."

"Why now? I doubt Felix remembers much about her."

"Last year, Felix's best friend's mother passed away. Ever since, he's been watching videos and pictures, asking about Isa, her whereabouts, and if he could speak to her. At first, Ellen didn't mind, but then she wanted to adopt Felix and Olivia. I think she felt Felix's attachment to Isa was preventing us from being a true family. I don't know. Maybe she was right. The reality is that Ellen is gone, Isa is gone, and I have to figure out how to cope with that."

Timo felt awkward and out of place. He shouldn't have asked. This was so personal.

Then Viktor offered his hand. "Thank you for taking care of him,

Inspector Paikkala. It won't happen again, I promise. And please... don't tell Isa."

Timo nodded, unsure if that was the right thing to do.

Felix, with a big smile, looked at Timo and waved goodbye.

* * *

Three days later, Timo and Isa were on a drive to visit the Lagers again, Tuva Norling's foster parents. As they traveled, Isa leaned her head against the window, taking in the wintry scenery of snow-covered trees rushing by. The chill in the air was unmistakable, and she hugged her jacket tighter, her breath fogging up the window.

"You look tired," he said and put his eyes back on the road.

"I didn't sleep well."

Isa had given Timo a brief rundown of her visit to Stockholm, which had not been productive. She had met with Fredrik, who had taken her to lunch and ranted about his troubled childhood and the ongoing tension with his brother. He had made another pass at her, which she had politely declined. She had found out nothing about Berg's plans, and Fredrik had given her a vague explanation why his boss had left the Grand Hotel so suddenly.

"Nick?"

"Nick is fine," she replied. "Well, that's not exactly true. I don't know how he is."

"Then what is it? You've been quiet all morning."

She took a deep breath, removed her gloves and cap, and placed them in her lap.

"I went to see Berger," she said.

"Oh," Timo let out.

She didn't know what it was—the sound of the heart monitor or the man himself. Either way, it reminded her of that day at Toby's bedside in the hospital. The son of her previous partner Magnus Wieland. A man she couldn't think about without her stomach tightening and her blood pressure rising.

A nauseating monotonous sound. Like that terrible day, almost a year ago.

Isa had caught herself staring at the calendar, hanging in the kitchen. The day was approaching. She wanted to skip over this date like it never existed. She had survived Alex's birthday last June. Time was passing, and yet he still felt so present in her life.

That afternoon, when she had finally been allowed to see Berger, everything had changed. Reality had hit her like a freight train. It was as if she'd been woken up from a dream, one where she'd immersed herself willingly to numb the pain of loss. And that deep sadness hadn't left her.

"The doctor said he was stable," she said.

"Was he awake?"

"Yeah, and in a lot of pain. I only had ten minutes with him, Solberg beat me to it."

"To be expected."

"Berger knows about Mila and Lars," Isa said.

"Shit. Did Solberg tell him?"

"He had to learn at some point."

"How was he?"

"Not great," she said. "I asked him a few questions about the wedding. I don't think he knows that he and Mila are considered suspects."

As the car turned onto a smaller snow-covered road, the tires slipped on the icy surface, and Timo struggled to keep the car on the road.

"What did you find out?" Timo asked.

Isa sighed. "Nothing good. Mila chose the wedding date and venue, despite Berger wanting to postpone until summer."

"That doesn't bode well for Mila," Timo noted as the car passed houses with snowmen in their front yards.

"Does he remember what happened?"

"No, he just needs time."

"Time is something we don't have," Timo pointed out. "He needs to clear things up about Mila. I have a feeling... he knows more. I think he remembers more than what he's telling us."

"It's not easy to accept that the person you trust most can be responsible for such a terrible crime," Isa said.

"We don't have enough evidence to condemn her yet. It's all circumstantial."

"Do you think we'll find evidence at the Lagers?"

"I don't know why we didn't realize it before but Hugo Lager, the father, worked for Tech4You, and the conductive thread found in Mila's dress has a proprietary coating developed by them. There's a link between Mila and Tech4You, and the Lagers," Timo explained.

"And Tuva Norling."

Isa gazed out the window, deep in thought as the car made its way to the Lagers' home.

"I met Viktor and Felix yesterday," Timo said suddenly.

Isa almost jumped up. "How? Why?"

"Felix was at the station."

"On his own? What was he doing there? That's no place for a child."

"No worries... he's okay," Timo quickly said. "He was looking for you."

Then he added calmly, "Maybe you should meet with him."

Her eyes narrowed and the expression on her face turned fierce. "That's none of your business, Timo."

"I just think...," Timo started, but trailed off as they pulled up to the Lagers' home.

She looked at him with her big green eyes. This was the last thing she wanted to talk about. Alex was on her mind. She couldn't deal with another painful episode in her life. "Leave it! You don't know anything about my previous life, and why I decided to leave them. I'm serious. Don't meddle!"

"Uhm, I only know there is a boy out there... a smart boy who just wants to reconnect with his mom, who misses his mom a lot. She might not think she's worthy of a family, but he thinks she is. I also think she needs to wake up and realize that not everything is about her. That's all. And now I'll shut up."

He smiled at her, in some strange attempt to make the message more digestible, but it wasn't the kind of smile that made her feel better or more comfortable.

She crossed her arms. She knew she'd look like a sulking little child, but she didn't care. This was her business, and he should stay out of it.

* * *

"Do you know this woman?" Timo held Mila's picture in front of Mrs. Lager, who was sitting across from him in the living room. She was alone. Her daughter was at work and her husband was visiting his father in the nursing home.

"Yes, that is Mila."

Timo quickly glanced at Isa before saying, "And where do you know Mila from?"

"She was one of our foster children."

"When was that?" Isa asked.

Mrs. Lager ran her fingers over the short gray strands of hair on her head. "I don't know exactly when it was. Maybe ten years ago? Her parents were killed in a car crash when she was a teenager, and she came to live with us for two or three years. Then she got a scholarship and went off to college."

"What was she like as a teenager?"

"Nice and helpful. She was quite smart and knew what she wanted. We never had any problems with her. Did she do something wrong?"

Timo ignored her question and continued, "Did she get along with your husband Hugo?"

"Yeah, but they weren't that close. Petra and Mila were very good friends. I think she was one of the few girls Petra actually liked."

"How come? Petra seems like an intelligent and nice young woman."

"Well, she's picky when it comes to friends. And she never had many."

"But Mila and Petra were close?"

Mrs. Lager nodded. "Petra and Mila were inseparable, almost like sisters. But after Mila left, they slowly grew apart. It was a painful experience for Petra, almost like a betrayal. It was hard on her."

Timo took a moment, but then steeled himself to ask the question. "Has Mila ever shown an interest in your husband's... uh, right-wing ideas?"

Mrs. Lager frowned, "What do you mean with my husband's right-wing ideas?"

"Oh, come on, Mrs. Lager. Your husband was and still is a member of the Swedish White Supremacy Group, and this group is known to have links with Aktivisterna."

"My husband has a right to his opinions. He does no harm," she said curtly. "And no, Mila wasn't interested."

"No harm? Aktivisterna has been linked to violence and hate crimes."

Mrs. Lager's expression tightened. "My husband had nothing to do with that. And even if he did have any involvement with this Swedish White Supremacy Group, that doesn't mean he's responsible for what others do."

"That's convenient. Close your eyes to what's happening around you."

Mrs. Lager's eyes flashed with anger. "I don't know anything about Aktivisterna or what my husband's involvement may be. And I'd like to see you come with some proof."

Timo calmly opened the file in his hands, pulled out a picture and held it in front of Mrs. Lager.

"This is your husband, isn't it?"

Mrs. Lager frowned and then nodded. "So?"

"This was taken in the 'Mille Birre' bar, here in Gävle. The pub has a questionable reputation. Our sources tell us that your husband is a regular visitor."

Only later, after analyzing Isa's pictures, had they noticed Mr. Lager in the crowd during the old man's speech. Isa didn't know for sure if Mr. Lager was part of the crowd that had met in the secret room, but if he was, she hadn't captured him on camera.

Mrs. Lager's expression darkened, and she crossed her arms over her chest. "I don't see how that proves anything. My husband could have been there for any number of reasons."

"You weren't at Mila's wedding," Isa interrupted since the tense conversation between Mrs. Lager and Timo was going nowhere.

Mrs. Lager relaxed and said, "Did Mila get married? Good for her."

"Mila is dead," Timo said with a straight face.

Mrs. Lager's face froze, her composed demeanor giving way to a momentary state of confusion. "How?"

"She died in the explosion."

"And you think she had anything to do with it? Just like my husband."

"Your husband worked for Tech4You," Timo said.

"So what? He worked for them only for a year."

"Then he was laid off," Timo added. "Why?"

"It was unfair. They accused him of stealing equipment and material but were unable to prove any of their accusations."

"And did he by any chance take some of their proprietary wires... to make bombs for example?" Timo said and gave her a sarcastic grin.

She folded her hands in her lap, then looked up at him with eyes that seemed to go for the kill. "You think we breed killers and terrorists here?"

"That's not what we said...," Isa started.

"No, that's exactly what we're saying," Timo interrupted, much to the dismay of Isa.

"Again... do you have any proof?" Mrs. Lager shouted.

Timo and Isa stayed quiet.

"Well, then I demand that you leave my house this instant!"

* * *

Outside, Isa slapped Timo on the arm. "Why did you have to screw it up?"

He huddled into his coat, the cold biting his cheeks. "Do you really think she would've opened up to us?"

"Yes, but you were too impatient. You never give anyone a chance."

He shrugged, his focus on his bare hands turning pink in the frigid air. He'd left his gloves in the car.

"You don't have anything to add?" she asked, stopping in her tracks.

"Nope," he said, continuing his way to the car.

Isa shook her head and trailed behind him.

"Have you noticed how the wall was suddenly covered with pictures of the foster kids? You could clearly recognize Mila."

"Uh... no," Isa said.

"Those pictures weren't there before. It's almost like they wanted us to know Mila had been one of them. Why? And why now? I don't understand."

CHAPTER

16

LEIF BERG LOOKED UP from his newspaper as Timo entered the room. "To what do I owe this visit?" he asked, setting his coffee down beside the paper.

The Minister had been having his breakfast when Timo walked in, escorted by a serious-looking bodyguard dressed in black. After checking his badge, the guard had made him surrender his gun and reluctantly allowed Timo into the room.

"SÄPO is taking good care of you," Timo commented as he closed the door.

"It's a bit much, but I can't deny that the extra security is comforting," Leif replied, pointing to a chair in front of his table.

"Coffee? I've discovered a new Colombian blend."

"I won't say no to that," Timo said. Coffee was one of his passions, and he felt a surge of excitement whenever it was offered.

Leif grabbed his phone and called for more coffee. "Anything else?" he asked, hand over the microphone.

Timo shook his head.

"So, what brings you here? Solberg has been keeping me informed of the progress."

"We've been tracing the origin of the threatening emails you've been receiving." For a moment, he was struck by how similar they looked. He'd heard it before, but the blue eyes, the familiar face, it was all becoming so real.

"And?" Leif took a bite of his omelet.

"They were sent by Lauri Valkama, on behalf of Karst Engersson."

Leif's hand, holding the fork, froze mid-air. "Karst?" He put down the fork and leaned back, shaking his head in disbelief. "I trusted that man."

"It looks like it," Timo said, glancing quickly at the door.

A young woman entered, with bobbed brown hair, a white blouse, and tight black jeans that accentuated her curves. Leif gave her an appreciative once-over. He was clearly over his breakup with Sandra Arvidsson.

Timo felt an unexpected surge of discomfort. He glanced at the door, feeling like he needed an escape. The feeling was intense, and he couldn't explain why he was suddenly feeling so uneasy.

"Go ahead and try it," Leif said after the woman left and Timo stared at the cup in front of him.

His grip on the cup tightened as he tried to quell his anxiety, trying to rationalize that the coffee was just coffee.

Then Timo took a sip and was pleasantly surprised by its taste. The bitterness was just right, perfectly balanced with a smoothness that coated his mouth. It was 'a damn fine cup of coffee'. Only the pie was missing.

"Excellent," Timo said with a smile.

"Your mother told me that you appreciate a good cup of coffee now and then," Leif said.

"How do you know my mother again?"

"I knew your father, Yrjo."

"You knew him well?"

"No, we were just acquaintances. In politics, you can never really consider anyone a friend. Everyone is competition, and you have to be careful who you trust."

"I see... and my father was competition to you?"

Leif gave him a faint smile. "Maybe. But let's talk about Karst. Are you sure it was him?"

"Yes. And not only that, but we found out that he was paying Breiner for information about police operations and to tamper with evidence."

"Do you think he's responsible for Breiner's death? If Breiner wanted to talk, then Karst was not a witness, but his killer."

"I wouldn't go that far. But coming back to the emails you received, Engersson was not the client, but someone else was. They communicated via email. We found the computer from which the emails were sent in Stockholm."

"And that's where Global Law's headquarters are," Leif said as he took another sip of his coffee.

"And the headquarters of the Social Democrats."

Leif looked at him with a confused expression. "Are you saying that the IP address leads to my party, not Engersson?"

"It looks like someone from within your party is behind it," Timo said calmly.

"Who would betray me like this?"

The scene unfolded like a scene lifted from one of his mother's melodramatic films. Leif Berg, with his flair for grandiose dialogues and exaggerated acting, was putting on a captivating spectacle. However, Timo saw through the facade; he was sure Berg knew about the betrayal in his own party.

"I want you to find whoever is threatening me," Leif demanded, tossing his napkin onto the table, and causing the half-full cup of coffee to shake. He rose from the table and approached one of his bodyguards, speaking in hushed tones. Moments later, he turned back to Timo. "You have my permission to access the computers. I'll have my men let you in, regardless of whether you have a search warrant or not."

Timo raised an eyebrow at the ease of the task at hand. Why wasn't Berg calling in SÄPO to handle this?

"I'd like you and your lovely assistant to lead this investigation," Leif said.

"Chief Inspector Lindström," Timo corrected.

"She's chief inspector? Interesting. Women don't often go into that line of business."

"We all could benefit from a more balanced mix of men and women in our workforce."

Leif nodded in agreement. "A few months ago, we had a workshop dedicated to these issues. Many of our party members have advocated for greater diversity and inclusion."

"Members like Eirik Lunde?"

Leif looked straight at him. "I don't want to jump to conclusions. If he did something wrong, he should be held responsible for his actions, but I know him, and I'm sure there has been a misunderstanding."

Timo was puzzled. Why hadn't Berg taken any action against Lunde? It seemed like an obvious course of action given the circumstances. Despite all the talk and media attention, Eirik Lunde remained a member of the party, and no consequences had been imposed.

"Well, I have to be going now," Timo said, rising from the table. "We'll work with the police in Stockholm and SÄPO."

As Timo walked to the door, Leif called out to him, "Oh, and send my regards to your mother."

* * *

"Timo," Isa said.

He looked up at her, putting his pen down on the table. "What is it?"

She sat in the chair at her desk and placed the file she had been holding onto the desk in front of her.

"Valkama's secretary," she said.

He leaned forward, looking at her with a confused expression. "What about her?"

"She disappeared. I wanted to talk to her again about Valkama, but I couldn't reach her by phone. I've already gone to her house, but she's not there."

"Do you think she's the next victim?" Timo asked.

"I got suspicious. Olga Morosov doesn't exist... at least not anymore. She's been dead for six years."

"What? How can that be?"

"She used a false name. I checked and she started working for mayor Pehr Ek more than a year ago. She came with many recommendations, likely from the real Olga Morosov, but I don't know why they didn't do a thorough identity check."

"Then who is she?"

"Sivert ran her picture through the Interpol database and found a name: Olga Tomčić. She has an Albanian background and a history of arrests for drug trafficking, prostitution, theft, and murder. But she was never convicted. She always managed to escape."

"You think she poisoned Valkama?" Timo said.

"Yes. She was with him almost every day, making his tea, bringing his lunch, and had access to everything. She could have poisoned him. Valkama's wife said he started feeling sick a little more than a month before his death, when Olga became his secretary, when his former assistant got injured in a strange car accident."

"What kind of accident?" Timo asked.

Isa opened the file and skimmed through it. "It says here that she was driving home from work when her car suddenly swerved off the road and crashed into a tree. She suffered a concussion and some broken bones but survived. The police investigated but couldn't find any evidence of foul play. Her statement reads that she didn't know what had happened. She suffered a blackout, either from the accident or…"

"You think Morosov was responsible?"

"Could be. It's very convenient. Morosov took her place, so she could get closer to Valkama. She was also the one who told us about Valkama's frequent lunches outside the office, likely to mislead us."

Timo leaned back in his chair. "But he did go out more frequently the weeks before his death. From CCTV, we know he crossed the bridge and usually headed east along the river towards the harbor, but no one seems to remember him. We checked restaurants in the area but found nothing. We need to send out an international APB. Morosov may have left the country already. And we need a warrant to search her office."

"Heimersson has to approve it," Isa said.

"We'll go through Solberg."

"But she couldn't have done this alone."

"Most likely she was paid to do it."

"Then who was the client?" Isa asked.

Timo ran his hands through his hair and slammed his fist on the table. "We've been too focused on Berg and lost valuable time."

"This is all connected. But you're right, we're not seeing the full picture." Isa got up. "Berg wants to meet with me. We agreed to have dinner tomorrow."

"Dinner?"

"Yeah, I don't feel so comfortable about it."

"I'll come with you," Timo said.

"I can take care of myself. You make sure we find this Olga Tomčić."

Timo's gaze bore a sense of concern as he looked at her. He wasn't comfortable with her having dinner with Berg. The man was a predator.

* * *

"So, I was the target of the explosion," Leif said, setting down his fork.

Isa's gaze drifted to her plate of risotto, expertly crafted by the culinary maestros of one of Sweden's most esteemed gastronomic havens. It was a bit overwhelming. The elegant ambiance of this top-tier restaurant, nestled within the illustrious walls of a distinguished hotel, exuded an air of sophistication. Initially hesitant, she had contemplated suggesting a more neutral venue such as a police station for their meeting. But she eventually relented, giving in to his unwavering insistence.

"They knew you were staying at the Grand Hotel. Can you think of anyone who knew but wasn't aware you had to leave at the last minute?"

"I already talked to your colleague Timo a few days ago."

Isa raised an eyebrow. "Timo? He didn't mention that to me. What did he want?"

"He asked for access to our computer system. We have a mole," Leif said.

"He talked to you about that?"

"I thought he told you. I thought you and he were colleagues and... close," Leif said apologetically.

"We're just colleagues. He's not my type."

"Really?"

"Yes, really," she snapped.

"I don't understand how a man wouldn't find you attractive. You're beautiful, smart, and kind. There must be something wrong with him," Leif said.

Isa put down her fork, crossed her arms, and glared at him. "This makes me feel very uncomfortable."

"Let's not beat about the bush. I know what you want."

"Oh, really? What?" Isa asked.

"Power."

"And sleeping with you will give it to me?"

A cruel smirk appeared on his face.

"Just like Sandra Arvidsson," she said.

"Sandra? I let her go because she didn't do her job. She was too soft."

"She's pregnant with your baby. How could you abandon her?"

Leif put his hands on the table. "Be careful what you say. I can have you charged for defamation. And Sandra had her sights set on someone else from the start."

"Who?" Isa asked.

Leif just grinned and took a bite of his lamb stew. "She's a smart woman. Don't underestimate her."

"And why are you so interested in Timo? He's your son, isn't he? You and Valesca Ignatova. Why are you so afraid?"

Leif hesitated before saying, "I don't like children."

Isa sat stunned, feeling a mix of emotions. "You don't like children? What about Anna? What about your son?"

There was a long pause before Leif said, "Children leave and break their families' hearts."

"Anna?"

Leif nodded, his gaze shifting down to his plate.

She shook her head gently and responded, "No, it's not just about that. It's about power and control. The need to exert dominance. You thrive on admiration, and you struggle when the attention is shared with a child."

Leif's voice took on a sarcastic tone as he retorted, "Oh, of course,

I'm just a womanizer who sleeps with every woman I fancy, impregnates her, and then discards her. You're painting me as a monster."

She took a sip of the water. She didn't like the risotto anymore. There was something rotten about taking dinner from a man who could only think about himself. "You're a narcissist. You are only interested in me because you thought Timo and I were a couple. Jeezes! Do you want to hurt your own son that bad?"

"No comment," he said with a straight face.

"Paikkala didn't make superintendent. Was it because of you? And why is his brother really working for you? Is Fredrik leverage?"

He shook his head. "Separation of powers, remember? And you make it sound like I'm some kind of evil mastermind. I'm not that clever."

"But you are that ruthless."

"That's how you survive."

"You even use your dead daughter for that."

"I owe a lot to Anna. It was thanks to her that I was able to achieve the success I have today. People like stories about loss and tragedy, stories about how someone overcomes their problems, and then makes something of themselves. My story."

She knew there was an expression of horror and disgust on her face. She took a last gulp of the water and moved the chair back. "I assume there will be repercussions?"

"Maybe. Depends…"

"I don't think so."

"Too bad, but it is what it is."

"To think of it," she said and put on her jacket, "I don't think there will be any repercussions."

"Oh, why not?"

She held up her phone and pressed the button. "… you even use your dead daughter for that…"

"You taped everything?" he said with big eyes.

She said nothing as she continued to stare at the man's face, marred by his years of time spent in the Mediterranean sun. The old man with wrinkles that had looked at her with a raw animal lust during the entire conversation. The handsome man with beautiful blue eyes that might have seduced her if she hadn't been so disgusted by what he had told her.

"You leave Paikkala alone."

He folded his mouth into a sarcastic grin. "Interesting how protective you are of him. And how he was of you."

She ignored his comment but knew he had found her soft spot. She couldn't hide the fact she cared for Timo.

"I'll fight you with everything I have if you decide to use this," he said.

She pressed the button. "Care to repeat this, mister Secretary?"

He just smiled. "My team will work with you. Do your job. Make sure I'll survive this conference."

He pushed his chair away from the table, got up and told the server, "Put it on my room tab."

As he disappeared through the door of the dining room of the hotel, she felt both relieved and anxious.

CHAPTER

17

SHE THREW HER BODY BACK, her fingers clenched tightly around the pillars of the bed, letting the orgasm run through her entire body. She didn't know why she was crying. It had been so long ago. The moan that followed was one of joy and satisfaction. Beneath her, she felt him stiffen and then relax. Then she lay down next to him. The cold, empty spot on the bed sent shivers down her spine as she caressed her sweaty body and tingling limbs, the fading echoes of passion still coursing through her. It was then that the truth hit her like a thunderbolt.

Was this who she truly was? A woman who sought satisfaction in the arms of any man who showed interest in her? The man beside her let out a satisfied sigh, but all she felt was disgust with herself. The reality of her actions was like a cold shower, drenching her in guilt and shame.

"Well, how was it?" he said.

She didn't want to have that conversation. The next moment, she sat up in bed, ready to take her clothes from the floor. Her body trembled with the lingering lust that refused to dissipate.

"And?"

"Okay, I guess," Kristina said.

"Just okay? I thought fucking a Paikkala would be more than okay."

"The wrong Paikkala."

Fredrik sat up, looking at her with a certain look of superiority and contempt. "You didn't have a problem with that when you invited me to dinner and started flirting with me."

"It was a mistake."

"A mistake? Tell me something: why do all women seem to lust after my little brother, but end up in bed with me at the end of the day?"

She frowned and then looked at him intensely. "Are there more? Who are they?"

He smiled. "That's for me to know and for you to find out."

"Jesus, you're enjoying this. That's exactly why. Women don't trust you. Timo is decent and kind. You are, on the other hand, a fucking bastard!'

The words didn't seem to have the effect she had hoped for, "Sure, but don't underestimate my dearest brother. He can be cruel and vindictive."

"I doubt that," Kristina said, her voice shaking. She pulled the sweater over her head.

His expression grew serious, and he stared in front of him.

"I can't believe you two haven't resolved your issues by now," she said as she continued to dress.

"Stay for a while." He looked at her with such intensity, she thought she saw tears in his eyes. It froze her on the spot. She had never seen him this way before. Timo had introduced her to his brother years ago when he was still in Stockholm. It was some benefit concert; she wasn't sure what anymore. The rivalry between the brothers had been very clear, almost as if they were jealous of each other.

"I can't... I need to go. I have an appointment tomorrow morning and I need to be rested and fresh. A new case."

He kept his gaze fixed straight ahead, his eyes hollow. "He will never love you, Kristina. Never. Caijsa is preventing that. Or that lookalike he's running after."

"I've seen her," she said. Ingrid Olsson. The moment she saw Ingrid, she knew her chances with Timo were slim, even slimmer than before. She'd seen the looks Timo had thrown at Ingrid—looks of a love-struck man, secretive and full of passion. And Ingrid had done the same. Kristina had put her attention on Anton in a maybe misplaced attempt to make Timo jealous or make him see that Ingrid valued her husband more than him. But it turned out differently.

"Then you must know," he said, turning to the bedside table and quickly checking his phone.

"I need to go." She threw her coat over her shoulders and stepped towards the door.

She put her hand on the door handle, but then turned back and asked, "Are you going to be okay?"

"Yeah... Fredrik Paikkala is always okay," he said quietly, pulled the sheet over his naked body and turned his back to her.

She stepped outside with a nagging feeling of sadness, which deepened when she started to think about it during the way down to the lobby and outside when she ordered a taxi to her hotel.

She felt sorry for him.

Sex with Fredrik Paikkala had been confusing and disturbing.

* * *

Nelvin sat down on the white leather sofa and looked around. "Nice place."

"I'm sure you didn't come here to compliment me about my apartment," she said, her face stern and cold.

Valesca sighed and sat down on a chair opposite Nelvin. "What did you want to talk to me about?" she asked again in a tired voice.

On that Thursday evening, an evening with snow and wind, Valesca had been happy to stay inside—the warmth and comfort of her apartment were exactly what she wanted. The doorbell had rung, and when she'd answered it, she found Caijsa's stepfather, Nelvin, on her doorstep.

She didn't know the man that well. In fact, she had never felt the urge to get close to Caijsa's family. For years, she had secretly hoped the relationship between her youngest son and Caijsa would end. She had never deemed Caijsa worthy enough. She had seen right through her. From the outside, she appeared to be an intelligent, kind, and beautiful woman; in reality, she was a manipulator who had pushed her son until he had lost all confidence and lust for life.

She looked at Nelvin.

The overweight man, who had just walked a few steps from the elevator to her front door, was still panting. She had been accused of being posh and she had no problems admitting she was. The man on her sofa didn't live up to her standards. Old, unkempt, and even rude the way he had barged in and had dropped, uninvited, onto her sofa.

She gave him a look that was supposed to make him feel uncomfortable, but it didn't seem to have any effect. Instead, he just looked back at her with an expression that said: "I'm not going anywhere until I've said what I came here for."

"Do you want some water?" she asked politely as she walked back towards the kitchen after looking at him for another moment.

"I can put some coffee on or maybe a beer if you want something stronger," she added as she opened one of the cupboards where she kept all kinds of alcohol in case guests dropped by unexpectedly.

"No, thanks."

Nelvin took the papers from the bag he had put on the floor.

"What do you want to talk to me about?" she said as she returned from the kitchen.

"I can't stay long. Cal is going to pick me up."

"Cal?"

"My son. We went to see Lyn, my daughter."

His daughter, the killer, the psychopath. She didn't know how to react and decided to stay quiet.

"Well, why I'm here is…" He stopped, took a deep breath, and then looked at her. "Marcel, Caijsa's father, lied to your son."

She frowned. "What are you talking about?"

"Timo came to see us a few weeks ago about Caijsa's old medical files."

"Why?"

Ignoring her question, he reached out to give her the papers. "These are Caijsa's medical files. Marcel keeps them in a drawer in the living room. He knew very well where to find them when he told Timo he didn't know if he still had them. Marcel doesn't know I'm here."

Valesca frowned, took the file, and opened it. "Why give them to me?"

"It's bad. I thought giving them to Timo, but I think it's best you decide what to do. They lied to him. Caijsa, Paulina and Marcel. I can't blame them, but it's not fair to your son. I might be less emotionally invested, although I always loved Caijsa as my own daughter. But she could be a spoilt princess at times."

Valesca hadn't heard the last words. She was staring at the words on the page. 8 April 2010. Pregnancy termination.

"She had an abortion," Valesca said.

Pregnancy termination. The words seemed so decent, as if it hadn't been the worst thing that could have happened to her son.

"Why?"

Her fingers held the papers so tight her knuckles almost turned white.

"She wanted to leave Timo," Nelvin said calmly.

"How could she?" She kept staring at the paper.

"Valesca, I understand you..."

"She killed my grandchild. And you all knew?"

"Paulina found out and Caijsa told her everything. And Paulina told Marcel. I only found out recently after reading the files. I think Paulina must have kept them and given them to Marcel just before she died of cancer."

Valesca finally looked up. "What else are you hiding from us?"

"There is nothing..."

"Stop lying! What else didn't you tell me? This is going to ruin my son. Who was she having an affair with?"

"I don't know."

"Stop lying!"

He sighed, then took a book from the bag at his feet.

"What's that?"

"Caijsa's diary," Nelvin whispered.

"Why do you have it?"

"I found it in Paulina's things when she died."

"You read it?"

"Not everything, but enough to know it's explosive."

"I... I can't take the responsibility," she said and put it on the table next to the one-seater. "What do you want me to do with this?"

"It's not my place either to decide," he said calmly. "I might not like him, but Timo is your son. You read it or not. It's up to you. You have a responsibility as a parent to protect him. We all have."

Her heart sank. The words hit her like a slap, and she felt them echo in her soul. He was right. Even though she'd never been a traditional mom, she needed to take care of her son, even if he were in his mid-thirties. He was still her baby boy.

Nelvin leaned over and looked at his hands. "She... Paulina was so devastated by Caijsa's death. When Thorgan Elker, Caijsa's supposed murderer, was arrested, and convicted there was a time when she found some peace of mind, but then he wrote to us. I think it was in 2015 or so, just before he died. He wanted to talk to her. She went, with Marcel."

He stopped for a moment.

"And?"

"Thorgan Elker told them he was innocent, but he remembered only bits and pieces. But it was enough. Immediately the suspicion was back."

"The suspicion?"

"For a while, Paulina thought Timo had killed Caijsa. She thought he knew that Caijsa wanted to leave him, and that he also knew about her abortion. After Thorgan's arrest, Paulina's suspicions went away, but after that meeting in prison, she was convinced Timo had set the whole thing up. Breiner poisoned her mind even more. She was adamant to prove your son's guilt and then Breiner died, and she got sick."

Valesca gasped for air. "So, all this time you thought Timo had killed Caijsa?"

She couldn't believe what she was hearing. All the people who had cared for her son—the people he had trusted—had lied to him.

"I tried to convince Paulina that Breiner was manipulating her, that it wasn't true, but she wouldn't listen."

"Is that why Paulina was reluctant to meet my son?" Valesca asked, her voice trembling. "When she became ill, he wanted so much to see her again... one last time before she died."

"I made up excuses for her. Let him believe that she didn't want him to see her like that, but she hated Timo."

"Why keep up the appearance? Did you think Timo would confess, or would finally betray himself? What was it?"

He took a deep breath and looked at her. "I know and I wish it hadn't gone that way, but you have to understand..."

She cut him off mid-sentence with a wave of her hand. "I have to understand? Really? How could any of you believe that my son could have killed Caijsa? She wasn't worth it. That bitch! I just knew it. That woman was nothing but trouble."

Nelvin got up without saying a word and shuffled to the door without looking back at her. "I need to go. Cal will be waiting."

She looked at him. "Who did she have an affair with? I ask you again."

Nelvin sighed and said, "Read the diary. Then you'll understand."

CHAPTER

18

"**You look bad,**" **Valesca said.**

Timo fixed his gaze on his mother as he took a sip of coffee. "I feel like I'm suffocating."

"What's bothering you, Timofey?" Valesca asked, her Russian accent lending a melodic quality to her words. "Tell me everything, my darling. It breaks my heart to see you like this."

Timo rolled his eyes. "Oh, mom... life isn't just a stage for you to perform," Timo replied, his eyes intense. "I guess I just thought you could listen for once instead of making it about you."

Valesca seemed stunned, then looked away. "If you don't want my help, then why did you ask me over?"

Timo drew in a deep breath, the frustration melting away. He had overreacted again. He cursed himself silently for pushing her away, a reaction that had become almost instinctive. He had to take control of the situation and defuse the tension between them.

"I'm surprised," he said with a serious expression on his face and took another sip.

"About what?"

"You haven't lectured me about my bad choice in interior design."

She smiled. "I wouldn't dare." Then she reached out and took his hand. "But I'm worried. You look sad, so very sad."

He gazed at her intently, seeing past the wrinkles and age spots to the stunning woman she had once been. She had given up everything—her homeland, career, and family—for Yrjo Paikkala, the dashing Finnish diplomat she had met at a movie promotion dinner. He wondered if she ever regretted it, the sacrifices she had made for love. A love that had been challenging and disappointing at times.

Timo grasped her hand. "Many things in my life are not okay. I'm just… glad you're here."

"Ingrid?"

He let go of her hand and then said, in surprise, "How do you know about her?"

"I'm your mother. I know everything."

"George told you."

"Perhaps," Valesca replied, her voice gentle but firm. "But I sense you may still be holding onto Caijsa too tightly. You need to move forward. You were doing so well the last years and now it almost seems like you're back to square one. You are desperately clinging to her memory, which is not a healthy way to grieve. And as for Ingrid, you must remember that she is married. Are you willing to break up a marriage?"

He hadn't noticed the tension in her voice when she mentioned Caijsa's name.

"Yeah... talking about married women and men, isn't it time you told me about Berg?"

She walked to the window and stood there looking out at the lake. The water sparkled in the weak sunlight, as if it were covered with tiny lights that danced over it.

"What do you want to know?" she said and turned around to face him.

"Is he my father?"

She stood still, like she needed a moment to contemplate, her eyes darting around the room as if she was fighting an inner battle with herself.

"Mom? Please, tell me."

She took a deep breath and then shook her head.

"But... I look like him."

She sighed with annoyance and then walked back to where he was sitting at the kitchen island. "Oh, Timofey. I'm sorry to disappoint you, but he's not."

He wiped a tear from his face. "Then who is?"

She shook her head. "No, Timo, I can't tell you."

"Why? Is he dead?"

There was a moment of hesitation. "Yes, he's dead."

He sighed and looked down at his hands, feeling defeated. "I don't understand why you won't tell me. Why keep it a secret?"

His mother's expression softened, and she reached out to touch his hand. "It's complicated, Timo. I'm grateful to him... for you, but that's all. He is out of the picture, and he should stay there."

Timo looked up at her, his eyes pleading. "I deserve to know."

"Why? Yrjo was your father. That's all you need to know. I'm sorry I told him about my affair. I know it made your relationship complicated. Yrjo was so disappointed. He loved you, but he couldn't hide that he felt different after my confession."

"I wish you hadn't told him," Timo said. He could barely hold his emotions.

"Oh Timofey, my dear," Valesca embraced him tightly, feeling his pain as he broke down in her arms. She held him as he released the pent-up emotions of recent days and all the hardships he had silently endured. Her gentle strokes soothed him as he cried, until he finally regained composure and pulled away from her embrace.

"I don't blame you... I know you never wanted this," he said and kissed her on the forehead.

"I love you with all my heart. Yrjo was your father and no one else."

"And Berg?"

"Yrjo knew him. He was this ambitious, young lawyer. I knew that one day he would go into politics. And he did."

"When did you meet him?"

"Fredrik must have been one or so, and there was a dinner organized by the Chamber of Commerce in New York. And there he was: Leif Berg. What a beautiful man he was, distinguished and with such a charisma that people wanted to talk to him and be with him. I'd never seen a man like that before. But he was already married at that time. His wife was pregnant with their first child. Anna."

He turned his head away from her and looked out the window. "Anna Berg."

She nodded. "It was a complicated marriage though."

He frowned. "Why do you say that?"

She dropped in the chair at the kitchen island. "It was a tumultuous relationship. Her jealousy was constant, and he took pleasure in fueling it, turning it into a twisted game."

"He had affairs back then?" Timo said.

"I don't think so. That only started after Anna disappeared. Rumor is Masja, his wife, resented herself for not being there when it happened. She withdrew from public life. They stayed together but I know Berg blamed his wife. And then he started to look for love elsewhere."

"Were there any signs he abused those women?" Timo said.

She thought about it for a moment and shook her head. "No, but then again everything was so different those days. Things were easily put under the carpet. There were rumors though that he had a relationship with a flight attendant, that he wanted to run off with her and marry her."

"What happened?"

"I don't know, but he stayed with Masja." She took his hand and squeezed it. "Look, there was never anything between Berg and myself. Yes, he flirted with me, and maybe I liked it, but he never did anything inappropriate. When I met him in Fredrik's office, I hadn't seen him for over ten years."

Timo ran his hands through his hair. "Then why is he behaving like that?"

"He's messing with you. He's good at it. It's like a game to him. I must say the Berg of today is not the same man as forty years ago. I could feel it when we had dinner. He's... slick and egocentric... hard on the people around him. Be careful."

He gave her a faint smile. "I'll be careful. No worries."

She smiled, let her hand slide over his face before taking his hands in hers. "You are such a beautiful man. I'm so proud of you. Caijsa doesn't deserve your tears."

He looked down. "She betrayed me."

The revelation sent a jolt of shock through her body, and she felt her fingers twitch in his grip.

"Did you know?" he said.

She took her hand away. "No, I didn't."

He narrowed his eyes at her. "Are you sure? The way you've been acting—it's like you know something."

"Timo... I don't know. I really don't know."

*　*　*

The next morning, Timo was consumed by uncertainty. The constant anxieties plagued him, hindering his ability to focus on work. He found himself gazing out the window, lost in thought and waiting for something that would never come. Thoughts of Anton, Caijsa, and Berg swirled in his mind, shrouded in a veil of confusion. The clarity he had felt before had vanished, leaving only pain and guilt in its wake. He was plagued by the pain of Caijsa's betrayal and the embarrassment he felt over her taking him hostage in his grief for so many years. She hadn't deserved it. He needed to speak to Marcel again, but he was afraid of what he might hear. Timo had picked up his cell phone so many times, ready to make the call, but each time he had put it down, unwilling to face the truth.

He checked his phone and saw a message from Isa. She was in Stockholm, talking to Berg and his entourage. Timo tried to refocus on his work, but the complete forensic report on Mila Hillborg was still missing, and thoughts of Ingrid occupied his mind.

In the past, Ingrid would have been there to help him navigate the report, and their work was often an excuse for them to spend time together. Now, she was gone, and Timo missed her. He had told her they couldn't be just friends, but now he felt foolish for even suggesting it. If being friends was all he could have, he would take it.

Feeling frustrated, Timo closed the file and decided to call it a day. He grabbed the papers, put on his jacket, and drove home.

*　*　*

In the comfort of his home, he found his energy back and his mind wandered from Lauri Valkama to the bomb explosion in the hotel. He had failed to convince Finn to allow Isa and himself to be involved in the investigation. And the more he thought about it, the more he was convinced that they had been left out on purpose. Kristoffer Solberg had passed Isa the information Finn had withheld from them. Those papers were now scattered over the table in his living room.

He looked out the large window and saw that it had stopped snowing. Darkness had settled over the land. At 3 p.m. it felt already like night.

The doorbell rang and he looked up surprised, not expecting anyone. Somewhere in the back of his mind though he had heard a car pulling into the driveway, but it wasn't until now that this fact registered.

He frowned as he saw Ingrid silhouetted in the doorway. Somehow, it seemed like a déjà vu. Only this time she didn't passionately kiss him as he opened the door. "Ingrid? Why are you here?"

"The full report on Lars and Mila," she said, pushed the file in his hands, and then walked inside without waiting for an invitation.

"Do come in...," he said surprised.

She unbuttoned her coat. "I thought you might be interested."

"Thanks, but this could have waited until Monday."

Her hands were almost balled into fists and her shoulders were hunched high. She was angry. Did he do something wrong? She had walked into his home with an air of confidence and arrogance, as if she owned the place. So unlike her.

"I'm all by myself today and the entire weekend with nothing to do," she said. "Anton took the boys skiing."

"Oh, okay... but still this could have waited," he said and then opened the file.

"Looking at the state of his body, Lars must have been close to the explosion."

Timo stared at the papers and frowned. "He probably confronted the bomber." He didn't want to think about Ingrid, who was pacing up and down the living room like she needed to blow off steam.

Women. It was best not to confront them when they were obviously in a bad mood.

"We found a gun in the debris," she said. "A 9mm."

He stared at her for a moment before responding. "We use 9mm Sig Sauer handguns."

"We couldn't trace the serial number. The heat of the explosion melted part of the gun. We still need to check if Lars' or Berger's gun is missing."

"What are you saying? Why would any of them bring a gun to the wedding?"

"I don't know. Berger still claims he can't remember anything."

"What about Mila?"

When she didn't answer, he continued, "No, there needs to be another possibility. It must be."

He looked at Ingrid, but it was clear she hadn't heard a word he had said.

"I'll talk to Solberg first thing on Monday and..."

"I want to ask you something," she interrupted him.

"Uh... what?"

"Do you love her?"

He was confused. "What do you mean? Who?"

"Kristina."

He couldn't speak, rooted to the ground by her question.

She continued like she needed to get it all off her chest, "You went with her to the wedding, and you have known her already for so long. Are you interested in her?"

Ingrid's eyes were locked on him, stern and staring, but on the verge of tears that made her look vulnerable.

"I..."

"I saw you, outside our house. Several times. Don't deny it! Why were you there?"

He gasped for air. Anton had seen him, but so had she.

"Do you want to be with me or with her?" she asked.

"You made it very clear we have no future, remember? I don't see why I shouldn't move on."

"So, you want to be with her," she snapped.

"You're jealous."

"No... maybe... yes, I'm jealous." She paused. "I just..."

She stopped and took a deep breath. "I just can't stand the thought that she would kiss you, touch you or even think of you. Because..."

He held his breath.

She looked out the window, as if to order her thoughts, to gather courage for what she was about to say next. "Because you're mine, only mine. I've been faced with death twice in the last months and that does something to a human being. It made me realize that waiting isn't an option anymore; it's time I went after my dreams before they slip away from me completely. And I... we have kept these feelings bottled up inside for far too long."

Her monologue wasn't over. And he was watching her, frozen almost, with the file still in his hands.

Ingrid took another deep breath and continued her speech. She was too focused on what she wanted to say to notice he still hadn't moved a muscle. "That evening, here in this house with your arms around me, has been going through my mind over and over again. It kept me awake at night as I thought about how it would feel to be held by you again. It has distracted me at work and has pulled me away from my role as a mother and a wife. I want that again. I want you. All of you. For me."

He couldn't resist it any longer. With a sudden burst of courage, Timo dropped the papers, seized Ingrid's face in his hands and kissed her. Her response was immediate, her arms wrapping around him tightly as she kissed him back with equal fervor. Then their mouths parted briefly, their breaths ragged as they gazed at each other with a newfound intensity.

In a desperate need for more, Timo kissed her again, and she moaned softly, her hands sliding down his back and pulling him even closer. His hands explored her body, trailing down her spine and gripping her hips, drawing her towards him as they deepened their kiss.

They allowed themselves to get lost in the moment, their bodies responding instinctively to each other's touch. But as they pulled away from each other, they both knew that it was just a temporary respite from reality.

"This... this can't happen," Timo gasped, his forehead resting against hers as they both tried to catch their breath.

Ingrid's eyes met his, and he could see the same strange mix of fear and longing reflected in them. "I know," she whispered, her voice thick with emotion. "But just for tonight, can we forget about everything else and be together?"

Timo hesitated for a moment, his mind racing with conflicting emotions. But then he saw the longing in her eyes, the same need he felt burning inside him. And in that moment, he knew he couldn't deny her or himself any longer.

CHAPTER

19

THE ROOM FELT FAMILIAR AND STRANGE at the same time. It was their old house, but everything felt slightly off, like the colors were slightly brighter, the shadows were deeper, and the shapes were more pronounced. The couch was new and the pictures on the wall were gone. Tuva tried to recall the memories attached to this place, but they seemed distant, as if they belonged to another person.

She was alone, but she heard a faint sound, like a voice in the distance, calling out to her. It seemed to be coming from upstairs, and she followed. The sound grew louder as she climbed the steps, until she reached her mother's old bedroom. The door was ajar, and the sound was now a distinct cry. Tuva forcefully thrust the door open, only to be confronted with a scene she believed she had long abandoned.

Her mother was lying on the bed, writhing in pain, just as she had on that fateful day. Her mother's eyes were wide and filled with terror as she saw things that weren't there. "Tuva! Make it stop! Make the demons go away!"

Tears streamed down Tuva's face as she watched the same horror play out before her. The voice in her head became her mother's voice, begging for help and calling out for her. Tuva tried to move, to do something, anything to save her, but she was frozen, unable to act.

She tried to scream, but no sound came out. The scene continued until her mother took her last breath and everything went silent.

Tuva woke up in a cold sweat, her heart racing, feeling like she'd just lost her mother all over again.

"Mom," she whispered.

Never had the absence of her mother been more profound than in that moment. Tuva had always known the loss was real, but now, it felt like a part of her had been torn away.

She sat up, trying to chase the chill from her bones. It was then that she realized the dream had felt more like a memory. She had truly been transported back in time to witness her mother's final moments. The fear was unmistakable, and she found herself looking around, as if seeking comfort from familiar surroundings. Her makeshift shelter, however, offered no solace. The bare, concrete floor and the thin blanket that served as her bed provided no comfort. Shivers ran down Tuva's spine as she longed for the days when she could rest peacefully in her own bed. The vivid memories of her bedroom back home, adorned with a comforting, vibrant comforter that cocooned her in warmth and safety, flooded her mind. The striking disparity between that cherished haven and the meager, worn-out blanket that barely shielded her now served as a painful reminder of what she had lost and the emptiness she felt.

She was homeless and on the run, constantly searching for a safe place to hide. The memories of her mother's suffering and the fear of being caught alternated with vivid dreams of Greta's dead body.

She tried to shake off the remnants of the dream and focus on the present. She needed to find a new place to lay low and figure out her next move.

She listened to the sounds. It was so quiet. And so cold. Her fingers felt numb. She couldn't recall if it had ever been so cold.

Her makeshift hiding place was made from scraps of cardboard and worn-out blankets, wedged between dumpsters and the unyielding wall of an apartment building. It was a desperate refuge, offering little protection against the harsh weather. She couldn't risk going to homeless shelters where the man would surely find her.

She wrapped the blanket tighter around her and lay back down, willing herself to fall back asleep and escape the haunting memories for a little while longer.

But no matter how hard she tried, she couldn't shake off the feeling of being watched. Her mind raced with paranoia again as she wondered if someone had discovered her hiding place. She was afraid of what might happen if she was caught. She knew she had to stay alert, to stay alive.

So, she stayed awake, listening to the sounds of the night and her own ragged breathing, until the first light of dawn began to creep through the alley.

* * *

Ingrid gazed at her reflection, taking in the curves of her body. As she ran her hands over her torso, she relived the sensation of his touch, the warmth of his embrace as he had drawn her into his arms. The memories brought a rush of excitement, quickening her pulse and making her yearn for it again. The lust in his eyes was unmistakable, a fiery passion that had consumed them both. Their lovemaking was beyond anything Ingrid had ever experienced, surpassing the bounds of simple pleasure and leaving her craving more. The emotion in his eyes at the height of passion was a breathtaking and bittersweet sight, a memory that would stay with her forever.

She glanced down at her belly, taking in the changes brought by two pregnancies. The once-toned stomach now carried a bit of extra weight, causing her confidence to waver. She wondered why he found her attractive when he could easily have his pick of more beautiful women. He was attractive, while she saw herself as plain and frumpy, lacking the appeal of someone like Isa.

She remembered the excitement and attraction of their first meeting and their first secret kiss. But those moments of happiness quickly gave way to overwhelming guilt and shame for her affair. The weight of her actions burdened her, and she tried to push aside the flood of conflicting emotions that overwhelmed her.

Deep within her struggle for emotional balance, a piercing question arose—what kind of mother was she, prioritizing her own happiness over her sons' well-being? And the thought of Anton, her loving husband who trusted her completely, weighed heavily on her. The memory of their wedding vows echoed in her mind. But despite her love for Anton, she dreamt of being with Timo.

Who was this woman in the mirror? She didn't recognize herself. This wasn't her. This couldn't be her.

She yearned for clarity and respite from the storm of emotions that threatened to engulf her. She longed to find a path that would reconcile her desires with her principles, but there was no easy way.

She heard the window slide open and then close again, jolting her out of her thoughts. It was a freezing -10° outside and she'd woken up to a fresh blanket of snow. He was nowhere to be seen. As she had made her way to the downstairs bathroom, she was reminded of a time months ago when she had stumbled upon a picture of his late girlfriend.

Now, she had taken her place.

She went upstairs to get dressed. Her clothes were scattered across the bedroom floor with his. The remnants of their passionate night together lay scattered on the floor of his room.

Then she made her way to the living room. There he was, sitting outside on a wooden bench, bundled up in a blue woolen blanket despite the below-freezing temperatures. He sipped steaming coffee from a cup, placed on an old metal table in dire need of a fresh coat of paint.

As she stepped outside, he turned his head and greeted her with a warm smile.

"It's breathtaking out here," Ingrid commented, taking in the winter wonderland before her. Snow clouds, a mixture of silver and dark, loomed in the sky, occasionally allowing rays of sunlight to peek through. The tree branches drooped under the weight of snow, adding to the idyllic scene.

This was a place where she could escape from reality and simply watch as snowflakes fell to the ground.

He sat silently, staring ahead. She could feel the tension in the air between them.

"I think I need to go," she said softly.

He suddenly turned and took her hand. She could feel the stubble on his cheek as she let her fingers run over his skin. Tears filled her eyes. This whole situation wasn't fair.

"Don't go," he whispered.

She knelt beside him and took his face in her hands.

"I need to," she replied, her voice filled with regret. "We knew this could never be."

She felt guilty for dragging him into this affair, but she had been so caught up in her own feelings. She was a selfish woman.

"I'll do anything you want," he said, his voice shaking. "Stay with me."

She took his hands and kissed them, feeling the weight of her decision. She put her head on his shoulder and looked out at the water. A sense of peace washed over her.

She had crossed a line that could never be mended. But despite the hurt and betrayal, this moment would be something she would always cherish.

* * *

Kristoffer Solberg removed his glasses and rubbed his face, looking even more tired than in recent weeks. He gazed at Berger's file in front of him as Isa watched him expectantly for an answer. The small meeting room, where she had summoned him to discuss the SÄPO report released that morning, was uncomfortably hot. Still struggling with the aftermath of her confrontation with Leif Berg over the weekend, Isa had woken up to a blazing headache. Every word that came out of Kristoffer's mouth grated on her nerves.

Isa took a sip of her coffee, the bitterness matching her sour mood.

"Let's start with Olga Tomčić," Kristoffer said.

"Yeah, let's," Isa replied, a hint of annoyance in her voice.

"Interpol informed us that she was spotted in Germany, but they failed to apprehend her. She arrived in Berlin airport a week ago, but we were too late. National authorities are still searching for her, but we have to assume we won't find her."

"Did you find anything more on her?"

"Not much, but with the help of CCTV, we found the house where she was staying in Varva. She used another false name. She left in a hurry."

"What did you find there?"

"Explosives, guns, and bottles containing..."

"Scopolamine," Isa finished.

He nodded. "But we still don't know who ordered Valkama's murder.

We have to assume it wasn't her idea."

"Any phone or financial records?"

"No," he replied. "She left no evidence."

"Any link to the hotel explosion? You mentioned finding explosives," she continued.

"Not the same type as what was used at the Grand Hotel. We don't think she was involved," he said.

Isa leaned back in her chair. She vaguely remembered the woman at the start of the wedding party. Could it have been Olga Tomčić?

"You believe Berger was involved in the explosion and Mila wasn't. That doesn't make sense."

Kristoffer's forced smile vanished and he glanced nervously at the door, as if making sure it was closed.

"What's going on?" Isa asked, sensing his unease.

"Nothing."

"Explain it to me. I'm lost. They found wires and evidence of explosives on Mila."

He was visibly torn about what to do next. "Mila was... an undercover agent."

"What?"

Kristoffer walked to the window, his face looking sad in the daylight.

"Why?" she pressed.

"Months ago, we received intelligence that there was a threat to public safety and Sweden's stability. Mila had been working to gather information about a network of corrupt cops and was attempting to infiltrate it."

"Here in Gävle?"

"Yes. But Mila got too involved. I don't think it was part of the plan, but her relationship with Berger made her biased."

"In Gävle? Why target Gävle?"

"I'm sorry," he said.

"You thought we were all dirty cops?"

He walked back to the table, placed both hands on it, and leaned in. "It wasn't about you or Wieland. It was about Paikkala."

"Paikkala?"

"As soon as we discovered his connections to Breiner and his eagerness to take on the Gävle assignment, we became suspicious of him. That's when Internal Affairs were called in to investigate the department, here in Gävle and in Stockholm where he worked before."

She studied his face. He avoided eye contact.

"No, it wasn't Paikkala," she said, shaking her head.

"Please, don't ask me more."

"You started it. It was Heimersson, wasn't it?"

Kristoffer closed his eyes as silence filled the room. She imagined the soft sound of snowflakes hitting the window, an illusion like so many things these days. But one thing she knew, he couldn't take away from her, was that Timo was a good cop. A man who genuinely wanted to seek the truth.

"Yes, Heimersson," he finally said. "It all started months ago."

"What did Mila uncover?"

"I can't reveal the information she obtained, but because of her we managed to set up the meeting between Berg and our informant," he said with a shrug. "And that failed miserably…"

"Who is this informant?"

Kristoffer shook his head. "We don't know his real name, neither did Mila. She tried for months and finally managed to find someone who was willing to talk. All communication went via chats and emails. He was going to reveal himself that evening. It was Mila's wedding, but we decided that it was best to involve her. She even proposed it. We haven't heard from him anymore after the explosion. He's lying low. This is a disaster. We worked so hard to get this done."

"Do you think she was framed?"

"We have witnesses who saw Mila leave the party a half-hour before the explosion. We don't know where she went, but likely to the second floor."

"Why?"

"She wasn't supposed to be there. She just needed to keep an eye, in case something went wrong. I can only speculate that Mila received a warning about something happening. The last message she sent to her handler before she died was short and didn't reveal anything suspicious."

"What about Berger?"

"Several witnesses saw him at the party, but not the entire time," he replied.

She frowned. "Are you suggesting that Berger was involved, and Mila discovered it?"

"I'm simply saying that there could be more to this than meets the eye. Mila's investigation may have initially focused on Heimersson and Paikkala, but she was determined to marry Berger Karlsson. Why? Perhaps she suspected him."

"And so, she decided to marry him. Looks farfetched to me."

"Maybe you're right," he said with a shrug. "But somebody wanted to eliminate Leif Berg. That much is clear."

"Or wanted to kill your informant?"

"Maybe," he said.

"And what did Internal Affairs discover about Heimersson?"

"I'm afraid I don't have access to his file. Only those with the highest security clearance can view it."

She stood up, convinced that a shadow had just flitted across the window. But she realized it was just her mind playing tricks on her. She turned to the man who sat slouched in the chair on the other side of the room.

"So, is Heimersson involved or not?" she asked.

"It's strange that Internal Affairs is keeping his file confidential, and that commissioner Eriksson sent him to Gävle."

"What is his role here?"

"I don't know for sure, but the planned police restructuring will transfer power from the regional bodies to the national level. Gävleborg is crucial to these plans. There's resistance from both the Left Party and the Sweden Democrats. Their conflicting ideologies are the only obstacle to the government's plans. And they clash over here. If the Social Democrats continue to support the Sweden Democrats' proposal for reinstating life imprisonment without parole, they'll lose the Left Party's support."

"So, what happens in Gävleborg could shape the future of policing in Sweden?"

"It could be the case," he said.

"But the Social Democrats just won the election."

"They did, but they lost votes to the right-wing Sweden Democrats. Prime Minister Olav Hult is facing a crisis after the Eirik Lunde sex scandal. And he's losing support within his own party."

"Lunde was Leif Berg's campaign manager, though," she said.

"Leif's popularity has barely been affected. Hult's has declined."

"We need to find out who Mila was investigating," she said, feeling overwhelmed by the magnitude of the situation. "And who the informant is."

Kristoffer straightened his shoulders and turned his head away from her. She could tell he was feeling unsure.

"I'll try to find out more, but I need to be careful. Berg knows more and so does Hult."

"There is another possible angle to the story," Isa said suddenly.

"What?"

"That Mila did this."

"No, no," he shouted.

Caught off guard by his intense response, Isa pressed further. "Why not?" But as soon as the words left her lips, she understood. The pieces fell into place. "Oh, Kristoffer... really?!"

"It's not like that," Kristoffer said. "I was her instructor and mentor in the police, and she was like a younger sister to me. I felt the need to protect her."

He tried to hide his tears and heartache over her death, but it was obvious.

"I remember the first time I saw her in a Stockholm coffee shop," he said. "She wore a bright red sweater and had a smile that lit up the room. Yeah, she was my friend."

"What was she really like? From what we know right now she was playing a role. We never got to see the real Mila. Even the descriptions we got from the Lagers felt distant and incomplete."

Kristoffer described Mila as a righteous and honest person, someone who would never be suspected of committing a crime. "I believe the bomber killed her after she caught him."

As he spoke, the city lights flickered on outside, casting a dim glow over the room. Isa shivered, feeling a sense of unease.

"Lars had a feeling that something was wrong," she said, her eyes narrowing in thought. "I think he followed Mila, which is why he was killed. And Berger knows more than he's letting on. We need to get him to talk, but it won't be easy. He's still in critical condition, and he'll need multiple surgeries and a long rehabilitation."

"I agree," Kristoffer said.

"Paikkala can help. Berger respects him, and I think he's hiding stuff out of shame. Timo is the right person to get through to him."

"I hope so," Kristoffer said, "because Berger's at the top of the suspect list right now."

* * *

Tuva stood outside the police station, her body frozen with fear and uncertainty. She had just narrowly escaped a knife attack in a deserted alley and could feel the tremors in her body from the adrenaline rush. Tuva knew she couldn't keep running. Fear had kept her going for so long, but now it was time to face the fact that she couldn't do this alone. She had to decide, and now was the time.

She took a deep breath and began walking towards the building, not daring to look back. The woman at the counter looked up from her papers as Tuva approached, and the fear and loneliness of weeks of hiding hit her all at once. Tuva broke down in tears and through the sobs she told the woman that she had seen a murder and needed help as she was being followed by someone who wanted to kill her.

The police officer took Tuva to a room and asked for her name and address. Tuva, her eyes fixed on her dirty hands, mumbled that she had no home and started to tell her story in fragments. The officer reassured her and promised to return with detectives to take a full statement.

Tuva stared at the white walls. A hooded man had tried to stab her. She tried to recall the last attack. Somehow it didn't feel like the same man.

An hour had passed by the time a man and woman in plain clothes entered. The woman introduced herself as Inspector Lindström and the man as Inspector Paikkala. They asked Tuva to recount her story once more.

"Do you know the name of the man who attacked you?" Isa asked.

Tuva's gaze shifted from Timo to her hands. Then she shook her head.

"Okay, can you describe him?"

The girl's eyes grew large. "It was dark, and I was so scared." Her words were soft, her tone barely above a whisper.

"We can have a sketch artist work with you," Isa said and looked at her partner.

Timo was quiet today. He looked worried. Isa decided to leave him alone. She had thought about telling him about Leif and their conversation, but she had backed off.

Tuva's eyes welled up with tears. "He knew where I lived. He knows my friends. Greta..."

She hid her face in her hands.

"Did he kill Greta?" Timo asked.

Tuva looked down and nodded silently, the tears now streaming down her face. "I think so. I found her."

"Why would he kill her?" Timo probed, but Isa shot him an angry look.

Tuva looked at them, her expression filled with confusion. "I don't know. Maybe he was looking for me."

"And you were looking for Greta. Why?" Timo asked.

"I needed help, and in the past, she was always there for me. I trusted her."

"If you want our help, you have to be more forthcoming," Isa told her.

Tuva let out a heavy sigh, her eyes filled with deep sadness. "Greta often hung around the harbor, and sometimes she would... uh... have sex with men for money. But if she wasn't with men, she loved watching the boats, so I knew I might find her there."

But there was a fleeting flicker in her gaze, a momentary pause that had caught Timo's attention. He pressed on, "I still don't understand why you were looking for Greta. How could she have helped you?"

"Rolf told me he saw her with two strange men, and I was worried they were after me. I wanted to know what they had told her. But I was wandering around the docks when I saw those two men. One of them looked familiar."

"Was it the man who attacked you?" Isa asked.

Tuva hesitated. "I'm not sure. Like I said, it was dark, and I was scared. I waited until they left and then I went over to see what they were doing. That's when I found her. Dead in the snow."

"And then?"

Tuva wiped away a tear. "I was so scared; I didn't know what to do."

"Why did you leave?" Timo asked.

"I panicked... I saw her lying there. So much blood. She died because of me."

"But you don't know for sure," Timo said.

"Why else would someone kill her?"

Timo's frustration became clear. "How did you know she was dead? Did you even try to help her?"

"I just knew," Tuva snapped, her voice laced with irritation. "I've seen my fair share of frozen bodies on the streets. Her skin was pale, and she was ice-cold."

"Did you touch anything else besides her face and hands?"

"I think I touched the knife too. But I was in shock, I dropped it as soon as I realized what I had done."

"Why did you go to the docks?" Timo continued his line of questioning.

Tuva narrowed her eyes. "I told you... I wanted to talk to Greta about those men. And she knew people where I could hide and disappear for a while."

"Where did you go after finding Greta?"

"Everywhere, nowhere."

Timo's voice grew stern. "That's not an answer. Where?"

Isa placed a hand on Timo's arm, but he pulled away. Then Isa said, "Let's give Tuva some time. We'll figure this out and get a description of the attackers. We'll keep you safe."

"Like witness protection?" Tuva asked.

"Yes, I'm not sure how it will work but we'll find a way," Isa replied.

Tuva's eyes flickered with a sudden calmness, and she leaned back in her chair. Isa looked at her for a moment, taking in her childlike face with its disarming smile and shrewd, knowing eyes. Despite her petite stature, Tuva had a natural beauty that captivated those around her. Her expression showed both innocence and wisdom, reflecting the deep understanding beyond her years. It revealed the strength and maturity she had acquired from her experiences as a homeless person.

Then Isa turned to Timo. It was clear Timo didn't agree with Isa's proposal, given the look on his face.

* * *

"What the hell was that?" Isa said and stopped Timo from walking back to his desk. "Don't you believe her?"

"What do we really know about her? Nothing."

"She's homeless and she needs help," Isa said.

"So why didn't she come to us after he attacked her a first time?"

"Homeless people are usually wary of the police. They like to fix things themselves."

"She's smart. She knows what's at stake. Why would she take the advice of unreliable people like Rolf and Greta? I think she knows who attacked her."

Isa frowned. "Why would she lie about that?"

For a moment he didn't know what to say, "I don't know... unless there is something else, she doesn't want us to know. What is she hiding?"

"She's scared. I don't think she's faking that."

He shook his head as if to get it all straight in his mind. "She's scared alright, but about what?"

"Tomorrow, we can question her again if that makes you feel better. I think it would be helpful if she sat with the sketch artist so we can get a better idea of what the attacker looks like. And we need to get her to a safehouse as soon as possible."

"Okay then," Timo said, "but I don't have a good feeling about this."

And usually, he was good at reading people, but maybe Isa was right. His judgement was clouded these days and he had no idea what was right or wrong. He had never felt so confused and out of control. It was difficult to focus on work. His mind kept wandering back to Ingrid.

He had to do his job. This was all so intertwined with emotions and personal problems. He couldn't be objective. Maybe he had projected his own sorrow and suspicions on Tuva Norling.

"Maybe you're right," he said.

"Of course, I'm right."

She looked at him for a moment. "Are you okay?"

"Yeah, yeah... I'm just tired," he said.

"I'll be busy with Berg's TV interview and the convention for the rest of the week, so you'll have to handle this case on your own," Isa informed him.

"Is this still going on? I thought Hult wanted to cancel."

"I don't like it myself, but these are direct orders from commander Eriksson."

"Be careful! I don't trust these guys."

"I know, but Solberg will be there. I'll be fine. After Friday this will be over, and I hope I'll never see or speak to Berg again."

He frowned. "Why? What happened?"

She hesitated. "Nothing... I'll be fine."

He wished that were true, but her silence and evasion indicated otherwise. Something was troubling her. He should've probed deeper, but she quickly retreated to her desk, leaving him in the dark. He pondered why he hadn't pushed further. Perhaps it was because he thought she expected him to open up about Ingrid, and he simply wasn't prepared to do so yet.

There were too many unresolved feelings and unspoken truths that still needed time to unfold.

CHAPTER

20

"**I WASN'T EXPECTING YOUR CALL,**" Fredrik said.

"Well, me neither," Timo replied.

Timo looked around and appreciated the ambiance. Ingrid had recommended the restaurant to him and told him the food was amazing. Then he shook his head to clear the thoughts of her from his mind.

"Mom called you?" Fredrik asked.

"To lecture me about being nicer to you," Timo said.

Fredrik went into defense mode. "I had nothing to do with that."

"Really? You have a way of manipulating mom, so she always thinks you're the one who's been wronged. Well... you are her favorite son."

"Her favorite son? Don't think so," Fredrik replied.

Timo didn't want to argue further. They had been through this many times before. "I saw mom recently. She was in Gävle. She's doing okay."

"She spends a lot of time in St. Petersburg with auntie Lilia, and we saw her on New Year's Eve," Fredrik said.

"I know."

"She almost drove Pam crazy... and me, for that matter," Fredrik added.

There was a tense silence as the waitress brought cups of coffee.

"Shouldn't you be with your boss?" Timo said as he took his first sip.

"I'll join him later... he doesn't need me there."

"Berg and Hult together in an interview? Looks to me you might need to do some damage control afterwards."

Fredrik shrugged. "Maybe... he said he could handle it, and frankly I don't understand that man anymore."

A subtle smile adorned Timo's face as he delicately placed the cup onto the saucer. "We need to talk about Lauri Valkama and Karst Engersson."

"I told you everything I know."

"No, you haven't," Timo said, taking papers from his inner pocket and putting them in front of Fredrik. "Tell me why you went to work for Berg."

Fredrik scanned the papers and looked up at Timo. "What is this?"

"Emails, sent to Berg. Death threats, warnings."

"So? We know he got them. That's why SÄPO is there. That's why you are helping us," Fredrik said.

"They are sent from your computer in Stockholm."

"Wait... what?! I don't understand."

"And this is you," Timo said, taking another set of papers from his pocket and putting them side by side in front of Fredrik, pointing to the man in the picture.

"This is Hugo Lager and you. Lauri Valkama and you, again. These are old pictures, taken at the 'Mille Birre' pub where, until recently, all those obscure nationalist meetings were happening. What is this, Fred?"

"I don't know what you're talking about," Fredrik pushed the papers away, took a nervous sip of coffee, and then looked up at Timo. "I don't know any Hugo Lager."

"God, Fredrik, don't play games. This is serious."

"I'm not playing games. You are the one who has been playing games... a lot lately."

Timo shook his head. His brother wasn't going to listen to him. Fredrik was being manipulated and he could prove it, but it seemed that Fredrik wasn't ready for that kind of confrontation yet.

"You're not making any sense. Do you have any idea what could happen to you if this became public?"

He had already crossed the line to protect his brother. Sivert had shown him the emails and the pictures, and he'd told the IT expert he would handle it. Sivert had looked at him with a mix of shock and suspicion, but he had eventually said nothing.

Timo had hoped that by confronting Fredrik with the evidence, it would make him open up and tell him everything. But instead, it only made matters worse. Instead of confessing, Fredrik went into denial mode. He not only denied any wrongdoing, but also feigned ignorance of the evidence presented to him.

"Where did you get these?" Fredrik asked.

"Do you seriously think that national security is not keeping an eye on this?"

"Am I under investigation?"

"I won't leave until you tell me what's going on," Timo said firmly.

Fredrik suddenly grabbed Timo's arm. "Timo, I'm trying to help you," he said, his eyes fixed on something behind his brother.

Timo turned around and saw a man in a black suit getting up and walking past them to the exit. He recognized him at once. It was the same man who had been at the interview for the superintendent position where ultimately Finn had won. The man, biased from the start, had called him incompetent and had poured his racist fit all over him. No one in the room had reacted and by then he already knew the interview was a mockup.

"That was the man from the interview," Timo said to his brother. "Wilhelm Özkan. He's commissioner Eriksson right hand."

"Timo, please stay out of it. I'm begging you."

"I feel so..." He felt manipulated—like a dancing monkey, being guided and forced to move in a certain direction, but not necessarily the right one. He got nowhere with his brother. Either he didn't know, or he had a lot to hide. That Fredrik would really try to protect him, that he was concerned about his little brother, was doubtful. He had never protected him. More so, he had belittled him and constantly undermined his confidence, leaving him to fend for himself.

"What were you doing in that pub?" Timo asked, trying one more time to get some answers.

Fredrik put his head in his hands. "I knew Lauri and Hugo. I'm not proud of it, but I was a member of the Swedish White Supremacy Group for a few years. I went to their meetings a few times, but I swear I didn't know what they were doing. I just wanted... "

"How can you be so stupid?!"

The young couple at a nearby table glanced at them, taken aback by Timo's stern voice, before returning to their own conversation.

"I used an alias," Fredrik stammered.

"Still, I found out," Timo said with an icy calm. "What else are you hiding from me?"

Fredrik shook his head.

Timo was convinced that Fredrik wouldn't intentionally harm anyone. Though he could be callous, resolute in his views, and sometimes unrelenting, at his core, Fredrik was a decent man. This was something

Timo had to hold onto. The same brother who had teased him, fought him, and tested him since their childhood was also the same one who had stood by his side in the hospital, comforting him after he discovered Caijsa lifeless on the floor of his living room. The same brother who had helped plan her funeral, and urged him to sell his house, despite knowing that there was still bitterness lingering from when she left him for Timo.

His brother needed him now, even if he didn't realize it.

"These guys are crazy," Fredrik whispered. "Calling for a revolution, putting society back to where the world was in Nazi times. You should be worried about how many people they're influencing and how much destruction they could cause."

He looked at his hands. "I wanted to get out, but they blackmailed me. They had pictures, videos, emails, everything. They knew about... Sandra."

Timo frowned. "What about Sandra?"

"I... am the father of her baby. Pam would never forgive me."

"Jesus, Fredrik. Really?! You couldn't keep it in your pants, could you?"

But then he paused, realizing the irony of the conversation. He had no right to lecture his brother.

Fredrik's lips trembled. "I... it takes two to tango."

"But you're the married man here. What did you have to do for them?"

"Keep them informed about Berg's whereabouts. Where he was, who he was meeting. Everything."

"And the emails?"

"I didn't do that."

"Who else had access to your computer?" Timo asked.

"In principle everyone," Fredrik said. "It's not hard to break the password."

"Berg?"

283

Fredrik frowned. "Why do you ask? Why would he send emails to himself?"

"Just humor me. Berg?"

"Yeah, of course, but also everyone in the campaign team."

"And how far was Lauri involved?"

"They were planning to cause a revolution, destabilizing the current government by causing political chaos. They intended to discredit high-placed politicians whose ideas did not align with their own."

"And this political chaos was supposed to be caused how?"

"Attacks on strategic targets."

"Leif Berg. Forsmark. What else?"

Fredrik swallowed. "Global Law."

"Fuck! Frederik, you're involved in a mass shooting. Ten people died!"

"No, no, I only found out later."

"But you said nothing," Timo said in a stern voice. "You kept quiet."

Fredrik looked at him with big eyes and an open mouth, unable to say anything.

"Who ordered the attack?" Timo asked.

"I don't..."

"Who?"

"Karst Engersson," Fredrik said. "With the help of Lauri Valkama."

"Okay... we knew that."

"But Valkama didn't realize what he was financing. And it turned out quite differently than what Engersson had planned. Berg was supposed to die, and Karst was only supposed to be injured, but he was murdered."

"But the incident put the far-right movement in a negative light."

"I know it was a stupid thing to do, but they were adamant to kill Berg," Fredrik replied.

"You're not telling me everything. Killing Berg is radical. Who would gain from his death?"

"Berg's influence on the party has increased substantially in the last years. It's no secret he wants to change course. More left, which is not to everyone's liking."

"Who?"

"Hult," Fredrik finally said.

"Olav Hult? The Prime Minister?"

"Please... you don't have it from me."

"This is huge," Timo said.

Timo's eyes widened in disbelief as the words sank in. He instinctively leaned back, as if the weight of the revelation pushed him away. His gaze drifted to the window, but the blizzard outside matched the storm within him. The darkness mirrored his clouded thoughts, causing chaos within. His mind raced, struggling to comprehend the enormity of what he had just learned. The world around him faded as he grappled with the implications. Was nothing certain? Were his beliefs and perceptions based on falsehoods? The idea of a world where truth and deceit intertwined felt almost unbearable.

"Hult wants to pull the party to the right. He wants to work together with the Sweden Democrats, but Berg has been blocking this for I don't know how long..."

"Wait! What about the explosion?"

"I think Hult is responsible," Fredrik sighed.

And then it hit him. The clouds of confusion lifted, and clarity set in.

"Wait! No, Fredrik! Think about it. Berg was supposed to be at Global Law but decided not to go at the last minute. Berg leaves for Stockholm just before the explosion. He knew. He knew and let it happen."

"But how and why?"

Timo ran his hands over his face. "He used you."

"But I have always been so careful," Fredrik stammered.

"No, you haven't. I was able to track you. And he has SÄPO."

"He used them?"

"Solberg is probably not even aware of it. Jesus!" Timo got up and quickly took his jacket.

"Timo," Fredrik tried.

"Give me a second... I need to think!"

Berg and Hult. Berg was on the TV interview today with Isa there to protect him. The perfect opportunity for one to eliminate the other. But who? Hult taking out Berg or Berg outmaneuvering Hult? Berg had proven to be the more cunning, always staying one step ahead, turning the tables on his opponent. He wasn't sure how far Berg would go.

Isa was in danger. And he needed to find her as soon as possible.

He got up, then looked at his brother and said, "Sandra. Do you love her?"

Fredrik didn't hesitate. "I do, but... I won't leave Pam. I might not love my wife, but I wouldn't do anything to hurt my children and if that means I need to stay in a loveless marriage, I will."

Timo put on his jacket. "But what about Sandra's child?"

"A child I will never know," Fredrik said and emptied his cup of coffee.

"How have we become so... dysfunctional?" Timo said.

"We are Valesca Ignatova's sons."

"No... we can't blame mom anymore. This is on us."

***

Timo stepped outside with his cell phone clutched to his ear. He had dialed Isa's number at least a dozen times and got her voicemail each time. He couldn't give up; he needed to speak with her before the TV broadcast started. There was still time if he hurried. He had to get out of here before the snow arrived and blocked the roads. Another bout of relentless snow.

"Come on, Isa, pick up!"

He felt uneasy and anxious. After ten calls and no reply, he got in his car and drove to the TV station hoping that she would already be there.

But Isa was nowhere in the neighborhood. She was driving Tuva to the safehouse.

"It's snowing," Tuva said, sitting in the back of the car. She was looking sad and distant, and she hadn't said a word during the entire drive.

"Yeah, heavy snow is coming. I'll drop you off, but then I have to go back. My colleagues will take care of you."

"Do you think he'll come after me?" Tuva said, shaking so hard that Isa was startled by the sound of her voice.

"You'll be safe where I'm taking you," Isa said, her brow furrowed in concern.

She turned the car onto a deserted street and pressed down on the accelerator. The thick snowflakes were hitting the windshield and melting immediately. Up ahead the streets were already empty. The orange glow from the streetlamp illuminated the falling snow for only a few seconds, making it hard for her to drive. She had no choice but to continue.

"Tuva, may I ask you something?"

The more she thought about it, the more she became convinced Timo was right. Tuva was keeping something from them.

"Yeah. What?"

"I think you know the man who attacked you."

Tuva looked out the window and remained silent. She sat in the back seat with her head resting against the glass, tears rolling down her face. The snowflakes shining in the light occasionally illuminated Tuva's features, making her tears sparkle like tiny diamonds on her cheeks.

"How...," Tuva started but needed a moment to recover. When Isa looked in the rear-view mirror, she saw Tuva's face, all red and wet. "It's my father."

"Your father?" Isa said.

Tuva nodded and wiped her face with the sleeve of her jacket.

"I'm not sure what his name is. My mother refused to talk about him, and I never found out. I only saw him twice. The first time was when I was five or six years old, so my memories of him are pretty blurry."

"And when was the second time?"

"The day I turned twelve," Tuva said. "He came by and assaulted my mother."

"What happened?" Isa said in surprise.

"She was already very ill at that time. She was so happy to see him, but he wasn't."

"Why was he there?"

"Later, I learned she had called him. She was worried about the medical bills and her cancer diagnosis. She asked him for a loan. But he started yelling at her, saying how selfish and manipulative she was. How she just wanted his money."

"Money? He's rich?"

Tuva nodded.

Isa turned the car to the left. In the distance, a rundown house appeared on the hillside.

"She sent me to another room, and their argument escalated. I heard a scream, then opened the door to find him shoving her against the wall. He struck her and she crumpled to the ground. I was stunned and didn't know how to react. I should have helped her."

"You were only a child," Isa said.

The car drew nearer to the house. The snow fell so thickly that the windshield wipers barely gave the driver a clear view of the exterior.

"And you never talked to him?"

"No, he didn't even look at me. My father... he's a stranger. A killer. He didn't hesitate... he wanted to kill me."

Rows of trees passed by, but Isa didn't look at them.

"Your colleague... the man. He doesn't believe me."

"Inspector Paikkala. And he was right, wasn't he?"

Tuva shrugged.

"To be fair, you did withhold some information from us."

"Not... on purpose," Tuva stammered.

"It's time to come clean. You told me about your dad. But you know very well who it is."

She pulled the car to a stop in front of the safehouse and turned to Tuva, holding up her phone. "Is this him?"

The display showed a picture of Leif Berg.

Tuva looked at it for a long moment before shaking her head and saying, "No, that's not him."

"Shit," Isa said. She had a dozen messages and missed calls from Timo.

Tuva suddenly cried out.

"What's wrong?"

The young woman sat up, her eyes wide. "I saw someone," she said and almost seemed out of breath.

Isa turned around and scanned the area. The snow made it hard to see anything, and the lights were off in most of the houses. It was dark and without any lampposts in the neighborhood it was difficult to distinguish anything. "Are you sure?"

"There's someone."

"Stay here. Keep the door locked." She took out her gun before she stepped out of the car.

Where were the others? She hadn't seen another car.

She ran to the house and walked slowly up the steps, feeling as though her feet no longer held firm on the icy pavement. She scanned the area again. Isa's doubts crept in as she questioned Tuva's claim of seeing someone. There were no footprints in the snow. At the door, she took a deep breath. She could feel fear starting to squeeze her chest, and she stared at the gun in her gloved hand.

She carefully pushed the door open and peered inside. The room was empty, save for a table and chair. She hurriedly looked around but saw no one and nothing out of the ordinary. Tuva had been wrong; there was no one else there.

She was just about to step into the next room when, suddenly, she heard a door open behind her. Isa froze; then she felt a hand on her shoulder and the blow to the head knocked her down. The blow was so quick that Isa didn't even have time to realize what had happened, let alone cry out. As she slowly opened her eyes, she noticed a figure standing in the doorway. The person's back was facing her, blocking the light from the other room, and making it difficult to discern any features.

Then everything went black.

CHAPTER

21

WHEN ISA WOKE UP, it was as if someone had whacked her in the head with a baseball bat. She could barely make out the contours of the person leaning over her and felt a surge of panic.

"Relax," a familiar voice said. "It's just us."

Police officer Varg Mårtensson was kneeling next to her, and she recognized sergeant Sylvia Ahlgren standing next to him.

"Where the hell were you?" Isa cried, irritated.

She tried to sit up, but her head was still spinning.

Sylvia reached out to help her. "We were called to check out a domestic dispute, but there was no one. Then we came here and discovered you lying on the floor. How did you get here?"

"What do you mean?" The nausea was barely manageable. "I got here in my car."

"Then the car is gone," Varg said.

"Shit! And Tuva?"

"We didn't see her."

"He must have taken her or maybe... she's already dead," Isa said and jumped up, but the nausea made her reach out and grab the wall for support.

"Inspector Lindström, you don't look well," Varg said. "We should get you to a doctor."

"It's fine," she yelled. "But we need to find Tuva."

Isa saw Varg Mårtensson's concerned face reflected in the darkening windows as the lights flickered on and off.

"Report back to the station but take me first to the Convention Center."

"Why?"

"Berg... the TV interview," Isa said, and then she suddenly went for her holster. "My gun is gone!"

She looked at the young man in fear. She hoped that it wasn't already too late, and that whoever had taken the girl, hadn't killed Tuva yet. Berg had to be responsible—Tuva had said no, but it wasn't the first time the girl had told them lies. Tuva just didn't trust them.

Sylvia said, "The snowfall has blocked some of the roads. Not sure how long it will take to get there."

"Jesus! My phone. I need to call Paikkala." And she frantically started to look for her cell phone, until she saw Varg holding it in front of her.

"It was lying on the floor next to you."

"Thanks," she breathed, but then frowned when she saw one bar of cell service. "We need to go. Now!"

* * *

"Are you sure you're ready for this?" Kristoffer Solberg asked. "We can still call it off."

Leif Berg stood with an air of confidence, his unwavering gaze locked onto his reflection in the mirror. With a swift motion, he adjusted his tie, maintaining a cool and composed demeanor on his face.

"Leif, listen to me." Kristoffer's voice shook as he spoke. "Someone wants you dead."

Leif let out a sigh and shifted his gaze towards Kristoffer, who was seated in a one-seater, weariness etched on his face as he ran his hands over it.

"I've received death threats before. Yet, here I am, still alive," Leif retorted.

"This isn't a joke," Kristoffer warned, standing up and checking his phone. "Engersson, Valkama, they're dead. Hult also received death threats."

A heavy scent of aftershave and makeup hung in the air.

A single, large mirror adorned one wall, stretching almost from ceiling to floor, providing Leif with a perfect view of himself. He moved closer to examine his face. He loved how the makeup evened his skin tone.

"Hult has arrived," Kristoffer said.

A mocking smile crept across Leif's lips as he meticulously groomed his hair, discontent evident in his expression. He disliked what they had done to his silvery locks.

"Did you hear what I said?" Kristoffer asked.

"I heard you... and so what?"

"Look, we need to talk about the hostility between the two of you. SÄPO has a responsibility to both of you, but we're not babysitters. I'd appreciate it if you didn't use my team to settle your differences."

"It will be over soon," Leif said.

"What do you mean?"

"I mean... when the elections come in three years from now, he'll be gone. Maybe even sooner."

Kristoffer shrugged, turned around and stared at his phone. It was vibrating in his hand.

"Solberg," he said.

On the other side of the line, there was a muffled gasp. "Finally," the voice said.

"Yeah, the connection is bad. What do you want, Paikkala?"

"Is Isa there?"

"No, I haven't seen her all day, but she's supposed to be here."

"I'm on my way back from Stockholm. Tell her to be careful when you see her."

"What's wrong?" Kristoffer said.

"It's Berg."

Kristoffer frowned and continued to observe Berg's meticulous routine in front of the mirror. Every gesture was calculated, every expression rehearsed to exude an aura of perfection. The man wanted to present the best version of himself.

"Yeah, Berg is here," Kristoffer said.

"Don't show him any reaction that can reveal what I'm going to tell you."

"I'll tell him," Kristoffer said.

"He sent the emails, and I think he killed Valkama."

Berg walked to the other side of the room. Kristoffer locked his eyes on him, as Leif took a black bag that was on the floor.

"Solberg?" Timo asked.

"Yeah... okay. And what do you want me to do?"

"Don't lose sight of him. He's going after Hult. I'll be there in thirty minutes. When Isa arrives, tell her. And... be careful!"

"Sure," Kristoffer said, pressing the button. The connection was interrupted. He stared at the phone in his hand, trying to take in what he had just learned.

"Was it Paikkala?" Leif's voice thundered through the room, causing Kristoffer to turn around. He looked straight in the barrel of the silencer. Instinctively he reached for his holster and felt the reassuring weight of his gun.

"I wouldn't do that," Leif grinned as he pointed the gun straight at his head.

Kristoffer's hand clenched tightly for a moment, the muscles in his arm tensing with anticipation, a sense of dread settling in his stomach. He realized he had made a grave mistake by letting Berg slip from his sight, and now he would have to pay the price.

"You'll have to thank Paikkala for it," Leif continued.

"For what?"

"Your death," Leif said.

Kristoffer had been threatened before. Death was nothing new to him. But when Berg announced his death, with an almost sarcastic grin and calm voice, that made the doom scenario so creepily real, he'd gotten goosebumps. Never had he felt so clearly that it could be a real thing, that he was going to die in this room alone over something he didn't even understand.

"You wouldn't dare," Kristoffer said.

"Really? Hult wants to kill me. He hired someone to do the job. Today, before the interview, he managed to enter my room and tried to kill me. You came in. There was a fight. I was injured and you were killed trying to save me. See... I even give you a hero's death. You should thank me."

"But why?"

"Haven't you figured it out yet? Even Paikkala and that bitch of his figured it out. Since you'll be dead anyway, I can tell you. I killed Valkama.

Engersson on the other hand did it all by himself. I just had to sit back and watch."

"You let ten people die," Kristoffer let out.

"Collateral damage unfortunately."

"Timo and Isa are on to you."

"Paikkala and Lindström will learn that their lives, careers, and reputations are worth nothing, and friends can be deceptive. Finn will take care of them."

"You won't get away with this," Kristoffer said, the horror of his situation suddenly becoming clear to him. He saw his wife and their three beautiful girls. Why was he still standing there like a coward? If he were going to die, he might as well go down with a bang.

"Enough talking," Leif said.

Kristoffer leaped forward.

He hung mid-air when the bullet hit the center of his forehead.

Kristoffer's eyes went wide as the bullet entered his brain, and he fell to the ground with a thud. His lifeless body lay there on the carpet, face down. The bullet hole, a shiny red circle in the middle of his forehead, was surrounded by a dark red ring.

Leif knelt and checked his pulse, then stood up and walked over to the mirror. He looked at his reflection in the glass and smiled while he removed the silencer, wiped the gun clean and put it back in the bag. He took off his gloves and walked over to the table where there was a bottle of pills. Antidepressants. Opening the bottle, he poured a few into his hand and swallowed them without water, feeling them dissolve on his tongue. He closed his eyes briefly, savoring the moment, before returning to the mirror.

"They tried to kill me," he whispered, molded his face in a terrified expression and then laughed. He straightened his tie and looked at the spot of blood on his hand.

* * *

Timo jumped out of the car. He didn't care he had parked in the wrong spot. The road was barricaded, and he had to hold his badge in front of him to get free passage.

"Did you see Inspector Lindström?" he asked the police officer at the entrance of the building.

The policeman shook his head. "She hasn't been in today."

"If you see her, tell her I need to talk to her. It's urgent."

He looked at his phone and saw he had gotten a message.

It read, "Tuva is missing. I think Berg has her."

She knew. She knew Berg was responsible for the murders.

He tried to call her, but she didn't answer.

He walked inside. A metal detector was installed at the entrance, and he showed the uniformed police officers his badge and gun. They waved him through without a word.

Just as he was about to ascend the majestic staircase, Timo's attention was drawn to Finn, who stood towering above the bustling crowd of people making their way towards the TV studio. Standing at an impressive two meters in height, Finn's commanding presence demanded attention. Amidst the cacophony of voices and noise emanating from the crowd, it proved challenging for Timo to discern the exact words Finn was shouting. Nevertheless, Finn's urgent gestures beckoned Timo to follow. Skillfully maneuvering through the throng, Timo evaded cameras and microphones wielded by journalists eagerly vying for a glimpse of the invited politicians and celebrities. Timo trailed behind Finn, ascending the stairs together, before swiftly veering left into a dark corridor.

"We need to talk about Berg," Timo panted, struggling to keep pace with Finn.

Finn halted, eyeing Timo with a piercing stare. "Not here," he growled.

Scanning the hallway, Finn searched for an empty room. He spotted one, jiggled the handle, and led Timo inside.

But as Timo stepped into the room, an overwhelming sense of foreboding washed over him. In a split second, Finn seized him by the shoulders and forcefully pressed him against the wall, his grip unyielding. Then, without warning, Finn tightened his hold, his hands constricting around Timo's throat. Timo struggled and thrashed, desperately attempting to break free, but Finn's grip remained steadfast. A look of sheer determination twisted Finn's face as he continued to apply pressure, causing Timo's face to turn an alarming shade of red and his breath to dwindle. Timo's heart pounded within his chest, threatening to burst out. He tried to utter words, but his choked throat rendered him unable to speak, fueling his panic.

In a desperate act of survival, Timo mustered all his strength and delivered a swift, powerful kick to Finn's thigh. Finn howled in pain, momentarily releasing his grip on Timo. He tried to flee, but Finn anticipated his move and swiftly tripped him, sending Timo crashing to the floor with a resounding thud. The next moment, Finn's weight nearly crushed him.

They tumbled and crashed through the room, wreaking havoc on everything in their path. The coffee table buckled under their combined weight.

Timo strained to overpower Finn, but the larger man proved to be too strong. Locked in a fierce struggle, each fought relentlessly for dominance. The floorboards groaned and creaked under the strain. Suddenly, Finn lunged at Timo, driving a knife deep into his leg. Timo howled in pain, but he instinctively dodged the subsequent strike.

The searing agony in his leg surged, blood flowing out in an alarming rush. Timo swiftly adjusted his position, leveraging his body to restrain Finn with his legs and arms. Summoning every ounce of strength, he delivered a powerful punch to Finn's jaw, sending him reeling backward and causing the knife to clatter loudly onto the floor.

Dazed but determined, Finn staggered to his feet, only to be met with Timo's heel crashing into his stomach. Doubled over in agony, Finn crumpled to the ground. Before he could regain his composure, Timo kicked the knife under a nearby chair and forcefully pinned Finn to the floor. Finn's agonized shrieks echoed through the room.

Timo swiftly secured Finn's wrists with handcuffs and then leaned against the wall, his body heaving as he struggled to catch his breath. Despite the searing pain from his stabbing wound, he noticed that the bleeding had begun to slow down.

Finn lay on the floor, thrashing to escape, and spat out a venomous, "I hate you."

Timo gazed at the red stains marring his jeans, grappling with the reality that a friend had attempted to take his life.

"Say something," Finn yelled.

"What is there to say? You tried to kill me."

"I've always hated you. You... with your rich parents, thinking you were better than us, thinking you needed to save us."

"You never objected when my family took you under their wings."

"It was humiliating," Finn growled.

"Sure," Timo said. "What did Berg promise you? Money? Fame?"

"Berg? You think I work for Berg?"

"You're not?" Timo said surprised.

Finn laughed loudly. "Oh, so naïve... as always!"

"Who then?"

Finn kept laughing. A denigrating, sarcastic laugh.

Timo got up, limped to the door, and then turned back to glance at the heavy man on the floor who was still trying to get free.

"You can't just leave me!" Finn shouted.

Timo opened the door and walked down the hall, with heavy heart.

He had to find Berg.

* * *

"Inspector Paikkala is looking for you," the police officer at the entrance of the building said.

Isa turned to Varg and Sylvia. "Find Finn and tell him everything. We need to find Tuva! I hope..."

"He hasn't already killed her," Sylvia voiced her thoughts.

Isa nodded. "We have to assume he hasn't. Let's split up. Then we have more chances of finding Berg and Tuva. And when you see Berg, call for back-up. Don't go after him on your own. He's dangerous."

"Got it," Varg said, and he disappeared into the crowd.

Then she turned to the police officer. "Give me your gun."

"But..."

"Now," Isa demanded, her eyes locked with the police officer's. "A woman's life is at stake, and we can't afford to waste any time."

The officer hesitated for a moment, his expression wavering between concern and duty. Then the officer handed over his firearm, and Isa quickly took the weapon.

Isa put her hand on Sylvia's shoulder. "Be careful."

Was it a good idea to take the rookies with her?

She looked at the gun in her hand. How stupid of her to have gone alone. She couldn't say it out loud, but she thought Berg likely had already killed Tuva.

"Where is Berg?" Isa asked the police officer.

"I assume he's still preparing for the show. He's been here since the late afternoon. I haven't seen him leave."

"Really?" Isa frowned. Maybe she was wrong, maybe Berg hadn't taken Tuva. "I'll find him."

She knew where to find the room Berg would use for his preparations. She had gone over the entire evening many times with his security team.

She climbed the stairs, checking her phone for messages.

"Shit!" The battery had died.

As the lights abruptly flickered off, the forceful wind relentlessly hammered against the windows, creating an atmosphere reminiscent of a raging war. The dim illumination from outside cast eerie silhouettes on the faces of the startled visitors, revealing their panic. The police officers at the entrance tried to reassure them.

She strained to hear their words, but all that reached her ears was the relentless gusts. Determined, she pressed forward, making her way towards Berg's room. Just as she approached, the generators roared to life, flooding the corridor with blinding light. She paused momentarily, waiting for her eyes to adjust to the sudden brightness before resuming her journey. And there, as she neared the door at the end of the hall, she observed that it stood ajar.

She took the gun from the holster and entered. The front of the room was lit with a single bulb on the desk. Isa approached the desk and looked around. The desk was covered with papers, and a jacket was lying next to it. She walked further into the room to the second part, which was dark until she switched on the light. She almost tripped over something on the floor. It was Kristoffer Solberg's body.

His lifeless body lay face down, arms stretched out. Isa's heart sank as she flipped him over and saw the blood staining his face. She hesitated for a moment before gently placing her hand on his shoulder, hoping for some sign of life, but there was none.

"Oh no..." Her mind immediately went to his wife and daughters. The pictures he had shown her with such pride. She made a silent promise to herself that she would do everything in her power to support them during this difficult time.

Then she got up and pivoted back to the hall. A man and woman were loudly quarreling in one of the rooms and the noise grew louder as she approached. The gun in her hand felt heavy, but she kept it trained forward. Upon reaching the room, she recognized the voices as Tuva and Berg.

When Isa entered the room, the first thing she saw was the anxiety on Leif Berg's face. Tuva was standing with her back to Isa, holding a gun aimed directly at Berg.

Tuva turned to face Isa, her expression a mixture of fear and desperation. "He tried to kill me."

Berg, however, wasn't backing down. "She's lying," he countered, eyes narrowed. "She was the one trying to pull the trigger."

"Tuva, lower the gun," Isa commanded, her voice steady despite the tension in the room. Berg shifted nervously, sweat beading on his forehead.

As she took another step forward, Isa tried to process what had happened. Tuva was no longer the scared woman she had seen earlier. The plan was now clear. Tuva had set everything up, from stealing Isa's car and gun, to waiting for the perfect moment to act.

With the gun still pointed at Berg's head, Tuva's hand wavered slightly. Isa knew she had to act fast to defuse the situation.

"Tuva. Don't!"

"Stay out of this," Tuva yelled.

"This is not the right way to punish him for what he has done to your mother."

Tuva didn't waver and kept the gun pointed at Berg's head. "He has to realize that he can't treat people this way and expect there to be no consequences. It's not just my mom." Tuva took a brief pause before continuing. "I'm glad they contacted me. He's done this to too many people for there to be no justice."

"Your mother?" Berg said. "I don't even know you or your mother."

"Shut up!" Tuva yelled. "You don't get to speak."

Isa stepped closer, taking in the tense scene. Tuva held the gun with unwavering resolve, her eyes gleaming with animosity. Meanwhile, Berg was frozen with fear, his eyes wide with terror.

"Who contacted you?" Isa asked.

"It doesn't matter. I knew I had to do this. Pay him back, no matter what the price was."

"And the price was Greta's life?" a deep voice sounded.

Isa saw Timo leaning against the wall with a pained expression on his face. He was clutching his left hand to his upper leg.

"Yes," Tuva said. "And I have no regrets. She shouldn't have meddled."

"She overheard you about killing Berg. Did she threaten to go to the police?"

Tuva shook her head in disbelief. "You give her too much credit. She wanted money. She thought I was being paid to kill him, but I told her to not get involved. When Rolf told me he had seen her with two men, I knew she wouldn't let go that easily. I had to do something about it."

"And you stabbed her to death," Timo continued.

Berg's smile got wide, and his eyes all ominous like he was hatching a plan.

"What do you find so amusing?" Tuva said, coming closer with the gun pointed directly at his head.

"What an entertaining little story," Berg said.

"Kristoffer Solberg is dead," Isa suddenly said. "Did you kill him?"

"I was attacked in my office. Solberg tried to stop him, but he was shot. I barely got away."

"Who attacked you?" Isa asked.

"I don't know but I wouldn't be surprised if it was the same person who sent me threatening emails and broke into my office. I wouldn't be surprised Hult is behind it."

"Why do you think that?" Isa asked.

"Don't you know he ordered the killing of Engersson and Valkama?"

Berg said.

"You killed Valkama," Tuva said. "I saw you."

"Really? What you saw was me taking his briefcase and checking if he was alright. I didn't kill Valkama."

Timo's voice was sharp as he spoke. "You were aware of Hult's plot against you from the very beginning, and you made a calculated move to infiltrate his inner circle. You established a relationship with Valkama and my brother, even though they had no idea of your true intentions. You saw the Global Law shooting as an opportunity to eliminate Engersson and consolidate your power. To that end, you hired Olga Morosov to monitor Valkama and Ek's activities, using a drug called scopolamine to extract information from them. And boy, did Valkama talk... he told you everything, but he was also a liability. Valkama knew about the threatening emails you had sent to yourself, the staged accident, and the incident outside the City Hall. He had become a threat to your carefully crafted facade, and you needed to eliminate him. Morosov was instructed to administer a lethal dose of the drug that day. I'm certain that she then contacted you, and you followed Valkama into the alley, where you retrieved the briefcase containing all the evidence."

Berg laughed. "Prove it!"

Timo continued, "You were always one step ahead of them and they didn't even realize it. But why? You are a popular man. You would have won. The entire party is behind you."

"They don't know what I really want."

"And that is?" Timo said, his face showing no emotion.

"The party needs to be led in a new direction. I will be the sole leader. I will make a new Sweden. I am everything—right and left. I am God."

Isa looked at Timo confused, and then turned to Berg. How could a man be so delusional?

"And now, how do we go from here?" Berg smiled and looked Tuva straight in the eye.

Tuva's eyes widened as she took a step closer to him. Throughout his entire monologue, her grip on the gun had tightened.

"You'll die," Tuva said.

"I doubt that Inspector Lindström will allow that. She's a law-abiding woman who will arrest you before you can pull the trigger. She might sympathize with you, but by law, she can't."

"Tuva, don't do this!" Timo said and the moment he said it, he fell against the wall.

"Timo?" Isa said.

"I'm okay."

Tuva's eyes were watery with tears when she looked at Berg. "You don't know what it was like. I held her hand. She was screaming and hallucinating. It was horrible. She didn't even recognize me. No one wanted to help me, and I sat with her for two days. Then she died. You poisoned her. You killed her. Just like you poisoned Valkama."

"I never hurt your mother," Berg said with a serious expression on his face. "In fact, I've never even met her. They manipulated you in thinking that I am your father, but it's not true. I don't know what you think I did to your mom, but it's a lie."

"No, liar! You never wanted us. You never wanted me. You killed her!" Tuva screamed. "And then you tried to kill me."

Berg frowned. "What are you talking about?"

"You sent people after me to kill me," Tuva said, her voice shaking with anger.

Berg looked confused. "I never hired anyone to find you."

"You never... ever wanted to talk to me. I tried to get your attention... I even broke into your home, but... then your wife started to accuse me of assaulting her. I just wanted to talk to you."

"That's you? I stopped the police from pressing charges," Berg said. "I'm sorry for Masja's behavior. She's not well..."

"I don't believe a word you said." Tuva's grip on the gun tightened, and she aimed it at Berg's head. The air in the room grew heavy with tension. Berg's sudden retreat, accompanied by a flicker of fear in his eyes, spoke volumes.

Isa stepped forward. "Let's put the gun down and talk this through."

Tuva didn't take her eyes off Berg, but she spoke to Isa. "You don't understand. He's a monster. It's too late for talking."

"Let justice deal with him," Timo said.

Tuva looked at Timo and whispered, "I'm sorry." Then she turned back to Berg. "Game over. You're dead."

"No!" Timo yelled, trying to stop her, but it was too late.

The gunshot echoed through the room. Berg fell to the ground, lifeless. Then Tuva turned to Isa, who had her gun pointed at the girl.

"I confess to murdering Leif Berg," Tuva said calmly.

"Put the gun on the floor," Isa ordered.

The girl complied.

Isa checked Berg's pulse. "He's dead."

Tuva smiled.

CHAPTER

22

"**How do you feel?**"

Timo slowly opened his eyes, trying to take in his surroundings. For the past half hour, he had been lying on a stretcher in an ambulance with a torn pair of jeans and a bandage wrapped around his left thigh. His throat felt soar, and the bruises on his neck from where Finn had grabbed him were painful. He didn't want to get up. All he wanted was to listen to the wind bouncing against the vehicle. Sometimes the gusts were so strong that it swayed the ambulance back and forth.

But he tried to sit up when he saw Isa leaning over him.

"I know what you're going to say," Timo said, trying to push himself up. The pain was sharp, and he let out a moan.

"I'm not saying anything. I'm just worried about you."

For a moment, he stared at the bandage where spots of red were already soiling the pure whiteness. "Did you find Finn?"

"He's arrested," Isa said.

"He won't say anything."

"I don't understand how we were so wrong about him."

"Yeah, I was wrong. He wasn't working for Berg. They were all on Hult's payroll. Breiner, Engersson, Valkama... all of them. My brother... my stupid, naïve brother."

"We'll have to question Fredrik," she said.

"I know, but he'll help you. Finn, on the other hand, won't."

"I'm so sorry," she said. "He was your friend."

"Well... that only shows how I am a bad judge of character," Timo said and shook his head. "But we still need to prove Hult is behind all of this."

"Tuva will be charged with the murder of Berg and Greta," Isa said.

As he swung his legs over the side of the stretcher and attempted to step down, a searing pain shot through his stabbed leg. The torn fabric of his clothing caught on the metal bars, adding to his discomfort as he maneuvered himself out of the ambulance.

"Tuva made her decision when she accepted to kill Berg. Now, I want Hult."

"If neither Finn nor Tuva are going to talk, it's going to be incredibly challenging," Isa remarked. She matched his limping gait as he walked down the pavement. His blood was burning with anger and his heart was beating fast.

Inside, a crowd of journalists had gathered around Hult.

"A young woman has been charged with the murders and will be questioned by the police." The moderator of the press conference cleared his throat and looked towards Hult, who was standing in the background. He looked haggard and exhausted, as if he had been through a war, but

Timo knew it was a lie.

Hult stepped up to the podium, his expression somber. "It is with great sadness that I inform you that our Secretary of Justice, Leif Berg, was among the victims." He took a moment to collect himself and looked down at his notes before continuing, "I extend my deepest sympathies to his loved ones and colleagues during this difficult time. We will be launching a comprehensive investigation into the events leading up to the tragic loss of life, and in the interim, my fellow ministers and I will work to find a suitable replacement for Secretary Berg."

When the reporters broke out into questions, Hult simply walked away from the microphone. The reporters' microphones began to squeal, and Timo was just about to step into the fray when Isa grabbed his arm. She pointed to Hult, who had just disappeared through the emergency exit.

"Let him go," she said, but Timo tried to run after him. He was just in time to see him exiting the building and stepping into his ministerial car. The doors slammed shut and the vehicle sped away.

"Shit," he said as the car disappeared into the distance.

"Timo."

"What's wrong?" He turned and saw Isa staring in front of her.

"That car," she said. "That black SUV."

It was parked on the opposite side of the street, a few cars away from where they stood. The tinted windows made it impossible to see if someone was inside.

"It's the car from the CCTV," she said. "Part of the license plate is the same."

The next moment, they saw a man walk up to the car, open it and step inside.

She swallowed a few times. "It's not Hult. It's Eriksson, the police commissioner."

* * *

Tuva sat in the back of the police car; her eyes fixed on the steel bars separating her from freedom. Her tears fell, and she wiped them away with the back of her hand. She glanced up at the officers in the front, realizing they had hardly uttered a word to her.

Tuva shivered, feeling uneasy. She had never found herself in a situation quite like this one before. She remembered the day clearly, more than a year ago, when a man had first approached her little makeshift shelter under the bridge near the train station. He was suited up in expensive clothing while she was a homeless kid, and yet he knew her name. Tuva tried to ignore him and his advances, because she knew all too well what men who looked like him usually wanted.

He started to talk about her mother and how he had known her when she had been a flight attendant. He spoke of how much he had admired her and how devastated he was when she passed away. It was a cruel and painful death that didn't seem fair. If only her father had helped her, maybe things could have been different.

She had blocked the memory of her mother's death and the few times she had seen her father until then. She had never talked about him, never even thought about him after that horrific incident when he had assaulted her mother—an incident where she had been forced to watch, helpless and terrified. She had never told anyone about it because thinking about it made her feel sick.

This man had not only told her about her mother, but also her father who he said was rich and powerful, and that no one dared to cross him. He told her that her father had forced her mother to get an abortion when she became pregnant with her. When she refused, he made sure she never told a soul. She lost her job and was humiliated, being forced to work as a cleaning lady for the people she once considered equals.

All this time, she had said nothing. The next day, the man had come back. This time, he told her how her mother wasn't the only victim; her father had seduced countless women and abandoned them when they got pregnant. He was a monster who had hurt the person she loved most in the world—her mother.

But was Tuva sure her mother had died of cancer? Maybe it had been something else. And that was when the memories of her mother's painful death started to take on another dimension. The seed was planted.

The man hinted that her father had probably something to do with her mother's death and that he wouldn't hesitate to do it again.

But she could do something about it, the man said. She could take sweet revenge. Until then, she hadn't even considered it. She had taken her life as it was.

The man had returned the day after, as she had known he would. She allowed him to plant the seeds of anger and resentment in her mind, letting him turn her into a murderer. They made plans for the murder as she sat in his car—a large black SUV, usually parked in an isolated area. She didn't know his name. Sometimes, he had a few colleagues with him. The bearded man and the tall, fat man. The only time she saw him again was in the TV studio, where he guided her past the metal detector and told her where to find Berg.

The road lined with trees flashed by. She didn't recognize the environment.

"This isn't the way to the police station," she said.

The police officers said nothing and stared ahead as the car drove further away from the city. The fear was rushing through her veins.

"Let me out of this car," Tuva yelled. "Stop!"

She could barely see the faces of the police officers through the grid that separated them.

She was trapped.

The sound of the engine faded as the car came to a halt. The next moment the officers got out, leaving her alone in the dark, deserted road.

Fear, desperation, and a feeling of utter helplessness consumed her as she realized the true terror of her situation. The once calm and composed Tuva was now a frantic mess, pounding on the windows and screaming for help, but no one came.

The silence was deafening.

"He deserves to die," the man had said, and he had handed her the knife. The knife she had lost when she had killed Tuva.

But she had found another way. When Isa Lindström had brought her to the safe house, a plan had formed in her mind. She told the inspector she had seen an intruder; then she had knocked her down and took her gun and car. She knew it would all lead back to her, but she was prepared to face the consequences.

"But you'll never talk about our conversations to anyone," the man had said. She had nodded, but how stupid she had been. They would never take the risk and when she saw the man dressed in a black biker's outfit, with the helmet hiding his face come out of the woods, she knew she was going to die.

In that moment, the truth dawned on her—Berg had spoken the truth.

She heard the lock of the door click open. It was over. Everything happened so fast.

"Mom," she cried, a single tear running down her cheek.

The man opened the door, pulled the screaming girl out, aimed the gun, and shot her in the head.

Her body fell on the ground, a line of blood pouring from the headwound.

A second bullet hit her in the chest.

The body was still.

He stood over her, waited for a moment, then turned around and walked back to the woods, leaving the body in the snow-laden landscape.

***

The investigation into the murders of Karst Engersson, Lauri Valkama, Kristoffer Solberg, Leif Berg and Tuva Norling kicked off a nationwide discussion about extremist opinions. Prime Minister Hult's reputation strangely improved. His image as a strong and decisive leader was enhanced even more when he appeared on television to emphasize how seriously his government took these atrocities. Police investigators were convinced that high-ranking individuals were involved in the murders, but they were unable to prove it, and the investigation was abruptly terminated after commissioner Eriksson became involved.

The public never learned who committed the crimes or discovered why they were committed. Finn Heimersson kept quiet. Emails and text messages, which showed he was the one who had planned the attack on Berg and had likely given the order to kill Tuva Norling, disappeared. He was released and given a position in Umeå, in the north of Sweden. But he wasn't able to enjoy his new life as two months later he was found dead in his home. The official report said it was an accident. He had fallen down the stairs. But Isa and Timo knew better.

All evidence who had planned the murders of Karst Engersson and Lauri Valkama and who had killed SÄPO investigator Kristoffer Solberg were equally missing. Ultimately, their deaths were classified as committed by persons unknown.

It annoyed Timo that he had failed. He had prepared for a storm that hadn't come. A storm where his own brother would be in the spotlight. Fredrik Paikkala's only crime was that he had been swept away by the propaganda of the right-wing extremists. But strangely, none of it reached the media. Timo didn't know if this was a good or a bad thing. When he learned of Finn's death, he knew it had been a dangerous thing. Sooner or later his brother would become a target, and he wouldn't be able to protect Fredrik. He didn't even know from what or who he needed to protect him.

.

* * *

The sun rays streamed through the windows of the church, illuminating the stained glass, and reflecting off the polished wood. The church was filled. Standing room was only available at the back.

Six officers marched into the church carrying the coffin, Timo among them. He surveyed the solemn scene: rows of uniformed police officers standing along both sides of the church entrance. When he caught sight of Isa in line, he saw the pain and sadness in her eyes, but also her resolve to remain composed.

As the funeral procession continued, Timo's thoughts were consumed with the loss of his colleague, Lars. He reflected on the life of this dedicated officer and the deep sadness that had engulfed their department. The eulogy from former superintendent Anders Larsen painted a picture of a man who was passionate about his job, his father, and serving the people of Gävle. Timo realized that despite working side by side with Lars for almost a year, he knew very little about him. This was true for his colleagues, Berger and Isa, as well.

If he had to be honest, it was a pattern. He had the tendency to keep people at arm's length, and he could try to rationalize it as much as he could, but it always came down to Caijsa. It was self-protection, an unconscious attempt to shield himself from the vulnerability of forming deep connections. He couldn't just let people in. Perhaps that was the very reason he had been drawn to Ingrid. He knew he could never have a relationship with her.

He reminisced on the journey they had taken as a team. He remembered meeting the young, blond man, Lars Nyquist, on his first case as superintendent. It was hard to believe it had only been a year since then. At first, he felt like an outsider and faced suspicion from his colleagues. His actions had resulted in Anders' layoff and increased scrutiny for the police department, making it a challenging year for everyone. However, over time, his colleagues had warmed up to him, and he cherished the moment when Lars respectfully had referred to him as 'boss'. Now, with Lars gone and Berger in a coma, the team he once knew no longer existed. As the new superintendent, he was faced with the daunting task of starting over, unsure if he had the strength to do so amidst the haunting memories, political challenges, and Berger's lingering suspicion.

Isa turned her head and looked at him. She was looking at him with an expression on her face—one of determination, but also one of compassion, saying they were in this together. No, he couldn't give up. It would be disrespectful to the memory of Lars.

* * *

Isa gazed at the freshly dug grave and let out a heavy sigh, her emerald eyes wide with a mix of grief and contemplation. The brilliant rays of the sun cast a serene glow over the cemetery, now hushed with a sense of reverence. She straightened the folds of her police uniform, taking a deep breath to steady herself before stepping forward.

Ingrid approached Isa, placing a consoling hand on her shoulder. "It was a beautiful ceremony," she said softly.

Isa nodded; her gaze fixed on the name etched into the stone. Mila Hillborg. "Lars' funeral was emotional, but..."

Ingrid looked at her.

"No one showed up at her funeral," Isa finally said, her voice heavy with emotion. "Not even the Lagers."

"We were there," Ingrid reminded her.

Isa nodded, but her mind was elsewhere. "It's just... tragic."

Her thoughts turned to the funerals of the past weeks. Leif Berg. A grand funeral splashed out in the media. Thousands of people. Lars. Kristoffer Solberg. Even Lauri Valkama. They all had people paying respect, while Mila had almost been dumped in a hole in the ground.

Ingrid nodded in agreement, understanding Isa's frustration. "Kristoffer would have been there," she said softly.

Isa's eyes were still fixed on the grave. "I just can't believe Mila would do this."

"They found evidence," Ingrid said. "Flyers about the White Power movement and emails with Mila's name on them. Countless messages between her and her foster parents. Hugo Lager has been charged."

"Kristoffer didn't believe it," Isa said, turning to face her friend.

"But he's not here, and the investigation is closed."

Isa shook her head. She couldn't tell Ingrid about her and Timo's suspicions. Eriksson. She still didn't know what to do with this. Someone in their own ranks. Someone in power. And they couldn't prove a thing. "Berger is left to believe his wife was a murderer. I can't let this go. I need to make it right."

"What does Timo say?" Ingrid asked.

"He's busy with other stuff," Isa replied.

Ingrid looked away, avoiding Isa's gaze. Ingrid and Timo hadn't spoken during the entire funeral, and they had barely looked at each other.

"I don't know what to think of it all," Isa said, breaking the silence.

"What do you mean?"

Isa stopped walking. "Take Berg... it's so easy to see him as the bad guy. But when we searched his house, we found a room full of pictures and memorabilia... a shrine for his dead daughter Anna. The grief was so tangible. It was so sad."

"Maybe her loss molded him into the person he became."

Isa nodded, lost in thought. "Maybe. But that doesn't excuse what he did."

She let the cold air fill her lungs as they continued to walk in silence.

"We also found paper clippings," Isa said suddenly.

"About what?"

"The Sandviken killer. A wall full of it."

Ingrid stopped in her tracks. "I thought he wanted to set him free."

Isa nodded. "That's what we thought, but maybe there was another reason why he wanted to have the Sandviken killer out of prison."

And that reason left her with mixed feelings. As a police officer, she had to condemn killing another human, but she knew exactly how he felt. She had thought many times about taking justice in her own hands. She remembered that one moment in Timo's office where her former partner had finally surrendered and confessed to murdering the man she loved. She would have taken her gun and pulled the trigger if her own moral code and duty to the law hadn't stopped her.

Ingrid looked at her with big eyes.

"We'll probably never know. Though... he was telling the truth. He didn't know Tuva's mother. We found love letters to a certain Ava Sjölander, a flight attendant he had an affair with ten, fifteen years ago. They had a child together, but the girl died when she was two. Ava was so heartbroken that she took her own life a year later, and that seems to have set off his delusions and his megalomaniac behavior."

"That's really... tragic," Ingrid said.

"I know. Tuva was convinced Leif Berg was the enemy."

"It's frustrating that most of them will never face the consequences of their actions. Just Mila and Berger. Their names will be dragged through the mud."

"I know, I know."

Then she took Ingrid's arm, and they walked back to the car.

"I'm going to miss you," Isa said.

"I'm not leaving Gävle, just... you won't see me every day. We'll still see each other outside of work."

"Is it because of him? Timo?"

Ingrid looked at Isa. "Yes. If I want to save my marriage, I can't be around him anymore. And... it's better for him. He'll get the peace he needs to think about his future."

Although Isa couldn't openly say it, she was glad Ingrid had finally accepted that a future with Timo was impossible. She knew how much Ingrid had come to love him. And she had come far enough to admit she was jealous of Ingrid and Timo.

Ingrid continued. "I will always be Caijsa's lookalike, not knowing if he really loves me or Caijsa."

As they continued to walk to the exit, a newfound feeling of obligation washed over Isa. She longed to take control of her life, just as Ingrid had. She envied her friend's unwavering selflessness, sacrificing her own happiness to protect those around her.

"Does Anton know?" Isa asked.

"I'm not sure. I think he suspects something."

"Will you tell him?"

Ingrid took a deep breath. "No... I'm not proud of what I did... no, that's not true. I don't regret it, but I can't tell him. He wouldn't forgive me."

They walked in silence for a while, when Ingrid suddenly said, "He won't stay."

Isa looked up at her in surprise. "Who?"

"Timo thinks he fits in here, but you can sense his restlessness. He'll come to see that Gävle is not where he can make an impact, it's not where he belongs. He won't stay forever."

Isa felt panic welling up inside her. She needed him. He needed them, too, she was sure of it. That's what she desperately wanted to believe. They were more than just friends; they were partners, confidants, and an integral part of each other's lives. She was grateful for their friendship and respected Timo deeply. She needed him by her side, but she often felt unworthy of his presence.

"Isa, you have to promise me to take good care of him. I couldn't bear... if he..."

Ingrid took a few deep breaths, the emotion in her voice clear and strong. "I couldn't bear if something happened to Timo."

She took Ingrid's hand in hers and squeezed. "I will... you can count on me."

"Thank you," Ingrid whispered. The same deep sadness overtook her as the morning when he had walked into her office with snow-drenched hair and skin as pale as the snowman Ingrid had seen in her neighbor's backyard. She'd looked up. After closing the door, he'd approached her, spun her chair around, and taken her face in his hands, kissing her with the passion of a young lover. As their lips locked in a goodbye kiss, Ingrid clung to him, remembering the tenderness of his touch, the warmth of his embrace, the passion they'd shared during that one magical weekend.

"You are leaving," he said.

She nodded. "I'm going to teach at the university of Uppsala. Forensic Genetics and Medicine. It's something new and at the same time familiar."

"I understand," was the only thing he said.

Then she kissed him again and they held each other for a while.

CHAPTER

23

FELIX'S EYES LIT UP as he turned to the woman beside him. "Do you know that Cephalopoda comes from Greek?" he asked, shifting his gaze to meet hers. "It means 'head-foot'. The tentacles are arranged in a circle around the mouth."

The tour continued, and Isa let her son chatter on. For the most part, she had been quiet and confused, amazed at how he had behaved around her—as if she hadn't disappeared from his life for five years.

"The first octopuses were discovered by the ancient Greek philosopher Aristotle. He observed them while they were hunting for food in a well," he said, his voice ringing with pride as if he were the one who had discovered them. He turned to look at his mother, his face full of awe and wonder. "They're so beautiful!" he exclaimed. "Look, mom," he said, pointing to one of the creatures. "Its tentacles are so cool!"

As Isa observed Felix wandering through the museum, she felt a profound sadness. She had missed so many key moments in her son's life, and it was heart-breaking to see how much he had grown without her. But despite her guilt and regret, she was overjoyed to see him so happy.

Lost in thoughts, Isa followed Felix to the next display cabinet, only to be confronted by a stuffed wolf staring straight at her. Her mind wandered to Timo, who had encouraged her to connect with her son. Although she found his involvement to be intrusive at times, she appreciated his efforts.

"Felix," Isa called out to him.

He turned to face her.

"I'm sorry," she said, and her voice broke.

"For what?" he asked, confusion written on his face.

"I left you and your sister."

"I know you didn't want to. You were ill," Felix said.

Isa was taken aback. "How did you know?" she asked and wiped the tears from her face.

"I overheard dad and Ellen arguing once. Dad told her about the depression. And I googled it," Felix explained, his eyes full of empathy.

Isa was stunned by his maturity and understanding.

"That's when I knew you loved me," he continued. "You wanted to save us."

Isa knelt down and embraced him tightly. She felt his heart beating against hers and it filled her with warmth.

Then Felix said, "Olivia doesn't understand... yet, but she will. You'll see."

Isa felt a surge of pride for her children.

"How did I ever deserve such great kids?" she thought to herself. "And a friend like Timo."

"I'm so glad you are here," Isa whispered, holding Felix close and never wanting to let go.

* * *

George opened the door and Valesca stepped inside without giving him a glance. She noticed that the hallway looked bigger than before. The hall was strewn with marble and crystal, lit by an elaborate chandelier hanging from the ceiling.

So George, she thought. The man claimed not to give anything about prestige, but all of his houses screamed the opposite. Every time bigger and more luxurious than the previous.

"To what do I owe the pleasure?" he said when she kept quiet and kept looking at him. "Your sister is not here if that's what…"

"How could you?" Valesca said with a serious expression on her face.

George frowned. "I don't understand."

Valesca didn't know where to start. She hadn't slept a wink. She had told herself she didn't want to know, but Nelvin's words had haunted her mind since his unexpected visit. She had taken Caijsa's diary and had read it in one sitting.

She wished she hadn't.

The next day, she called her son with the request to come by. She had been so determined to tell him. He had stood on his porch, with a cup of steaming black coffee, and had glanced over the lake and the white-covered trees as if it was a postal card. He had told her about Ingrid and the heartache he was going through. Then she had backed off. She couldn't drop another bomb on him.

She would have to take care of this alone.

"Valesca, what do you mean?"

"How long?"

"What?"

Valesca didn't want to take her eyes off the shiny statue on the table near the door. White, innocent, like snow. Why couldn't her life and that of her sons be uncomplicated? There was always some drama lingering in the background. And regardless of what people thought of her, she was so tired of it.

"You and Caijsa," she said and then turned to George.

The man stood transfixed and looked at her in horror.

Valesca paused, taking a deep breath, before continuing with a mix of anger and sorrow in her voice. "I keep going over it in my mind, but I don't understand. I can't understand. Eight years we've shed every tear for that woman. Timo doesn't know, but I know he wallowed in shame and guilt, thinking he was the bad one, the one willing to pull out of the engagement, while she had given up on their relationship. She had an affair... with one of his best friends, nonetheless. You. Nelvin told me. Caijsa told Paulina weeks before her death. She wanted to leave Timo. For you. A man twice her age. Jesus!"

"Valesca, I...," the old man took one step toward her, but she signaled him to stay back.

"Spare me the excuses! Why her? Why? Tell me!"

"There is nothing I can say," George said and looked at the floor. "Almost a year if you must know. I never wanted it to happen, but it just... did. She was in a bad place at that moment."

"So, it's my son's fault," Valesca snapped.

"I didn't say that."

"But you implied it. He must have made her so unhappy."

"I'm not going to deny my love for Caijsa. I've tried to deny it for so long."

"So, what was the plan? To run away together. What?"

"She was going to tell him, but then..."

"Yes, let's talk about that! The baby. She told you she was pregnant."

George looked down.

"Whose baby was it? Yours or Timo's?"

George shook his head. "I like you to leave now."

"Whose?!"

"If you must know… Timo's! But she didn't want it. She had enough of him. She wanted to move on with me. She missed the thrill, the excitement."

"And so you decided to kill my grandchild?" Valesca said.

"We… she…," George stammered.

"Stop it! The pregnancy thwarted your plans. You couldn't live with the thought of raising someone else's child. So, you let her have an abortion. And after that what was the plan?"

"She was going to tell Timo about the affair, but then she died. And I couldn't… for years, I had to hide my sorrow. I saw how it almost destroyed him, but I had to keep up appearances. I had to pretend, I had to help him. You can't imagine how devastatingly hard that was. Her death left a hole in my heart."

Valesca looked at him. The vibrant man, the man she had once looked up to, the man she had once loved. That man was a lie. What she saw was a pathetic, old man. A dirty old man who couldn't keep his hands from another man's wife. It disgusted her. It upset her. It made her angry. But there was one more bomb to drop.

"Are you now saying we should feel sorry for you?" she asked.

He shrugged and looked at her with contempt in his eyes.

"After you did that… to your own son," she said and couldn't help smiling. A sarcastic smile. She wanted to hurt him with everything she got.

His eyes widened. A moment he looked like the statue on the table. White, frozen in the moment. He opened his mouth, then closed it again. His breathing became heavy and difficult like he had run a marathon.

"What?" He shook his head. "No, you're lying."

"You are Timo's father."

"No… I asked you over and over again and you told me… you told me..."

She gave him another sarcastic grin.

"But... why?" he stammered.

"I didn't want you to meddle with my family. What we had was a mistake. I was at my lowest. In my eyes, he's Yrjo's son and will always be."

He hid his face in his hands. The next moment, she heard him cry. "How could you do this to me? I..."

"You did this all alone," she said. "You betrayed your son. You killed your grandchild. That's all on you!"

"I never meant..."

"You had no regrets until I told you he's your son."

He looked up, his face wet with tears. There was nothing left from the lively man who had opened the door. He looked ten years older now.

"Does he know?"

"No. And let's keep it that way, but George, I never want to see you again. I don't want you near my family. Ever again."

"But Lilia..."

"You're going to break up with her. It's going to be painful, but she'll get over it. And you'll disappear from my son's life."

"He's my son too and... my friend," George said.

"Oh, really? Fine by me. If that's what you want. Let's have that conversation."

"Fredrik knew," George blurted.

This time, Valesca was speechless with shock. "Why would you say that?"

"Because it's the truth. He saw us together. Then he approached Caijsa. I thought he would tell Timo everything, but he actually seemed happy. He advised Caijsa to get rid of the baby. It wasn't me. I would have loved the child, I would have cared for it, but by then it was already too late. How will you explain that to Timo?"

325

"This is the lowest of the lowest," Valesca yelled.

"Believe what you want. I'm done pretending. I loved Caijsa and she loved me. I would have given up everything to spend my life with her. I was prepared to give up everything, but just know that not everything was a lie. My friendship with Timo was true. My love for you was real."

She shook her head, the words almost strangled in her throat. "You know the worst thing is that so many people knew. Nelvin, Marcel, Paulina, and now Fredrik. I have to wonder... did you also think Timo had something to do with Caijsa's death? Did you believe he killed her?"

"No, no...," but there had been hesitation and his words didn't feel true.

"Oh, my God! How could you?"

"What was I supposed to think? Caijsa had an abortion just a week before. She was going to tell him. But after they arrested Elker, I knew I was wrong."

Valesca said nothing and walked to the door, but suddenly felt his hand on her arm. "I'll do what you want me to do. I just hope one day you'll be able to forgive me."

"You don't want my forgiveness," she whispered as she pushed him away. "You'd better hope Timo never finds out."

She opened the door and stepped outside.

As George saw her walk away, his eyes rimmed with tears. Tears for Caijsa, tears for a son he had betrayed, tears for the grandchild they had killed. For a friendship that had been a lie. He took a deep breath, ran his hands over his face, and in an instant, a surge coursed through his body like thunder. He dropped to the floor and burst into tears.

* * *

The sound of footsteps echoed through the hall. It was quiet in the house of commander Eriksson. He stopped at the stairs and listened, but he couldn't hear anything. Where was everyone?

"Ilsa?" he called out.

There was no answer, and he continued his way to the study.

The study was enormous, with a huge window overlooking the courtyard. The walls were lined with books, which were all in order and alphabetized. Two big leather chairs were placed in front of the fireplace and behind the desk, there was a sofa. The fire burned low in the large fireplace, casting flickering shadows on the wall.

He jumped up. In one of the chairs, a woman was sitting. The hair on the back of his neck stood up. He recognized her.

"How did you get in?" he said. "You shouldn't have come."

"Your wife let me in."

"Where is Ilsa?"

"I don't know. We don't need her, do we?"

The woman was wearing a white dress with short sleeves, a jarring sight against the cold winter weather outside. Her blonde hair was pulled back into a tight bun, and he noticed the expensive ring on her finger. Her skin was as pale as the snow outside, almost bluish in its lack of warmth.

"I almost didn't recognize you," he said, trying to break the silence. "You changed your hair color."

"Do you like it? I did it for you."

"Uh... it's nice," he stammered.

She put her hands in her lap and watched the fireplace.

"What do you want, Petra?" He walked up to the desk and put his hand on the tabletop.

"What do you want me to do next? I did good, didn't I?"

He sighed and straightened his back. "Petra... it's a disaster."

She turned around and frowned. "What do you mean?"

"You didn't listen. You went behind my back and arranged Tuva's murder."

Her smile twisted into a sneer. "We couldn't let her live."

"And Finn? Jesus, Petra, you made a mess."

She narrowed her eyes. "I sacrificed two sisters for you… for this cause. And that's how you thank me."

Eriksson felt a cold knot form in his stomach. He had known this woman for too long to underestimate her. "Petra…," he said.

She got up and walked over to him. "Don't you see, I did it for you. For old times' sake. I can still remember the first time we met… in that pub. I was with my father. You were so cute, trying to hide in that corner, hoping no one would notice. But I did. My own police commissioner."

"Yeah… but we're not talking about stupid speeches and secret meetings anymore. People got killed."

She let her finger run over his cheek and lips before she kissed him. Then she stepped back. "It's a bit late to have doubts. We need to move forward."

"No. We need to lay low for a while. I don't like it that your father got arrested. They'll find out."

"Relax. We designed it that way. He would take the fall. He and that bunch of Aktivisterna amateurs. And Hult will do the rest. You're in his circle of confidants. Step by step we'll push him a bit further to where we want to have him. The next elections will be a victory for the right."

He felt a chill run down his spine. The last days, he had felt invincible. No one knew about his involvement. But Petra was a different story.

"Okay."

"Good," she said and let her hand run over his cheek. "Everything will be okay. You'll see."

She walked back to the chair, took her bag and coat, and moved to the door.

"Oh, and one more thing," she said. "I think I can trust you, but just in case… I have evidence that implicates you in all of this. Emails, phone calls… your black SUV. If something should happen to me, it will be sent to the police, and Timo Paikkala in particular. I'm sure he'll be very interested to hear about your plans to destroy Berg and move this country into a new right-wing direction."

She put on her coat. "Too bad you and Berg didn't get along. You could have made a nice duo. But then again, he was a lunatic. Anyway, you did well by making a hero out of him. The man would have damaged the party beyond repair if this all came out."

As she opened the door, he sank back into the chair at the desk, his head in his hands. He had lost his independence, his freedom. There was no way out. He felt trapped—a prisoner of his own decisions. He wanted to stop. Forget all of this had happened.

No, there was always a way out.

He just had to find it.

* * *

Petra Lager walked to the stairs and as she descended, she thought about Mila. Her foster sister had been remarkably susceptible to manipulation, and her role as an undercover agent made her an asset to their cause. Unbeknownst to Mila, she had provided Petra with confidential information, and Petra had exploited Mila's upcoming wedding as a pretext for positioning her in the same location as Leif Berg.

Mila craved a family, and Petra had played the part of the loving older sister to perfection.

Suddenly, Petra felt her body tense.

She stopped halfway the stairs. She remembered everything. The explosion, Mila's death.

Mila had turned to Petra for help with planning her wedding, and Petra had eagerly jumped at the opportunity. She had suggested the perfect venue and planted a seed in Mila's mind about the exact date when Leif Berg would be there. Mila hadn't objected to the idea. She had seen it as the perfect opportunity to keep an eye on the secret meeting and to intervene if things went awry.

The informant was a problem. For months they had tried to figure out who it was. He could do so much damage. The network of dirty cops Engersson and Breiner had built up over the years would have been exposed, and the consequences would be disastrous.

It was a marvelous opportunity. They could kill two birds with one stone. Leif Berg and the informant.

But they needed scapegoats. Petra had helped Mila with finding a dress. It was a perfect excuse to plant the wires to make her foster sister look suspicious. The wires would lead the authorities to her father, whom she had long wanted to get rid of. She just had to find a good excuse not to be at Berger and Mila's wedding party.

On that particular Saturday, Petra, impersonating Mila's handler, had used a burner phone to call Mila and had instructed her to check if Berg had arrived and ensure that everything was in order. The bomb had been planted in a room next to where Berg would meet the informant. She had planned to detonate the bomb as soon as she knew Mila was outside Berg's room, using her as a scapegoat. But when Mila ascended the stairs to the second floor, the plan took a dark turn.

It was too quiet, and it looked as if no one was there. Petra, who had followed Mila, knew something was wrong.

But to Mila's surprise, someone else turned up. Lars.

For a moment, Lars and Mila had stared at each other, each letting the reality of the situation sink in.

"Lars? Why are you here?" Mila had said.

He didn't answer but kept looking at her with a strange expression on his face.

Then Mila's eyes widened in shock. It finally dawned on her.

And all the pieces of the puzzle fell nicely together.

He was the informant.

"No, this can't be true," she said. "Tell me you…"

The color drained from his face as he looked at her in disbelief. His voice shook as he spoke, "I knew it. You were watching me. How did you know?" His eyes searched hers for any sign of reassurance, but all he found was a blank stare.

"I didn't know it was you," Mila stammered.

He shook his head. "No, I don't believe you. This is why you tricked Berger into marrying you and having the wedding at the Grand Hotel on this day."

She cast down her eyes. "Lars… I…"

His eyes became watery with tears. "Berger knows?" He took a deep breath. "I wanted to wait until everything had been cleared up. I need to explain to him… he'll be so disappointed."

"Lars, how did it come that far?"

He looked down and shook his head before answering. "It started after the Sandviken case. I was so angry and frustrated because of what Lindström had done. So stupid. She had compromised such an important case. Heimersson knew that and he used that to manipulate me. He offered me a way to get back at Lindström. And I took the bait. I did whatever he asked me to do. I was blinded by anger, and I let myself be used."

"What did you have to do?"

"Give him information, make evidence disappear. By then, Breiner was already dead, and Heimersson took over, but the network still exists and there are more… many more."

"Who?"

"It doesn't matter… not anymore. I'm not proud of what I've done. I just thought that I could make amends by telling everything I know."

"You're doing the right thing," Mila said softly.

"Really? Is that so? I can't trust you. As far as I know, you are working for them. I knew I couldn't trust you. Is your name even Mila

Hillborg?"

"I am Mila Hillborg, 25 years and I studied forensic anthropology. That is all true. I didn't know it was you. SÄPO asked me for help with the informant."

A sarcastic grin appeared on his face. "Where is Berg? You are trying to frame me!" And in a split second, he pulled his gun.

Mila looked at him in shock. "Lars, think about what you're doing!"

"How stupid have I been? I wanted to come clean... But now I see this was a setup."

"Lars," Mila pleaded as he aimed the gun at her. "It was me you talked to. I sent you the messages. I swear."

Lars frowned and for a moment he stared at the floor, "That's... why everything felt so familiar."

The next moment, they heard a noise coming from the darkness, and suddenly Berger appeared before them.

"What the hell is going on?" Berger said.

Lars and Mila turned towards Berger, both startled.

Lars slowly lowered his gun, but the tension in the air remained thick.

"Lars, why...," Berger said surprised.

Lars hesitated for a moment before finally dropping the gun to the ground.

"We have to talk," Mila said, her voice shaky.

Lars closed his eyes and put his head in his hands, "I did something so stupid... I'm sorry!"

Berger turned to Mila. "What is he talking about?"

And Petra had seen the entire incident. She looked at the message on her phone: "Berg is not there. Blow off the operation. F."

But in that moment, she made the decision to kill Mila. Her sister was compromised, and Lars, the traitor, deserved to die. She walked downstairs and activated the bomb. The resulting explosion killed Mila and Lars, and injured Berger.

As Petra took a few short breaths, she couldn't ignore the guilt weighing heavy on her chest. She had betrayed Mila. Despite her claims of loyalty, Petra had always intended to sacrifice her foster sister. Her pragmatism always took precedence over sentimentality. Besides, Mila had betrayed her first, leaving her behind with her abusive parents, especially her father, who was the worst kind of brute.

Then Petra thought about Tuva.

Just like Mila, Tuva was easy to manipulate. A young woman searching for her father and consumed with anger due to her mother's death. What more could she have asked for?

But why was she so emotional?

These women meant nothing to her.

They had betrayed her.

Then she straightened her back and put her chin up. Mila and Tuva were collateral, the sacrifice she had to bring for the good cause: a Sweden going back to its roots, a Sweden she could be proud of.

She smiled, walked downstairs, and out of the door.

THE END

Printed in Great Britain
by Amazon